DEFY NOT
THE HEART

DEFY NOT THE HEART

Johanna Lindsey

This title first published in Great Britain 2000 by
SEVERN HOUSE PUBLISHERS LTD of
9–15 High Street, Sutton, Surrey SM1 1DF.
This first hardcover edition published in the USA 2000 by
SEVERN HOUSE PUBLISHERS INC of
595 Madison Avenue, New York, N.Y. 10022
by arrangement with Avon Books,
a unit of The Hearst Corporation.

British Library Cataloguing in Publication Data

Lindsey,   Johanna
    Defy not the heart
    1.   Love stories
    I.   Title
    813.5'4 [F]

ISBN 0-7278-5546-8

Printed and bound in Great Britain by
MPG Books Ltd, Bodmin, Cornwall.

Chapter One

Clydon Castle, England, 1192

*B*ang! Again, again—bang! The sound of the battering ram took precedence over the screaming confusion on the inner battlements, over the death cries below in the outer bailey as arrows struck true, over the thundering headache that pounded inside Reina de Champeney's head. Bang! Again.

It had happened too quickly, the attack. Reina had been aroused from sleep by the cry "To arms!", to find the outer bailey already breached by trickery. The supposed pilgrim she had given succor to the night before had opened the gate on the outer curtain wall at dawn, letting in a small army. Thank God she had not let the cur bed down in the inner bailey or in the keep itself, or she would not now be directing a defense from the battlements above the inner gatehouse. But that was all she had to be grateful for.

The attacking army might be no more than a hundred men, but Clydon was presently grossly undermanned for a castle of its size. After her father had depleted the garrison for the army he took with him on Crusade, she had only fifty-five men left, not all of whom were present. Twenty men-at-arms and ten crossbowmen and archers were about. But at least six of that number were dead or trapped on the outer walls, which the attackers were not even bothering to secure, since there was no archer of any skill there to cause damage to their flanks.

"Put more fuel on that fire!" Reina shouted at one of the menservants, all having been commandeered to help with the defense. "We need that boiling water now, not after the gate gives way!"

She leaned over the parapet in time to see a fat rock drop at least three feet away from the battering ram, then roll harmlessly into the dry ditch below the wall. She turned a murderous glare on Theodric, her most trusted servant. The gangly youth of eight years and ten had insisted on helping even though Reina had tried to send him below after he brought her specially made armor and dressed her right there on the battlements.

"Idiot!" she snapped at him in disgust. "You are supposed to break through the ram's thick cover, not stir the dust to coat their feet!"

"These rocks are heavy!" Theodric snapped back peevishly, as if that could excuse his wasting their supply of missiles.

"Aye, and you have not the muscle for lifting them, so leave off and do what you *can* do, Theo. We need more water up here for boiling right quickly, and another fire, too. We are running out of time."

She turned before seeing if he would swallow his prickly pride and do as she ordered, only to nearly knock over little Aylmer, who had come up to stand by her other side. The seven-year-old boy wrapped his skinny arms around her leg to keep from falling, but Reina's heart jumped into her throat, for the fall could have taken him right over the wall, since with his crippled foot he had not the balance or the dexterity to save himself.

"What do you here?" Reina shouted, furious at the scare he had given her.

Tears formed immediately in the brown eyes looking up at her and caused a like moisture to gather in her own eyes. She had never yelled at the child before, never had aught but a kind word for him or a soft shoulder onto which he could cry his hurts. She was the closest thing he had to a mother, orphaned as he was and unwanted by any of the villeins because of his crippled foot. He was only a serf, but she had brought him through so many childhood illnesses that she thought of him as her own—at least hers to protect and care for.

"I want to help you, my lady," was Aylmer's answer.

Reina knelt down before him to wipe the wetness from his smoke-smudged cheek, hoping the smile she offered now took the bite out of her earlier surliness. "I am glad you have come, Aylmer," she lied as she moved him to put her mail-clad back between him and any arrows flying over the wall. "I came up here so quickly there was no time to set my ladies to what is needful inside the keep. Do you go and tell Lady Alicia to cut bandages and make ready for the wounded. Stay with her and Dame Hilary and help them as you can. And, Aylmer," she added with a forced grin, "try to assure the younger ladies there is no reason yet for alarm. You know how silly they can be."

"Aye, my lady. They are only girls."

And you are only a boy, she thought tenderly as she watched him hobble to the ladder, his pride at

least intact. Now if only she could think of something
to get Theodric out of the way as easily. She saw him
about to help another man tilt the large cauldron of
boiling water over the wall and opened her mouth to
shout him away, only to have an arrow fly past her
cheek. In the next second, she found herself tackled
to the floor by Aubert Malfed.

"*Jesú,* my lady, you almost—"

"Get off me, you beef-witted oaf," she growled
into Aubert's ashen face.

"But, my lady—"

She cut off his protest furiously. "Think you I want
to be here? But with Sir William taken sick last eventide, no doubt poisoned somehow by that false pilgrim, there is no one else to lead the defense."

"I can."

"You cannot," she said with less rancor. How she
wished he could, but Sir William's squire was only
five years and ten, and she was the one William had
dragged up here just this past week for a thorough if
quick lesson in defense, not Aubert. " 'Tis me they
want, and I will hold my own fate in hand, thank
you. If I am taken, it will be my own fault, no one
else's."

"At least stay back from the wall," he beseeched
her as he helped her to her feet.

"Aye, I—Theo!"

Her screech caused both lads to jump, Theodric
then turning an indignant glance on her after he had
to jump back even more to avoid the sloshing water
that nearly boiled his feet. Reina lost her temper completely, seeing that.

"To hell with your pride, Theo. Get you below—
now! I love you too much to see you scorched or

ventilated with arrows because you *think* you can do a man's job with those skinny sticks you call arms.'' When he did not move immediately, she yelled, ''Now, Theo, or by God, I will have you chained inside the keep! And you, too, Aubert. I need brawn up here, not babes to get in the way. Your sword is useless unless they bring up ladders to scale the walls, or breach the gate. So begone, and not another word, from either of you.''

Aubert flushed at this set-down because he knew she was right. His skills, such as they were, were useless without the enemy right before him. But Theodric grinned as he passed her on the way to the ladder. Without that ''I love you too much'' he would be smarting sorely, but with it he could retreat gracefully, and thankfully. He might be a year older than she, but he would have fainted at the first sight of blood anyway, and they both knew it.

Reina sighed once they were both gone, and turned her attention to watching as the boiling water was finally tipped over the wall. There were some new screams from below, but after only a few seconds, another loud bang. Curse and rot them! They had probably killed *her* animals for those wet hides that made the improvised ''turtle'' to shield them as they rammed the gate. The raw hides resisted both fire and water, though the splash of the latter had surely reached some exposed legs underneath the covering. A bridge to span the ditch was a wall ripped off the smithy. She knew they were using one of her wagons they had found in the bailey to support the large tree trunk that was hammering at the gate, a tree they had cut from *her* woods.

''My lady?''

She turned to see her steward, Gilbert Kempe, offering a chunk of bread and cheese, with a flask of wine. His tunic was soaked from helping to water down the gate and buildings in the inner bailey, though the attackers had not fired any flame-pitched arrows yet.

"Thank you, Gilbert," she said with a grateful smile as she took the food, even though her stomach was too knotted up just now for her to eat anything.

He winced, hearing the ram's noise from this closer distance. "Know you who they are?"

"Sir Falkes' men," she replied at once.

Gilbert had not thought of that, and was alarmed to think of it now. "But they wear no colors," he pointed out. "Nor are there any knights among them. And they did not come prepared to give siege."

"Aye, they thought they would have an easy path straight into the keep with their man inside to open the way. And nearly they did. If someone had not seen what the pilgrim was about and given the alarm, there would have been no time to bring in the castle-folk from the outer bailey and secure this gate. But who else, Gilbert, would dare to take me?" Her voice lowered to add, "Who else knows my father is dead?"

He shook his head. "Anyone could know by now. It has been nigh a year, though we only learned of Lord Roger's death four months ago ourselves. Think you no one else with King Richard writes home as your father did to us? And the earl informed his castellan at Shefford of the loss of his vassal just as he did us. There is no knowing who Shefford's castellan could have told in these past months, and told also that you are not yet wed. Did he not write again just last week for the date of your wedding?"

All of that was true, though it annoyed Reina to admit it. She still found it hard to speak of her father's death at all, or the dilemma it left her in. She had been so undone by grief that nigh a month had passed ere she got around to writing the letters that would secure her future. That month had cost her dear, witness Clydon under attack now. But she still had no doubt that these were Falkes de Rochefort's men trying to get at her, and she reminded Gilbert why she thought so.

"Be that as it may, you forget the visit de Rochefort paid us a fortnight ago. Did he not ask me to wed him then? And when I refused, did he not sneak into my chamber that night to rape me to see the deed done in that foul manner? If Theo had not heard my scream—"

"My lady, please, you need not mention that unfortunate night. This could indeed be Sir Falkes' doing, and with revenge in mind, too, after you had him thrown out of Clydon right into the moat. I only point out that he is not the only lord who would risk much to have you."

"I am not a great heiress, Gilbert," Reina said in exasperation.

He frowned at her. "To tempt an earl, mayhap not. But with so many knights' fees yours, there is more than enough to tempt the countless petty barons in the realm, as well as the greater ones. Clydon alone is enough to tempt them."

He said naught that she was not aware of, but again, it was annoying to admit it. She could have been married two months ago if she had not taken so long to write her letters. She knew how vulnerable she was with her overlord, the Earl of Shefford, on Crusade, and half her vassals with him, three now dead with her father. And this attack had come so quickly, to surround her so thoroughly, she had not been able to send for aid from Simon Fitz Osbern, her nearest vassal.

"These could even be those accursed outlaws living in our woods," Gilbert was continuing.

Reina had to force down a laugh to keep from offending Gilbert, but the levity relieved her fear for a moment. "Those pesky wood rats would not dare."

"There are no knights below, my lady, nor even a single man in mail," he reminded her.

"Aye, de Rochefort is too cheap to invest his men properly. Nay, enough, Gilbert. It matters not *who* is knocking on our door, as long as we keep them out."

He said no more, for he would not dream of actually arguing with her. When he went away, Reina's fear returned. And she truly was afraid. If Clydon were merely besieged, she could hold out for months, but that would not even be necessary. Simon would come before then, and Lord John de Lascelles was due sometime next week, finally in answer to her letters to him. But these curs below had to know she was so undermanned. Why else would they have immediately attacked after she refused to give herself over to them? They were determined to get at her with all speed, to win victory before help *did* come, for their numbers were not that large, though far larger than her own.

She had done all she could, considering the battle was half lost. Her greatest defense, the outer curtain wall with the deep, wide moat that would have taken men days to construct a bridge for the crossing, was already breached. True, she did not have enough men to man such a long wall, for Clydon was no small castle. But the enemy would have lost a good deal of their number in trying to take that outer wall, and mayhap would even have given up. The inner wall was not nearly so long, enclosing only a quarter of the entire area where the keep sat in a corner; and was easier to defend, with four sturdy towers, including the second gatehouse, facing the outer bailey, on which the enemy was concentrating their efforts.

She had had time to prepare after she heard the demands from the wall and had replied to them in the negative. While the ram was being cut down, her buildings torn apart for protection against arrows and a new bridge to cross the dry ditch, her animals slaughtered for the hides to shield the enemy's covers, she had put to use all Sir William had prodded her to learn, having weapons checked and readied, water and sand heated for pouring from the walls, poles found for pushing ladders back, all near flammables wetted down. And with such a shortage of men, every male servant was enlisted, which did double her numbers. The menservants knew naught of fighting but could throw stones, push away ladders, wind crossbows for those with the skill to use them. But they would be of little help once the battering ram did its job, and then all Reina could do was retreat into the keep, the last defense—if there was time.

Chapter Two

The meow woke him, Lady Ella letting him know she did not like to be kept waiting for her morning viands. Ranulf Fitz Hugh stretched a long arm out without opening his eyes and picked up the bundle of scraggly fur to plop it down in the center of his wide chest.

"I suppose it is time to get up?" he grumbled sleepily to the cat, and got more answer than he wanted.

"My lord?"

Ranulf cringed, having forgotten he had taken more to bed yestereve than his pet cat. The light-skirt, one of a half-dozen camp followers who serviced his men, moved closer to rub a bare leg over his. Ranulf was not interested. The whore might have come in handy last night when he felt the need, but this was morning, and he did not like to be bothered when he had work to do.

He sat up and gave her backside a sharp whack, then caressed the smarting area to make his rejection more palatable. "Begone, wench."

She made a moue of her lips that did not impress him. She might be the prettiest of the current lot, but beauties came easily to him. He could not even remember this one's name, though this was not the first time she had warmed his pallet.

Her name was Mae, and as soon as a coin was

found and tossed to her, she knew she was forgotten. He was not. It was impossible not to think of him at least a hundred times a day, for Mae had made the mistake of letting her emotions get involved with her livelihood, something she knew better than to do, though it was too late. She was already in love—along with every other woman who had ever set eyes on him, including her fellow camp followers, who despised Mae because she was the only one of them he ever called for. If they knew he sent his squires for "the blonde," that she meant so little to him that he could not even remember her name, they would not be so envious of her. To him, she was what she was, a whore, a convenience, no more.

She sighed as she watched him leave the tent bare-assed naked to relieve himself. Like most men, he thought nothing of his nudity as long as there were no ladies around to be embarrassed by it. Whores did not count. But Mae imagined a lady would not be so very embarrassed to get an eyeful of Ranulf Fitz Hugh. Few men had such presence of height as well as magnificence of form. That Sir Ranulf avoided ladies as he would a shit-clogged privy was their misfortune.

Mae gasped to realize she was wasting time with her musing. Sir Ranulf might have woken with his usual morning grouch, but if he returned to find her still in his tent, his grouchiness could turn much uglier.

Ranulf was actually in what was for him a pleasant mood this morning, a miracle as far as Lanzo Shepherd was concerned. Instead of the usual foot to his backside to wake him, he got his red hair tousled and Lady Ella dropped in his lap for feeding.

"Think you Mae gave him a better ride than usual?" Lanzo asked his fellow squire, Kenric, who was already busy rolling up his blanket.

The older squire shook his head as he watched Ranulf saunter off into the bushes. "Nay, she always gives him better than the rest of us are like to get," Kenric said without rancor.

They, like the other men, were used to being invisible to women whenever Ranulf was around. And Lanzo, only four years and ten, had not got much yet to speak of, so it made no difference to him.

"He is just glad to have this particular job near done," Kenric continued, turning turquoise eyes back to Lanzo. "Old Brun, who recommended us for this one, said there would be little challenge to it, but you know how Ranulf hates dealing with ladies."

"Aye, Searle said he would not accept the job at all."

"Well, and so he has not, not really. At least he did not take Lord Rothwell's money yet, even if he did allow Rothwell's men to come along with us."

"Slowed us up is all they did. But I do not understand why—"

"Gossiping like little girls again, are you?"

Lanzo blushed and scampered to his feet, but Kenric only grinned as Searle and Eric joined them. Both men were newly knighted, Ranulf having arranged it with the last lord they had hired out to, in lieu of payment.

He could have knighted them himself, but wanted them to have the sense of ceremony involved, as well as witnesses other than his own men. They were both eighteen, Searle of Totnes taller, blond, with light, merry gray eyes, and Eric Fitzstephen with hair as

black as Kenric's and hooded hazel eyes that always
gave him a sleepy appearance. They had been with
Ranulf and Sir Walter de Breaute much longer than
Lanzo and Kenric, and yet the four of them had much
in common. They were all bastards, born in the village or castle kitchen and denied by their lordly
fathers, so lost the hope of ever bettering their lot.
Half villein, half nobleman, shunned by both classes.
If Ranulf had not recognized them for who they were
and bought their freedom, they would still be serfs tied
to the land owned by the very men who had sired
them. But like recognized like, for Ranulf was a bastard himself.

"We were wondering why Ranulf refused to take
the first half of the money for this job from Lord
Rothwell," Lanzo said in reply to Searle's teasing.

"If you think about it, little Lanzo, the answer will
come to you."

"But the only answer is that he might not complete
the job."

"Exactly," Eric replied.

"But why?"

Eric chuckled. "Now, that answer is not so clear.
What think you, Searle? Did Ranulf just take a dislike
to Rothwell, or was it that he did not believe Rothwell's story about a broken betrothal?"

Searle shrugged. "He has worked for other men he
had no liking for. And others have lied and it made
little difference. Money is money."

"Then it can only be the nature of this job, that it
involves a lady."

"Mayhap that and the other reasons combined. But
whether he has made up his mind yet—"

"But we have come so far and have arrived,"

Lanzo pointed out. "He must have decided by now. And he would not really turn down five hundred marks. Would he?"

No one answered, and Lanzo turned to see what they saw: Ranulf was approaching. Only then did the boy realize he still held Lady Ella in his arms, for only then did she let out a meow as if to wake the dead, or to let Ranulf think she was starving. Pampered bitch. Sometimes he wanted to wring her scrawny neck, but Ranulf would flay alive anyone who plucked so much as one of her short brown hairs. Ugly thing. How could a man love such an ugly thing?

"You have not fed my lady yet?"

"Ah, no, sir," Lanzo was forced to admit.

"Mayhap I did not wake you properly?"

"I was just going," Lanzo squeaked, holding one hand to cover his threatened backside until he was out of Ranulf's reach.

Ranulf chuckled as Lanzo scampered away, then went on to his tent. Searle's eyes met Eric's and they both grinned.

Searle voiced both their thoughts after hearing that chuckle. "He has decided. We will escort the lady to her new husband. Lanzo was right. Five hundred marks is too much to turn down when it will make the difference of owning land or not. And land is all he thinks about."

"Then mayhap he was never undecided. Mayhap he did not commit himself only to make Rothwell nervous."

"Aye, that is possible. He well and truly disliked that old lord. We should have asked Sir Walter—"

"Asked Sir Walter what?" Walter inquired quietly from behind them.

The three young men turned about to face Ranulf's foster brother, shamefaced until they noted the dark brown eyes twinkling.

There were no two men so different than Ranulf Fitz Hugh and Walter de Breaute, in temperament as well as in looks, and yet they had taken to each other like true brothers from the first day they met. At an impressive six feet in height, Walter was taller than most men. Ranulf stood a half foot taller, a giant among his peers. Walter was night with his olive skin and dark brown hair. Ranulf was sunshine, golden-skinned, golden-haired. Ranulf bellowed even in a good mood. Walter spoke so softly, sometimes you had to strain to hear him. Walter would laugh at the poorest jest. Ranulf rarely laughed at all.

Walter's was a carefree spirit. The third son of a minor baron, he was as landless as Ranulf, the difference being he did not care. He would be as happy attached to the household of a great lord as to a minor one, or to none at all. It made little difference to him. He had no ambitions, no driving need to make a name for himself or acquire wealth and power. His older brothers loved him, so there would always be a home for him if he was ever in need.

Ranulf did not have that security. His father might be a great lord, might have taken him out of the village where his stepfather had raised him for the first nine years of his life, might have arranged for his fostering and training to become a knight, but Ranulf hated the man, would never ask him for aught, even did his life depend on it.

Ranulf had no home, but it was his burning ambition to correct that lack. It was his only goal, yet it was an all-consuming one. It was all he worked toward, hiring out to any man no matter the task, no matter the difficulty, no matter his own feelings in the matter. His ambition did not allow for scruples. He had wrested keeps for other lords, fought wars for them, routed thieves from their towns and outlaws from their forests. Whatever he did, he never failed. He had built up a reputation to that effect, which was why he could no longer be hired cheaply, which was why Lord Rothwell was willing to pay the exorbitant fee of five hundred marks to assure the wife he wanted was delivered to him.

"Well?" Walter grinned when no one spoke up to his question. "Did Lady Ella steal all your tongues?"

It was Kenric who answered. The curiosity of a fifteen-year-old does not allow for much subtlety. "Sir Ranulf talks to you. You know his thoughts and feelings better than any man. Was it only because he felt such strong aversion to Lord Rothwell that he would not take his money to commit us to this task?"

"He did not tell the man he would not do it."

"Nor did he tell him he would," Eric replied.

Walter laughed at that. "Aye, I thought that 'we shall see' was most eloquent coming from someone of Ranulf's surly disposition."

"Think you that is why Rothwell insisted we take fifty of his men?"

"Certainly. Men like him are not given to trust, especially when something is this important to them. The man cannot even trust his own vassals, or he would not have needed to hire us, would he? If that gout had not laid him up, he would be here himself. He no doubt thinks his men, in greater number than our own, will be incentive enough to see the task done."

"Then he does not know Ranulf," Searle said with a laugh.

"Nay, he does not," Walter agreed, smiling himself.

"But what did Ranulf object to in the man?" Eric wanted to know. "He seemed harmless enough, if somewhat crafty."

"Harmless?" Walter snorted. "You should have talked to his men to learn what manner of man he is."

"Did you?"

"Nay, I saw what Ranulf saw, that he was another like the Lord of Montfort, with whom we both were fostered. Montfort took us both as his own squires, rather than giving us to one of his knights, and if you think Ranulf has been a difficult master, you do not know what hell is truly like. Pure meanness was what Ranulf sensed and reacted to in Rothwell."

"But what of this task?" Kenric asked. " 'Tis not by any means unusual, though *we* have never been hired before to bring a reluctant bride to her betrothed. Was Sir Ranulf truly reluctant to do it, or simply unwilling to assure Lord Rothwell that we *would* do it?"

Laughter sparkled in his brown eyes as Walter smiled at each of them. "Now if I told you that, children, what would I leave you to gossip about?"

Searle and Eric both glowered to be called children when Walter was only twenty years and four himself. But Kenric's groan drew their attention to see Ranulf leaving his tent, fully armored.

"God help us, Lanzo is too quick this morn," Walter said, his humor flown. "Fie on you, Kenric, letting me stand here in my underwear gabbing like a woman. Move, lackwit, or he will ride off without us!''

Which was a very real likelihood and would have happened if Lady Ella had not scorned Lanzo's offering and gone off to stalk her own meal. Ranulf would not trust the cat to find him, even though their destination was less than an hour away. They had to wait until the feline returned with her field mouse and was set in the supply cart to enjoy her meal.

Chapter Three

*R*eina caught the wounded man before he fell, but his weight was too much for her and they both went down to the floor. He had pulled the arrow out of his shoulder before she could stop him, and now there was a gaping wound there, and she had nothing at hand to stop the flow of blood. She did not even know who he was, he was so covered with ash and smoke from tending the fire, but he did not take well to pain, promptly fainting to avoid it, and she could not leave him there to bleed to death.

"Aubert, I need a scrap of cloth, something . . ."

Aubert was not listening, or else he could not hear her over the continued pounding of the battering ram. The closed drawbridge had been smashed through, as well as the first of the two portcullises inside the gatehouse. The men working the ram were inside the gatehouse now and could no longer be reached with boiling water or sand, though the fires needed to be kept burning, the water dumped again when the army finally advanced.

It was time to retreat into the keep. The others who had attended the fires were slumped against the walls in exhaustion. The men-at-arms were still firing arrows when a target moved out from behind cover. The rest of the army were patiently waiting for the ram to do its work, though they too sent an occasional arrow over the battlements.

"Aubert!"

He stood right next to her, looking out over the bailey, but still he did not hear her. When this was over, whether she was taken or not, she was going to get even with Aubert Malfed for causing her nigh as much exasperation as the army below. She finally hit his leg to get his attention.

"Give me your knife—or sword."

She had no weapons of her own, for there was no point in adding them to her armor when she had no skill for their use, and the mailed tunic she wore was heavy enough without adding the weight of a sword to it, though it weighed only fifteen pounds. William's idea had not been to have her actually fight, but only to disguise her and protect her enough to parley from the walls if she ever had to.

This idea had come about just days ago, when he had panicked, realizing she had sent her other two household knights off on duties, leaving only him to see to the defenses. And although Reina had gone along with the idea grudgingly just to humor him, she had never thought the need would actually arise. But it had, and her disguise, much as she hated it, had worked well enough this morn. She had addressed the men below as a knight, speaking for his lady, not as the lady herself. And with her head coiffed and helmeted, they had not guessed she was a woman, the very woman they demanded be handed over to them.

Aubert's green eyes widened now that he saw her position half under the fallen man. "My lady!"

"A knife, lackwit!" was all she shouted at him.

He handed over the dagger in his belt without thought, but Reina's hands were so slippery with blood from holding the wound that she dropped it.

Aubert collected his scattered wits enough to retrieve the knife and hack away at the man's tunic until he had a strip of cloth to hand her, which she stuffed inside the hole in his tunic over the wound. Aubert then had sense enough to rouse one of the other servants to help the wounded one below, but not sense enough to help her out from under him first; and annoyingly, she found she could not get out without help. Only Aubert was distracted before he accomplished anything, and Reina heard his gasp, followed by a groan, followed by another bang of the accursed ram.

"What?"

"*Jesú!* Sweet *Jesú!*"

"What?!"

Aubert crossed himself before stammering, "They—they are reinforced, my lady. More men are coming through the outer gate—mounted. *Jesú,* more than thirty mounted and more still coming on foot—and—and knights . . . they have knights leading them."

Reina's blood turned cold. *Now* what was she to do? Sir William was mad to think that she could handle such a crisis when she was so frightened she could barely think. If only she had not lost the outer walls, or if the enemy had done the *normal* thing and settled down to a long siege, there would be no problem. But de Rochefort, that bastard, that lecherous swine, he *knew* she was undermanned. That was probably him there now, thinking the battle would be over. And it would not last much longer, not with knights come to lead the attack. A few ladders, which could be found in the barn if they bothered to look, and the walls would be scaled in as few minutes.

And here she was stuck, pinned to the floor, her arms so tired from supporting the long mailed sleeves she wore that she could not budge the weighty back that pressed her down, could not even order retreat.

"Aubert!" She tried again. "Help me up!"

But he was still mesmerized by the scene below, still telling her what she did *not* want to hear. "They are still coming, seventy—eighty—doubling the number and more— Wait! *Jesú!*"

"What?" And when he did not answer at once: "Curse you, rot you, Aubert! *What?!*"

He looked down to give her a smile to outshine any other. "My lady, *we* are reinforced. We are saved!" She could hear it herself then, the clash of swords, screams aplenty, cheers from her own people spread out along the wall. Aubert continued, laughing. "They did not hear the newcomers approach, and now 'tis too late. They are scattered. Look at them run, the cowards!"

"How can I look, you dolt?" she said, though she was grinning now.

His face turned nearly as orange as his hair when he realized she was stuck. Immediately he rolled the unconscious man off her and helped her to rise. And when she saw the battle taking place below, the knights cutting down a man with each swipe of their swords, the new men-at-arms chasing the attackers across the bailey on foot, she laughed, too. There was no contest. The newcomers were routing the enemy with such ease, and so swiftly, 'twas nearly over already. Reina was so relieved she could even forgive Aubert for all his "help" this morn.

"Do you let them in as soon as it is safe, Aubert. *Jesú,* I must change. I cannot receive them like this!"

She made a face as she looked down at her masculine attire, a face that then pinkened with shame at the thought of being seen like this by someone other than her own castlefolk. "Make them welcome, Aubert!" she added, already heading for the ladder.

"But who are they, my lady?"

"What matters that when they have saved Clydon for me?"

Chapter Four

Ranulf did not remove his helmet until he had entered the Great Hall and saw that it was filled with only women and children. It still made him uneasy, however, a place so big, with so few men. He could not help thinking there must be an army of soldiers yet hidden away, waiting to decide if he were friend or foe ere they showed themselves.

From what he had seen thus far, there were more servants than soldiers here, which likely explained the pitiful display of defense he had witnessed on arrival. The castle had nearly been taken, and by a ridiculously small number of men, without even a knight among them. But even so, those outer walls alone should have taken weeks to be breached, if it were possible, and that only with every available siege engine brought into use. Whoever was in charge of the defense either was an imbecile or had been slyly losing the battle apurpose.

"If . . . if you will wait here, my lord, the lady—Lady Reina—will soon make you welcome."

Ranulf eyed the young man, who appeared no older than Kenric. Aubert Malfed, he claimed to be, squire to Sir William Folville, whoever that was. Malfed had met Ranulf and his men inside the inner bailey and had led them straightaway into the keep itself without asking so much as a single question. Ranulf was used to intimidating men, but this was ridiculous, and he itched to take the boy to task for his foolishness in literally turning the keep over to them. But then that would be defeating his own purpose.

He had intended to ask for Roger de Champeney, Lord of Clydon, as if he were unaware that the man was dead. His business could have been anything to do with the lord, and would have kept his true reason for his presence here from being suspected by the lady. But that was if he had come in alone, with only a few men as retinue, as he had planned to do.

Arriving to find Clydon under attack changed things considerably. Having to bring in his own troop of thirty men-at-arms, as well as Rothwell's fifty, made his presence threatening, and if he was not to alarm the lady into hiding, he needed a new reason for being there.

At the moment, he was being made to feel most welcome, after sending the besiegers on their way. But to say he was just passing by and, as a lark, decided to come to Clydon's defense was not likely to be believed. Knights did not travel with so many men without a military purpose, and so being, they did not stop to join a war they just happened across.

The squire was too nervous by half, rambling on about some neighbor named de Rochefort being in league with some outlaws nesting in Clydon's woods, supposedly the besiegers. What he was doing was stalling, it seemed, talking nonstop so that no questions could be asked. The lady of the castle should have been there in the hall to greet them, and Ranulf had to wonder why she was not, or had not come by now. Was she at that moment being spirited away, out of his reach?

Ranulf at last held up a hand to silence the squire.

"Where is your lady, sirrah? I would know that she is safe."

"Ah—she is safe. The last I saw . . . ah . . . where she is now, I am not sure." That was no answer to relieve Ranulf's mind, and his resultant frown half terrified poor Aubert, so that he added quickly, "I will find her," and practically ran from the hall.

"What do you make of that, Ranulf?" Walter asked thoughtfully beside him as they watched the young squire disappear up some stairs in a corner turret. "Think you the lady's chambers are up there?"

"This keep is so big, there is no telling what is up there, so keep your eye on that stairwell." His own eyes moved to scan the hall, passing over the women briefly, marking one beauty in particular for later consideration, before turning to the others with him. "Eric, go and—Eric!" The lad had to be jabbed in the ribs before he tore his eyes off the same stunning blonde Ranulf had noted. "This is no time to be ogling the wenches," Ranulf growled low.

"Aye, but God's wounds! Did you ever see such a—" Eric grunted to a stop when Searle jabbed him from the other side, and he finally noted Ranulf's darkening scowl. "Ah, yes, sir?"

"Go and set a man at each gate. I want no women leaving the castle, not a single one." As Eric left, Ranulf turned to Kenric. "Go and ask the servants where the lady is," but when Kenric headed straight for the blond beauty, Ranulf called him back. "Give me an excuse to cut it off and I will. We attend to business before pleasure."

Kenric blanched, his hand going protectively to cover his groin, but he nodded before starting off again. Walter and Searle laughed to see him steer a wide circle around the blond wench this time.

"Come, Ranulf, if we must wait, let us at least sit down," Walter suggested, pushing one of the stools in front of the hearth at Ranulf before seating himself on another. "Lanzo, see if you can locate the steward or someone who can fetch us some ale. I could use a drink after our little sport, but as usual, everyone is too afeard of our leader here to approach us with refreshment." Walter grinned at the sour look Ranulf turned on him. "You know 'tis true, brother. The women might crawl all over you once they know you are not as dangerous as you look, but not before then."

"You are mad, Walter, to tease him now," Searle said in a whisper, though Ranulf did sit down.

"Not so," Walter replied just as quietly. "If I do not, he is like to lose his patience waiting on the lady, and woe betide her if that happens."

"It has already happened by the look of him."

"Nay, not yet." Walter grinned. "But she had better appear right quickly."

Unfortunately, Kenric returned to say no one had seen Reina de Champeney since dawn, and Ranulf did explode then. "Christ's toes! She flew before the attack began. She has escaped!"

"Nay, Ranulf, be easy. 'Tis as like she wisely hid herself and no one has yet told her 'tis safe to come out."

"Aye," Searle added. " 'Tis her ladies would know where she is and should have been asked. I will find one and . . . thank the Blessed Mother! Here is the lady now, Ranulf."

Ranulf turned around to see Aubert Malfed returning, following behind a young girl who was indeed a lady, garbed richly in blue samite, with copper-colored hair neatly tucked beneath a sheer white veil. She was much younger than he had somehow imagined she would be, no more than twelve or thirteen, he would guess; but as that was the age at which most heiresses were married off, he could not feel any but the slightest aversion to be taking her for Rothwell, and that only because she was so young, and lovely as well.

It was too common a happening, the old lords taking children to wife, and he had already grappled with his conscience about taking *any* wife to someone like Rothwell, deciding a man in his position could not afford to involve himself with the right or wrong of it. If he did not take her to the old man, someone else would, so why should he give up five hundred marks simply because Rothwell personally disgusted him? If he had been dragging his feet over the whole affair, 'twas only because of his own reluctance to actually have to deal with a "lady." Personal experience had taught him well that they were not what they seemed to be.

This one, for all her look of sweet innocence and nervousness, too, as she approached him, could be as vicious and cruel as any other he had known; reminded of that, Ranulf gritted his teeth now that he must actually speak with her. 'Twas sheer perversity that he did not rise for the sake of chivalry, or even because her rank was so far above him. Ladies had long been calling him brute and churl because he did not hide his contempt for them. But because he *must* deal with this one, he schooled his features to a blandness that did not reveal what he really felt.

She, in fact, curtsied before him. Well, why not? He was accustomed to being called lord by servants or anyone who did not know he was no more than a landless knight undeserving of that title.

"I bid you welcome to Clydon," she said as she rose, her voice soft if a bit hesitant in her nervousness. "Do forgive us for not greeting you sooner, but we all thought our lady would have met you in—"

"Your lady? *You* are not Reina de Champeney?"

"Oh, nay, my lord. I am Elaine Fitz Osbern of Forthwick. 'Tis my honor to be fostered here at Clydon with my father's overlady."

"Now, Ranulf . . ." Walter began as he saw his friend's expression darken dangerously, but he was too late.

"By Christ's holy blood!" Ranulf bellowed. "I will know why the lady will not receive me, and I will know it now! You, Malfed, were sent—"

"My lord, please!" Aubert cried, fearfully backing away even as Elaine Fitz Osbern was doing. "My lady was not where I thought she would be, but she means to make you welcome, I swear!"

"Five minutes, sirrah, or by God—"

He did not have to finish. Aubert turned about and ran away again, this time toward the bailey. Ranulf then fixed his eyes back on Lady Elaine, who began to stutter.

"May—may I—offer—" With a tiny gasp, she gave up and fled, too.

"Well, there goes our refreshment, thank you very much," Walter grumbled. "And that thunder of yours has frightened away everyone else as well. I suppose I could *try* to find the buttery myself, but God's wounds, it might take days to locate it in a place this size.''

Ranulf's reply was curt and to the point. ''Searle, stuff something in his mouth if he says another word.''

Chapter Five

Aubert nearly ran Reina down on the stairs as she mounted them with Theodric at her side. If Theo had not caught her, she would have gone tumbling backwards, yet the squire was so agitated he did not even think to apologize.

"Thank God you are come at last, my lady! The lord has somehow taken insult that you have not received him. He affrighted Lady Elaine to death and—"

"And you as well, I see," Reina snapped impatiently. *"Jesú,* I told *you* to make them welcome, Aubert. Did you offer refreshment, see to their comfort?"

"I—I did not think you would be so long, and—and he is monstrous, my lady. I have never seen a man so—"

"Lackwit! Do you tell me all this time no one has attended them?"

"I thought *you* would be down."

"I never came up! There were wounded who needed immediate attention and—oh! Never mind. I swear, Aubert, you have me so wroth, if I do not see you for a sennight, 'twill be too soon. Do *something* right and pull me up these stairs. I am tired unto death and, thanks to you, cannot even sneak past them to get to my chamber as I intended. Theo, do not just stand there grinning like an idiot. Help!"

"You must admit, my lady, that we do not often see you in such a grouch." Theo chuckled as he pulled on one arm, and Aubert the other, to maneuver the last few stairs. " 'Tis most novel and enlightening. There, can you manage now?" he asked at the top of the stairs.

"Aye, and you will find yourself demoted to the kitchens if I am treated to any more of your humor. You overstep yourself, but then you always do. I am in no mood for it just now. And where the devil *is* everyone?" she said as she looked across the hall to find it empty except for those few men by the hearth at the far side of it.

"I *told* you he was fearsome," Aubert said indignantly.

"What you said was 'monstrous.' Do you mean this lord has frightened everyone into hiding?"

"I did not see them leave because I was leaving too quickly myself, but they are wise to hide. He is not *normal,* Lady Reina, and do hurry."

"Do I have reason to fear, Aubert?" she asked in all seriousness now.

"Nay, he wants to see that you are safe, is all. He would not believe me when I told him you were. Methinks he suspects something amiss because you have not appeared to him yet, and the longer he waits, the more suspicious he is become."

"Well, run ahead and tell him I am found. I simply cannot hurry, Aubert, to save my soul, not with this armor now weighing as much as a horse."

"Please, my lady, he is like to wring my neck before I get the words out if you are not beside me. Let us just go."

She sighed and did just that, with one of them on

each side of her, yet several feet behind her, she noted in disgust. Her "protectors." She would feel safer with her ladies around her, even if most of them were children.

Shoulders slumped, her head aching from exhaustion, her body feeling as if it had been battered, and so it had been when that wounded man had fallen on her, Reina presented herself to her "savior," started to curtsy—whether she would be able to rise by herself afterward was another matter—and found herself lifted clear off the floor instead.

"I am done with excuses, delays, and evasions, so if you have not come to tell me where the lady of this castle is, you are a dead man."

Reina's mouth dropped open, but not to utter any words. Words were stuck halfway down her gullet and were not likely to come up soon. He held her off the floor with his fist hooked into her mailed tunic just above her breasts, one fist, one single fist supporting her and her accursed mail more than a foot above the rushes, bringing her face up to a level with his. A peek down revealed that much; revealed, too, that *he* was not standing on anything to account for this height. Monstrous, Aubert had said? Sweet *Jesú*, this was a giant, as wide across as he was tall—well, that was an exaggeration—but he was incredibly wide across the shoulders and chest, easiest to see in her present position of looking *down* on things. No tall reed this, but a bear, with a bear's growl.

She was not the only one in momentary shock. Theodric and Aubert were likewise rendered speechless, that this giant would dare, *dare*, to treat her so, to speak to her so, and not only that. He shook her!

He actually shook her when she did not answer him soon enough.

Aubert was the first to regain his senses, only to lose them again in thinking he alone could do something. Instead of speaking up to inform the giant of his mistake, the fool lad chose *that* moment to finally be courageous. He leapt on the giant's back, to be shrugged off as if he were no more than a pesky squirrel. The giant was annoyed enough by it to shake Reina even harder.

Reina then heard the most reasonable voice suggest dryly, "Mayhap if you set him down, Ranulf, the fellow would remember he has a tongue."

But it was Theodric who did the remembering and said, " 'Tis the Lady Reina you are throttling, my lord."

Oh, curse and rot that boy for not being more subtle! The giant was so surprised he dropped her, just let go, and Reina went crashing to the floor at his feet.

They stood around her, three towering knights too stunned to move, let alone speak, staring down at her with the most ridiculous expressions. If Reina did not hurt so, she would have laughed, for this truly was the perfect topping to an otherwise rotten day. But she did see the humor in it. Later she would be mortified. Just now, it was their turn.

"Well, this is one way to discover if the rushes need changing."

She could not have said anything to embarrass the giant more. If it were possible, his face would have gone up in flames, it burned so red.

Reina felt better already, until she tried to rise by herself and could manage no more than getting to her hands and knees. *Jesú,* she had to get this armor off her back—immediately. Nothing had ever made her so graceless and bone-weary, and the minute it was off, it was going straight into the fire.

Two hands slipped under her arms, and she became weightless again for a second as she was lifted and then set on her feet. Directly at eye level now was the giant's chest. Reina refused to look any higher until she stepped back several feet so she would not have to crane her neck. And then she felt her own surprise.

That face had been a golden blur before, but now she saw each feature clearly. Golden brows, straight and thick, and far darker than the light golden hair, of a length to set on those immense shoulders. A well-shaped nose between broad cheekbones covered with sun-kissed skin. Firm lips over a square-cut jaw shaded with dark bronze stubble. It was a face harsh in its masculinity, yet even so, incredibly handsome. And he had violet eyes, piercing, narrowing now as she stared. Violet! Imagine that.

Ranulf could feel his anger returning, and centering solely on the lady, if lady she really was. He had thought her a man, albeit a little one, but a man nonetheless, and who would not think so with her shapeless mail hauberk that fell to her knees, mailed chausses on her legs, a mail coif clinging to her head, leaving only a small oval of her face visible. Even her brows and chin were covered by the coif, and there was dried blood on her sleeves and hands.

She might not be wearing a sword or any other weapon, but she in no way appeared to be a woman—except her voice was soft and melodic, but heard too late to keep him from making a fool of himself. He did not even have the appeasement of seeing her react to him as most females did. She might have been surprised, but for no more than a second. Her large blue eyes, as pale as the morning sky, held no admiration or fascination as they looked him over. They were direct now, without fear, with just the barest trace of curiosity.

"Thank you," he heard her say in response to his assistance.

"Nay, I must beg your pardon," he heard himself answer, when what he wanted to do was rip that coif off her head to see if he could then determine if she was child or woman. He did not like not knowing.

And then she surprised him by taking full blame for his mistake, when she had every right to upbraid him instead. "Nay, my lord, 'tis I who must beg pardon for receiving you like this, and so causing confusion. I had hoped to change first, but Aubert said you were—impatient—to be assured of my safety."

The dark-haired man beside the golden giant laughed suddenly. "And so you were safe, demoiselle, until you came before my friend here. Allow me to present to you this chagrined fellow who is feeling much the fool, Ranulf Fitz Hugh, and our young friend, Searle of Totnes."

"And you are?"

"Walter de Breaute, at your service."

She inclined her head to each of them, though she was waiting for the giant to speak again. But he did not, did no more than glower at Walter de Breaute for making light of his embarrassment.

They might have given their names, but Reina was aware they had not really said *who* they were. Still, courtesy demanded. "I am Reina de Champeney and

I bid you welcome to Clydon. Your arrival was most timely, as I am sure you have realized.''

Walter was quick to forestall her thanks. ''How long were you under siege?''

''There was no siege. They attacked with the dawn, after their man who had passed the night with us opened the outer gates to them.''

''And you went out to fight them yourself?''

Now that the giant was heard from again, his contempt unmistakable, Reina could have wished he had kept his mouth shut. ''To fight, nay. My man, Sir William, was bedfast, and there was no one else capable of taking charge.''

''You sent for help?''

''There was no time,'' Reina answered without thinking, then paled to realize what a fool she was to give him that information before knowing his purpose there.

He might have saved her from one devil, but he could as like as not be another. And she would swear he seemed relieved with her answer, that his lips were not so tightly drawn now, his stance more relaxed.

''Why have you no—''

Reina cut him off. ''You have not said what brings you to Clydon Castle.''

''We come from your lord.''

Reina relaxed at once. That was a strange way to say he was from Guy of Shefford, but then he was a strange man. They no doubt had been asked to deliver another letter from the earl's castellan on their way past Clydon, since she had not yet answered the last one as to the date of her wedding. Nor could she answer this one, at least not until John de Lascelles arrived next week and she knew whether he would be agreeable to marrying her or not. Lord Richard, whom she would have preferred to wed, was still in Ireland, according to his castellan's last reply, seeing to his father's lands there. The man had been unable to tell her when Richard would return. But these were her problems and must await another time.

Since these men were vassals to Shefford, as she was now herself, it was her due to have their help, so she need not feel quite so beholden. But they were indeed welcome, even if they were only Shefford retainers.

"Forgive my abruptness, Sir Ranulf. I must confess I am sore overset by this morning's happenings. I will answer all of your questions, but allow me, please, to see to your comfort first." At his reluctant nod, she sighed with relief and turned to Aubert, who was just now dusting off his clothes from his sprawl in the rushes. She was too tired to bother with her own. "Get the servants back to set up the tables for dinner, then send my steward to me for further orders. He will see to Sir Ranulf's men, so you report to Lady Margaret. I wish to know how Sir William fares. Theo, find Dame Hilary and have her prepare several chambers, with baths for each, and wine. Do not forget the wine. And send Lady Elaine to the wounded. I took care of the most needful, but there is still minor stitching to do, and 'tis time she learned to apply her needle to flesh. Then you may see to me."

Walter watched her walk away from them and shook his head. "She can barely stand up, let alone get to her chamber, and God's wounds, did you hear the way she took command, and she such a tiny thing? Mayhap I should help her . . ." His words trailed off as Ranulf left his side, and his mouth dropped open when he saw Ranulf had left to follow the lady himself.

Ranulf reached her in only three strides and scooped her up in his arms. He heard her gasp but ignored it, continuing on to the stairs she had been heading toward.

"You should not wear armor if you cannot carry its weight," was all he said.

Well she knew it but did not say so, too afeard at the moment of his intent. But that fear lasted only as long as it took him to mount the stairs, mere seconds, even though the stairwell in the east corner tower rose the two-storied height of the Great Hall to reach the third floor of the keep. At the top he set her down and, with a curt nod, immediately returned below.

How chivalrous, she thought, then thought of him no more. The door to the lord's chambers was right there, with the stairs continuing up to the battlements surrounding the roof, but Reina moved slowly down the narrow passage that cut through the thick wall of the keep, lit by several window embrasures. She passed the women's quarters, where most of her ladies slept in a chamber beyond, with the weaving-and-sewing room in front where the chambermaids slept, and finally reached her own small chamber in the north tower. She could have long since moved into the spacious lord's chamber, but her grief had kept her from it, and when she married would be soon enough to take up residence there.

Her room was empty, as it should be this time of morning, and Reina slumped back against the door with a weary sigh, too tired to move even a few feet more to her bed. She could not think of the rest of the day, the entertaining she must do, the questions she had promised to answer for her guests. It was so hard speaking to visitors, never knowing how much to say, who might be aware of her circumstances, lying to anyone who was not. The lying was the worst, and it was her father who had started it all, thinking he was doing as she would want.

If only Lord Raymond had not died, she would have wed before her father left to follow King Richard on Crusade two years ago. She had been betrothed to Raymond when she was only three, had never thought to object to the match even though she barely knew Raymond, had seen him no more than a half-dozen times in her whole life. But when it was time for them to marry, he had become a favorite of Henry's court, and the old king had made much use of him, sending him hither and yon to do his bidding. There never seemed to be time for Raymond to send for her, or to come himself to Clydon so they could speak their vows. And then she had received the news that he had died while crossing the Channel, drowned while trying to save a child who had fallen overboard.

Reina was saddened by the news, but 'twas not as if she knew the man well enough to truly grieve for him. Yet his dying had certainly put her in a fix, for her father had already taken the vow to go crusading with his overlord, Lord Guy, and the new king, Richard Lion-Heart. There she was, fifteen, unwed, and Roger de Champeney about to depart for the Holy Land, with no time to find her another husband.

So he had bidden her to make some choices of her own and send them to him for his approval, and this she had done. But her first letter to him had not reached him. She heard from him first, of how they had stopped to conquer Cyprus, and of the king's marriage there to Berengaria of Navarre. He had taken four of his vassals with him and had lost one to fever in Cyprus.

There had been a cart full of loot with that letter, but she had been loath to sell any of it no matter how much she needed the money, for it came from the Crusade, and that made it almost holy.

Her second letter had reached him still in Cyprus, for the king had stayed long there, and her father wrote again, approving of two of the men whose names she had submitted: Lord John de Lascelles, who used to be one of her father's retainers until his brother died and he inherited the family lands in Wales, and Richard de Arcourt, heir to Lyonsford, and already in possession of Warhurst Keep and town, which was only a few hours' ride from Clydon. Both men Reina knew fairly well and liked; both she felt she could deal well with as husbands. Both men were young and fair to the eye. Richard was possessed of a fine humor and could make her laugh; John was good and kind. She would be happy with either, but her preference was Richard.

Her father died in the siege of Acre just a month after he had written his last letter, so he never knew of her preference. The letter she got from the earl, informing her of his death, also mentioned that Roger had told him she *was* betrothed again, only he had apparently been delirious before he died and had not given the earl a name. "I have no fear that whoever Roger chose for you will be acceptable to me and willing to do me homage. He loved me too well, and I him, to put an enemy of mine in Clydon, so this is to officially give you my permission, and my blessing

on your wedding.'' But the earl also went on to say
he wanted the deed done within a few months for her
own safety, and news of it sent to him.

Reina had been confused, until she realized what
her father had done. He had lied to his friend and
overlord to give Reina her preference, one of the two
men he had approved for her; otherwise Lord Guy,
who became her guardian on her father's death, had
the right to choose a man for her, or even to sell her
wardship instead, keeping her unmarried, though he
was not likely to do that. Although he had always
been kind to her and loved her because he loved her
father, such things were not considered when making
an alliance. And without his permission and his approval of the man she married, she could lose her
inheritance.

So she had written to Richard, asking him to come
to Clydon. She had not said why, unwilling to propose an alliance in a letter, but she had conveyed an
urgency. He had been difficult to locate, and after a
month had passed and she had yet to hear from him,
she had written to John, too, willing at this point to
take either one of them, especially with the earl's castellan pressing her for a date. After this morning and
Falkes de Rochefort's effort to take her, the urgency
was far more critical. She was lucky that in all these
months, he was the *only* one to try.

Reina started to push herself away from the door,
only to have it push back at her as it opened. Her
shout stopped Theodric from sending her flying.

"Reina, you should have seen that slut Eadwina
wagging her tail in his face," Theo said in disgust.
"And Dame Hilary will send her to bathe him unless

you say otherwise. Let me see to him, Reina, please? Eadwina always gets—''

"See to who?"

He gave a dramatic sigh. "The golden behemoth. Who else?"

Reina sighed normally. Who else indeed? "Go." She waved a hand. "What do I care?" And then: "Wait! Get this devil's weight off my back first."

He did, stripping her down faster than he ever had before. She almost laughed at his impatience. And he had called Eadwina a slut?

When only her underwear was left, the sweaty short shift and braies, she collapsed on the bed. "Did you at least see to my bathwater ere you rushed up here?"

"Of course," he replied indignantly as he tossed her armor into a corner.

"Then send Wenda to me. And, Theo?" She leaned up on her elbows to warn him. "If your 'behemoth' is not interested, best get out of his way right quickly."

The boy nodded, grinned and was gone.

Chapter Six

Lord Rothwell did not deserve to be so fortunate. A man who had gained his extensive lands through the wedding of five rich wives, and now he was doing it again, increasing his vast wealth with Clydon.

Ranulf did not know if there were other fiefs or subtenants involved, but Clydon alone was a magnificent holding by any standards. He had seen the numerous fields planted with spring crops on his approach to the castle; the large village, large enough to contain at least two hundred villeins, with sturdy cruck cottages made with timber trusses to last, a stream flowing behind it, giant oaks shading it. There was a water mill in the distance, and a manor house, and an immense stretch of woods where he and his men had camped yestereve and left the supply wains and camp followers this morn.

But it was the castle itself that was most impressive. Not even Lord Montfort's demesne keep was as large, nor Ranulf's father's, for that matter. The outer bailey was several acres at least protected by the thick curtain wall with its many towers projecting at regular intervals. Numerous buildings stood back against the walls inside the bailey: a large stable, a thatched barn with animal pens on either side, a smithy, a brewhouse and several storehouses. There was a fish pond in the left field as well as a large dovecote, but the entire right field was allowable for an exercise yard.

The mews were in the inner bailey, as were a granary and a smaller stable and more storehouses. Here too were the kitchen and a garden complete with beehives, though a newer kitchen had been added inside the keep, following the example of keeps built in recent years, in an attempt to have food passably warm by the time it reached the table.

The whitewashed keep itself, with immensely thick walls, rose at least a hundred feet, the corner towers rising another twelve. Divided by a cross-wall to support its height, the keep boasted three floors above a basement, with garrison quarters and wellhead sharing space now with the new kitchen on the second floor, the Great Hall on the third. Entrance to the keep was through the forebuilding, a substantial extension on the left side of the castle. It rose three stories itself, the external stairs leading up to the second floor protected at the top by a collapsible bridge, the chapel on the top floor of it, off the Great Hall.

Ranulf had seen much of this himself. The squire Aubert had supplied more detail during his rattling discourse as he led them up to the Great Hall, and the servant the lady had called Theo was also a font of information, answering whatever questions Ranulf put to him. 'Twas the only reason Ranulf had let the boy attend him at his bath when he offered his service, sending Lanzo off straightaway to clean his bloodied armor and sword.

Usually a female servant was sent to assist a guest at his bath, though if the guest was important enough, the lady herself would do it—the lord's wife, that is, rarely his daughter. Ranulf had never been considered important enough to have the lady of the house attend him, which he was grateful for, but he did usually get the cream of the wenches fighting for the honor, and he could remember many a pleasant hour spent not just in bathing.

At the back of his mind, he had expected to see that luscious blond wench from the hall show up in the tower chamber he had been led to, but instead the boy had arrived with the menservants carrying in the large tub and heated water, a tray of wine, cheese and fine manchet bread to tide him till the afternoon meal was served, and even a change of clothes, which he was not usually offered, mostly because of his size, then again, because he was not an important guest. He allowed the Lady of Clydon did consider him important, not only because he had said he came from her lord (he was not unaware she assumed he had meant a different lord than Rothwell) but because he had literally saved her and Clydon from her enemies, whoever they might have been.

That he was not getting a wench to assist him did not matter. He was not in need of a woman after his indulgence last night. He was instead intrigued by Theo's presence. Not full grown yet, the boy was lanky with a slow grace of his movements that was almost womanish, surely to be outgrown eventually. Dark blond hair curled about his ears and nape, and his brown eyes were too boldly direct for a servant's. But he was a handsome boy, or would be once his face matured past its prettiness.

Ranulf had noted the way Lady Reina had put her hand on the boy's shoulder as she gave him her orders in the hall. The gesture was noted because it was not usual to see a lady touch a servant, for any reason, especially a male servant. He had also heard her say to him, "Then you may see to me." What that could mean he could not imagine, but the boy was obviously special to her in some way. So being, 'twas likely he had her confidence as well as trust, and would know just about all there was to know about her. That he was here must also be at her order, and could only be to gain information from Ranulf for her, though he had yet to ask any questions himself, and had not hesitated to answer all of Ranulf's inquiries about Clydon.

Stripped down, Ranulf stepped into the large round tub, the weight of his body as he sat down raising the water up to his chest. He did not notice the way Theo's eyes watched his every move, glittering with anticipation.

Theodric was fair drooling, but frightened, too. He had never seen a body so beautiful or so big. Iron-hewed strength rippled from every muscle. Arms like that could break bones without even trying. Long, long legs, a tight, exquisitely curved arse, a broad back that went on forever, all golden-skinned and rock-hard. Theo could be killed. He must take the chance. But he did not know how to proceed with one such as this.

He had removed the knight's clothes, fingers lingering and touching as much as he dared without offending, but the man had not noticed, had barely even looked at him as he asked questions Theo answered by rote, his thoughts centered on only one thing. He did not usually have to be so obvious. A sultry look was enough, but not apparently for this man, whose interest seemed wholly for Clydon—until now.

"How old is she, your lady?"

Theo saw the knight reaching for the washcloth and

soap on the stool by the tub and dived for them himself. "Do let me wash you, my lord."

Ranulf shrugged, though he had not expected the boy's help to extend this far. But Lanzo or Kenric often scrubbed his back for him, so he leaned forward to expose it, yet did not forget his question.

"Your lady?"

Theo soaped the cloth, but hesitated in both answering and touching. "Why do you ask?"

"Because I saw no breasts, no hips, no curves of any kind to help me to even come close in guessing. Is she no more than a child?"

Theo might have been offended to hear his lady's breasts and hips and curves mentioned by a stranger—by any man, for that matter—but he grinned instead, though Ranulf did not see it. Reina was not in fact as shapely as most women, but what she had was just right for her size. The trouble was, her size was extremely petite. For anyone not allowed into her chamber where she could be seen unclothed, there was no way to tell that her legs were perfectly formed, that she had the prettiest, most enviable little derrière, a gracefully sloping back as smooth as silk. Her breasts might not be a handful, but, freed of restriction, they were pert and upthrusting, with large nipples that would make a man's mouth water—most men's, anyway.

Theo had to force the smugness from his tone when answering, for he might know all this, but this knight never would. "My lady has not been a child for many years. She might not appear so, but she is a woman full grown."

Ranulf was aware his question had not really been

answered as to age. If the boy would not speak of the lady, he would know it now.

"If she is so long past childhood, why is she not married?"

Theo moved the washcloth caressingly over the golden skin. It was difficult to think with that beautiful, thick-muscled back under his hand.

"She was betrothed, but he died two years past."

"But she was betrothed again?"

Theo frowned, trying to concentrate. This was now a dangerous subject. The man was from Shefford, so he should think Reina was betrothed as Shefford thought she was, when in fact she was not, not yet. So why would he ask about it?

"Certainly she is betrothed. Did Sir Henry not send you here to inquire of the date for the wedding? Lord Guy's castellan must come to witness and accept the new Lord of Clydon's homage to Shefford in the earl's stead."

Ranulf was grateful to have an excuse for being here given to him so easily. And 'twas obvious now that Rothwell had been right in at least one thing. If there really had been a contract with Rothwell, the lady was indeed ignoring it. She was planning to marry someone else.

"Then the date is—finally fixed?" Ranulf asked.

Theo took advantage of the giant's distraction to lean closer and bring the washcloth around to his chest. "Only my lady can answer that."

"And who is the fortunate husband-to-be?"

Theo was out of his league now, for Reina usually fended off such questions. How could he say it was de Lascelles, when if de Arcourt should miraculously show up first, Reina would pick him instead? He took a chance that Ranulf Fitz Hugh did not know that a name had never been given, and would not admit to being excluded from that knowledge if he thought it was known by the man who had sent him.

" 'Tis not widely known, but surely Sir Henry would have told you?"

Ranulf grunted in answer. The boy was being evasive again, and he liked it not. If the planned wedding was to be soon, and the lady would certainly want it to be soon after coming so close to capture this morn, what was so secretive about the name of this man she was taking in Rothwell's place? He could not be her father's choice, if Rothwell had spoken the truth. So it had to be the Earl of Shefford's doing, done after Roger de Champeney's death. No woman would presume to arrange an alliance for herself or break a betrothal. The scorned man would doubtless send an army after her, or a mercenary, as Rothwell had done. Then why would the earl leave her unprotected all this time? If he wanted to give her to another man, it should have been done immediately, for she was fair game until the deed was done.

It was a puzzle, but one that did not really matter. Ranulf's duty was to take the lady to Rothwell, and so he would. It was nothing to him who eventually held Clydon through her. He could envy the man such a prize, for Clydon was magnificent. That it came with a tiny, childlike woman who gave orders like a general was the only drawback, but of little account, for she could be a crippled hunchback and still be desirable as long as Clydon was hers.

With his thoughts wandering, Ranulf had not been paying attention to Theo or what he was doing, so it was a jolt to find the boy on the side of him now, his

arm in the water in front of him, his hand with the
washing cloth in it moving up the inside of Ranulf's
thick thigh. He stiffened, disbelieving the suspicion
that leapt to his mind. The lad could not be that sui-
cidal. And yet giving him the benefit of the doubt
hanged him, for that hand continued on. In the same
second that it touched Ranulf where it had no business touching, he turned to the boy and caught the
glazed eyes on him, and then his reaction was instan-
taneous.

His bellow of rage shook the rafters, and with a
single swipe of his arm he sent Theo tumbling across
the room. "Christ's toes! She sends me a catamite!"

Theo scrambled to his feet, but in his disappointment he said sulkily, "You could have just said nay."

"Nay?" Ranulf shouted incredulously. "You misbegotten little cur, you are lucky I do not rip your
prick off and shove it up your arse! Get you gone
before I change my mind!"

Ranulf watched with fire-banked eyes as Theo
tripped over his own feet racing out of the chamber.
He should have known by the girlish manner, should
have been more alert, but the lady had sent the boy
to him, so all he had suspected was that he was to be
grilled for information—which he was not. By the
rood, did she think he was a God-cursed sodomite,
then? Did he look so? But there was no look to it,
was there?

His temper moved down to a slow simmer as he
admitted that to himself. Even the king, an intrepid
warrior, a giant among men, was rumored to prefer
a boy in his bed. There were men who would have it
either way, and men who would have it only one way
or the other. He heard enough church preachings

about it to know it was a perversion that was rife. But Ranulf had never been approached before. No man had dared. That girlish Theo was lucky Ranulf had not torn him apart.

Chapter Seven

Reina rarely used the bathing stool that would be placed in the center of the large, cloth-lined tub for her to sit on, and this time was no different. But today her need was to sink down into the hot water to help ease her sore muscles, and as she was so small, she did not need that much water. Oil of myrrh had been added to her bath, and its delicate, exotic sweetness soothed and relaxed her; it had been her favorite scent ever since she discovered it in the cartload of treasures her father sent home.

The opening of the door had her sitting up in the tub, since Wenda had already brought in the last of the hot water heated over the hearth in the lord's chamber, but she sank back down again when she saw it was only Theodric. She heard him dismiss Wenda and wondered why he was back so soon, but she waited for him to volunteer the information. She had a foreboding that she would not like it, and so was in no hurry to hear it.

She had already spoken to her steward and was sure everything would be nearly back to normal below, but she knew she should not be tarrying in her chamber, not with guests in the keep. Yet her chamber was the one place, the only place, where she could be assured of privacy without demands being made of her, which was what she needed at the moment. No one but Theo or Wenda would ever enter here without her permission, and when she was here, which was not often, everyone knew she did not like to be disturbed.

These rules had come about because of Theo. Her ladies knew that he served her, but not in what capacity. They knew that women held no attraction for him—how could they not know when he was so *obvious* about his preferences? Still, they were most of them too young to understand if they should walk in, like now, and find him in the chamber whilst she was in her bath.

His twin sister, Ethelinda, had been her chambermaid since Reina was twelve. That the twins were nigh inseparable had gotten Reina used to having Theo in her chamber, at first attending to the chores allotted to menservants, but soon, when Ethelinda was busy, taking over some of her duties. His touch was more gentle, so he was better at combing and arranging her hair, kept her clothing neater; abhorred filth, so kept her chamber cleaner.

When he was fourteen he had his first affair of the heart, and although she was shocked that it was with another male, she soon became used to that, too. Afterward, she no longer dived for cover to hide her nudity whenever he unexpectedly entered her chamber. He became just Theo, a male, but not a male in any threatening sense. So it seemed only natural, when Ethelinda died in a tragic accident not long after Reina's father left for the Holy Land, that Theo should assume all her duties.

Reina had already been attached to him, as she had been to his sister. They consoled each other in their grief over the loss of Ethelinda and became even closer. There grew a bond between them. Theo was not just her servant but her friend, which was why he took liberties with her that no other would dare to take. But her father would not have allowed it, no man was likely to understand, so no one except Wenda actually knew that Theo was her "chambermaid," that it was he who bathed her, dressed her, saw to all her needs.

The "secret" had been necessary while she was younger, and to protect her even younger ladies from any undue influence, but now Reina was a right unto herself and did not care who knew, for no one would dare gainsay her. Not even her husband could say aught about who should serve her, not with all she would bring to him, especially after knowing the circumstances. But if necessary, she would have it included in her marriage contract.

Theo was still silent, and Reina's water was growing cold. "Well?" she called from deep in the tub.

"Well, what?"

She sat up at that sulky reply to rest her arms on the edge of the tub. It took a moment for her to locate Theo sitting dejectedly on the floor in the corner, his arms wrapped around bent knees upon which his chin drooped.

She obviously did not need to ask, but did, gently. "He was not interested?"

"Not even a little."

"What is wrong with you? You do not usually take rejection so to heart."

His head snapped up. "You did not *see* him, Reina, all golden-skinned and so beaut—"

"Spare me his praises, Theo," she cut in dryly. " 'Tis ever the same with you each time a new, handsome face comes along. And you never stop to think of your current lover and what he would do if he learned of it. Is he not one of the men-at-arms? I do not want to have to send him to Roth Hill as I did the last one because he beat you for your unfaithfulness.''

"Can I help it that men are so possessive?''

Reina laughed at his long-suffering tone. "If you want to be like Eadwina and flit from one man to another, then you should not commit yourself to a single one.''

"You compare me to that slut, who has crawled into every bed in the keep?'' he demanded indignantly. "She is too stupid to know how to please a man for more than one day!''

"But smart enough to avoid any jealous beatings, which you are not,'' she reminded him. "I do not like putting you back together after they are done with you. If you cannot be faithful, Theo, at least pick your lovers smaller than you, or build up your muscles.''

"But I *like* to feel helpless, as a woman would feel. Would *you* want to be stronger—''

"We are not discussing me,'' she retorted as she stood up. "And I do not know why I bother to talk sense into you, for you will do as you always do, no matter what I say.''

Theo was quick to come forward with a drying cloth and to help her out of the large tub, which she was only just able to step over. He was loath to tell her he had made the giant angry, but he could not let her face the man not knowing. She brought up the subject again herself.

"Did you at least discover what this Sir Ranulf is doing here?''

He wrapped a cloth around her wet hair, washed earlier by Wenda. "There was not much chance of putting a question to him with all those he was asking. He was curious about Clydon, as most everyone is who comes here for the first time. But he was also curious about you.''

''Oh?''

Theo grinned, remembering. ''He was vexed, I think, that he could not tell how old you were.'' He was not about to repeat the man's exact words. ''He asked your age, when the wedding was to be, and who your betrothed was.''

''And what did you tell him?''

''Nothing to set his teeth into, so he is like to repeat his questions to you—that is, if he calms down enough.''

Reina became very still. ''Theo, tell me you did not offend him?''

''Of course not . . . but . . . he might think otherwise.''

''Tell me!''

Theo blushed, looking away. ''He was so distracted that when I . . . well, I did not get out of the way as quick as you suggested. He was ready to tear me apart. I did not wait around to see if he would.''

''Oh, Theo,'' Reina groaned. ''Could you not sense that he was not interested *before* you went so far as to make him wroth?''

''I told you, he was distracted.'' His tone turned defensive. ''There was no easy way—''

''You could have just asked him right out! Sweet *Jesú*, what was I thinking to let you near him? I do not need this on top of everything else.'' She threw open her clothes chest and yanked out whatever was on top. ''Well, do not just stand there. I must hurry now so he will not be kept waiting a second time. Did you at least send Eadwina to finish his bath?''

Theo tossed a linen shift over her head. "She was already busy with one of the others.''

"Who did you send?''

"Amabel.''

"Theo! Fat Amabel? How could you?''

"What did I do?'' he replied in all innocence as he tied the laces on her long-sleeved chemise. "She was available.''

Reina glared at him, ready to box his ears. "If he was not insulted before, he is like to be now. And I swear, if your silly spite causes me difficulty with him, I will myself nail your hide to the wall.''

Theo protested. "He had so much on his mind he was not interested in a tumble, from anyone. He will not even notice Amabel.''

"You better have the right of it. Oh, *Jesú*, you still have to dry my hair! Do hurry, Theo. I must be there when he returns to the hall.''

Chapter Eight

*R*anulf came down the tower stairwell to find Walter sitting on the bottom step waiting for him. "I was beginning to think you were lost up there. And here I thought I would be the last to return to the hall after that stunning little blond wench saw to me."

Walter could not have said anything worse, not after Ranulf had lingered apurpose in the tower chamber to give his temper time to cool off. First he was given that catamite, then a female so hefty even he could not get his arms around her if he had wanted to, which fortunately he did not.

"How was she?" Ranulf said curtly.

"Need you ask?"

Ranulf growled low in his throat before demanding, "Has the lady come down yet?"

"Aye, a while ago," Walter said with a curious look. "And what is wrong with you?"

"Naught that *she* cannot fix," Ranulf replied and passed through the archway that opened into the Great Hall.

With anger near choking him, he headed straight for the raised dais and the large hearth in the center of it, where Searle and Eric stood amidst an entire group of ladies. Even the thought of going among so many "ladies" did not daunt him. But he did slow down and feel rather deflated as he rounded the long table now set with white linen for the afternoon meal, realizing belatedly that he would not know which of the women was Reina de Champeney.

There were four older women, the young Lady Elaine, whom he had frightened earlier, and three other girls who looked no more than twelve or thirteen. Which of the older women was the Lady of Clydon was impossible to guess, for even the oldest could be no more than a score and ten years.

It was the youngest of the four women who stepped away from the others to greet him. That her eyes, as well as the others', were lowered demurely kept him still in the dark, for at least he would have recognized those cerulean-blue eyes he had seen earlier.

"Sir Ranulf, allow me to make known to you Lady Margaret, wife to Sir William Folville, who is still bedfast and unable to join us."

Lady Margaret was the oldest. One down and three *women* to go.

"Lady Elaine says she has met you." Was that censure he heard in her tone? "And this is Lady Alicia, Sir William's daughter."

A pretty twelve-year-old. He was obviously being introduced by rank.

"Dames Hilary and Florette are widows now," the spokeslady continued. "Their husbands were Clydon knights, lost with my father in the Holy Land."

That demanded a response, even though he now knew for certain after this introduction which was the lady he meant to have words with. Dame Hilary was a stout woman of a score and five years, Dame Florette a winsome brunette with green eyes that peeked up at him shyly. And that took care of the women present except for the one beside him.

"I am sorry to hear of your recent loss," Ranulf

said to these·two, getting no more than a halfhearted
smile and nod in reply.

"Cecilia's and Eleanor's fathers also joined mine
on Crusade. We are hoping these knights will return
safely with Lord Guy."

These were the last two younger girls, each too shy
or frightened to look up at him. "The honor is mine,"
Ranulf allowed, bowing to them all.

And now that that was over, Ranulf was damned
well done with politeness. He turned to the Lady
Reina with every intention of taking her off somewhere and blistering her ears with what he was feeling.

She spoke first, however, placing a tiny hand on
his arm and leaning closer to him to say in a soft,
half-whispered voice, "Sir Ranulf, do you come with
me, please. I would have a private word with you ere
we sit down to table."

For all that "please" she included, it was still a
command to his ears. That it suited him and was what
he would have said, though not so nicely, did not
change the fact he did not like being commanded by
a woman. But she did not wait for his response, taking it for granted he would not refuse her. She turned
away from the others, her hand not just resting on his
arm now but gripping it, as if she meant to pull him
along with her, as if she could if he chose not to
follow. But he did follow her, only because *he* wanted
that private word, too.

She led him to a window embrasure on the side of
the hall between what appeared to be wall chambers.
There were two steps up into the arched alcove, an
area five feet wide and as deep as the thickness of the

walls, with two benches facing each other, lit brightly by afternoon sunlight.

She entered first, sitting on the left bench to face away from the dais. Ranulf took the other bench, though this left him in clear view of those still gathered at the hearth. He did not think that would stop him from venting his anger, as justifiable as it was, but again she did not give him a chance to have the first word.

"Thank you, my lord, for allowing me to apologize to you in private. The incident that resulted from my inattention is embarrassing for me to speak of, as I am sure it is for you, so I will be brief. I meant no insult to you in sending to you my personal servant. I was not thinking clearly when he beseeched me to let him attend you. Theodric is not usually so clumsy in giving insult, but in this case he tells me he did, and for that I beg your forgiveness, for myself and Theo. There is no excuse for his thinking you would be . . . he was simply besotted . . . oh, *Jesú*, this is more embarrassing than I thought."

Reina squirmed uncomfortably, her cheeks flaming with color. The man was not helping her to end this. She had not been able to meet his eyes during this recital, but knew he stared at her, his own color high, waiting to see what more she would say. What more could she say?

With a sigh, she floundered on. "One has only to look at you, Sir Ranulf, to know you are not like . . . well, you must realize by now that Theo is different, that he is attracted only to . . ." She could not go on in that vein. "Verily, I am putting my foot in it."

"Aye, you have that aright."

Reina stiffened to hear his surly bass rumble at last.

So he was still in high dudgeon, was he? She finally met his eyes directly and did not like what she saw in their depths, darkened now to indigo.

Coldly, offended herself that he could not be magnanimous after her apology, she said, "The mistake was mine. Theo cannot help how he is, but he has been with me for five years and is dear to me. I have already chastised him and will assure that you will not be reminded of the incident by his presence. But if you cannot see your way clear to forgetting the matter and wish to leave immediately, I will understand."

Forget it or leave? Ranulf had to choke back what he would like to say to that ultimatum. The little bitch. She was forcing him to let the matter rest, denying him a chance to vent his fury now that she had put it this way. Of course he could not leave, not until night came and he could take her with him. But, by God, she had seen to it that he no longer had any regrets at all about delivering her posthaste to Rothwell. The two deserved each other.

With difficulty, Ranulf got out, "As you say, the matter is forgotten."

"Forsooth, I cannot say I feel forgiven, Sir Ranulf. Do you wish to shake me again? Will that help?"

He glared at her for reminding him that he had also made an unforgivable mistake, and he had little doubt the reminding was done apurpose. And she had the audacity to smile at him now, revealing a row of pearly white teeth.

Nor did she await an answer. She reached across the narrow space between them and placed her small hand on his knee, then drew it back as if recalling she was not familiar enough with him to touch him. Yet she still smiled.

"I was not serious with that offer, you know. Does no one ever tease you?"

"Aye, Walter risks his life often to do so."

She laughed, a soft, pleasing sound. "Fie on you if that is so. I hope 'tis only an empty belly that has you so surly, for that I can amend."

Ranulf had the grace to blush. The lady was still teasing, but if he did not let go of his bad temper right quickly, she would not be offering him a chance to leave, but demanding that he do so.

"Your pardon, demoiselle. And your viands will indeed be most welcome."

"Then we must not make you wait any longer. Come, and you shall share a trencher with me."

Christ's toes, did he have to? She was honoring him, but *he* did not see it so. To sit next to her and have to observe all the courtly rules, to feed her the best portions, cut her meat, make sure her cup was never empty, to in effect do all he could to please her? When a man was hungry he ought to be able to eat his meal in peace, but how could he with ladies present demanding you serve and amuse them?

Ranulf closed his eyes with a groan, then snapped them open again to watch her as she returned to the dais, once again assuming he would follow. His eyes fixed on her narrow hips, swaying gently as she walked, or more likely glided away. How old *was* she? Fifteen? Sixteen? She could not be much more than that, not as tiny as she was. But he had to allow she did have breasts. Two small mounds, but notice-able despite several layers of clothing.

Sitting across from her, he had gotten a good look

at her at last whilst she avoided his eyes due to the
nature of her apology. There was nothing childlike
about her face. It was small but clearly defined, the
face of a woman. Slanting brows were nearly hidden
beneath a fringe of thick bangs. Almond-shaped eyes,
a narrow, straight nose, a wide mouth with full lower
lip, and a small chin completed the picture. It was
not a beautiful face in the ordinary sense, but certainly interesting with that lush lower lip and unblem-
ished skin, a creamy, white softness that almost
demanded touching. But what was unusual and striking about her was the combination of those light, light
blue eyes with hair as black as pitch, brows just as
black, thick lashes blacker still. Not beautiful, but by
no means ugly.

She did not attract him, however, not in the least.
It was the strong, robust wenches who caught his eye,
women capable of withstanding a rough tumble,
which was all he was interested in. Small, delicate
women scared the hell out of him, and if they were
ladies, he liked them even less *because* they were ladies. And this particular lady he liked least of all for
thinking a few paltry words of apology could appease
the insult she had dealt him. Now she had added teasing to the list of grievances he had against her. He
might have to put up with such annoyance from Walter, but not from her.

Noticing Walter grinning at him brought Ranulf to
his feet. He might as well get this over with, the
sooner he could then make plans for their leaving.

A horn sounded, calling the castlefolk to the trestle
tables set up below the dais. Ranulf could scarce believe the small number of soldiers who trudged in,
some wounded. A demesne this size and so obviously

rich could support a garrison of several hundred, so where were the men needed to protect it? He itched to know the answer, but it would have to wait.

He had decided not to question the lady here, where he must guard his temper. She annoyed him too easily with her commanding air, and the less he must talk to her, the better. When he had her away from Clydon would be soon enough to demand answers. She would not be so haughty then.

So he let Walter do what came natural and monopolize the table talk with his jocular humor, even if some of it was at Ranulf's expense. At least Walter kept Lady Reina amused, which kept her attention diverted, and Ranulf did not have to suffer her direct gaze more than once or twice. And after the meal was over, he was able to escape entirely with the excuse of dispatching most of his men, which she did not object to in the least, for his greater force obviously made her nervous, and rightly so. That he could simply take her with that greater force and be done with it was not an option he allowed himself. That would only lead to the unnecessary killing of her people, which stealth would prevent.

Chapter Nine

"What did you find out, Walter?"

"Her chamber is in the north tower, but can only be reached by that stairwell in the east tower you mounted with her this morn."

Ranulf turned away from the narrow arrow-slit window where he had been observing the activity in the inner bailey. "Aye, I do recall seeing a long passageway running directly through the wall, as in the gallery over the hall. Did your source mention what else is up there?"

"The lord's chamber and the women's quarters, where her ladies and their maids sleep."

"Then there can be no mistakes, and no noise to disturb the women. Is that our supply cart I noticed in front of one of those storehouses?"

"Aye," Searle replied to this. "Eric got Rothwell's men back to camp as you ordered and sent one back with the cart. It has already been loaded with the grain Walter was able to purchase."

"Not enough to fill it, I hope."

"Nay, there will be room enough for the lady."

Ranulf nodded before looking toward Kenric and Lanzo. "Have you decided which of you will ride with her?"

"Lanzo will," Kenric answered, "since he is smaller and will take up less room in the cart."

"An inch smaller," Lanzo grumbled, "which is hardly any—"

"Skinnier, then." Kenric grinned.

Walter chuckled, watching this byplay. "So Kenric decided that Lanzo decided to volunteer? Buck up, Lanzo. Yours will be the most important task. You must see to it the lady does not rock the cart, nor make the slightest noise to alert the guards ere we pass through the outer gate. What think you, Ranulf? Can he do it? He is not much bigger than she is."

"A whole inch bigger," Kenric snickered.

"Can you, Lanzo?" Ranulf asked the boy directly and in all seriousness. "Because if you cannot, and the lady makes her presence known to her sentries, we will have to fight our way out of the keep. Know you how many lives will be forfeit if it comes to that?"

"I will do it," Lanzo said firmly and with eagerness now, then tossed Kenric a superior look before asking, "But what is my reason for being in the cart?"

"You should not draw notice, but if you do, you are ill, so ill you could not sit your horse."

"A few moans and puking sounds will help to convince anyone, and serve to cover any sounds the lady might make as well," Walter added. "And our men will surround the cart, though not in an obvious way. They have all been warned to prevent anyone from drawing too near."

"Any more questions?" Ranulf queried. Met with silence, he concluded, "Then we will begin at midnight. Kenric and I will collect the lady. Searle, do you wait outside under the short bridge on the stairs. While Walter distracts the guard in the forebuilding, I will pass the lady to you, so be ready as soon as the door opens. You must secure her in the cart and wait with her there until Lanzo comes to take your place. Be sure you are well hidden when the gates open to admit Eric. His message that our camp has been attacked by outlaws is all the excuse we need to depart. I will have the steward roused to escort us out so there is no delay.''

"And what if he wants to wake the lady?'' Walter asked.

"Then you will put your glib tongue to use to see that he does not. But what need to wake her? We are a force leaving, not begging entrance. So there you have it. Get what sleep you may ere 'tis time to begin, for Eric has already sent Rothwell's men ahead, and we will ride the rest of the night and on through the morrow once we join up with the others. Only one man need stay awake to rouse you, Searle, but see that the rest are prepared to leave the moment they are roused, so that only the horses need be seen to. Kenric will wake us here in the keep to get the lady out, and we should be back in our beds to be roused again when Eric arrives.''

"Then there is naught else to do for now,'' Walter said, dismissing the others.

Ranulf moved to the table to refill his goblet with imported wine. "Did you obtain parchment from the chaplain and write out the warning?''

Walter nodded, removing the note from inside his tunic to hand it over. " 'Twould be best left in her chamber. Whoever enters to wake her in the morn will find it. But do you really think 'twas necessary? With this Sir William still bedfast, there is no one here likely to give chase.''

"Did you not learn that she has other vassals? She

could have sent off for one or more of them today, and likely did, after the morning's attack. She would see the need now to have herself better protected until this wedding that is planned takes place. 'Tis not inconceivable that a large force could arrive on the morrow or soon after.''

"Aye, I see your point," Walter allowed. "But will they heed your warning?"

"They know not what manner of man I am or what I am capable of doing, so why should they not? Do you really think they would risk her life to have her back, when she will eventually be returned to them unharmed?''

"Unharmed, but with a husband not to her liking, nor to theirs."

Ranulf shrugged. "That is nothing to us. 'Tis up to Rothwell to get her men and Shefford to accept him once the deed is done."

Walter swirled the wine in his own cup, staring at it thoughtfully. "In matters such as these, the man usually waits until a babe is on the way to strengthen his position. Rothwell is a mite old to have any fertile seed left. He might be able to bed her, but he will get no child on her. Shefford will know that, and know there will be no heir forthcoming. He might decide to forsake the lady and reclaim Clydon for his own."

"Again, that is no concern of ours. Once we deliver her, we are done with this job. With the money from Rothwell, I now have more than enough to meet de Millers' price, enough even should he think to raise it again."

This last was said with such rancor, Walter had to laugh. "The man does not know what he wants. I thought you would kill him when he added another thousand marks the last time. Mayhap this time you will find he had decided not to sell Farring Cross at all.''

''Bite your tongue, Walter. I want that southern holding. I want it so bad 'tis all I can think about.''

''There are other properties for sale,'' Walter reminded him reasonably.

''Aye, with worthless land, or keeps in such ruin I would have to continue to hire out my sword for another ten years just to pay for the repairs. Farring Cross might be a small keep, but 'tis in excellent repair, its defenses strong, the land not overworked, and the villeins healthy.''

''But 'tis not worth the price de Millers is now asking for it.''

''To me it is, Walter. So the man is greedy. 'Tis why I have waited until I have an extra thousand to meet a new price should he dare to make one. I will have Farring Cross by the end of the month.''

''Aye.'' Walter sighed. '' 'Twill be nice to lay my head in the same spot night after night for a change. Verily, I am tired of sleeping out in the cold and trekking back and forth across this island.''

''You could have gone your own way at any time,'' Ranulf reminded him.

''And leave you with no one to yell at save those young-uns you adopted?''

''Coxcomb,'' Ranulf snorted, but with a softening at the corners of his mouth. ''Begone and leave me in peace. And make my excuses to the lady, for I will not join you for the evening meal. Tell her I have not slept for two days and you are loath to wake me. The less I see of her the better.''

Walter chuckled. ''Annoyed you, did she?''

"You do not know the half of it."

"Would you rather I collect her when it is time?"

"Nay, trussing her up is the only pleasure I will have of this job," Ranulf replied.

Chapter Ten

*I*t was a piece of work, getting from one end of the hall to the other without waking any of the castlefolk bedded down there or alerting the few sentries passing the open arches of the gallery that looked down on the hall. The second time Kenric stumbled over someone's feet in the dark, Ranulf picked him up and toted him under his arm the rest of the way to the stairwell.

"S'wounds, if we had a candle—"

"We would be easier seen," Ranulf growled low.

He set the boy down to traverse the narrow stairs and they lucked onto a wall torch at the top, which Kenric borrowed to light the long passageway.

"Is this it, then?" the boy whispered when they reached the door at the end.

"If Walter's wench did not misguide him. And block the light when I open the door. I do not want the lady waking ere I reach her."

The door was not locked, but it was blocked by a pallet spread on the floor in front of it. Ranulf closed the door again and swore under his breath.

"What is wrong?" Kenric asked.

"One of her maids sleeps in front of the door. You will have to squeeze through the crack and see to it she continues to sleep."

Kenric's eyes widened to great turquoise circles. "You want me to *kill* her?"

"*Sleeps,* lackwit, not 'never wakes up.' A light tap on the head with your dagger hilt should do it nicely. Just be quiet about it."

Kenric set the torch in the wall bracket beside the door before he slipped through. In half a minute he was back and opening the door wide.

" 'Twas not a she, but a he," Kenric whispered, his surprise still evident. "That boy—"

"I can guess who," Ranulf replied in disgust. "Just bring the restraints. We will see to the lady first; then you can tie up her 'guard.' "

" 'Tis done." At Ranulf's raised brow, Kenric amended with a grin, "Just his hands. You said to be quick."

Ranulf grunted. "So I did. Let us have this over with, then."

With the door left open, torchlight spilled a few feet into the room, but only dimly lit the rest of the area. However, it was enough light for what they had to do.

The chamber was not large, though not too small either. It was in fact nearly identical with the one Ranulf had been given for his use. Theo was slumped beside the door where Kenric had shoved him. The bed sat in the center of one wall, the curtains closed about it. A number of items cluttered the room, several tables and stools, a wooden chest at the foot of the bed, a large brazier where a fire had burned earlier, needed even for this warmer weather of late spring.

Carefully, Ranulf drew back the curtains on the bed just enough to lean inside. She was there, no more than a tiny mound beneath her covers, topped by the raven locks spread across her pillow. It was she. Even in the darker gloom inside the enclosed space, he could see the whiteness of her small, piquant face, the dark slanting brows, that full lower lip forming a pout as she slept.

For a moment he hesitated. Once she woke to see him in her chamber, there would be no turning back. She would belong to Rothwell, for better or worse. And he knew it would only be for worse. But he would then have Farring Cross, his own land, earned by his own labor, not given to him, as his younger half brother had come by his land. Ranulf had had to work for what he wanted because his mother had been no more than a village wench, whereas his brother's mother had been a lady—not wed to their father, but a lady nonetheless. For that and that alone, her son, a bastard as Ranulf was, younger than Ranulf was, had been named their father's heir, had been raised with all the privileges accorded a precious heir.

No, Ranulf could not afford to feel anything for this lady sleeping so innocently in her chaste bed. There were little enough ways for a man to earn the kind of money he needed without stealing it, so he could not pick and choose as his conscience might dictate. And she was just another heiress to be fought over and won by the stronger man, Rothwell being that man because he had hired Ranulf. She was no more than a job to him, hopefully the last. So being, he hesitated no longer.

Her eyes opened the instant Ranulf's hand slid across her mouth, colorless in the dark, wide and fearful. The softness of her lips registered, but only for a second, for he had to apply more pressure when her small hand came up to push against his arm. He leaned across her to keep her other arm trapped beneath the cover whilst he exchanged his hand for a gag and quickly secured it with a strip of cloth. Her free hand was ineffective in stopping him, useless no matter how she pushed or pulled.

She moaned, for no other reason than he had pulled her hair in tying off the gag, but Ranulf stiffened, not knowing what caused it, and immediately leaned away from her. He had thought his mind hardened against her, but that soft sound pricked him on the raw, enough to make him furious with himself, with her, with life in general.

"Kenric!" The boy instantly poked his head through the curtain. "Get her hands and feet tied." But the boy did not move, and Ranulf swore under his breath when he looked down to see that the cover had moved enough to reveal the lady was naked beneath it. "Hold her down."

Ranulf angrily left the bed to rummage in the chest he had seen. He returned and thrust a sleeveless shift through the curtain.

"You want *me* to put it on her?" he heard Kenric squeak in horror.

Ranulf gritted his teeth. "Just do it and be quick about it."

Kenric gave Reina an apologetic look before he slipped the shift over her head. But that was as far as he got. She had both hands loose now, and it was all he could do just to keep her in the bed. He was not Ranulf.

"She will not let me!" Kenric called out desperately.

"She *will* let you, or she will be carried out of here naked."

No more was heard from behind the curtain after

that. Ranulf waited several moments more for the lady
to be clothed, then threw the curtain wide to swipe
the cover off the bed. While Kenric struggled to bind
her wrists with the cloth strips they had brought along
for that purpose, Ranulf spread the cover on the floor.

"You are not finished yet?"

"She does not *want* to make this easy," Kenric
hissed in answer.

With a low growl of irritation, Ranulf returned to
the bed and grabbed Reina's hands to hold them together whilst Kenric finished wrapping the cloth
around her wrists. He did the same with her feet,
ignoring the furious looks he was now getting from
her. That done, he lifted her off the bed.

"Secure the boy now," Ranulf told Kenric before
laying Reina down on the cover. One hand on her
chest, just below her breasts, held her there. "Be easy,
lady," he unbent enough to tell her. "We do not take
you to harm you." There was a spate of garbled
mumbling from behind the gag, loud enough to make
him lean closer to add, "Do you go quietly, no one
will be harmed. Do you draw attention to yourself,
make no mistake, there will be killing aplenty. Think
you your men, such as they are, can stop me?"

He was satisfied to hear no more noises from her,
and she stopped squirming beneath his hand as well.
In a moment Kenric returned to kneel beside him,
and together they rolled Reina up in the thick cover.
This not only secured her more completely but also
concealed her and would better muffle any more
noises she might make.

"Should she not have more clothes than that shift?"
Kenric asked as Ranulf picked up the long bundle to
toss over his shoulder.

"She can go to Rothwell naked for all I care,"
Ranulf said, only to recall that it would be days yet
ere she would be turned over to Rothwell. "Very
well," he amended surlily. "Find a gown or two in
her chest and bring it along."

In another few moments they were both moving
back down the passageway to the stairwell. Below,
Kenric went ahead, ready to use his dagger hilt again
should any of the servants wake to see them, but 'twas
unnecessary. The castlefolk's labors had been much
increased throughout the day, and they were now dead
to the world.

Across the hall, Walter waited by the stairwell leading down to the second floor and the forebuilding
where a guard stood duty at the entrance. With a nod,
he went down to draw the guard away, and in only
another minute Ranulf was able to pass his burden on
to Searle, outside the door.

Back upstairs, they waited for Walter to return. He
was grinning when he did.

"You had no trouble with the lady?"

"Nay, we need only wait for Eric to arrive now."

"It has gone too easy," Kenric remarked. "What
if Eric is delayed, or—"

"Bite your tongue," Ranulf retorted. "Eric will
come within the hour, so return to your beds that you
may be 'awakened' for his message."

"Idiot, only one layer of those sacks! Any more
will smash her."

Those were the last words Reina heard for a long
while. And she was not only smashed but had nearly
been suffocated by a sack unknowingly set directly on
her face. If she had not managed to twist her head to

the side, they would have had a fine surprise when they got around to digging her out.

She did not have to see to know she had been put in their supply cart, hidden under the sacks of grain Gilbert had sold to them earlier. 'Twas the only way they could smuggle her out of Clydon, and from what she had heard, that was obviously their intent.

Other things were known to her as well without her having to be told. Of course she had seen who was abducting her. And there could only be one reason for it. That it was a planned abduction, rather than a lark, was indicated by the mention that she was going to Rothwell, whoever that was. The stupid giant was not even taking her for himself. *That* she could have understood. Whoever wed her, be he landless knight or great lord, would have Clydon as long as he swore homage to Lord Guy. But to go to all this trouble for someone else? Fitz Hugh must be earning a fortune to do it. That was the only answer.

Reina had also gathered from his manner that Fitz Hugh was still angry with her because of Theo, that he had not accepted her apology. She wished now she had never made it. How did he dare be wroth because of a little insult when all the while he had been planning this?

It galled her to the teeth to know she had welcomed the viper into her home, had in fact been grateful to him. The truth was, he had saved her to suit his purpose, not for any noble service to her benefit. Trickery, deceit, *lies!* Some chivalrous knight this. But her own gullibility could not be corrected now. She was well and truly captured. Even should their ploy be discovered, Fitz Hugh had it aright. Her men could not hope to defeat his, would only forfeit their own lives trying. And the soonest she could anticipate help would be several days hence. She could be wed before then, depending on how far away this Rothwell was. Who the devil *was* he?

Reina grunted, feeling a new weight atop her belly, but it was quickly removed. Not the sack, however. So she had company, did she? Aye, someone was definitely moving around in the cart, shaking it. And she could hear other sounds now, just barely. The cover and sacks meant to conceal her and keep her quiet made hearing most difficult. Were they leaving now, or was she just being guarded, to see she stayed put? As if she could move even a little, as tightly as she was wrapped up.

"Here, Lanzo, keep this with you."

"What is it?"

"Some clothes for her. There was not time to dress her proper."

"Oh?"

"Oho, best get rid of *those* thoughts. She is too old for you, and spoken for besides."

"What has age to do with it, when Rothwell is old enough to be her great-great-grandfather?"

"How you go on. One 'great' was enough. And quiet now, they are opening the inner gate. Remember to moan if you have to."

"I know what to do, Kenric. You best mount up yourself ere you get left behind."

The cart began to move and right quickly. Reina wondered what possible excuse they could have used to leave before morning, but soon she felt the jarring bumps of the new bridge crossing the dry ditch and had no thoughts but of her own discomfort. The lad was bounced around, too, at one point right onto her.

She moaned as his knee slid between two sacks to gouge her thigh.

"Shh, lady!" she heard him hiss at her. "You will not have to stay under there much longer."

Reina ground her teeth against the wad of cloth in her mouth. The sneaky little cur, him and that other sweet-faced lad. All along they had known what they meant to do, yet all afternoon the two young squires had been smiling and flirting with her younger ladies, and were naught but innocent looks when she happened to gaze on them. The others, too, the young knights and Sir Walter, with his smiles and jests and friendly manner, all deceivers, all despicable knaves in their pretense, their foul plans already made. At least Ranulf Fitz Hugh had had the decency to avoid her the rest of the day. Whether in anger or because he could not dissemble as easily as the others, at least there was *some* honesty in that—but not enough to warn her or do her any good.

Chapter Eleven

"God's wounds, I have never seen so many disgruntled faces," Walter remarked as they rode slowly into the new camp about an hour after sunrise. "Did the light-skirts all run off yesterday, Eric?"

"With as much as they earn of a night with us?" Eric snorted. "Not likely."

"Then what is wrong with Rothwell's men?"

"You do not want to know."

Walter frowned to see Eric shaking his head, yet grinning, but he was distracted and shouted to those near, "Hold tight! Lady Ella has seen her master."

A brown blur came racing across the camp to leap onto Ranulf's destrier. The huge horse did not even snort, used to this particular presence, though the other war-horses reared and snapped, and it took several moments to get them back under control. There were curses aplenty, but at last Ranulf was smiling, so no one cursed very loudly. And the creature who had caused the commotion was oblivious to it, settled now in her favored spot atop Ranulf's wide shoulder, wrapped half around his neck.

"You were saying, Eric?" Ranulf said now from his position on Eric's right.

"I was?"

"About Rothwell's men?"

"Oh." Eric was chagrined to have been caught ribbing Walter. Neither had known Ranulf had been listening to their exchange. "Mayhap you should talk to their master-at-arms. 'Tis doubtful you will believe it coming from me."

"Do you tell me anyway."

That tone was not one to argue with. "The way I understand it, had we been delayed just one day in taking the lady, we would have been fighting Rothwell's men as well as hers."

"How so?"

"Their one year of service with Rothwell ends today."

"So?"

"So they do not mean to return to him. Had they been still at Clydon today, they would have offered their service to the lady."

"And told her our plans?" Walter demanded, outraged.

"Aye. Apparently they hate Rothwell, but he had paid them in advance, so they could not leave his service. So until that service ended, they remained loyal to him."

Walter whistled. "Incredible. A matter of a few hours made the difference in our success, because those louts clung to the very letter of their contract. That is carrying misplaced loyalty a bit far, especially when the lady would have been eternally grateful to them if they had joined her, and they must have known it."

Eric nodded. "So there you have the reason for their sour faces this morn."

"Did Master Scot tell you all this?" Ranulf asked.

"Aye."

"Think you he will still approach the lady?"

Eric shook his head. "You have her now, so she is

no longer in a position to hire anyone. They are only fourteen stronger than us, and our four knights even those odds. They might be stupid, but not that stupid.''

"Will they hire to us, then?" Walter asked.

"Aye, and gladly."

"Then why were they willing to join the lady's service?" Ranulf demanded.

Eric chuckled. "For revenge. They hate Rothwell enough that they do not want to see this good fortune come to him. But since that opportunity is lost, and well they know it, they will see to themselves now."

Ranulf grunted, satisfied for now, but he would have to talk to the master-at-arms himself. "Farring Cross is not large enough to support them all, not with my own men, and I do not even have it yet. Mayhap I can use twenty . . . tell Master Scot I will work something out with him, to come to me after we make camp tonight. Right now, I needs unwrap the lady and listen to her screams and demands the while my patience lasts. We ride within the hour."

"She will not remain ungagged for long," Eric predicted as Ranulf turned about to head back toward the supply cart.

"Mayhap," Walter said thoughtfully. "But you were not long in her presence yesterday, as we were. You did not see how easily she assumes command. She has been long on her own, after all, nigh on two years with no man to gainsay her. 'Tis as like Ranulf will be doing the screaming and demanding if he must deal with her."

" 'Tis as like he will do that anyway, no matter her reaction." Eric laughed.

* * *

Somehow Reina had managed to sleep the remainder of the night. Given that she could not see or move or do aught toward an escape at present, there was not much else to do but sleep, especially when she was still quite exhausted from one of the most grueling days of her life. And cushioned as she was between sacks, and with her thick cover adding to that, the ride was not as bumpy as it would have been otherwise, not enough to keep her awake. Nor did the removal of her blanket of sacks wake her. But being picked up none too gently has a way of breaking through the deepest slumber.

She was being carried in a pair of sturdy arms, but whose arms she could not say. No word had been spoken near enough for her to hear it, though there were numerous sounds all around her, vague and distant-sounding through the thickness of her cover. Was she to meet this Rothwell now? Was she at least to be unwrapped?

Fast on that thought, she was set down and literally unwrapped, *rolled* out of her cover and several feet farther with the impetus. She came to rest facedown, her nose buried in thick grass, the strong verdant smell of it nigh choking her. Well, what did she expect? Fitz Hugh had said he did not care if she went to Rothwell naked. Rolled out at his feet and nearly naked was just as bad. But when she rolled to her side and managed to use her bound wrists and an elbow to push herself to a sitting position, she found only the giant and his youngest squire present.

She had been brought into a tent, not a very large one, and quite empty, though there was a place or two where the grass was flattened, indicating something had been there earlier but had since been removed or packed away. His camp, then, but where had the rest of his men gone? The light coming through the walls revealed it was morning. She could assume they would not be here long.

The boy, Lanzo, stood next to the giant, looking rather startled, as if he had not expected Reina to be treated so carelessly. He held a bundle of clothes in one arm and a stool in the other, which he finally recalled and set down. Fitz Hugh was crouched on his haunches, likely to avoid stooping in a tent not large enough for his impossible height. He looked no more friendly than he ever had to her, golden brows drawn together, lips tight over clenched teeth. Obviously he would prefer not to be anywhere near her, though for some reason felt it his chore to deal with her himself.

He proved her earlier conclusion when he stood up to come nearer but could not stand straight. Then he was back on his haunches next to her, reaching for the bound hands she had resting in her lap.

"Take care of her feet, Lanzo," he ordered without looking back at the boy. "We do not have all day to waste here."

He had not said anything to her, had not met her gaze directly, nor did he now, looking down instead at the knot on her wrists he was trying to pick apart. Lanzo had moved to kneel by her side where she had her legs tucked under her, and without being asked, she moved her feet farther to the side so he could reach them. Unfortunately, that threw her balance off and one shoulder slumped lower than the other, causing the loose material of her shift to slump also, halfway down her arm.

Cool air against bare skin brought instant color to

Reina's cheeks. She could not have been more horrified if she had been sitting there completely naked, for that would have been intentional, meant to humiliate her and put her at a disadvantage. This was accidental and much more embarrassing because it should not have happened at all, regardless that it was not yet noticed. And worse, when she tried to raise her hands to slip the material back on her shoulder before it *was* noticed, the stupid giant refused to let go of her wrists, probably thinking she was trying to resist his efforts to free her, though why he should think she did not want to be free was beyond her.

A glance to the side showed the boy was not as unobservant as the man. He was paralyzed, his eyes agog, his mouth dropped open as he stared at her. But he was just a boy, she told herself, even as she turned a shade darker in color. 'Twas the man's eyes Reina wanted to avoid. Righting her shoulder was the *wrong* thing to do, however, for it only bared more skin, though she found that out too late.

Desperately, she tried again to raise her hands—to have the horror finally realized. Fitz Hugh's eyes came up in irritation, but rose no farther than the bared breast staring him right in the face.

Reina groaned behind her gag, but nobody seemed to hear it. In his surprise, Fitz Hugh was holding even tighter to the ties about her wrists, though his fingers had stilled on the knots. She still could not raise her hands and he just stared at her breast, just as the boy was doing, as if neither of them had ever seen one before. Reina could not even try getting to her feet to turn her back on them. Even if the man would let go of her wrists, to raise up on her knees to get to her feet would shove her breasts right in his face. Though this might snap him out of his bemused stare, she did not care to try it. Some men might construe something like that as an invitation, and if *he* should think so . . .

It was Lanzo who came to her rescue at last, though he seemed pained to do so. Hot color had rushed into his cheeks when his senses returned to realize Reina could not correct the matter herself. His hand moved toward her hesitantly, thumb and forefinger extended, trembling; and carefully, as if he would die if he actually touched her skin, he plucked the material off her arm to set it back on her shoulder.

That the top of the shift caught on the tip of her breast and shriveled the nipple before covering it was of no moment to anyone but the man still staring at it. Reina was simply relieved to be halfway decent again. Not even those violet eyes meeting hers for the briefest second before lowering to her wrists could discompose her again. The damage was done. Best forget it as he appeared willing to do.

But she did wonder what had happened to the angry visage for that brief moment when he looked up at her. Angry, Ranulf Fitz Hugh was still handsome. Bemused, he was devastating. She liked the angry visage better. She could breathe easier when he was merely handsome, though why that was so she did not know.

And the frown was back when he still had no luck untying her. At last he drew his dagger, and though it was a tight squeeze between her wrists, the ties were quickly severed. A flick by her feet and at her cheek, and the rest of the cloths fell away, too.

If only he had done that to begin with, Reina thought resentfully, then she would not have this embarrassing incident between them to color what she was feeling. She had every right to rail at him for what he had done to her, but at the moment, she wished he would just go away.

But he did not. He drew the stool to him and sat down right in front of her. That he had not offered *her* the stool was no more than she could expect after everything else. The man was the most unchivalrous knight she had ever met. And if he thought she was going to remain sitting in this demeaning position at his feet, he was crazy.

Reina ignored him for a moment whilst she spat out the cloth in her mouth and flexed her jaw to ease the stiffness from it. She took another moment to rub her wrists before slowly getting to her feet. With as much dignity as she could manage with her hair streaming about her in a tangled mess, and wearing no more than a thin shift that fell only just past her knees, she walked to where her cover had been tossed at the side of the tent and drew it around her like a mantle. Only then did she deign to face the enemy.

"So, Sir Knight," she began in a deceptively pleasant tone. "If you have aught to impart to me, do you get to it right quickly. I cannot stomach your presence for very long."

That stung enough to bring him soaring to his feet, only he forgot the tent would not accommodate him. Reina almost laughed to see his expression when his head struck the ceiling, shaking the walls so much the tent was in danger of collapsing. He was forced to sit back down, where his newest anger was still intimidating, but not nearly as much as it would be were he towering over her.

"I see the feeling is mutual," she said before he

could, thereby stealing his thunder and making his expression darken even more. "At least we have that in common, so if you can find a tongue that knows aught besides lies, do bring it forth."

She saw he had to strain this time to remain sitting, but he did discover his voice, a very loud one directed at Lanzo. "Gag her!"

Reina stiffened and rounded on the hapless youth before he could take a step toward her. "Touch me, boy, and I will box your ears so hard you will hear bells for a sennight. If he is too cowardly to hear what I have to say of him, let him gag me himself. He does it so *gently.*" And her cerulean eyes seemed that much lighter as they came back to rest on the knight, daring him to just try it.

"Cowardly, lady? I care naught what you think of me, but you waste time—"

"Aye," she cut in with a sneer. "A baseborn knight would not care, which your manner claims you to be."

"You have that aright," he growled back.

It was deflating for an intended insult to turn out to be a truth instead. And perhaps she was pressing her luck just a little in deliberately provoking him. He looked now as if he were about to come apart, his body was straining so hard not to come after her and throttle her. Well, she had made her point and her disdain clear. Best get on with hearing what he had to say.

"Well, then," she said on a sigh, "let us waste no more time, the sooner to part company." And yet she just could not seem to stop herself from adding, "What has your duplicity accomplished?"

"You harp on lies and duplicity, lady, but you opened your gates to me."

"Because you pretended to give aid!"

"I did give aid. What I did not do was slaughter the rest of your people to take you out of Clydon yesterday, which would have been more easily done. If your misplaced dignity is not worth those lives, say so."

That effectively knocked the steam out of her. She knew very well that to have taken her any other way than he had would have left countless bodies behind.

"None of that discounts that you had no right to take me at all," she said in a quieter, though no less bitter, tone. "You did *not* come from my lord as you claimed."

"There you are mistaken, lady," he was pleased to tell her. "As your betrothed, Lord Rothwell *is* your lord, and I act on his behalf. And he does have the right to take you and force you to honor your betrothal contract with him. Whether 'twas your idea or Shefford's to put him aside is of no moment. He does not choose to be put aside."

Reina listened to this quite calmly, and then confounded the man by smiling at him. "If you believe that nonsense, you have been duped. My betrothed died two years ago, just before my father left for the Holy Land. There was no time before he left to arrange another alliance. He charged me to see to the matter, and through correspondence with him, I had two men he and I both approved, and 'tis one of these I would have been wed to within the week."

"Who?"

"That is hardly a concern of yours, other than this Rothwell you mention is not one of them. I have never even heard of the man, and if he says he has a contract, he lies.''

''Or you do.''

Reina's chin came up sharply. ''I have my father's letters to prove what I say.''

''Then produce them.''

''Idiot!'' she hissed in exasperation. ''The letters are at Clydon.''

''So you want me to believe, but I *would* be an idiot the day I take a lady at her word,'' he snorted.

Her eyes narrowed on him at that left-handed insult. ''Then you still intend to take me to your lord?''

''He is not my lord, but aye, for five hundred marks, you most definitely will go to him. What I want to know from you is why my task was made so easy. Why were you so poorly protected?''

Reina was still reeling over the paltry sum he had been offered to ruin her life. As for his wanting answers from her now . . .

''Go to hell, Fitz Hugh. I am done talking to someone so unreasonably pigheaded. For that matter, I am done suffering his presence.''

So saying, she took flight, and with no one standing between her and the front of the tent, 'twas not difficult. That she blundered into the midst of his entire camp gave her only momentary pause. The thunderous roar she left behind was incentive enough to quicken her step; and, barefoot or not, she raced straight for the nearest horse she spotted, sending up a word of thanks that it was a gelding rather than a war-horse, and still saddled, too. The men lounging all around her, under trees and in front of cooking fires, merely gaped at her as she sped through them, too surprised to do anything.

For not having planned her escape, she was doing remarkably well, and even believed she could actually make it now that she had reached the horse. The cover had to go in order for her to hoist herself into the saddle without a boost up, but that was a small sacrifice to make for success. The horse was not that many hands tall, and once her foot found the stirrup, she managed to pull herself up the rest of the way.

But there her problems began. That her shift rode halfway up her thighs as she sat astride was the least of them. The horse did not care for her light weight on its back and made haste to let her know. That was not her main problem either, for she was not inexperienced with difficult mounts. Her biggest problem was that every man in camp had stood up by then, fully aware now what she was about. There was a solid wall of them blocking the three directions that would take her away from the enraged knight, too close for her to pick up the speed to break through them. The only opening available was back the way she had come, right though the heart of the camp. As long as she could generate enough speed to knock away anyone who tried to stop her, there was still a chance.

She wasted no more time thinking about it, but drew the horse about and dug her bare heels into its sides. Disdainfully, it would not budge, and after all its sidestepping and head tossing until then! Furiously, Reina gave it a sharp taste of the reins she had gathered in one fist, then almost lost her seat when it bolted. But that was the speed she needed, and the first few men who dared get in her way dived for cover when they saw she would run them down rather than stop.

Unfortunately, the closer she got to the end of the camp, the braver they got, reaching for the reins, banging into her knees as they missed, trying to frighten the horse with wildly waving arms. One fellow succeeded in latching onto her arm, but a sharp twist made him loose his grip before she lost her balance. And then she saw Walter de Breaute coming at her, taller than all the others, more able to reach up to her because of his extra height, and she steered away from him, only to find herself riding right at Fitz Hugh on her other side—too late. He did no more than hold out an arm as she passed, and she was plucked right off the horse, the animal riding on without her, while she felt as if she had run into a stone wall.

She lost her breath at the impact of his arm with her belly, and that it still squeezed her while holding her to his side did not make it easy for her to start breathing again. But once her lungs finally filled with air, she let out a screech of outraged fury, half for being stopped, half because she was being hefted back to the tent rather than being allowed to walk.

"Cretin! Devil-spawned lout! Put me *dow*—"

The word ended on a whoosh when he tightened the iron band about her waist. She started to struggle then, kicking backwards at him, hammering at his arm and the shoulder she could reach. But he seemed not to notice her efforts at all, just kept marching along, with her practically sitting on his hip, her feet a *long* way from the ground.

When he did set her down, it was directly in front of the tent opening. She got a look at his face then, and it was thunderous.

"Lady, you are more trouble than you are worth," he rumbled out.

If he had not said that, she might have become truly afraid of him at last, for his visage was terrible to behold. But those words rubbed her on the raw. And besides, if he ever did strike her with one of those clublike fists that he was clenching at his sides, she would not be alive to worry about it ever happening again.

"Nay, that is where you are so stupid, Fitz Hugh," she said with contempt. "My worth is well known and makes your Judas fee insignificant. Clydon earns four times as much in just one year. Your friend Rothwell knows it, even if you do not. Well he will laugh at how little he had to pay to steal a fortune and the power behind it."

For that she got a light push on her shoulder that sent her stumbling backwards into the tent. "Five minutes you have to dress yourself ere this tent comes down. In ten we ride out."

That was all he said, or rather shouted in at her. No comment on what *she* had said, just change before the tent was dismantled. He really was a loutish bear, in size as well as intelligence. *Jesú,* he could ask for anything and she would give it, just to get out of this fix. His bargaining power was unbelievable, because she was at present in his possession. But did he see that? Nay, all he saw was the five hundred marks he would be earning, and unfortunately, that was the one thing she could not offer him, thanks to her father having emptied their coffers for King Richard's Crusade.

Chapter Twelve

The march that day seemed longer than usual to Ranulf, though actually they made good progress considering the slow pace they kept to accommodate Rothwell's men, none of whom had been supplied with horses, and the supply carts. Ranulf's own thirty men, who had been with him now for four years, some longer, had mounts he had bargained for long ago, not the best or the youngest in horseflesh, and not nearly as expensive as the destriers he had supplied for Searle and Eric when they were knighted, but adequate to their needs. The thirty horses had not come cheap; had cost him four months' service to a northern horse breeder beset by Scottish reivers, but having his men all mounted made the difference in getting certain jobs where speed was a necessity.

Usually, the time in the saddle sped by quickly for Ranulf, spent in planning the current job or even the next one, or on thoughts of the future when he would finally achieve his goal and have his own keep, rich fields to support it, his own villeins to care for. He had learned where he could about farming and animal husbandry, and about baronial court laws, for he had not received a proper education.

He had spent the first nine years of his life with the village smith, the brutish man his grandfather had given his mother to wed when she claimed the lord's grandson had been planted in her belly. She died the year after he was born, so the smith got no bargain, only a babe to raise who was no use to him until he could learn the craft. This was sooner than he was ready, which accounted for Ranulf's overdeveloped muscles at a tender age.

Known to be the future lord's bastard had made his lot harder, not easier, for the village youths shunned him, the smith resented him and worked him until he was ready to drop each night, and his father, a youth himself at six years and ten when Ranulf was born, cared not what happened to him. His lordly grandfather came around from time to time to check on his development but never offered a kind word or a hint of kinship, and his father was seen rarely, and only at a distance.

He did not even meet his father until the day he was told he was being sent to Montfort to become a knight, and that likely came about only because his father had been wed five years by then, yet had produced no legitimate child in all that time. He had another bastard, one he had already made his heir in case a true heir was never born, which had indeed come to pass, for his wife was barren and yet still lived. But Ranulf did not know that at the time. For many a year he had thought he was being groomed to inherit, which was why he never complained about the hardships of being trained by a man like Montfort, and why it had been such a bitter blow to him when he did learn his bastard brother would inherit all instead.

His education at Montfort was only in the use of arms, with a bare smattering of knightly courtesies thrown in, for Lord Montfort was nowise a chivalrous knight himself. But Ranulf *was* knighted, had in fact earned his spurs on the battlefield when he was only six years and ten, during one of Montfort's petty wars. That he stayed on to serve Montfort for another year was only because Walter, a year older than Ranulf, had to wait that extra year before he was knighted, too, and they had already vowed to seek their fortunes together.

If his manner bespoke his baseborn heritage, as *she* claimed, it was partly a result of his particular "education," but partly deliberate, too, his dislike and distrust of ladies in general coloring his attitude toward any he must deal with. And it was his dealings so far with the Lady of Clydon that made this day drag out, for instead of pleasant thoughts of the future to occupy him as he rode along, he was plagued by anger, bewilderment, and horror over the events of the morning, or, more specifically, over what he had felt when he saw the lady up on that horse.

She in no way looked like a lady with that cloud of raven locks flowing down her back and over her shoulders, whipping about her hips. The too short shift had become shorter still, revealing legs that should have been spindly on a woman so narrow of build, yet were too shapely by half, and longer than he would have imagined them to be. Or was it that he saw so *much* of them?

She sat the horse with shoulders thrown back, head high, with a skill no doubt learned from the cradle, and while she galloped across the camp, she had appeared beautiful somehow, when he knew very well she was not; but more bewildering than that, she had aroused his lust.

'Twas no doubt because he had seen that breast of hers. No, that in itself had not done it. He had seen

too many breasts for one to fire his blood just because
it happened to be staring him in the face. And yet
that single moon-white globe of hers *was* different.
'Twas barely a handful, though quite perfect in shape,
without the slightest droop to it, as was common with
larger breasts. But it was the rose nipple that made it
unique, so large for such a small shape, and so sen-
sitive! His mouth had gone dry when he saw it pucker
as it was scraped by the cloth. After that, to see her
with her legs spread wide in the saddle was enough
to inflame his senses to lust.

And yet he still could not understand why, when
she was everything he did not like, and he was horrified that it had happened at all.

He stole glances at her all day where she sat in the
supply cart, just to make sure that, since she was
completely clothed, there was nothing about her that
was desirous, and there was not. Covered from head
to toe, she was the lady again, prim and stiff, wrapped
up in haughty pride, and shooting venom at him
whenever their eyes should meet.

And that was another thing that aggravated his fury.
Why had he not been able to intimidate the tiny shrew
into giving him no trouble? He had certainly given it
his best effort. Grown men quivered like jelly when
he turned his wrath on them, yet not her. She threw
insults at him whilst she was within his reach. No one,
no one, had ever dared such a thing before.

"Do we stop at the abbey again, Ranulf?" Walter
said as he rode up next to him. " 'Tis just ahead."

"Nay, not with the little general among us."

"The little—oho. Her. But she can be left in the
camp whilst we—"

"And let her get to another horse with no one to

stop her next time? Nay, I am not letting her far from my sight or hearing, though the latter is like to drive me crazy.''

Walter chuckled, recalling what he had overheard before Ranulf had sent the lady back into the tent. ''She does have a forceful way with words.''

''You heard only a small sampling.''

''Know you, then, what she meant about Rothwell stealing a fortune?''

''She claims he has no right to her, that he is not nor ever was her betrothed.''

''Did you not have that doubt yourself from Rothwell's craftiness?''

''It matters not,'' Ranulf replied stubbornly. ''We are not being paid to discern who has what rights.''

''But—God's wounds, Ranulf! Do you not realize what that means? If the old man has no true claim to her, why give her to him? *You* have her. Why not keep her yourself?''

''Bite your tongue!'' Ranulf snarled, horrified. ''I want no lady to wife, least of all *that* one.''

''Not even for Clydon?''

For a fraction of a second, Ranulf hesitated, but that was all. ''Not even if she offered the whole kingdom.''

''Clydon is just as nice,'' Walter noted with a grin, only to earn a black look before Ranulf spurred his mount ahead, refusing to listen to more.

But the notion had taken root in Walter's mind, and he turned about to find Master Scot, Rothwell's master-at-arms, and brought his horse to a walk beside him. ''How did your lord learn of Roger de Champeney's death, Master Scot?''

''Like as was in that letter he had from his nephew,

the one who went crusading with the king. I heard
him mention the man's name just after the messenger
arrived with it.''

"Had you ever heard of the betrothal with Reina
de Champeney before then?''

"There was no betrothal,'' the man snorted. "All
I heard was Lord Rothwell saying as how the girl
would be easy pickings with her liege lord still in the
Holy Land.''

"Do you not think that is something you should
have mentioned ere now?'' Walter said irritably. He
had not expected exact confirmation, just more doubt
to offer Ranulf.

Master Scot shrugged. "The doings of barons is
no concern of mine, but I did not see as how it would
matter, when you had already been paid to deliver the
lady.''

"Ah, but you see, Sir Ranulf has not accepted payment as yet.''

Master Scot stopped walking on hearing that.
"Then why are we taking an innocent young lass like
her to a devil like Lord Rothwell?''

"A good question,'' Walter replied and rode off to
walk his horse alongside the supply cart where the
"innocent young lass'' was suffering a bumpy ride
due to Ranulf's annoyance with her and refusal to let
her ride a horse again. "I thought you would like
some company, my lady.''

She gave him only a single cold glance before looking away from him. "Not from any friends of *his,*
thank you.''

Walter flinched, but tried again. " 'Tis true Ranulf
is not easy to deal with when you know not his ways,

but compared to your betrothed, you will remember him as a saint.''

''Not likely, de Breaute.''

Walter shrugged for her benefit and said no more, but still rode along beside her. He was waiting for her curiosity to get the better of her, unless of course she had lied about there being no betrothal. Then again, even if there was not, she still might know of Rothwell and so have no questions about him. In that case, he would have to try a different approach to set his idea before her.

But his ruse did work. She finally glanced toward him again, and her expression was not so frigid this time, though not openly friendly either.

''Have you met this—this craven lord who means to steal my inheritance?''

Walter had to bite back a smile at her choice of words. ''Aye, I have met him. But tell me something, demoiselle. If he is not your betrothed, who is?''

Her eyes fell to her lap and she did not answer for several long moments, making him think she would not. Then she did, but 'twas not what Walter was expecting to hear.

''I have no betrothed.''

''You mean the Earl of Shefford means to keep you as his ward, as old as you are?''

''Nay, I have his blessing to marry, and would have seen the matter done within a sennight if you and your *friends* had not interfered.''

She was controlling her anger well to say that with only a little bitterness, but Walter still did not understand. ''How can that be? If Shefford is sending you a man, then he has made contract for you, so the man must be your betrothed.''

"Nay, Lord Guy is sending no one. Not that it makes a difference now, but he had it from my father before he died that the matter was taken care of, when in truth 'twas not yet settled."

Walter was frowning now, still not understanding. "But Shefford had to have a name to give his blessing, as well as to make contract for you, if as you say 'twas not done by your father. How, then, can you claim to have no betrothed and yet claim you were to wed within the week?"

Reina was loath to admit the unthinkable, that her father had allowed her to make her own contract. Fitz Hugh had not bothered to pick apart what she had said to him. Why could his friend not leave it alone?

"What does it matter the why or how of it, Sir Walter? The fact remains you are taking me—"

"Wait! If you have no betrothed, then you have no contract as yet. And with Shefford not here, who then will make it for you?"

Reina hissed through her teeth, "I will. And before you yap and yammer over that, know that 'tis as my father wished it. He offered me my choice of two men he approved of, but he died ere he knew my preference and could make contract himself. In telling Lord Guy 'twas done, he assured that I would still have one of these men. He could not know that it would be so difficult to reach them to put the matter to them, or that the news of his death would spread so fast that other men would be tempted to take me by force."

Walter stared at her incredulously. "What you have said is simply not done, demoiselle."

"Under these circumstances, 'tis most easily done. You forget Lord Guy believes my father already made contract, and on that belief I have his permission to

wed. Lord Guy's castellan, Sir Henry, was to come
to the wedding to accept my husband's homage to
Shefford, and to obtain copies of the marriage contract. That is *all* that is necessary to see the matter
done legally and without further consequence.''

''Nay, it sounds to me as if your willingness is also
needed to prevent further consequence. Yet Rothwell
means to have you. What do you think will be the
end result?''

''Forced marriages are not familiar to me, Sir Walter, so I do not know what you expect me to say. I
can tell you that unless this Rothwell kills me ere
Lord Guy returns, I will see to it he knows I was
forced. What will happen then is a matter between
men. But I can also tell you that Lord Guy loved my
father and so loves me also. 'Tis as like there will be
war to have me back, whether there is issue from the
union or not. But that is not your concern, is it?'' she
added resentfully. ''From what I understand, your
duty is only to deliver me to Rothwell.''

''But if you were willing to wed Rothwell?'' Walter
had to know.

''Then who is to know he is not the man my father
chose for me?''

''God's wounds, lady, you are mad to tell me that!
If I so informed Rothwell, he *would* have reason to
kill you ere Shefford returns.''

''Then he would also have to kill those close to me
who know the truth, and thereby kill everyone at Clydon, for I will die under torture rather than reveal any
names to him. One way or another, Lord Guy will
know if I am forced or not, so do you tell him that,
too, if you mean to tell him aught. Now 'tis your turn
to answer questions, Sir Walter.''

"Aye, fair is fair," he agreed.

"Then do you tell me if there is a chance I might agree to wed this Rothwell without coercion. He obviously lacks honor, but is there aught else to recommend him?"

"You want the truth, demoiselle?"

"That would be helpful," she replied dryly.

"Then as to his character, there is naught to recommend him. But whether you could be persuaded to accept him regardless of that depends on what you would deem important. He is wealthy enough, if that matters to you. He is a great lord with vassals aplenty, come from his many previous marriages, if that matters to you. That none of these men like or respect him is due to his manner, which is offense to one and all. If children matter to you, you will get none from him, but will have to wait until you are widowed and remarry, and that only if his large family is willing to give up any portion of your inheritance, which is doubtful. They are a greedy lot, just as he is. As to—"

"I think that is enough, Sir Walter," Reina cut in, her complexion paler than it had been. "Just tell me why children would not be possible. Is he crippled or for some other reason unable?"

"Nay, just old, my lady, though not too old to—ah—try."

She had paled even more, as he had hoped, though her eyes were ready to fry him when she hissed, *"That* is who you would sell me to?"

'Twas not easy to pretend indifference at this point. "When you need the money, you do not question the job too closely, and 'tis our livelihood, selling our service. If we did not accept the job, Rothwell would

only have hired someone else to do it. But his offer
was too tempting to ignore, especially when it will
enable Ranulf to buy the fief he wants.''

''If 'tis land he wants, I will give him a rich fief
myself, does he take me back to Clydon.''

Walter groaned inwardly. Ranulf would kill him if
he ever found out that he was going to refuse in his
behalf. '' 'Twould take much more than that to make
him change his mind. He has a reputation to uphold,
after all, one that has never failed to finish a task
begun, nor failed to succeed at that task.''

''Is that all? He did not give his word or accept the
fee already?''

''Nay, he did not.''

''Is that normal?''

''It is not,'' Walter admitted. ''But he liked Rothwell no more than you will.''

''Then there is no problem.''

''There is a very big problem,'' he countered. ''A
reputation is naught to scoff at in our profession.''

''Is it worth two fiefs?'' she offered.

Walter nearly choked. Ranulf really would kill him
if he heard about this, and he would deserve it. But
he was determined to hold out for all or naught.

''You seem to forget your present position, Lady
Reina. Why would Ranulf settle for so little when he
holds you and could have all by wedding you himself?
'Tis too bad he cannot be persuaded to do so, for I
think you will agree he is the lesser of two evils.''

Her color was back with more besides. ''Mayhap I
would *not* agree. Your friend is a churlish lout with
the manners of the meanest villein!''

''Aye, he is that.'' Walter grinned. ''But then he
has not had much association with ladies willing to

correct his manners. He is also young, strong, and not without means. He might be landless now, but he has the wherewithal to correct that, a small fortune that he has been saving to do just that.''

''A few thousand marks?'' she scoffed.

''More like fifteen thousand,'' Walter was very happy to tell her.

''How?'' she asked suspiciously. ''Mercenaries do not earn such high fees, no matter how good they are. How is it, too, that Rothwell was willing to pay so much?''

''Rothwell was desperate to have Ranulf for the job after hearing he never fails at any task. He had meant to offer only a hundred marks, a high enough fee for so easy a task, one taking so little time. But Ranulf refused that and each higher offer, until it reached five hundred, an amount *too* high to refuse outright. As for the other, 'tis true mercenary work does not pay well. 'Tis the possibility of loot and ransom that makes it worthwhile, and in that we have been fortunate. In one skirmish several years ago, Ranulf captured fourteen knights single-handed. The ransoms for these account for the bulk of what he has now. So you see, he would not come empty-handed to a wife. But I should not even have mentioned it. As I said, he cannot be persuaded—''

''*He* cannot be! As I see it, I am the one who must be persuaded if it is to be done with the earl's blessing. Do I not clear the way in saying he is my father's choice, then his position would be no different from Rothwell's. And how dare he *not* be tempted, when his fifteen thousand marks do not come anywhere near the equal of Clydon and all it entails?''

"Methinks he does not see it as plainly as that, my lady. He sees that you do not like him—"

"And so I do not," she retorted stiffly.

"Well, there you have it. He would not force you to wed him, so he rejects the idea altogether. That you might prefer him to Rothwell does not even occur to him."

"What I would prefer is neither of them, de Breaute, and well you know it. And you are discounting the fact that my vassals will come after me, and not at this snail's pace that we are traveling."

"Will they? Even should they think you will be killed if they attempt to take you back?"

Her eyes narrowed on him like glowing blue coals. "Why would they think that?"

"Because that is the warning I put in the letter Ranulf left in your chamber."

"*Would* you kill me?"

"Nay, but will they risk it?"

She did not answer, too furious for several moments to say anything, and then she hissed at him, "Why have you bothered to imply I have choices when you also say I have none? What is your purpose, de Breaute?"

"Curiosity, I suppose, on which choice you would make if you were given the choice. And I did wonder if I *could* bring Ranulf around to the idea. If anyone can, it would be me, since no one else dares to browbeat him as I do, and even I dare only so far. But there is no point in trying unless I have your leave, so it comes back to 'what ifs.' "

"You could be lying to me about Rothwell," she pointed out bitterly.

"True, but you need not take only my word for it.

The men who march behind us served him this past year. Ask any one of them and you are like to have the same opinion. I doubt they are smart enough to lie, but neither do they have reason to lie. They every one of them hate the man for his meanness and cruelties.''

''I have a neighbor like that who inspires the same sentiments in his people. You crossed swords with some of his men yestermorn, for which I *was* grateful at the time.''

''But not now?''

That did not even deserve an answer, or so her expression told him. ''Let me see if I have this aright. If I tell you I will willingly wed Fitz Hugh, offering him the same contract I would have offered the man of my father's choosing, then you will make the effort to convince him he should wed me himself, cutting Rothwell out of it?''

''Correct.''

''How long do I have to consider this?''

''Only until we make camp in those woods,'' and he pointed to what was no more than ten minutes away. ''I will need time to work on Ranulf, and if he *does* agree, it needs be done tonight—''

''How can it be?'' she gasped.

''Those woods belong to an abbey that is a bit farther up the road. If Ranulf agrees, there is a resident bishop who can marry you. It must be done tonight, for Ranulf cannot be allowed time to think long on it or he is like to change his mind.''

''I know I am not beautiful, de Breaute, but I also know I am not *that* sore on the eyes. Why would thinking about it—''

'' 'Twould have naught to do with you personally,

demoiselle, but with Ranulf's distrust of *all* ladies. He has had bad experiences in the past that have soured him against them. So being, I will use Clydon to tempt him, you understand? You will have time enough to bring him around to trusting you after you are wed.''

''You do not further your cause by telling me *that*, Sir Walter.''

''Mayhap, but you must allow that Ranulf is young enough to change his ways, whereas Rothwell is not.''

''Then begone, for I will need every single second I have to consider it.''

Chapter Thirteen

Walter was ready to pull hairs. He had been at it for nigh an hour, and although Ranulf had not lost his patience yet, was still listening to his arguments, he was not changing his mind.

They sat before the fire near Ranulf's tent, forcing down the last of the unappetizing camp food that had been quickly prepared. The lady under discussion was across the camp at another fire, Searle and Eric both sent to guard her under the guise of keeping her company. Even so, Walter noticed Ranulf's eyes going to her repeatedly as they spoke, though she had not once looked their way.

If he thought there was something there that was attracting Ranulf, he would change his tactics. But although he might himself find the lady quite comely with her powdery blue eyes and delicate features, he knew his friend was drawn to more stunning wenches, certainly more robust ones. But mayhap he should change his tactics after all, though he had a few more things to say yet in Clydon's favor.

"I do not understand you, Ranulf. I know of no other man who would not leap on this incredible chance, none who would not hesitate to wed the lady even by force, and *you* can have her willing. Have you not considered the power behind the annual income Clydon has? One hundred knights' service!

Imagine how many fiefs she must have besides Clydon Castle, to allow for that much income.''

"I am surprised you did not ask for an exact accounting while you were at it.''

Walter flushed. Ranulf had not been pleased at all
that he had approached the lady, especially for the
reason he had. Walter had related to him everything
she had to say, except about her offer if they would
simply return her to Clydon, but it did no good. Ranulf was simply not interested.

"Do you realize Clydon is like to equal your father's lands?'' Walter threw in, then quickly added
before Ranulf could react to mention of his father,
"And have you considered that you would only need
swear fealty to Shefford? You would have had to swear
to King Richard for Farring Cross. Better an earl than
a king, especially a king who so loves war. The demands would be much less—''

"From my overlord, mayhap, but what of the extra
demands in holding such a large fief? Did you ask her
how greatly subinfeudated it is? How many vassals
she has? How many people she is responsible for?
All I wanted was a small fief to farm and settle on,
Walter. I never entertained the idea of becoming as
powerful as my father.''

"Because it was an impossible notion. You could
sell your sword the rest of your life and still never
earn enough to buy a fief like Clydon. But here 'tis
being *given* to you, costing you naught but the taking
of a wife. You do not even have to fight for it.''

"Nay? Think you Rothwell will just give up, that
he still will not come a-calling? She also has neighbors who visit with drawn swords, if you did not notice.''

Walter shrugged aside that sarcasm. "But you will no longer be only thirty men strong, Ranulf. You will have your own army, and another to draw on from Shefford should you need it. And there is another thing. 'Tis easier getting aid from an earl than from a king."

"Be that as it may, there is naught that could compensate for the headaches I would have from the lady and *her* ladies. Christ's toes, Walter, did you count how many she has in her care?"

"Is *that* what you object to?"

"*She* is what I object to. I want no lady in my life, least of all a tiny one who thinks she is seven feet tall and has not the sense to know when to push a man no more."

Walter almost grinned, for he knew now that Ranulf could be brought around, that he was only still smarting under the insults the lady had heaped on him. "She may be a mite big on audacity, but she has long been in control of all around her. She only needs a husband to put her in her place." At Ranulf's grunt, he opted for his last arguments. "Did you never intend to take a wife once you had Farring Cross?"

"Aye, a lusty village wench will do nicely."

Walter stared at him aghast for a moment, but he now had the ammunition he needed. "And who would see to your household, to the making of cloth, to the cleaning, the cooking? Think you the servants will work just because there is work to do, or that they will take direction from one of their own just because you elevate her to wife?"

"If I say—"

"Ranulf, my friend, that is your stubbornness speaking through the mouth of a fool. Nay, hear me out," he added quickly at Ranulf's scowl. "Can you hand a villein a sword and call him a knight?"

"Do not be stupid," Ranulf growled.

"Aye, it takes years of training to make a knight. But so, too, does it take years to make a lady. She has no skills from the cradle, Ranulf. She is trained to her duties just as we were. Will you live like a pig for years whilst your village wench learns the skills of a lady? And who will teach her if not a lady? And what lady would condescend to do so for any price?"

"Enough, Walter!"

"Aye, enough, de Breaute," came a new voice as Lady Reina stepped into the circle of their fire, Searle and Eric not far behind her. "If you have not an agreement by now, you are not like to get one, and I do not need to be forced on any man. This was your idea—not mine, and certainly not his. I agreed for only one reason. You painted a better picture of *him* than you did of Rothwell. But Rothwell is obviously the better man, at least a man who feels himself capable of being Lord of Clydon, whereas your friend must doubt his own ability to rule so great a fief."

Walter groaned aloud. She could not have said anything worse if she had tried. To compare Ranulf with Rothwell was bad enough, but to say Rothwell was the better man! To question not only Ranulf's ability but his courage as well, implying he was afraid of the challenge that Clydon presented!

Ranulf shot to his feet well before she had finished speaking, and Walter would not be surprised to see him throttle the lady for these newest insults. He was so angry he could not speak at once, his eyes dark indigo as they glared at her, and heaven help her, she did not seem the least bit afraid, dared to taunt him even more.

"If I am wrong, Fitz Hugh, say so. Or do you want me to believe that you would refuse Clydon because *I* frighten you?"

The air came hissing through Ranulf's teeth. "Saddle her a horse, Walter! We ride for the abbey now!"

As Ranulf stalked off to fetch his own mount, Walter looked at the lady incredulously, to see her smiling at him. "You did that apurpose!"

She shrugged. "You appeared to need some help. As you said, better him than Rothwell."

"But he is not like to ever forgive you for what you just implied, lady."

Again she shrugged. "If he is too stupid to realize he was goaded into making the right decision, for his own benefit, mind you, then that is his problem."

" 'Tis more like to be your problem," Searle said softly from behind her.

Eric was quick to agree. "Are you certain you want him, lady?"

"Ask me instead if I want Rothwell, whom you were all so eager to give me to."

She left the three flushed faces behind and went to find a horse for herself.

Chapter Fourteen

Ranulf was well aware he had been goaded into marrying the lady, and he would do it for the sole purpose of making her regret manipulating him in such a way. But this was no time to let anger get in the way of his reason. She was prepared to make contract with him, and whether he liked it or not, he knew it was necessary, was in fact considered to be the most important aspect of any marriage. She was also too shrewd for him not to pay close attention when she dictated the terms to the young monk who had been lent to them as scribe.

They had been allowed the use of a small room for the discussion, with Walter and Searle there as witnesses for Ranulf, and the monk for her. Ranulf would have preferred talking over the terms with her privately first, but she had insisted that it would not take long, and that he should find everything agreeable to him, as she was offering him the same as she would have Lord John de Lascelles—he finally had the name! Whether this was so or not remained to be seen, but if it was not, he was less likely to argue with her in front of the monk, which she was surely counting on.

Ranulf had not realized until after they had spoken to Father Geoffrey, and he had agreed to marry them, that Walter's little plot could very well have backfired in their faces. The lady could have sought sanctuary with the bishop, the very reason Ranulf had not

wanted to bring her to the abbey to pass the night.
He had to wonder why she did not, for the notion
must have crossed her mind. She could not truly *want*
to marry him, not with her low opinion of him that
she had made abundantly clear. Yet in no way had
she appeared reluctant before Father Geoffrey. And she
had been naught but calmly controlled ever since they
arrived at the abbey.

"Before we get to the terms, 'tis your right to know
what you are getting, Sir Ranulf."

He snorted upon hearing she was back to address-
ing him in a courteous manner, and she heard him,
giving him a smile meant to annoy him before continuing. "Because my father is dead and I am his only
heir, I do not come to you with a mere dowry, but
with my full inheritance. Besides Clydon Castle with
its large farm and mill, there are two other keeps,
Brent Tower and Roth Hill, not quite as large, but not
small either. There are also two other farms near Roth
Hill, and three fortified manor houses with hamlets
closer to Shefford."

Ranulf was impressed, but it was Walter who
thought to ask, "Which do you want as your dower
property?"

"I thought I made it clear I do not come with a
dowry, but with everything my father owned. So being, I wish to keep half my inheritance should aught
happen to Sir Ranulf ere there are any children of this
union. If there is a child to then inherit, I would request only Clydon for my own, for the duration of
my life, to go to the child on my death. If I die before
Sir Ranulf, then of course everything remains his, for
I have no other family to fight over it."

"Does that sound reasonable to you, Ranulf?" Walter asked his friend.

It was more than reasonable, since she was in effect giving him everything for the duration of his own life. But not trusting her, he knew there had to be a catch. He just could not see it.

Instead of answering Walter, he said to her, "You say you want only half of your inheritance back should I die. Who, then, gets the other half?"

She looked at him as if he were daft. " 'Tis usual for the husband's family to fight over the property should he die. Ofttimes they try to keep it all, though Lord Guy would prevent that in this case. But Lord John's family would have expected half, as would Lord Richard's family, had he answered my summons first. So I was willing to give half to form either alliance. As I said before, I offer you the same terms. You need but match them, pledging half you possess to me, the amount to be given only should you die. But I thought we agreed to wait on discussing the terms."

"You were not finished?" Ranulf frowned.

She shook her head. "What I have mentioned are the demesne lands, held only by me. Though I should mention now that two other fiefs have returned to me due to those vassals dying, one without heirs and one with a baby daughter now in wardship to me. Actually three vassals died with my father on Crusade, though the third had three sons, the oldest of whom has already sworn to me for the manor he holds now."

Ranulf ignored Walter's groaning. Neither of them had thought she was this well landed. "How many vassals did your father take with him?"

"Four," she replied. "William de Bruce remains

with Lord Guy, as do our household knights, though
we have lost two of them as well, as I already told
you when you met their widows. Sir William's son
has already sworn to me for his father, who holds a
manor and a toll bridge of me.''

Ranulf was almost afraid to ask, "Is that all?"

Again she shook her head. "I have three other vassals who did not join my father. Sir John holds a farm
and four hundred acres near Bedford. Sir Guiot, a
farm and mill worth three knights' service. And Lord
Simon, whose daughter Elaine you met, holds Forthwick Keep, a mill, and two rich manors.''

Walter was groaning louder. Ranulf was not sure
what he thought now. Clydon did not just equal his
father's estate, it surpassed it.

For want of something better to say, for he was
frankly overwhelmed, he asked, "And how many
knights' service does Lord Simon owe you?"

"Twelve knights for the forty days if I need them,
but if 'tis the income you are interested in, that
equates to two hundred and forty marks a year.''

"And the others?"

"Fifteen and a half knights' service.''

Ranulf calculated quickly and then said suspiciously, "But that is only five hundred fifty in income, my lady. From where comes all the rest you
claimed? Surely not all from your demesne lands.''

Patiently she replied, "Nay, the demesne amounts
to eight hundred marks a year. The wardship is two
manor farms with villages accounting for one hundred fifty. 'Tis Birkenham Keep and Town—''

"Birkenham!" all three men gasped in unison, but
it was Ranulf who demanded, "Birkenham Town is
yours?"

"And the keep that guards it," she said. "You know Birkenham, then?"

"Lady, who does not know Birkenham? 'Tis nigh as large as Lincoln!"

"So it is," she replied without the least smugness in her tone. "But as I was saying, Birkenham is the richest of the holdings, with dues and fees amounting to five hundred marks a year. 'Tis also the fief that has returned to me, though I have yet to see the additional income that that entails, nor will I until Michaelmas."

"But why would your father subinfeudate a fief that must be worth more than Clydon, if the dues alone are five hundred marks a year?"

She finally smiled. "Have you never dealt with merchants, Sir Ranulf, or their guilds? Birkenham may be the richest fief, but 'tis also the most troublesome, as well as time-consuming if you are not in residence there. My father was glad to have done with it."

"And now it will be my problem?" he fairly snarled.

"It need not be a problem at all." She frowned at him. "You need only decide whether you wish to keep it or give it to your own man or one of mine. Give it to Sir Walter," she sneered. "His tongue is glib enough to deal right well with demanding merchants."

"God's wounds, Ranulf!" Walter groaned, horrified. "Do not even consider—"

" 'Tis no more than you deserve for getting me entangled in this," Ranulf growled low, and then, to Reina: "Now if *that* is all, let us get back to the terms, which have been so far one-sided. What do you want from me, demoiselle?''

''I am rich in land and priceless trophies from the Holy Land, but there is no money at present, as you may have surmised, nor will there be until after the harvest and the rents due at Michaelmas.''

''How is that possible? Were you robbed? Those outlaws in your woods—''

''Nay, nothing like that,'' she assured him. ''Crusading is not done cheaply, Sir Ranulf. My father took more than half our wealth, gold stuff, and jewels to support the large army he brought with him. He also took most of our horses, and fifty of the men-at-arms from Clydon.''

''Is *that* why you were so little protected?''

This brought a look from the monk and a blush from the lady. ''Partly. I was to replace the garrison as well as the horses and did half, replacing the men, only to lose thirty of them in war. Immediately my father left, both Forthwick and Brent Tower were attacked. The crops and village were burned at Brent Tower ere my men arrived, so there was no income from there last year, and much cost to me to rebuild the village and see they did not starve. But Lord Simon was captured and ransom demanded, which took nigh all the money I had left. And losing those men I had just paid a year's wage to did not make it easy to replace them, not when one thing after another kept occurring to put it off. So for the rest of that year I took what was left in knights' service as castle guard, though it has never been my father's policy to do so. I was then able to hire new men for a garrison of fifty-five soldiers when the rents came due last year.''

"A small number for such a large castle, but not all accounted for," Ranulf reminded her.

She gave him a baleful stare before replying. "I was caught short only this past fortnight. Lady Margaret's married daughter had been visiting this past month and needed an escort of ten to return her to London. Sir Arnulph, another household knight, needed another ten to accompany him to Birkenham, where I sent him in my stead. And one of my bailiffs requested assistance with a killing at one of my manors, so I sent him a knight with five men just four days ago." When Sir William had gotten his crazy idea that *she* could be taught to defend her own castle, and had quickly instructed the armorer to piece together her mail. "I know the number is small. As I said, there has simply been no extra money for long now."

"But you had your income from last year."

"And more catastrophes this year than I care to mention. A fire at Roth Hill took every building in the bailey, including the grain sheds, only just replenished. The walls there have long needed repair, too, which was begun but not finished. More than a hundred sheep have been stolen, preventing me from selling any, and my entire herd of cattle. I suspect Falkes de Rochefort had a hand in that. The cattle had to be replaced, as well as the horses for the garrison, though I still do not have enough for all my men. And—"

"So from me you need money?"

"Aye, but not overmuch, just enough to finish the repairs at Roth Hill and to meet any other emergencies occurring before Michaelmas. You already have men to increase the garrison, though Roth Hill and Brent Tower could use more as well. And it would not be amiss if we had more horses. Is this too much for you to meet?''

His answer was accompanied with a surly glare. ''You already know what I am worth and that this will not tax me at all. But what of the obligatory payment due from your vassals on your wedding?''

'' 'Tis due on the wedding of the lord's oldest daughter, but technically I am no longer that. I am now their liege lady, and there is no aid due on the wedding of their lord or lady. But that payment would only have offset the costs of the wedding, which will be no burden. Clydon has an abundance of food and stores. We were never in danger of starving.''

Ranulf was still so far dissatisfied he could barely stand it. How *could* she give all this to him, with almost naught in return? Granted, some man had to have it, but doubtless that Lord John or Richard she had wanted would have brought her untold wealth and the power of his family. *There* was where she was being shafted. *He* had no connections, no family to give aid, naught of power to draw on should the need arise. But she could not know that, or she would not have mentioned giving half her estate to him to remain with his family on his death.

Ranulf stiffened, recalling that and what it actually meant. He would have to speak to her about it, but not in front of the monk.

Looking at the monk, he asked, ''You are not writing all of this down, are you?''

''Nay, my lord, only the extent of the lady's holdings as will come to you through the marriage, the stipulations upon the death of either of you, and what you have agreed to pay for. I need only list now your holdings before you can return to Father Geoffrey to speak your vows. The legalities of these terms will be added later, the copies of the complete contract ready in the morning.''

Ranulf said nothing, loath to mention how little he was bringing to this marriage. But the monk was waiting. . . .

. ''His marriage portion is seven thousand marks, to give it an even number,'' Lady Reina said.without the slightest inflection in her tone. ''Half his wealth.''

The monk was aghast at the small amount. ''But—''

''There are no 'buts,' '' she cut in forcefully, only to add more moderately, ''Sir Ranulf also agrees to give me children, protect my people and property to the best of his ability, and—and not to beat me, for as he is a man of such unusual size, one blow is like to kill me.''

All eyes turned to Ranulf to be treated to the bright color flooding his face. That last stipulation was unheard of, for a man had a right to beat his wife if she was deserving of it, even if she was not. The monk would be the first to say so. And yet she had made a point that Ranulf had not considered. He did not dare take his fist to her as small as she was, for it *was* like to kill her.

But children! To have it stated in contract that he could not ignore her. Did she think that was his intention, to take all she had and put her away somewhere? It was a tempting notion, but he would not do it. Christ's toes! He was getting so much that it would be a matter of honor to treat her with the tenderest of care!

''Do you—ah—agree to this, Sir Ranulf?'' the monk asked with hesitancy.

"Aye." He nodded grudgingly. "But I need a word with the lady ere the terms can be finished."

So saying, he rose and snatched Reina's hand to pull her out of the room before she could gainsay him. She thought he meant to beat her now ere the contract was sworn to and he lost the chance. She had dared much considering she was in no position to make any demands at all. But she had gotten away with it. He *had* agreed before taking her out of the room.

She held her breath when he stopped just outside the door. She wanted to squeeze her eyes shut, too, but did not want him to know she was afraid of him. If he did beat her, it was no more than she deserved for deciding to accept him. It was madness to be "under the rod" of such a man, a complete stranger. To be unable to gainsay him even if he sold her land. To have no rights whatsoever, not even to appeal in court without him. To allow him such *control* over her, a man who gave every indication of actively disliking her. But what was the alternative? An old, greedy man who would not care about Clydon, who only wanted to drain its wealth.

She shuddered each time she thought of Rothwell, after what she had been told of him—and she *had* asked some of his men, not trusting Sir Walter any farther than she could throw him. At least this Ranulf would care for the land. That he had saved so long to own land told her that. And he was more than capable of being Clydon's lord. That really had been the deciding factor and why she had not tried to enlist the monk's help, which was no guarantee, really. Neither John nor Richard would be able to do as well as this giant when it came to actual fighting. From the size of him, 'twas doubtful *anyone* could beat him.

"What was the reason, lady, for those ridiculous demands?" Ranulf demanded in a low rumble. "Think you I cannot see to you and yours?"

Reina let out her breath. That had to be the softest she had ever heard him speak, and it boded well that he would not be stomping all over her.

"Not at all. I think you will be quite able to protect Clydon."

He was not sure he had heard her aright. A compliment! From *her?* Unbelievable!

"That was not your sentiment earlier in camp," he reminded her.

"Do not be stu—" She bit her lip. *Jesú,* she would have to learn to watch her tongue with this man. "Ah, I ask your pardon for what was said earlier. I was upset and did not really mean any of that."

"So if you think I am capable, why insist on seeing it in writing?"

"That stipulation and the other were only a cushion, so to speak, to lessen the impact of the last."

He was frowning now. "Which you press your luck in demanding at all."

"True," she allowed, lowering her eyes to his broad chest. "But you have agreed. And as for making mention of children, I know 'twas unnecessary. To get me with child will be to your benefit, to strengthen your position should Rothwell or anyone else still think to have me by killing you."

"You talk freely enough of the bedding, lady. Are you prepared for it?"

She knew he asked that just to fluster her, and it worked. "Aye," she whispered.

"Tonight?"

Her eyes flew back to his. "But this is not the ceremony that counts! We must be wed again at Clydon, with my vassals and Sir Henry attending. I thought we would wait—''

"And have you return to Clydon not truly wed, so once your vassals are there you can put me out? Nay, lady, you will have no grounds for annulment. You stipulated children, so we will get started on them soonest.''

She could feel her cheeks heating rapidly, and with it, her temper. He would do this just to get even with her. She was aware she did not attract him, that he did not *want* to bed her. 'Twas likely he would never have gotten around to it if she had not embarrassed him by making demands about children in front of the others.

Tight-lipped, she asked, "Is that all?''

Surprisingly, his expression grew uneasy. "As it happens, that was not why I asked you out here.''

She could have said he had not asked but had dragged her out, but she did not belabor the point. Whatever it was he wanted to say was obviously difficult for him to speak of.

"You called me a baseborn knight.''

"And you admitted you were,'' she agreed, amazed that he might be embarrassed about *that*.

"Then why do you mention my family when you know me to be a bastard?''

"I assume that one of your parents must be of rank, or you would not have been trained to knighthood. As it is usually the male who spreads his seed about with so little thought or care, I also assume it is your father who has the rank, not your mother. Am I wrong?''

He was now tight-lipped and frowning again. "Nay, you have that right, too."

"Is he dead, then?"

"To me he might as well be. I have spoken to him only twice in my entire life, lady. I was nine ere he first deigned to notice me, though he knew about me well enough, for I was born in the demesne village."

"But he must have acknowledged you, to have had you fostered."

"That matters not. He has his heir and has no need of me, nor I of him. Even should my half brother die, I would not accept aught from him now. 'Tis too late."

"Fie on you, sir, to be so bitter," she dared to admonish him. "Your father could not overlook a legitimate heir to elevate you, and you should not—"

"Did I say there was a legitimate heir, lady? My half brother is a bastard, too, but one younger than me by several years. His good fortune stems from having a mother who was a *lady*. A whore, but still a lady."

Reina was not sure what to say after that. She should just leave it be but could not, not after he had trusted her with such a confession. It made him seem no longer a stranger, and, *Jesú,* she actually felt incensed on his behalf.

"I would not call that anywhere near fair, and it seems I must again ask your pardon. You do indeed have reason to be bitter. If a man must choose a natural son to succeed him, it should be no different than if he were choosing among legitimate sons. The oldest inherits by the law. Who is this man?"

Ranulf was taken aback by the heat in her response. *He* knew 'twas unfair, but that she should think so was unexpected. A lady, not championing another of her kind?

But he waved her question aside. "It matters not who he is, only that I want him to have naught of yours. Should I die, I want your entire inheritance returned to you, and not just half of what is mine but everything I then possess as well. And I want *that* put in your contract."

She stared at him wide-eyed with disbelief. "If—if you say so."

"And you understand that an alliance with me does not bring you aid from anyone other than myself?"

"Aye." She got her voice back under control. "But only your aid was ever needful. We will have all the additional aid we could need from Shefford."

Ranulf felt strange, hearing her say "we" like that. He had never been a "we" before, not in his entire life. And she was proving she could be reasonable—at least during this discussion. Of course, he was forgetting the stipulations she still wanted included in the contract; and reminded of that, he picked her up under her arms to bring her face up to a level with his.

"We are agreed now and can finish this business, but do you understand one thing more, little general. You may have protected yourself from ever feeling my fist, but do you ever deserve it, your backside will become acquainted with the palm of my hand. You will *not* feel free to provoke me at your will."

With that he set her down to drag her *back* into the room for the swearing and the kiss of peace. Peace? Reina wondered if she would ever know that state again.

Chapter Fifteen

Reina found it hard to reconcile being afraid of a man when she had never before been afraid of any man. She had been protected all her life, kept from the harsh realities other women suffered, though not unaware of them. She had been loved and indulged, first by both parents, then even more by her father after her mother died six years ago. She had not even been sent away to foster at Shefford, her mother too fearful of letting her only child out of her sight. She had been taught at home to work with needle and shuttle, to read, write, and speak Latin, French, and even the rarely used English. She knew all things to know about managing a demesne, inside the castle as well as without, even to making financial and legal decisions, though those were most tedious, and she would be the first to admit she was not very good with money.

Certainly she had been afraid before, when her mother died, when her father went crusading, leaving her alone and in control of Clydon with only a few vassals to advise her—when she learned of his death. And when Falkes de Rochefort sent his men to take her, she had been afraid they might succeed, but she had not been afraid of de Rochefort himself. He had not even engendered fear in her the night he sneaked into her chamber to pounce on her with his foul intentions. She had felt outrage then, enough to have him tossed into the moat on his way out.

Of course, if he had managed to get her and somehow force her to wed him, then she might have been afraid of him—enough to kill him. Her father had never liked him, and she trusted his judgment in men, the reason she had not even considered Sir Falkes when he asked to wed her.

But another had got her instead, and this one she did fear, though she did not entertain the thought of killing *him*. She would be too afraid to even try—not that she actually wanted to. The fear was there, but it was not complete, and not for the same reason.

Right now it was all-consuming, for she was on her way back to camp and the promised bedding. Aside from that, however, the man deserved the benefit of the doubt. She had agreed to have him. He was not her first or even second choice, but he could possibly have been her third if it had been put to her under different circumstances. After all, Fitz Hugh did have a lot in his favor.

She would certainly never grow tired of looking at him, though she was not silly or foolish enough to let him know how attractive she found him. She had seen him use his sword, and his skill was most impressive, more so if his friend Walter could be believed. He was accustomed to leading men, but not only that, they wanted to be led by him. There were not many men who could inspire loyalty like that. He was young. He was strong. He was kind to animals, as she had seen with the brown cat that rode today perched on his shoulder. And he did not have any other obligations. Both Lord John and Lord Richard would have had to divide their time between her holdings and their own, and even those of their families. That Ranulf would devote himself solely to Clydon made him the better choice, actually.

Aye, there was much in his favor—but much against him, too. Her main and immediate worry was his size, a weapon in itself. Then there was his anger, which she had seen more of than not. And his manner, which was atrocious. The fact that he distrusted and disliked ladies, as Sir Walter claimed, was not going to be easy to deal with either. And he was unpredictable. Who would have thought he would have balked at being given an estate like Clydon?

There was going to be a problem with Theodric, too, unless Ranulf could be talked into forgetting that unfortunate incident between them. And how he would handle her villeins remained to be seen.

What Reina feared, she supposed, aside from his size, was that he would have no care for her feelings. She knew he disliked her. He had already been rough in his treatment of her. That he now had the power to hurt and shame her at his will was shattering to her peace of mind. But again he deserved the benefit of the doubt. She could only hope that marrying him would not be the biggest mistake of her life.

Her horse plodded behind his on returning to camp, neither of them in much hurry now. She had hoped they would spend the night at the abbey, where, if she was going to be doing any screaming, someone who might care would hear it. No such luck there.

Father Geoffrey had offered, separate rooms, of course. Her new husband, resourceful as he was, could have found a way to come to her there for the bedding. It would have alleviated at least some of her fear. But he had declined.

Reina did not *feel* married, but she would ere the night was through. Her inner trembling would not stop, the more she thought about it. She knew what would happen. She had often imagined it happening with Richard, even with John, but never with a giant. Before, she had looked forward to her wedding night, for she was old not to have experienced lovemaking yet. Now—she could only berate herself for prodding Ranulf into bedding her tonight, when she still could have had days to get used to the idea if she had kept her mouth shut about wanting children.

But she did have a small reprieve. Dismounting before his tent, Ranulf nodded toward it. "Do you do whatever needs be done. I will join you anon."

His "soon" turned out to be two hours, proving he was as reluctant to get to the bedding as was she, needing the bolstering of the two flagons of wine Father Geoffrey had pressed on them in honor of the occasion. She could have used some of that wine herself. What she got was water from the pitcher set inside his large tent and an opportunity to meet his leman, a big, hefty girl nigh as beautiful as Eadwina, who, if not exactly sprawled across his bed, came damn close to it sitting on the edge, resting back on her elbows, with knees spread in the most provocative, sluttish position Reina had ever seen.

The meeting surprised them both, for the girl was obviously not there to assist Reina, but had been awaiting Ranulf's return. That no one had told her the reason for his absence from camp was obvious in that she *was* there, expecting only him to enter the tent for her blatant invitation.

Reina was not annoyed, however, especially since the girl was horrified to be found there by her, scrambling to her feet and stammering something about presuming she might be needed, and begging Reina not to tell the lord she had come without being summoned. Obviously she had *not* been summoned, or Ranulf would not have sent Reina inside to find her. Or would he? *Nay, give him the benefit of the doubt, Reina.*

"Since you are here . . . ?"

"Mae, my lady," the girl told her quickly. "My name is Mae."

"Well, Mae, you might as well help me with my laces this one time," Reina said matter-of-factly. "Since I have wed the lord, this is the last time I expect to see you. We will return to Clydon on the morrow. You will understand if I ask that you do not linger there."

Mae did no more than nod, incredulous that she was being let off so lightly under *these* circumstances. She had been whipped once by the order of a lady who had no more than suspected her husband had visited Mae. She had heard of other light-skirts who had been done away with by jealous ladies. That was one reason she had become a camp follower, where ladies were not likely to be, and the women of soldiers had no real power over her, at least not the power of life and death. If the lord had wed, glory be, Mae wanted naught else to do with him. Love was not worth risking her life for. Let the other Clydon whores see to him henceforth, and he would have use of them if *this* lady was as indifferent as she seemed.

Reina took pity on the nervous Mae and dismissed her ere she was more knotted up than unlaced from the green woolen bliaut. She finished the chore herself, no more easy task than it had been donning the clothes earlier without help. Minus her braies and hose, which Kenric had overlooked when he swiped up clothes for her in the dark, she had felt nearly naked all day. But at least the boy had found a pair of her shoes. To have been married barefoot would have really been the crowning touch for this horrid day.

There were a number of things in the tent, but come to think of it, a mercenary as her husband had been up until now was likely to carry with him most of his possessions. There was a strongbox under lock, a small chest that could not contain *too* many clothes. On top of it was a basin of water with a drying cloth Reina had every intention of making use of, since she would probably not get a bath here. Several stools around a low table with the water pitcher and goblets on it, as well as several fat candles, were set off to the side of the tent. The sleeping pallet was actually a thick mattress, very long and perhaps five feet wide, made especially for the giant, no doubt. The bedding was rather fine, a soft woolen blanket and linen sheets, better than she could have expected. In the corner was a war chest for the instruments of his trade, with an assortment of longer weapons that would not fit in it, including another sword like the one Ranulf had been wearing—and one brown cat.

Reina was surprised at this second guest for a moment, seeing those glowing yellow eyes staring out of the shadows at her. But then she was delighted, welcoming company that would not talk back. She was fond of cats, made sure the Clydon felines were as well fed as the hunting dogs, for they served their purpose, too, keeping down the rodent population.

The cat's presence in Ranulf's tent proved what she had earlier suspected when she first noticed it atop his shoulder. The animal was a pet. What was so unusual was that such a large, gruff man would want such a little pet, and an ugly one at that. Its tail was bent at the end, probably from being stepped on at some time or other. Its coat was short and scraggly, in need of fresh milk and an occasional egg. There were patches of reddened skin from what was no doubt a bad flea infestation.

Aside from that, it certainly seemed friendly enough, coming forward when she made soothing sounds to attract it, rubbing up against her leg. She bent down to scratch it behind the ears to gain a very loud purring of contentment, and smiled. At least someone around here liked her.

Wearing only her shift now, Reina took care of her toilet, keeping up a running chatter with the cat, which continued to move in and out between her legs, and answered her with that overloud purring that was a rather soothing sound. She was in need of soothing. She did all she could do to avoid getting down on that pallet, including rummaging in Ranulf's chest until she found a comb to make use of.

But coming her hair took only so long, even as snarled as it was. Wondering what was keeping Ranulf was pointless. He would come when he was ready. She thought about sleeping while she waited, but knew she never would.

Finally she picked up the cat and settled in the center of the bed to pass the time picking fleas. The cat, which she discovered then to be a female as it stretched out on its back to let her have at it, seemed to enjoy the grooming. She became so engrossed she did not hear her husband enter—but the cat did. One second it was purring in utter contentment, and the next, hissing, and Reina got a sharp scratch for her presumption that the cat was friendly.

She stared incredulously as the feline bounded away from her to actually leap up into Ranulf's arms. Since he was not surprised, this was obviously a normal occurrence. But Reina was a bit piqued as she rubbed the scratch on the tender inside of her thigh. That was the last time *she* would offer to groom the fickle thing, and after she had allowed its fleas into what would be *her* bed.

Since Ranulf had not deigned to even notice her yet, but was busy greeting his pet, Reina took a moment to dust the sheets. And then Kenric was entering, unannounced, and she quickly stuck her legs under the covers.

She supposed she would have to get used to this. The squire had his duties, and disarming and undressing her husband was one of them. But the lord's chamber at Clydon had an antechamber. Perhaps she could persuade her husband to have his disrobing done there—on the other hand, she thought as she silently watched the process, perhaps she would not.

Sweet *Jesú*, were those bulges under that tunic real? Off it came, and with it a tiny gasp from her. They were real, all right, thick cords of muscle bunching and rippling as he moved. Theo had tried to tell her, but she had refused to listen. All golden-skinned and beautiful, he had said, and it was more than true. She felt a tiny bit jealous that Theo had seen all of him, whilst she was waiting with bated breath for those chausses to come off. But she had to wait. Ranulf dismissed Kenric and moved to the basin, splashing the cold water all over him. It was only when he used the cloth that was already wet from her use that he finally seemed to be aware of her presence, turning about abruptly to impale her with those violet eyes.

"You are—not asleep?"

Reina felt the little kernel of expectation curl up and die in her chest. She had seen for herself what kind of woman he preferred, and she did not even come close. Of course he had been hoping she would be asleep. He had made a promise in warning that he now regretted. Why else would he have taken so long to join her, and weaving unsteadily on his feet, too?

Well, she would not stay where she was not wanted. The bedding would have to come sometime, but it could wait until they *both* got used to the idea.

She stood up in the center of the bed, perversely feeling something of a disappointment when she should feel naught but relief. "Nay, I do not sleep yet. I waited to hear where you wished me to sleep," she said calmly, though with raised chin, daring him to call her a liar.

He did not call her anything. He stared at her hard, for an unnerving long time, and then the cloth fell from his hand unnoticed.

"You sleep there—with me," he said huskily, surprising her and perhaps himself, too.

But he continued to stare, as if he doubted what he saw. Then he was yanking at the laces on his chausses, tearing them in his haste. Reina's eyes widened. She had the distinct feeling he was going to jump on her, and she was not far wrong. He took her down to the pallet with one arm as he crashed on it. She lost her breath and, in the next moment, her shift.

"Wait—"

"Are you a virgin?"

He did not wait for an answer. She knew he did not care if she was or not, and that hurt. Obviously he had decided that if he must do this, to get it over with as quickly as possible. Why else would he slash his mouth across hers for one measly second, then climb atop her the next? Well, she could assume that attitude, too. Best to have done with it right quickly, to find out how much she would have to fear of it next time—if there was a next time.

Reina braced herself to be crushed, but was not. Instead she felt his entry, and it did not rip her asunder, but was smooth and easy. Had staring at him done that, got her juices flowing without his even touching her? She was amazed, and felt a fluttering niceness like nothing she had ever felt before. *Then* she was ripped asunder.

Her scream was cut in half by the return of his bruising lips. How he managed to reach her lips and thrust into her at the same time, she did not know. Perhaps because most of his height was in his long legs. Perhaps because his back was bent over her; she was still not crushed as she had expected to be. Just her lips. He could use some lessons in that area. But in other areas . . . sweet *Jesú,* what was that she was feeling now? Whatever it was, she was left to wonder about it. Her husband, with a loud roar, was done.

Chapter Sixteen

*R*eina moved carefully in taking inventory ere she got up, but she was not really battered. Her lips were a mite tender, and there was a definite soreness between her legs, but naught had been broken when Ranulf had collapsed on her for those few moments after he reached his pleasure.

But she had been misled. Wenda said it was wonderful. Eadwina must think so, too, to like doing it so often. Reina would not call what she had experienced wonderful, but it certainly was not as terrible as she had thought it would be with a giant. With the rending of her maidenhead behind her, she supposed she had naught left to fear from this business of coupling, but there was naught to recommend it either.

She dressed quickly while her husband slept on. Staring at him in that helpless state was not conducive to clear thinking, and she had much to consider, particularly what she would tell Lord Simon, who was likely to be at Clydon when they returned.

It was the stirrings of the camp that had woken her, and stepping outside the tent, she saw there was activity everywhere as nigh a hundred men broke their fast and prepared for another day's march. She found some bushes to relieve herself whilst no one was paying attention, and when she returned, Lanzo approached her with a cup of ale and a chunk of day-old bread.

She thanked the boy but offered him no smile, and he quickly retreated. He might be learning skillful arms under Ranulf's tutelage, but knightly courtesies were sadly lacking. It would do no harm for either squire to think she was still displeased with him for his part in her abduction. Both must become aware that the arts of warfare were not all that made a knight. The social skills and graces must be learned, as well as the courtesies due a lady, especially the treatment of a lady at all times. Those courtesies were due even during an abduction, but they had not been accorded her.

She was approached again, this time by Ranulf's fickle cat, who once again rubbed up against Reina's legs. "So, 'tis to be that way, is it?" Reina frowned down at the animal. "Think you I am not wise to your ploys?"

She got a meow in answer; then the creature bounded off toward Lanzo, who had just set down a tin of scraps for it. Reina shook her head, not sure whether she wanted to play silly games with a cat. She supposed she might have to, if her husband intended to bring the animal home with them.

She then heard rumblings from the tent and returned to it. Ranulf squinted up at her as she opened the flap, letting in the bright sunshine of a beautiful spring morn.

"Where is Lady Ella?" he asked in a grouchy tone.

Reina stiffened. "I was not aware there was another lady in camp."

"My cat," he clarified.

"Oh," Reina said dumbly, then, "You named your cat *Lady* Ella?"

"Aye."

Reina was treated to the first really pleasant expression she had seen on her husband. Whether it could actually be termed a smile, she was not sure, but 'twas devastating to behold.

"Her namesake is the cleverest cat I know," he continued. "So it suited."

She now had to wonder who this namesake Ella was, but she was not about to ask him. He obviously did not think highly of her.

"Your Ella—"

"Lady Ella—"

"*Lady* Ella is breaking her fast," Reina gritted out. She was insulted to give that scrawny creature a title, *her* title, but was not ready to have her first argument with her new husband. "Do you wish me to summon your squire so you may—"

"Not yet."

He sat up as he interrupted her, so that the blanket fell to his lap. Reina looked away. That wide expanse of golden chest was like a magnet for her eyes, but she staunchly resisted the pull.

"Take off your clothes."

Her eyes flew back to him, wide in disbelief. "I did not hear you aright."

"Aye, you did." His tone was mellow for all its deepness. "I wish to know if I was dreaming last eventide, if I really did bed you."

"You have only to look beside you at the sheets to see that you did indeed bed me."

He did, and swore at the size of the bloodstain there. "Christ's toes, have I killed you?"

"Hardly," Reina replied, bringing those violet eyes back to her. "Do I look dead?"

That brought a frown. "What you look like is the

lady I wed. What I want to know is if I dreamed what you look like beneath those clothes. Do you get them off and right quickly, or I will—''

''Stay where you are!'' she ordered in her most authoritative voice when he threw back the blanket. It was an effort to keep her eyes on his face, but she managed. ''Before you get more silly with this notion of yours, recall what must be done today. If we do not ride, and soon, leaving the foot soldiers to follow at their own pace, we will not reach Clydon while 'tis still light enough for me to be easily recognized. I will have enough trouble explaining to Lord Simon, who is like to be there, why I wed the very man who made off with me. I do not also want trouble getting into my own castle just because you chose to dally this morn and we do not arrive before dark.''

He said nothing for several long moments, just stared at her. Then he finally shrugged. ''Very well, I suppose it can wait until this eventide.''

That is what *he* thinks, Reina said to herself as she escaped the tent with relief. She had every intention of doing as she had originally planned and sleeping in her own chamber until the second wedding. Until Sir Henry came and accepted Ranulf's fealty to Shefford, *she* did not consider herself truly wed, bedding or not.

As it happened, Reina changed her mind about what she would tell Simon Fitz Osbern and her other vassals. She told Ranulf her reasons as she rode before him on his huge destrier, denied her own horse because he did not trust her yet. He wanted her within reach in case she tried turning her people against him. And since he would be returning to Clydon with only his men who were mounted, she did not try to convince him his fears were groundless. He would have to see for himself that she was now committed to their marriage and had no plans for doing away with him.

But as for her vassals, she made Ranulf see that it would be easier to convince them that marriage to him was what she wanted if they thought it had not been done yet. To say she had willingly married him so quickly would be to cast doubt on her willingness with the deed done and too late to rectify. She wanted her vassals to accept him without reservation, and they were more apt to do that if she informed them Ranulf was the man she *wanted* to marry, then proceeded to do so.

He agreed, if grudgingly, but of course to his way of thinking, he had the copies of the marriage contract to produce if she had tried anything underhanded. He had to tell his men, all of whom knew she had spent the night in his tent, but they none of them objected to pretending the wedding had not yet taken place.

Reina hoped she had every probability covered, but she could not be sure. It was not easy to think clearly with those thick, hard arms on either side of her, and then, too, she was still shaken and confused from the morning's incident.

She could not reason why it would now matter to her husband what she looked like naked. It was not as if he still had the option to repudiate her if he found her body unacceptable. That chance was lost when he took her maidenhead. So why embarrass her by making her disrobe? Did he like what he had seen? Was he appalled? Did he just want verification, or did he feel annoyed that he simply could not remember?

That he was not sure if he had dreamed his taking of her or not was annoying to *her,* as well as insulting. It might not have been pleasant to her, but she would like to feel she had shared the experience. Obviously she had not. If she had known Ranulf was so sotted with drink he knew not what he was doing, mayhap she could have put him off—or mayhap not. Yet 'twas done, too late to speculate over. All she could do was brood about it, and make sure he was not drunk the next time.

Chapter Seventeen

Ranulf remained silent throughout the numerous effusive welcomes his wife was receiving, all cut short as soon as it was noticed who held her. He did not like leaving so many dumbstruck people behind him as they advanced through one gatehouse, then the other, cutting off his retreat, but it could not be helped. He did not actually grow uneasy until they had reached the inner court, where more than a hundred men-at-arms waited, and at least fifteen knights, some merely wearing swords, some fully armored, some still hurrying down the stairs of the keep, all obviously only just warned the lady had returned.

"Be easy, my lord," Reina said quietly to him when he halted his destrier to face this small army. " 'Tis merely two of my vassals with their knights and men. I told you I had sent for Lord Simon, telling him about the attack. He no doubt picked up Sir John on his way here."

"John, your hoped-for betrothed?"

"Nay, my vassal, John Radford. He is a man set in his ways, inflexible even, so his first impression of you is the one he will adhere to. Three knights are his, and twenty of the soldiers. The rest are Simon's men, though I see Sir Meyer has returned. He is the household knight I sent to assist my bailiff. He and Sir Arnulph have been with us nigh on four years now. Both have given excellent service, but as they are retainers, 'twill be your decision if their terms are to be renewed or not.''

"You want no say in that?''

"It would be nice did you ask my opinion on anything you are not sure of,'' she replied, "but nay, the final decision is henceforth yours.''

"And is that your Lord Simon stomping toward us with his hand on his sword?''

Reina flinched at his suddenly aggressive tone. "Aye, but do you let me handle this. 'Twould help if you set me down and took your hands off me so they do not think I am still your prisoner.''

"Is that an order, lady?''

"I would not presume to order you, my lord.''

"Oho,'' he grunted. "Like you did not do this morn in my tent?''

She blushed at that reminder, just in time for Simon to see, which did not help at all. But Ranulf did dismount and lift her down in front of him. And he did keep his hands off her, though 'twould be no hard thing to change that with as close as he stood behind her.

"Lady Reina, you are not hurt?'' Simon asked immediately he reached her.

"Not in the least,'' she replied with a smile. "If you must know, Simon, 'twas a high adventure I quite enjoyed.''

Ranulf at that point met the man's blue eyes, which were not unfriendly yet, though not easy either. He was a man of middle years, robust of health and frame, but only of medium height, which meant he had to look up to Ranulf, far up, a fact no man of rank liked.

Since he was studying Ranulf, Reina quickly intro-

duced them. "Let me make known to you Sir Ranulf
Fitz Hugh. Sir Ranulf, my liege man, Lord Simon
Fitz Osbern."

"But is he not the man who—"

She cut him off swiftly with the assurance, "That
was all a mistake, Simon. He did not take me for
himself but for a Lord Rothwell, who had lied to him,
claiming I was his betrothed and had refused to wed
him. Naturally, as soon as I informed Sir Ranulf that
I had never even heard of this Rothwell, he was honor-
bound to bring me home. 'Twas no fault of his that
he was misled by a craven lord who thought to have
me at any cost. Rothwell is no different than de
Rochefort, and I am glad you answered my summons
so quickly, for we need to discuss what to do about
my presumptuous neighbor, though I am inclined to
let the matter be with my wedding pending—which
we also need to discuss." When his eyes returned
suspiciously to Ranulf, she added, "When did you
arrive?"

"This morn, to be given that letter that was left
behind," Simon replied surlily.

"Oh, that," she said with a forced grin. "Come
now, Simon, admit 'twas cleverly done and it worked,
but not a word of it was true. Look at him. Does he
look like a man who would kill a defenseless woman
just to avoid a little skirmish? I would have been perfectly safe had you followed, though 'tis well you did
not, for de Rochefort is likely watching Clydon for
another opportunity, and 'tis not likely he knew I was
absent, leaving after matins as we did. I cannot tell
you how much I had worried over that, and how it
eased my mind, hoping you were here to defend
against another attack."

He took her soothing and pacifying words as they were intended, relieving his guilt that he had done naught to get her back, and praising him for doing naught to get her back.

"Come, John, Meyer." She beckoned the other two knights forward. "I would have you meet the man who has given up a fortune just on a lady's word. This is Ranulf Fitz Hugh." And to Simon: "He did not have to believe me, you know. 'Twas only my word against everything Lord Rothwell had told him." She had to grin at that point, knowing without looking at him that Ranulf would not like what he was hearing, that doubt was rearing up in his mind as he wondered if she was the one who had lied. Mischievously, she waited a long moment before adding, "I am sure confirmation at this point would not be amiss. Do one of you gentlemen relieve Sir Ranulf's mind. Am I, or was I ever, betrothed to a Lord Rothwell?"

There were three ready "Nays" to that, but it was John Radford, even older than Simon, who added gruffly, "She is to wed John de Lascelles, if the boy can ever find his way back to Clydon, which is become doubtful."

"Do not be cruel," Reina admonished gently. "Lord John has had his troubles, which have kept him from coming sooner. But as to wedding him, I have had a change of heart. Do you all come inside and we will discuss it over supper, but I really must let my ladies know I have returned safely, and see that my servants have not grown lax in my absence. Simon, do you assume my honor and introduce your men to my guests and make them welcome for me." At last she turned to Ranulf. "I will join you in the

hall anon,'' and then with a grin: ''You may be sure
my 'soon' is sooner than yours, my lord.''

She knew he hated to let her out of his sight, but
there was naught he could do as she rushed up the
stairs and into the keep. He was left standing amidst
her men, and with the lady gone, the other knights
converged on him. But he need not have worried. Her
having informed Lord Simon that he and his men were
guests and welcome was all that was necessary to
assure there would be no antagonistic questioning.
Simon did no more than she had bidden him, introducing the two groups of knights, then slowly leading
the way into the keep, talking about anything and
everything *except* the lady's abduction.

Chapter Eighteen

"*T*heo! What means this?"

"Reina, thank God!"

Entering her chamber and finding the boy trussed up in the corner was not at all what she had expected. "Do you tell me you have been like this since I left?" she asked incredulously.

"Nay, Wenda found me yestermorn and untied me. We took the letter left here to Sir William, still bedfast but no longer delirious. But when he read the letter aloud, I—I was so afraid for you I meant to go after you. Sir William refused, but Aubert, that scurrilous cur, caught me trying to go anyway last eventide and ordered this. I will kill him when I get my hands on him," Theo vowed.

"Nay, you certainly will not," Reina said sternly, but failed to keep a grin from appearing as she began to untie him. "You silly boy, what did you think you could do? Do I look as if I suffered from my little adventure? I was in no real danger, which you should have realized. I am too valuable to kill until *after* I am wed."

"How could I know that when 'twas *him* who took you?" he demanded.

"Well, as to that, he is not so terrible after all. He brought me back, did he not?"

"Aye, but wed to him," Theo groaned.

"How did you know that?"

The boy's eyes turned into perfect circles. "I was but jesting!"

"But I am not."

"Reina!" he cried. "How could you? You know how I felt about him!"

"Are you jealous, my dear?"

"Well—no, I guess not," he admitted thoughtfully. "If I cannot have him, you might as well. But *him*, Reina? Were you given no choice?"

"Not much, but if anyone had to be browbeaten into marriage, 'twas he," she said matter-of-factly. "I was not taken for him, you see, but for an old lord who hired him. He was not easy to convince he should have me instead."

"You mean you *wanted* him?"

" 'Twas either him or the old lord." This needed no further explanation. "Now help me change and quickly. I cannot leave him alone for long with my vassals."

"What did *they* say about this sudden marriage?"

"They do not know, nor are they to know, so you do not tell anyone what I have told you, not even Wenda. There would have to be a second wedding for their benefit anyway, so I mean to let them think the second is the first. I will tell them Ranulf has agreed to wed me and 'tis he I want. That way, they will not harbor doubts about why I wed him, thinking I was somehow forced to it even though I would say not. That could only lead to distrust of him, which I do not want."

"But if you would like to get rid of him, Reina, now is the time, ere you tell Lord Simon you want the giant."

"But I do want him, Theo. I have thought it

through and he is actually the better man for Clydon. John and Richard could neither of them devote themselves exclusively to Clydon, but Ranulf Fitz Hugh will. He has no land of his own, no family he will claim, no other obligations to take, him away from protecting us. And he is not poor. He will see to all that needs doing, that I have been unable to do.''

''So Clydon will love him, but what about you?''

Reina looked away. ''Once he set his mind to do it, he made sure it could not be undone. Whether I regret my decision remains to be seen.''

''How was it?'' Theo grinned now.

She knew what he referred to, and gave him a glare for daring to ask. ''None of your business.''

''Come on, Reina,'' he wheedled, his grin widening. ''Tell me what I missed.''

''If you must know, 'twas rough and quick.''

''Oh, now I *am* jealous.'' He sighed.

''Lackwit,'' she snorted derisively. ''It takes me longer to piss, so you cannot tell me you like it *that* quick. Now stop teasing me or you will find your ears boxed.''

Reina had wanted to wear her best for this important conference with Simon and John, but Theo pointed out she would need her best for the wedding, so she settled on her second best, a crimson velvet bliaut with loose bell-shaped sleeves that were shorter in the front to reveal the closely fitted long sleeves of her undertunic, a bright yellow chemise, revealed also beneath the deep V of the bliaut's neckline and at the sides where the gown was left open up to her thighs. Her girdle was golden links that hooked just below her waist to hang down to her knees.

And for this occasion, Theo talked her into wearing her hair plaited over her shoulders, the braids wrapped tightly with yellow ribbon, the short white headdress covering little. Reina felt the braids made her look younger, which she did not want just now, but Theo disagreed, swearing she had never looked lovelier. Vanity won out, something she did not succumb to often. Theo made sure she realized it, claiming that since her vassals knew her well and would not be affected one way or the other by how she looked, she was in truth dressing only for her new husband, which was natural and as it should be.

Whether Reina agreed with that or not, she could not deny she seemed somehow prettier than usual. Her costly glass mirror, which gave a much clearer image than polished steel, said so; Theo said so; and who was she to argue with the adage that a husband well pleased with his wife's appearance was a man easier to deal with. It was worth finding out if it was true, for Ranulf Fitz Hugh was no doubt *displeased* that it was taking her so long to return to him.

She found him deep in a discussion of crop rotation with Simon and John, a subject he seemed to find fascinating. So much for his displeasure at her long absence. He obviously was no longer worried about letting her out of his sight, and she was of a mind not to make her presence known at all, to retreat back the way she had come. There were other things that needed doing, and she was a fool to attach so much importance to one man's anxieties, be they natural or not.

But before she could slip away, John noticed her and greeted her, and she put on a smile as the other two men then turned to her. That she could see no reaction to her appearance at all from her husband deflated her even more, though she was too adept at concealing her feelings to show it.

"Do not let me interrupt your conversation, gentlemen. I only stopped to let you know I have not forgotten you. There are a few more things I should see to ere I join you."

Ranulf opened his mouth to protest her leaving again, but Simon beat him to it. "My lady, please. You know I am a patient man most times, but not when my curiosity has been aroused. Do you tell us what has happened to change your mind about young de Lascelles."

She looked at Ranulf with wide-eyed innocence. "You did not tell them? Fie on you, sir. Did you think they would doubt you?" After getting in those licks that he could not possibly answer, she felt vindicated in her disappointment that he had not even noticed her improved appearance and turned back to address her vassals with an explanation. "My acquaintance with Sir Ranulf may be of short duration, but sufficient to conclude that he is the man best suited to Clydon and myself."

"He wants to wed you?" John Radford asked without much surprise.

"He has agreed to wed me," Reina clarified. "Actually, it took some convincing to get him to see the benefits to himself. He was reluctant because he comes landless, though he has the means to buy a fine estate does it please him to do so. That he is sworn to no other lord is what makes him ideally suited to Clydon."

"So this was your idea?"

Her expression gave truth to the lie. "Aye, mine.

After considering all aspects, and finding naught that you might object to, I went ahead and offered Sir Ranulf contract, which he approved. *Is* there any reason you might be reluctant to accept him as your liege lord when you know him to be the man I have chosen?''

Put that way, and in that particular tone, if there were any objections, they would not be voiced now. She had quick assurances from both men that Sir Ranulf was acceptable to them.

''Think you my other vassals will feel the same?'' she put to Simon.

''I do not see why not. They are as aware as we of the urgency in getting you wed quickly—to a man your father would have approved of.''

''Good, because I have already sent messengers off to summon them and Sir Henry. The wedding will take place as soon as all are gathered. And yes, Simon, my father would have found much to admire and respect in Sir Ranulf. You knew him well, and know he valued honesty, honor, strength, and ability, above all things. Sir Ranulf's strength and ability cannot be in doubt, and I have had firsthand experience of his honesty and honor. My father would have been well pleased.''

That more than anything settled their minds to the matter, and the rest of the evening went by smoothly, especially since she invited Sir Walter to the lord's table again, which seemed to put Ranulf at ease and made for lively conversation. The man really was never at a loss for words.

But there was a moment after supper when Simon managed to corner her with his one remaining concern. "Are you certain, my lady? You have not let that pretty face of his sway you in your judgment?"

She had to laugh at this. "Come now, Simon, you know me better than that. Would I let a man's looks come before what was best for Clydon? I do not delude myself that 'tis me Sir Ranulf covets. He succumbed to the same inducements John or Richard would have succumbed to had I put the offer to them instead. Love and infatuation have no place in forming alliances, and neither influenced me in choosing Ranulf over anyone else. He is strong, able—"

"Strong? The man is a giant, my lady, if you have not noticed."

She chuckled at his expression of awe. "Aye, he is that. You should have seen how quickly he sent de Rochefort's men fleeing for their lives, killing half of them ere they could escape. He will do you well do you need him, Simon. You need have no unease on that score. But more important, he will be available do you need him, not off seeing to other estates that have naught to do with Clydon."

Simon was well satisfied after that, but then Reina had her last difficulty of the day to face, the sleeping arrangements. Left alone with Ranulf at last, she could no longer avoid it. She had to put him in the lord's chamber, since Simon always had the west tower chamber when he was at Clydon, and he had already gone off to retire there. The lord's chamber was now appropriate for Ranulf. She just would not be sharing it with him yet.

Of course, that would doubtless relieve him, rather than annoy him. That she suspected it might annoy him was only because of what he had said that morn about wanting her to disrobe for him—that it could

wait until tonight. In all likelihood, he would have
forgotten that by now. But just in case he had not,
she had prepared what she would say. Whether he
would accept it or not was what had her worried.

She forestalled him when he was about to speak,
now that they were alone before the hearth. "Do you
come with me, my lord."

A servant waited at the bottom of the stairwell to
light the way. Lanzo had earlier been directed where
to place Ranulf's armor, which had been removed just
after he arrived, save his sword. The lad was waiting
in the antechamber, half asleep on a pallet there,
though he perked up as they entered.

"Wait until you see this place, Ranulf!" Lanzo said
enthusiastically. " 'Tis like a treasure room."

Reina smiled as she led the way into the larger
room. Both chambers were well prepared and brightly
lit with numerous candlestands.

"These are some of the treasures my father won in
Cyprus," she explained, indicating the finely woven
Turkish rug that covered a goodly portion of the floor,
and two huge tapestries of foreign design. "Had you
heard that the king stopped there to successfully conquer the island?"

"Nay, what happens far from England has never
concerned me overmuch," Ranulf replied absently.

This time she smiled to herself, for he was frankly
overwhelmed by the amenities the chamber supplied.
The four-poster bed was large and curtained in rich
blue velvet with the de Champeney coat of arms hung
above it. In the two thick outer walls there was a
personal privy, flushed by a cistern on the roof to
keep down the smell; two deep window embrasures
with seats covered in ermine pelts; and an aumbry,

which was a cupboard recessed in the wall to store valuables, this one large enough that her parents had used it as a wardrobe for their expensive formal clothes.

There were numerous clothes chests for everyday wear, as well as a large one with a lock for valuables, this one containing only the precious gold plates, exotic oils, and jewel-encrusted chalices from the Holy Land. A like chest was in her own chamber with her family's important documents, silver plate, rich cloth she had got from the merchants of Birkenham, her costly spices, and what few jewels and money remained.

The hooded fireplace was cold, since the tapestries and rugs kept down the drafts in this room. There was a rare chair placed before it, like the two at the lord's table below, a large fur rug, several stools, and a small table, at the moment set with a jug of wine. The large tub had been pulled out from where it was kept screened in the corner and was filled with water. Steam could still be seen rising from it. Thick drying cloths sat on a stool next to it with a fresh cake of imported, sweet-scented soap, also gotten from her Birkenham merchants.

"Do you—do you wish my assistance with your bath?" Fortunately, she sounded nervous enough about it that he shook his head, giving her the opening she needed to leave. "Then I bid you good night, my lord."

She was gone before he realized that was her intention. She thought she would escape that easily, but she was wrong. He stopped her just before her own door, his deep rumble no doubt waking those women already asleep in the women's quarters between them.

"What means this, lady?"

She waited until he had reached her at the end of the passageway before replying. "Surely no explanation is needed. You sleep there, I sleep here—until we are wed."

"We *are* wed," he reminded her with a frown.

"But no one here knows that, my lord, and you did agree to that. Would you cause a stir that would besmirch my honor when in only a few days we will be wed again?"

"What happens to your honor when there is no blood on the wedding sheets for all to see?" he threw back at her.

But Reina was prepared for that question, and withdrew a small vial from her sleeve, filled with red liquid. "This will see to that matter right well. Now again, good night."

If she could have seen his expression when she closed the door in his face, she would have laughed. But she was too afeard at the moment that he would bang on the door to still insist on his marital rights. He did not, however, and Reina congratulated herself on the victory of this small reprieve, refusing to think of what would happen in just a few more days when she could no longer avoid the rough marriage bed she had made for herself.

Chapter Nineteen

"Come, Ranulf, if you feel like pacing so much, let us get out of here and walk the battlements," Walter suggested.

"I cannot leave now."

"Then at least sit down and get your eyes off that door. It will not open the sooner for your watching of it, and someone is like to notice your tension do you not sit down."

Ranulf sighed and joined Walter at the table, though he could not relax. The Great Hall was more crowded than ever now that Sir Henry had arrived late this afternoon with a retinue of twenty knights and as many squires. The number of ladies had also more than doubled, Simon's and John's wives and daughters sent for, the other vassals' and castellans' women arriving with their men, six ladies coming with Sir Henry, including the earl's wife and two married daughters. The air was as festive as if the wedding celebration had already begun, though the wedding was planned for the morrow.

The lower tables had been cleared away right after supper, and most of the crowd was dancing to the rousing tunes of a group of minstrels set up in the gallery. A few older men were playing chess or tables, despite the noise. There were dice games going on at the other end of the hall amidst the squires. And servants weaved in and out of the crowd, keeping ale and wine cups replenished.

Ranulf was finally not under such close scrutiny as he had been throughout the meal, though there were still ladies who could not keep their eyes from him. Walter was right. He was showing himself to be as nervous as any groom, making a first-class fool of himself, and all because Reina had closeted herself in one of the wall chambers off the hall with Sir Henry.

"You know," Walter said, breaking into his thoughts, "I could have sworn you were the man who had to have his arm twisted to accept this glorious prize, yet here you are making it a matter of life and death if you do not get it."

"How would you like a little arms practice?"

Walter chuckled. "Feel like running me through, do you? Instead, tell me what turned you about in favor of Clydon."

"You know very well 'twas taking a lady to wife that I objected to. Never Clydon."

"Aye, I know it. And she still comes with the prize. So what changed your mind about her?"

"Naught has changed my mind. She is still not to be trusted farther than I can spit, but as you said, she comes with the prize."

"She has kept to her end of the bargain so far."

"Walter, you are being a pest!"

Walter blithely ignored the warning. "Well, has she not? She has presented you so favorably that every one of her men is now eager to swear fealty to you. Not only that, they *like* you." That got a dark look that Walter could not resist laughing over. "And even now she is working toward overcoming the last possible obstacle."

"Is she?"

"Is *that* what has you worried? How can you think she would undo everything she has done at the last moment? 'Tis not reasonable to think so."

"But women think differently than men do, and now is the perfect time to drop the sword, when 'tis no longer expected. Know you where she sleeps? Not with me. She does not consider herself well and truly wed yet."

Walter's mouth dropped open, and then he burst into guffaws of laughter. "Incredible. I should have realized your restlessness had more meaning to it. God's wounds, Ranulf, if you need a woman, why have you not taken one? 'Tis not as if there are not dozens here who would gladly have your notice."

Ranulf did not answer, refusing to mention that he was so irritated with his wife's attitude that he *had* looked the wenches over, and every time he thought to approach one or even indicate more subtly his wishes that she come to him later in his chamber, he found that infernal catamite Theodric watching him, almost as if the boy could read his mind. 'Twas frustrating beyond belief, but he was not about to risk displeasing his wife before she became his wife in the eyes of her people. He had little doubt her "maid" was deliberating thwarting him. And the more he was denied a woman, the more he wanted one.

But *she* would denounce him for a lecher, that he could not abstain for a mere few days. He was not going to give her that pleasure. Ladies loved to moralize, even those who were hypocrites and played as much as their husbands. Cursed lot of them.

"You do not desire a long life, do you, Walter?"

"All right, all right, I will plague you no more.

But at least I took your mind off what is happening in that room. I do have my uses, you know."

"But he has no property, Lady Reina, not even a farm. How could your father have picked him over all the landed lords available to choose from?"

Reina had not worried about this meeting. Henry was a smallish man, no taller than she, clerkish in stature, yet in Lord Guy's absence, he held the power of Shefford in his hands. But he was not a man who gloried in that power, delighting in the fear it could invoke. He was sensible, intelligent, and a reasonable explanation was all that was necessary to make him see her point of view.

"A man with no other duties or concerns of importance will make Clydon his main concern," she told him. "My father was not as interested in enlarging Clydon as in protecting it, and keeping it as intact as when the earl gave it him. Sir Ranulf will have no other overlord to conflict with his homage to the earl, as would most any other lord. How can you object to that, when 'tis in the earl's best interests to have a man sworn only to him, just as my father was?"

"I had not considered that, but you are right, of course."

Reina grinned at him. "Besides, Sir Henry, he is rich. He has been a mercenary for long, and you know how much they have been in demand recently, with so many nobles gone off to Crusade." She handed over the copy of the marriage contract that he would take to Shefford Castle, waiting until his eyes widened when he came to the part indicating Ranulf's portion before adding, "He could have bought land long ago, but has been too busy earning more money to get around to it. He still can, if we feel there is a need. Think you it is still important?''

"Nay, not at all. You should have told me sooner that he comes to you so prosperous."

She shrugged. " 'Tis his capabilities that matter to us.''

"True, true," he agreed absently while glancing over the rest of the contract. And then: "He gives back *everything?* How did your father manage to get him to agree to that? Most men fight like mad to give nothing, yet he gives back everything of yours, and gives everything he possesses as well!"

"You know my father was more generous than that," she replied. "Those were Ranulf's terms, because he has family he does not wish to acknowledge or see benefit by his marriage to me. It was to our benefit to find no fault with this idiosyncrasy of his."

"Certainly not," Sir Henry agreed. "I have never seen a more advantageous contract for a bride. Lord Guy will be most pleased."

The bottom of Ranulf's stomach dropped out, or so it felt, when he saw the smug little smile Reina wore as she emerged from the wall chamber with Sir Henry.

"Shefford will accept your fealty and gladly, my lord," she told him, the smug smile turning into a wide one.

He did not believe her. He could not. She would not be happy that she was stuck with him. How could she be? The denouement would come, sometime between now and the ceremony on the morrow, or mayhap during the ceremony, but it would come.

Ranulf went to bed that night so morose he was

certain 'twas the last time he would sleep in the lord's
chamber. Clydon his? It had been a nice fantasy for
a short while.

First thing in the morn, he had Lanzo sharpen his
sword. If he had to fight his way out after the denouement, so be it. He also had the lad warn the
others to be prepared. Walter was going to laugh his
head off, but better that than have it hacked off. He
was *not* suffering "before-wedding" nervousness.
After all, today was no more than a formality. He
was already wed—though his wife would like that
changed.

'Twas cruel beyond words what she had done. The
honest approach would have been to disclaim him as
soon as they were met by her men in force. But nay,
she had to wait until Shefford's man came with even
more men, to let Ranulf be deluded into thinking Clydon really could be his, that she truly wanted him for
her lord. The only honest indication of her feelings
had been when she refused to share his bed. That
should have given him warning instead of merely irritating the hell out of him.

The arrival of his wedding finery was noted with
little enthusiasm on his part, though Lanzo fairly
swooned in awe. The royal purple mantle of velvet,
trimmed in white ermine, was finer than anything he
had ever owned, but then he had never been one to
waste money on rich clothing when he had no one to
impress and better needs for that money. The long-
sleeved tunic was shot through with so much silver
thread, from a distance it appeared a glittering silver
cloth rather than the fine white sendal silk it was.
Even the chausses were of the best quality, and a belt
had been included with a silver buckle to match the

brooch for his mantle, both decorated with small purple gems and looking newly made.

That the clothes were made especially for him was indicated by their perfect fit. That Ranulf did not care was indicative of his mood, still sunk in gloom.

He heard little of the praise from his friends for his new finery, did not even recognize his wife when she entered the hall, and was barely aware of being ushered out of the keep for the short ride to the village, where the ceremony was to take place before the village church. With prodding from the priest, he managed to repeat the terms of the marriage contract, what he was to contribute to the marriage, and give his wife a ring in token of the dower, as well as a gift of gold coins. The ring and the moncy represented a pledge, in Old English, a *wed*, whence a wedding. The vows were then exchanged for all to hear, and before Ranulf knew it, they were moving inside the church for the nuptial mass.

Yet even during the long mass, it did not dawn on him that it was actually accomplished. He had wed his lady wife again. He had warned his men to be prepared for anything, but he was so in a daze himself, he could have been struck down from any side and not seen the blow coming. Not until the mass was over and Sir Henry approached him right there in the church to hear him swear homage to Shefford, did Ranulf begin to suspect what an idiot he had been. That done, the Clydon vassals were quick to do likewise, and swore fealty to him for their honors then and there.

No longer dazed but still thoroughly bemused, Ranulf looked at his wife, who held to his arm as they left the church together. "You married me?"

She trilled a soft laugh before she leaned closer to whisper up at him, "I am glad you were at our first wedding, my lord, for you surely have not been much present at this one."

It was a red-faced groom who was greeted by the cheering crowd outside the church.

Chapter Twenty

If Ranulf thought he had been served a feast yesterday in honor of Sir Henry's arrival, his wedding feast was worthy of a king. A total of six courses was served, double the normal number, each course consisting of numerous dishes each of meat, fowl, fish, eggs, vegetables, desserts, and ended with a subtlety, a sugar, paste, and jelly concoction shaped to depict something, in this case scenes of courtly love.

Complete ceremony was observed, with the pantler arriving first with the bread and butter, followed by the butler and his assistants with the wine and ale. Squires lined up behind tables to serve their respective knights, and to cut and replace the trenchers after each course.

With such variety, everyone's appetite was well satisfied. Roasted were venison, boar, lamb, veal, partridges, and peacocks. There were partridges also in a mustard and ginger sauce, or stuffed with eggs and herbs, and a number of stewed meats for those with not so sturdy teeth. For different tastes in fowl, woodcocks, mallards, herons, plovers, larks, and redshanks were also served. For those who preferred fish, there was turbot basted with verjuice and spices, oysters served on a bed of parsley soaked in vinegar, haddock cooked with garlic butter, boiled mackerel with mint and sorrel sauce, or fresh herring, crawfish, mussels, lamprey, and fish tarts. The desserts were too many to name, from spiced fruits to pastries with every kind of sweet filling.

His wife had not lied when she said she had no lack in food stores at Clydon. With such abundance, the feast naturally lasted the remainder of the day. Entertainment was nonstop, with music, or jokes and stories provided by the guests so inclined or by the dozens of wandering performers hired for the special occasion.

When Ranulf returned from the privy, it was to find the lower tables gone and a noisy carole in progress, where the dancers joined hands and sang as they circled. His lady had joined in, and as he watched her laughing and singing with the others, he realized it was the first time all day that he was really *seeing* her, though she had been near his side ever since leaving the church.

She glowed with a special loveliness that had naught to do with her glittering attire. Her chemise was the same white silk as his tunic, shot through with silver, her bliaut a bright blue sarcenet silk edged with silver embroidery, and girded about her hips was a belt sparkling with red and blue gems. She wore no mantle or veil to detract from the richness of her clothes, and her lustrous black hair was unbound and flowing about her as she danced, crowned with a circlet of silver that slanted endearingly to one side.

Her cheeks were flushed, her lovely blue eyes gleamed with pleasure, and without warning, Ranulf's body came alive as he watched her. Annoyance quickly followed.

He resumed his seat at the high table, the seat of honor, aye, the lord's chair, *his* chair. It did not matter that this had been the chair offered him every time he had sat at this table. Today it was truly his. Yet when he thought of the agony of doubt he had taken to bed last night, he could dredge up no satisfaction. And she had been amused by his surprise in the church, teasing him about it. 'Twas more than likely that she had deliberately provoked his suspicions with that smug little smile of hers last night, just so he *would* suffer through the night. She was devious, spiteful, everything he knew a lady like her to be—yet he looked at her carefree abandon in the dance and felt lust for her. He must be mad.

She was out of breath when she returned to him, the short hairs curling damply about her face, laughing at some jest called out to her from a noble across the room. She did not glance at Ranulf once, so he was surprised from his dark thoughts when she spoke to him.

"You do not dance, my lord?"

"Nay."

"I do not much either, though 'tis expected today."

Ranulf was in no mood for frivolous conversation. "When do you . . . that is, will your ladies escort you from the hall soon?"

"Oh, but 'tis early yet."

It annoyed him that she still would not look at him, enough to ask, "Have you your little vial handy?"

"Of course," she replied absently.

That had not gotten a reaction from her either, and he was of half a mind to pull her across his lap to see if *that* would. But then her cerulean eyes did turn to him, proving she had been attentive to his questions. Only she had misunderstood his motive.

"You need not be nervous about the bedding ceremony," she told him in a soft murmur. "There is no question that you will repudiate me, nor I you, so we need not be stood naked before each other and the guests for inspection."

He grunted, even more annoyed with her. Why was it she never blushed when speaking so plainly of such matters? The control she had of her emotions was commendable, yet thoroughly irritating just now.

She interpreted his frown correctly. "You are not enjoying yourself, my lord? Is there aught I can—"

"You can get yourself to bed, lady, and right quickly. I want the last formalities of the day concluded."

Now she blushed, and her eyes dropped to her lap. She sat there silently for a long moment, but at last she gave a stiff little nod and rose to leave.

Ranulf sat back, feeling the tension flow out of him. He had not realized how important her response had become to him in those long seconds of silence. If she had tried to gainsay him—but she had not. She had taken his words as an order and obeyed, giving him a most satisfying feeling that lasted all of two minutes, when it dawned on him that the hour *was* early yet, and that his wife had been enjoying herself immensely until he had visited his dark mood on her. And, verily, he had no *reason* to be in such a grouch. Was he not lord of all he surveyed? The most fortunate man there? As powerful now as his own father? Aye, but what had he done to earn it?

"What is *that* doing up here?"

Reina saw the "that" in question lying smack in the center of her wedding bed. She had had Lady Ella doused for fleas when the cat showed up with the rest

of Ranulf's men, but she had not realized the creature
had been sharing the chamber with her master.

" 'Tis Ranulf's pet," she replied to Dame Hilary's
huffy question.

"Truly?" One of the other ladies giggled.

Reina had to smile, too. If they thought *that* was
funny, wait until they saw the ugly creature wrapped
around the giant's neck.

"But animals have never been allowed on this
floor," Dame Hilary persisted.

Reina shrugged. "Clydon has a new lord now. If
he desires his pet in his chamber, who is to gainsay
him?"

"You are, my lady."

My, what confidence they had in her. If they could
have seen how hastily she had scurried off to collect
them for the bedding, they would not be so quick to
think she could get rid of one scrawny cat. Of course,
it might be called the lord's chamber, but the sleeping
quarters were traditionally the lady's domain. She
would have a say about whom she shared those quarters with—aside from her lord, that is.

Thinking of him and how flustered he had made
her with his growled order to get herself to bed, she
told Dame Florette, "Take it to the kitchen for some
warm milk." Then, thinking how the cook would not
appreciate that, she added, "Explain to the kitchen
staff who it belongs to, so they do not chase it out to
the stables."

"Does it bite?" the young widow asked warily.

Hilary picked Lady Ella up by the scruff of her
neck and shoved her at Florette. "If it does, bite it
back."

That brought a round of laughter, and Reina's nervousness eased somewhat as she joined in. She had already experienced the first bedding, which was the worst, so she had no real reason to be nervous now—yet she was. Mayhap she should not have ordered her husband's wine watered down so much that it was nigh colored water. He might have enjoyed himself more if he were a little drunk, and not rushed her up here. Mayhap she should not have teased him today either. His behavior had been strange all day, waxing between bemusement and plain sourness, no mood to take teasing in fun, as it was meant.

What could she expect from a sober, disgruntled giant? Rough and quick again? Or rough and long? *Jesú*, she must have been mad to bring this on herself! Or mayhap there would be no bedding at all?

That thought brightened her considerably. After all, she had told him about the vial of "blood" for the wedding sheets, which Theo had earlier hidden in here. Ranulf did not have to bed her simply because everyone in Clydon expected him to. And he had only said he wanted the formalities over with, not that he meant to . . .

She had worked herself into full nervousness again, but as that was the expected state for her to be in, it did not draw comment other than the normal gentle teasing and ribaldry suited to the occasion.

She remained silent while her clothes were carefully removed and put away in the aumbry, but seeing the white, silver-threaded chemise in Hilary's hands reminded her that her husband had not even mentioned his new clothes. Her ladies had worked long hours at her behest to finish his mantle and chausses in time. She herself had sewn his tunic to match her own clothing from an extra bolt of the precious sendal she had been saving. Though why she had bothered she did not know, and was not likely to do so again when the man showed such little appreciation.

Yet he had looked fine, so fine. Did she really need to hear his thanks when she had felt so proud on first sight of him in his splendid attire?

She sighed, then recalled where she was and blushed. But no one had heard her. The women were too busy giggling at each other's jests.

Lady Margaret produced a comb and began stroking it through Reina's long hair, but after a moment they heard the men coming, and Reina was quickly put into bed. There she was to sit waiting like the sacrificial virgin on the altar, which was just how she felt.

If anyone had thought Ranulf would be carried over the threshold on the shoulders of his merry escort, as was usually the case, Reina could have told them 'twas not likely to happen. Who could lift him? And no one tried. But if Reina had known he led the pack himself up the narrow stairwell, her fear would have increased tenfold.

The ribaldry continued, now more coarse with the men's arrival. Reina refused to listen, or watch as Walter dared to wrest Ranulf's tunic from him. She concentrated on the hunt she had planned for the morrow; on what to prepare for dinner if at least half the guests stayed on another full day, which was likely; on the visit she owed the village to tend its ills, which she had neglected these past days. She dredged up anything likely to distract her, and then the door closed, breaking her concentration, and she swallowed, with difficulty, to see she was alone with her husband.

He had closed the door, and he wasted no time in coming directly to the bed. He still wore his braies and chausses, though nothing else. Reina held her breath. Was he going to jump on her again? Nay, not this time. He yanked the covers away from her instead.

She gasped, though it was a tiny sound only she heard. He was staring at her body so intently the roof could have fallen on his head and he would not have known it. She still was not breathing, afraid to move, afraid to cover herself even with her hands, afraid of what he would do next, this unpredictable giant she had married.

"So 'twas no dream," he said.

Her eyes moved warily up to meet his, which were darkened now to indigo. He seemed surprised by whatever he had discovered, and there was some other emotion there she was not quite sure of.

"Is that good—or bad?"

Ranulf only grunted in response. She wanted compliments after all she had put him through? She had best not hold her breath waiting. But Christ's toes, he was glad it had *not* been a dream he had carried in his mind these past few days.

He remembered clearly now her standing in the center of his bed in her short linen shift, looking like a little Valkyrie about to do battle with him. He had been fired with lust again, just as he had been earlier that day when he had seen her astride that horse. But her body stripped bare! Who would have thought the woman hid such a perfect form beneath her clothing? She might be small of stature, but no limb was too long or short, every part of her shaped just right.

He wanted to just stand there and look at her. He

wanted to plunge right into her. It was vexing that he could not do both at once, but at least he knew he could not. Last time he was not sure of anything, even doubting that there had been a last time. This time his lust was no less rampant, but he had control of it—he hoped he had control of it. Christ's toes, would he always find himself at a disadvantage with this lady?

One knee came down on the bed, then the other. This time he heard her gasp and he met her eyes again, seeing what he had missed before.

"You are afraid?" he asked doubtfully.

Her nod surprised him, especially when he clearly recalled her telling him the morning after with heavy sarcasm, "Do I look dead?" when he had stupidly asked if he had killed her.

He began again. "Surely you know—"

"I know."

"Then what do you fear? Think you I am different from any other man?"

She made a choking sound that produced a quick frown from him. But then he looked down at himself and conceded grudgingly, "Aye, mayhap a little different." The sound turned to strangling, and brought his brows together more sharply. "You do not have to belabor the point. And you have withstood my size once without dying, as you were so quick to tell me. So what do you fear?"

"I—I suppose 'tis the unknown, of—of not knowing why you were so impatient to have us alone here."

He stared at her incredulously. "Not knowing . . . lady, why else would I send you to bed?"

"But your impatience—"

"What do you expect when the one woman who

now belongs in my bed keeps herself from it? Abstinence I can deal with as well as any man if needs be, but *forced* abstinence does not suit my nature. Better you know it now. I do not like being denied something I want."

And then he frowned again, realizing how cleverly she had got him to admit to wanting her, getting her compliment after all, when all he really felt was momentary lust. It was only lust, was it not? Certainly. Any woman would do to satisfy this craving, even though *she* had caused it. Then why had he forced her to leave the festivities below, when he could have slipped away for a few moments with any likely wench and not have been missed in such a crowd?

He was startled from his thoughts by her fingertips on his brow. "Why do you do that?" she asked.

"What?"

"Frown so often, for no apparent reason. Do you know I have never seen you smile?"

"You want smiles, lady, you should have married Walter," he replied sourly.

"Aye, he does have a certain merry charm, that one—but I married you."

"So you did, but why did you? And I want the truth this time, lady, for 'twas not a matter of me or Rothwell being your only choices. You had ample opportunity to put me aside since you returned here."

"But you heard what I told my vassals. That *was* the truth, Ranulf. I felt you were the better choice for Clydon."

"And yourself?"

"Clydon comes first."

It had taken her a moment to answer, and the answer was most unsatisfactory. But he supposed he had better not hold his breath either, waiting for compliments from her. She had never in any way given him reason to think she wanted him for herself. She was the first woman he had ever met who did not look at him with at least *some* interest, sexual or not. And he had married her, a woman who showed fear when she should not, boldness when she should be afeard, a woman who would rather avoid him, especially his bed, when other women fought to get into it. Well, she was in it now, and whether she liked it or not, he would have her.

"Are you still afraid?" he asked tersely.

"Nay."

"Good, because you have put me off long enough with this silliness."

"I do not think 'twas—"

"Christ's toes, do not argue *now*, lady!"

She made a noise that sounded suspiciously like a giggle, but he did not care anymore. He had held his lust in check this long because, in truth, he did not *want* her to be afraid of him, at least not in bed. But as he talked her into relaxing, that fluff of hair between her legs had drawn his eyes repeatedly. Black gloss against pale white skin, 'twas a magnet for his eyes—and his touch, which he gave into now.

She sucked in her breath sharply as his finger slipped inside her. But that was not why Ranulf progressed no further. She was dry, without a drop of moisture to encourage him, something else he had never encountered before.

Even knowing what was to happen, she had not been ready for him, nor was she now, a frustrating development considering his own need had not diminished in the least. And what did he know about

arousing a woman, especially a lady? Most times *he*
was the one not ready, not the other way around. But
he should have expected this from a woman who was
so completely indifferent to him.

And then a new thought occurred to him, and he
glanced at her sharply, demanding, "Were you this
unprepared for me last time?"

If she was, her pain would have been so much the
worse for it, which would account for her reluctance
now, and her earlier fear. Yet his answer was a blush
that spread even across her lovely breasts, and this
was a lady who did not blush at plain speaking.

Was he wrong? Was the little general not as immune to him as she seemed to be? Even as he wondered that, his finger became drenched with warm
moisture, though he had not moved it further, and
her blush darkened even more.

His laughter was spontaneous, he was so relieved
and, in truth, delighted. It surprised his wife and
made her look at him as if he were mad, but he did
not care.

"Is—is aught wrong, my lord?"

"Nay, 'tis just right."

He sat back to tackle his laces, though his eyes
remained on her. Although he did not remember it,
once again his impatient fingers broke the ties to shed
the rest of his clothing. And he was impatient again.
She wanted him. So he was not just for Clydon. Hah!
The little witch would not give an inch, would make
him think anything but the truth, but some things were
impossible to hide, and she knew that now.

"If you intend—" she began nervously, then started
over. "Will you not close the curtains first?"

"Later," Ranulf said.

He disallowed further questions by covering her mouth with his as he moved over her into position. And she tasted so good . . . how could he have forgotten that? . . . that he delayed entering her—until her tiny hands hesitantly circled his neck. His undoing, that small response from her. He plunged into her warmth with a groan. She felt so good! . . . how could he have forgotten that, too? . . . so tight, like a soft hand squeezing, pulling him deeper into her.

Ranulf had never felt anything like it before. Of course, he had never experienced a virgin ere this one. But for the first time in his brutish life, he wanted to take his time with a woman, rather than rushing toward what fleeting pleasure could be found.

What had always been no more than a bodily need, just like eating or pissing, now seemed different somehow, and he wanted to savor the feeling. But wanting and doing do not always mix, and he found, in this case, that his body was not willing to hold off, could not hold off. And he no longer cared as he became mindless in the throes of the most incredible climax of his life, vaguely hearing a roar loud enough to shake the rafters, unaware it was his own.

Chapter Twenty-one

*T*he window embrasure was shadowed still, and cool with the night air emanating through the costly glass panes. Reina sat on the fur-covered seat, arms wrapped about legs drawn up close to her chest, chin resting on one knee as she stared pensively at a sky turning slowly to mauve, now lavender. Her husband still slept, had slept peacefully all night long, commencing the moment he rolled off her last night. She had not been so fortunate.

Long hours she had lain next to him listening to his soft, even breathing. She had hoped he would snore loudly so she would have something to complain about, since she could not complain about what was really bothering her, but he did not give her that satisfaction any more than he had satisfied her earlier. She had come so close to—what? She was not sure, but it had to have been worth having if it could produce the primeval roar of pleasure when *he* got it—whatever it was.

It had been so different this time without the pain, so nice having that part of him inside her. She had felt so strange, but it was not a frightening feeling; warm and languid at first, and that fluttering in her belly had come again. Then the warmth got hotter, for some reason breathing became difficult, and something had started to build deep inside her, centering in her loins, something so very, very pleasant.

And then it was over, and she had felt such keen frustration to have those feelings ended that she had almost hit her instantly sleeping husband.

But she was not mad enough to do *that*. And the frustration had not lasted all that long. 'Twas other thoughts that had kept her awake, thoughts about that strange conversation they had had.

The whole thing had a quality of unreality to it as she recalled it. She would never have believed Ranulf would show concern for her nervous fear, but he had. And he had been so amusing, claiming he was no different from any other man, when he was not only a giant but an exceedingly handsome one. But then to say his impatience had stemmed from being denied something he wanted. Her? She could not credit it.

She knew she was not beautiful. Her mouth was too wide and full for her small face, her hair an ugly black, her breasts so small they were not worth noticing. Her skin was good, her one saving grace, and people always seemed to notice her eyes first; whether that was good or bad she did not know. She could pass for pretty on her better days, she supposed, but that would be generous. She had servants more pretty, some truly beautiful like Eadwina. And she had seen for herself the type of woman Ranulf found attractive. She did not even come close.

So why would a man as magnificent-looking as Ranulf Fitz Hugh say such a thing? Her worth was in what she could bring to her marriage, not in herself. She had always known that. And yet he had said it, and for a moment she had felt such heady pleasure in hearing it—before she discredited it.

And then their roles had somehow been reversed. She had listened to him doubting *his* own worth, giv-

ing her an inkling of what had been bothering him
these past days, that he truly did not believe she could
think he was the best man for Clydon. Why would he
even care what she thought? That had made no sense
at all.

His impatience had then returned and she discovered he really did want her. 'Twas no pretense. The
coiled tension in him had been palpable all along, but
the reason for it became clear only then, when his
hand had followed his eyes to the apex of her wom-
anhood, and her glance in that moment happened to
take in the hard bulge in his braies. For whatever
reason, last night he had felt a powerful lust for her—
probably because she *had* denied him, and he had just
warned her he did not deal well with denial.

That triumphant laughter, though, that had so
amazed her, she still did not understand, especially
coming after that embarrassing question of his about
whether she had been unprepared for him last time.
He obviously remembered naught of last time or he
would not have had to ask. And recalling that she was
so prepared for him before brought that same moist
warmth into her loins. And then his laughter, the first
she had ever heard from him, changing him, making
him seem an entirely different man, one not so churlish and gruff and unapproachable.

But it had not lasted. If he had not jumped on her
the second time, it still seemed as if he had, in such
a feverish haste had he been to have from her whatever it was he got. Remembering that reminded her
of the frustration she had felt, and her brows drew
together. Would it always be like that, quickly on and
quickly off? Was that normal, and the fault her own
that she was not fast enough with her responses?

Sounds from the bed drew her attention, and she saw with surprise that daylight had banished all shadows from the room. The lone candle she had lit to don her bedrobe and prepare the evidence on the sheets had sputtered out, but was no longer needed. She had not even thought of those sheets last night, so 'twas fortunate she did awake early, allowing time for the "evidence" to dry before her ladies arrived for the traditional collection of those sheets.

Her twice-wed husband was sitting up in the bed, a frown creasing his brow that did not exactly disappear when he finally located her in the far corner of the window embrasure. "Hiding, lady?"

"In plain sight, my lord?"

His grunt was heard clear across the room. "Why did you not wake me?"

She uncurled her legs and found them stiff, so did not stand up just yet. " 'Tis early, though you might wish to rise and dress now. There is no telling how soon our company will arrive."

"Company? Ah, yes, how could I forget." It was no question, and it was said most dryly. He looked down then at the few measly drops of blood she had smeared on the sheet next to him, and one golden brow shot upwards. "You do my manhood an injustice, lady, when in truth it wrought from you a full puddle of blood. Mayhap I should have produced the true sheet for inspection."

She could not believe it. Her grouchy husband making a joke? Or was he joking?

She stepped down into the room slowly. "You— actually kept that sheet?"

"Aye, 'tis in yonder chest, and mayhap you should

fetch it. This deception we have practiced did not sit well with me. I want your men told the truth.''

Her eyes flared for a moment, but then she relaxed. The deception had bothered her, too. And now that her second wedding was accomplished, there was really no need to continue it.

''Aye, they will accept the truth more readily now and be glad to hear it. I will tell them today.'' He appeared surprised that she had not argued, but she was not finished. ''However, the women are a different matter. In order for speculation not to arise to start gossip, they must be certain you have no doubt about my virtue, and only you can assure them of that. You may deal with the matter of the sheets however you like, but *you* must do it.''

She thought he would balk, he looked so displeased, yet he gave her a curt nod. He was not so hard to deal with after all, which put one of her worries to rest. However, she still was not finished.

''But what I told Sir Henry must stand.''

''What *did* you tell him?''

''That you were my father's choice for me. 'Twas a deception my father began with Lord Guy, and I will not have him called a liar.''

''*Would* he have approved of me, lady?''

''Aye, I believe he would.''

''So be it.''

''Good. And while we are clearing the air, so to speak, do you not think 'tis time you started calling me by name? You do remember my name?''

''So the little general is back, and with sarcasm, no less. Just what I need to wake up to.''

Reina stiffened. ''I do not like *that* name either, husband.''

"What you like is not of much concern to me right now—wife."

She reassessed her opinion about his being easy to deal with, about as easy as a wild boar, whose temperament could also at times be likened to her husband's.

"An argument is no way to start the day," Reina said coldly.

"It suits me fine," he growled back, just to disagree, she was sure.

"Does it? Just what you need to wake up to, eh?" She threw his own words back at him. "Best I leave you—"

"Where do you go?"

She stopped on the way to the door. "That hardly—"

"Where?"

So already her life was no longer hers to control. That was the one thing she had suspected she might be giving up in choosing him over Richard or John, whom she knew she could have handled with ease.

Reina sighed as she turned back to face him. "Only this robe was brought here last eventide," she said, indicating the white velvet she had wrapped around her. "I was going to my old chamber to dress, and to arrange to have my belongings moved here whilst we are away on the hunt. Unless, of course, you have changed your mind and prefer not to share these chambers?"

He glowered at the hopeful note that had entered her voice. "You will sleep here, where you belong."

Just what he had said last night, she recalled. Why was he being obstinate about it when he obviously did not really want her there?

With a nod of acquiescence no less stiff than his had been earlier, Reina continued on her way. She absolutely refused to ask his permission to withdraw. She would stay in this room the rest of her life ere she would do that. He did not stop her again, which should have improved her mood, but did not.

And her mood was certainly not ready for Theo, who was waiting in her chamber to ply her with eager questions.

"Well? How was it this time?"

"You want the gory details, or will a few words do?" she snapped at him.

"So 'twas rough and quick again?"

"Not so rough," she allowed grudgingly. "But over before I barely knew 'twas begun."

Theo sat down hard on a stool, his young face a study in disappointment. "So he has not pleasured you yet?"

"Pleasure?" she snorted, heading toward the coffer at the end of the bed. "Tell me something, Theo. Is a woman actually supposed to feel something special when coupling, or is it only a desire to give the man she favors what he wants?"

"You are asking the wrong person, Reina. *I* certainly enjoy it."

"Well, *I* certainly do not."

"But you know something is missing, or you would not be this annoyed about it." He grinned at her. "Ask Wenda. Mayhap she can describe to you what 'tis like for a woman."

"I do not want to ask Wenda," she said with a pouting turn to her lips. "Just tell me this. Is it normal for it to be done so quickly?"

"Not normal, nay. But look at it this way, Reina.

That lovely man either pays you the supreme compliment that you so arouse his lust he simply cannot hold off, or—"

"Lackwit, be serious!"

He dodged the shift she threw at him, protesting, "I am. Or, as I was saying, 'tis just his way and he does not care whether you find any pleasure in it or not. Some men are like that, unfortunately."

"And I am married to one." She sighed, sitting down on the bed with a bliaut in one hand and a chemise in the other. "What can I do?"

"You can tell him you are not satisfied with his—"

"Are you mad?" she shrieked. "I could not do that!"

Theo shrugged. "Then arouse him again when he is finished. A man is usually always slower the second time."

That caught her full interest. "You mean—right after?"

"Aye."

"But he goes to sleep."

"So you wake him."

She frowned. "He is not like to appreciate that."

"He will not mind if you do it right."

"How? And how do I arouse him?"

"Reina!" He rolled his eyes. "Did your mother tell you naught about pleasuring a husband? You touch him, caress him all over . . . oh, would that I—" He blushed, but quickly continued. "You caress him— especially where it counts."

Her eyes widened. "You mean *there?*"

"Just so."

"Oh, well, I suppose that would not be too difficult." What was she saying? How could she ever bring herself to do *that?*

"Then I will expect to see you smiling on the morrow."

She glowered at him. "This was only one small problem. You would not believe how insufferably annoying that man can be. If I ever smile again, 'twill be a miracle."

Chapter Twenty-two

*R*eina sighed as she looked about the clearing. They had stopped while the hounds sniffed through the bushes, momentarily having lost the scent of the big buck that had been spotted earlier. Her thin woolen bliaut was ideal for riding, but the weather was unseasonably warm, and trickles of sweat were annoying her temples and soaking her linen chemise. Usually she would not notice, caught up in the excitement of the hunt. Today she had too many other things on her mind.

She ignored her husband, who had stopped his horse beside hers; at least she tried to ignore him. The insufferable lout *had* shown the ladies that other sheet, and Reina had suffered looks of horror and pity that were likely to continue until someone bothered to recall that she had returned to Clydon in perfect health. But that was what she got for telling him to do as he liked. And he seemed to think it amusing.

She had actually got a smile from him when he joined her in the hall to break their fast. She should have suspected that smile, but at the time she was too flustered by feeling that funny fluttering in her belly again. Caused by that smile? *Jesú.* Better he stuck to his boarlike disposition.

"Are these not the woods where those brigands I heard mention of abide?"

Reina was forced to give him her full attention now.

"You mean those terrible outlaws who attacked your camp and caused you to leave in such a hurry that night?"

Ranulf did not take the bait. He had the nerve to give her another smile at the reminder of the ruse he had used to get her out of Clydon that fateful night. Two smiles in only a few hours. His mood had definitely been improved by that incident with the sheets. Perhaps he found it perversely amusing that the women of Clydon were temporarily frightened of him, thinking he had a monstrous weapon inside his braies instead of a normal prick. Reina was not amused.

"I do believe I do mean those same terrible outlaws," he told her in what was for him a most pleasant tone. "Think you we will see some sign of them?"

Reina decided to bridle her annoyance for now, since he did seem serious in his interest. "Mayhap you will see signs that they have been about, but you will see no sight of them. They always seem to know whenever a large group leaves Clydon or Warhurst, and they scatter east and west, leaving the woods entirely."

"Warhurst?"

"The small town on the other side of the woods. Actually, Warhurst is more plagued by them than we are. Occasionally they steal a sack of grain or a crock of butter from my villeins—"

"What of those large thefts of cattle and sheep you mentioned before?"

"They could be responsible for that, but I do not think so. They are only outlawed villeins themselves. Who could they sell the animals to? And the woods provide all the meat they could need. Nay, the thing they do best and most frequently is rob small groups of travelers on the north road, which cuts through these woods, especially merchant caravans on their way to Warhurst. As I said, Warhurst is more plagued by them than Clydon.''

''You have not tried to rout them?''

She could not help smiling in fond remembrance. ''My father used to take his men in every month or so and scour the whole area. He actually looked forward to it, enjoying the hunt, and letting off steam when he returned, cursing the brigands, for he never caught a single one. As I said, they seem to know when they are threatened. The castellan at Warhurst sends out patrols more often, but the man is an imbecile and easily outsmarted. The outlaws might be villeins, but they are clever.''

''Think you they watch both Clydon and Warhurst?''

''With the woods so near to both, 'twould not be difficult to do.''

He studied her for a moment before saying, ''You do not feel them to be a true menace, do you?''

''You mistake me, my lord. They gave my father sport, and that amused me and him. But they have been more troublesome since he left. 'Tis true they have killed no one I know of, but visitors to Clydon have been set upon, one lord robbed of nigh a hundred marks, which I felt conscience-bound to replace. They are my woods, after all.''

''And so your outlaws?'' he snorted.

''Aye, mine—now yours.'' That got a glare from him finally, and she almost laughed. ''You have to take the bad with the good, my lord.''

''There is more bad?''

"Certainly." She grinned. "Let me see—there is Tom Smith. Every few months he drinks too much and tries to set the village afire. No one knows why, not even Tom."

"And you have not hanged him?"

"Why would I hang him? He is a good smith, and pays for the damage he causes in ironwork. I hope hanging will not be your answer to everything."

"And if it is?"

She stiffened, her chin going up in a challenge. "Then we are like to have many arguments."

"Mayhap we will, but not about that. Whether I will be quick to hang anyone remains to be seen, but 'twill be my decision as lord. Is that not so, my lady?"

He had met her challenge and thrown it back at her. She stared at him for a long moment, at the implacable set features, the obvious tension in his body. What could she say? *She* had given him the power to do as he would when she married him. But she had married him to have him protect her people, not to hang them arbitrarily.

Yet she could not have been so totally wrong about him. He had to be only testing her when asking about hanging Tom Smith. How else was he to learn how she dealt with her people unless he asked questions? She should not have got upset about it.

But the upset was not quick to go away, and her tone was stilted when she answered, "Aye, most all decisions are yours as lord."

"Most all?"

"You want my duties, too? If all I am to do is apply my needle to a strip of embroidery, do you say so."

Ranulf said nothing. Watching her eyes glitter with rancor, her small body trembling with it, brought a

hot thickening to his groin. Christ's toes, not again!
But it was there, tearing at his gut, making him forget
their conversation, forget the hunt.

The dogs caught the scent just then and the party
took off after them, including his wife. Ranulf was
filled with an unreasonable rage for a moment, as if
he were the stalking animal and had just lost the scent
of his own prey. And then it dawned on him that he
had nothing to be angry about. What he had been
hesitant to accept, even last night, even this morn,
crystallized in his mind finally as truth. Reina de
Champeney was now Reina Fitz Hugh, his wife. *His.*
She truly belonged to him.

He set spurs to his own horse, but with a different
quarry in mind.

Reina had just begun to relax, thinking she had left
Ranulf behind and would not have to be bothered by
him and his infuriating manner again, at least for a
while. She was wrong. His large destrier sidled up
next to her palfrey again, but this time 'twas not to
ride next to her. Before she realized his intent, Ranulf's hand reached out and took the reins from her,
and her little mare was suddenly following him into
the brush.

No one noticed. That was her first thought. The
others in their party just rode on, not even looking
back. Her second thought made her pale, remembering her defiant attitude just moments ago. She could
only imagine that he had taken exception to it and
was going to chastise her here and now.

But why? So she had been angry and let him see
it. 'Twas not the first time. Was that worth a beating?
He might think so, and he now had the right, whereas
before he did not. But he did not now either, she

reminded herself. He had sworn he would not when they had made contract—but not that he would not blister her backside. He had in fact warned her he would.

She paled even more and leaned forward to see if she could grab the reins back, but just then her horse halted behind his. She held her breath, watching him dismount, too frightened to do the same, to even think of running now.

She found her voice only when his hands gripped her waist. "I did not mean to—"

She got no further in her bid to appease him, for she was dragged off her horse, slammed against his chest, and smothered by his mouth covering hers. Kissing her? Aye, she supposed he might call it that. She was not sure what it was, especially when his tongue stabbed at hers. She tried to push it out of her mouth with her own tongue. That made him groan and squeeze her tighter, strangely not hurting her, stranger still causing a thrill to leap in her breast.

Her legs were not steady when he set her down. Neither was her breathing. And her thoughts had scattered hither and yon. By the time she had them back and in some semblance of order, Ranulf's mantle was spread on the ground, his sword belt removed, and he was fumbling with the ties of his underclothing.

"What—"

The fierce look in his eyes cut her off. "Are you or are you not my wife?"

That look and tone should have warned her, as challenging as it was, but it did not. She was simply surprised by the question.

"Of course I am your wife. Did I not twice marry you so there would be no doubt?"

"So you did, and so being, I desire use of my wife."

Her eyes flared in disbelief. *"Now?"*

He shrugged, though there was nothing nonchalant in his look. "I am young and lusty, which is what *you* insisted on, is it not?"

"But—"

Again she could not finish the thought, much less any protest. He caught her about the waist with one arm and bore her down to his spread mantle to begin kissing her again. In the back of her mind there was the thought that she still had time to explain reasonably that the Lord and Lady of Clydon did not couple in the woods. He had to stop kissing her to undress her, and she would make him see reason then.

More fool she.

He did *not* stop kissing her. He did *not* undress her. He did no more than yank off her braies and pull down his own and then he was inside her, riding her with a swift urgency that reached its peak in less than a minute.

Reina felt nothing, and *that* more than anything else let loose her temper when he rolled to her side. "Curse and rot you, Ranulf! You may be used to tossing up the skirts of any serf girl you come across and going right at it, but I will not have it! I am your wife, not some wench you found in a field. Do you want me, you will have the decency to remove your clothes and mine first."

"If you say so."

He reached for her skirt and she gasped, scrambling away from him and to her feet. "Not *now*, you beef-witted lout! I have had enough of your brutish skills for one day."

He did not take offense. In fact, he rendered her speechless by laughing. And he was still grinning like a sated mongrel as he put his underclothes back to rights.

"Mayhap it has taken me longer to have it set in my mind that you belong to me," he told her with that maddening grin, "but you have yourself confirmed it, and I will no longer fight it. 'Tis best you get used to my ways right quickly, for I will have you, will you nill you, whenever 'tis my wont to do so."

"Anywhere?"

He glanced about at the low bushes surrounding them that were no real concealment and had the audacity to chuckle. "Aye, anywhere. It makes no difference to me."

She huffed past him, tight-lipped with fury. "It does to me, and I will be certain not to leave Clydon with you again if this is your idea of a romantic tryst!"

For that she got more laughter that had her close to screaming in frustration. She was not about to ask his help to remount her horse. Yet while she was struggling to pull herself up, his hand came to her backside for the boost she needed. She gave him no thanks, did in fact blush mightily as she whirled about.

She would be lucky if she found the hunting party ere she was missed, but she had no doubt she would find them. Hopefully her husband would not. 'Twould serve him right did he become lost in the woods and not return to Clydon until dusk—in a mood to match hers.

Chapter Twenty-three

Ranulf watched his wife trot off in the direction in which they had come, unaware he was still smiling. She was like the other ladies he had known, yet different, too, in a way that was a welcome relief. Most ladies would cry or plead, cajole or bring forth every available wile when they did not get their way. Not his lady. Her manner was too direct. She either cut softly with stinging sarcasm or let loose her temper, which he found he did not mind at all. Her temper in fact amused him, coming from such a little baggage.

Why she was wroth with him this time, he was not quite sure. Could she really have objected to a quick tumble in the woods on such a fine spring day?

Lady Anne had never objected. She had in truth been the one to instigate most of their encounters together, and in the most unlikely places. Lady Montfort had also tried to seduce him in the woods, after arranging for him to accompany her hawking. That he had not accommodated her was not owing to where they were or who she was, for he was as randy then as now and took his relief where and when he could. But he liked his wenches a bit younger than two score and ten years. Grandmothers just had not appealed to a lad of fifteen.

Ranulf shook off thoughts of the past before they threatened his good humor. And his humor was good, ever since challenging his wife this morn and coming out the winner. That had been unexpected. He had wanted her vassals told the truth about their first wedding, but if Reina had given him valid reasons why they should continue the deception, he would have conceded. After all, she knew those men well and so was better able to judge their reactions. That she still wanted Sir Henry kept in the dark was all right, too. Perhaps one day, when he came to know his new overlord, he would tell him the truth. Or mayhap not. If Reina wanted her father's memory to remain unsullied, he could not object to that.

But she had agreed with him, at least in part, proving she was not as inflexible as some ladies were wont to be just out of sheer perversity. He suffered from that himself at times, as he had this morn, being unable to resist tossing the true wedding sheet at that group of giggling women who had barged in on him just as Lanzo finished dressing him.

The women had been surprised to find him alone, and surprised more when he told them the truth. But their reaction to that sheet was truly laughable, almost as bad as his own reaction when he had first seen it. At least he had had his wife standing before him, proving he had not killed her. The ladies did not have that to ease their horror, since Reina had conveniently absented herself.

Reina? Aye, Reina. 'Twas a lovely name, and not one he was like to forget, as she had accused him of doing. But what difference what he called her? And what difference where he tumbled her? Could that really be what she had objected to? She had tried to protest, and yet she had turned soft and yielding once he kissed her. Or was it more that he had not undressed her? Not that he had had much choice. To do so would have taken time that that traitor in his braies was not willing to allow, may it fall off and rot. Never had he had so little control over the cursed thing. And 'twas becoming a habit.

Verily, 'twas not such a bad habit to fall into, Ranulf thought with a grin as he swiped up his mantle. There were worse things than to lust after one's own wife. And then his grin widened and became a chuckle when he saw the scrap of white linen on the ground. She had been so wroth with him, she had ridden off without her braies!

He picked up the forgotten underwear, made of the softest linen he had ever felt. He could not recall feeling that softness earlier when he had stripped them off her, aware then only of what lay beneath them. He rubbed the linen against his cheek, thinking how his wife did pamper her body with luxuries—but that was a mistake. Her essence came to him, and his manhood stirred at the scent. Again!

Disgruntled, Ranulf stuffed the material inside his tunic. But his annoyance did not last. He imagined the little general's expression when he returned her braies to her, and that had him chuckling to himself again.

And so he was when Walter found him, at least after Walter's close scrutiny and exclamation that he had thought the lady had done him in.

"And can a man not tarry for other reasons than to get himself done in?"

"What was I to think," Walter grumbled, "when you disappeared with her in woods unfamiliar to you? And when I just passed her, she like to smote me with her eyes."

"Aye, she was in high dudgeon when we did part."

"So you stopped to have words?"

"Why we stopped is none of your business, my friend," Ranulf replied.

Walter accepted that for about five seconds, then burst out, *"Tarry* for other reasons? God's wounds, Ranulf! Say you did not . . . you would not . . . God's wounds! In the woods? No wonder she is again wroth with you. Do you not know ladies like to be wooed gently?"

Ranulf's snort was loud. "What needs to woo a wife already won?"

Walter gave a short bark of laughter. "Methinks you have avoided ladies too long. You have forgotten what 'tis like to live among them, subject to their moods and spites. And your lady rules your household. Remember your thoughts on wooing when your clothing lacks repair, your dinner comes ill-done, and there are no warm bricks in your bed come winter."

Ranulf grinned despite these dire predictions. "All things I have always done without."

"But now you have a wife who will or will not see to your comfort. There is no reason to do without, *Lord* Ranulf."

It was Ranulf's turn to bark with laugher. "Lord Ranulf? You are determined to tease me from my good mood, but it cannot be done today. I am well pleased with my lot, so do you let me worry about my wife and her humors."

Walter shook his head, but finally shrugged, then added a grin. "Well pleased, eh? And nary a word of thanks did I get for convincing the lady to have you."

"Convincing her? 'Twas my handsome face that did it. Did she not swoon at first sight of me?"

"She fell at your feet right enough."

They continued jesting back and forth until they came upon the hunting party again. The kill had been made, the huntsmen now attending it, the group in high excitement discussing it. Walter joined right in to this, but Ranulf was subdued at the sight of his wife again, especially as she made a point of deliberately ignoring him now.

He had to wonder if there could be some truth to what Walter said. *Had* he been too rough with her? He had somehow forgotten how really small she was, at least small to him. Had he hurt her? Was she too stubborn to tell him if he did, reverting to anger instead?

What he knew of ladies he did not like, but in truth, he knew very little about them. The two who had turned him against their kind had done a good job, for he had avoided gentlewomen ever since. Now he was married to one, a woman he had no understanding of at all, and who set him to doubting his own behavior when he knew no other way to be.

She was right about what he was used to with women. Getting right to it was necessary when the moments were stolen, for a servant or villein rarely had any free time to herself. And they had always been easy to come by, costing no more than a cheap bauble or a decent meal, or nothing at all because they found a man his size a novelty and wanted to try him.

He had never had to woo a woman, not even Lady Anne, for she had been the one to start their affair. Yet she had never complained of his roughness, if rough he had been. He could not recall much of their passionate encounters except that they had been hur-

ried, too, the fear of being discovered very strong.
But he had been only ten years and five at the time,
and well and truly smitten. By the time his head had
come out of the clouds, it was too late for him to see
through the sweetness to the rotten core beneath.

Rationally, he knew 'twas unfair to compare all ladies with that bitch Anne, yet he had done exactly
that. As for his wife, she had had fair warning of how
he had been raised, as well as a sample of his manners *before* she had decided to settle on him. A man
learns by example, and his example had been first his
blacksmith stepfather, then Montfort, both men as
churlish as they come and ever quick with a blow.
Walter had tried to show him differently, and teased
him mightily about his lack of courtly ways, but
Walter's own were nearly lost during their years at
Montfort.

Ranulf was what he was, a product of his upbring-
ing. If his wife wanted different, she would have to
find it elsewhere. . . .

That thought cut deeply into his good humor. There
would be no finding aught elsewhere, not for her. The
lady had stuck herself with him and would just have
to lower her expectations accordingly. But he supposed he could not call his treatment of her gentle
thus far.

Since he had met her, he had dropped her on the
floor, bound her and rolled her up in a blanket, ordered sacks of grain dumped on her, literally rolled
her out of same blanket, and God only knew in what
manner he had taken her on their true wedding night,
for he had been too sotted to remember his part in it.
In all fairness, she deserved none of that, and what

would it cost him to be less—brutish? Aye, that was her word.

He could at least try to be as she would like. There were those comforts Walter had mentioned as a reward. And she had given him so much, more than he had ever expected to have. He would try.

Chapter Twenty-four

*R*eina's good spirits had returned somewhat by the time they crossed over Clydon's first drawbridge. Her guests had enjoyed good sport, even if she had not. They were still quite merry. They had returned early enough to refresh themselves ere they sat down to another feast that was awaiting them. And most would be leaving after that, to take advantage of the rest of the afternoon to get back to their own homes. Clydon could then return to normal, at least by the morrow, which would be a welcome relief.

As much as Reina usually enjoyed company, insisting her guests stay as long as they liked, this time she did not. She needed some time alone to acclimate herself to this drastic change in her life. She had even thought of a way to get rid of her husband for a while, if he would only agree.

But she was not to get rid of all the guests, did in fact have a new one, as she saw when she entered the hall with the hunting party. John de Lascelles rose from the bench by the hearth, where Lady Elaine had been having a conversation with him, and crossed the hall to meet Reina halfway.

Her own step had slowed. She felt raw anger at first sight of him, for at the moment she was none too pleased with her choice of husband, and John could have changed all that if he had just arrived one week sooner. One cursed week! Then she felt contrition.

He had his own troubles in taking over his brother's lands. She could not blame hers on him, no matter how much she wanted to blame them on someone. And she was forgetting that Ranulf *was* her choice, and for all the reasons that were important. It was just her misfortune that she was beginning to dislike him personally.

Aside from those feelings, Reina was glad to see her old friend, for it had been more than a year since he had visited Clydon. He had lost weight in that time he could ill afford to lose, and looked a bit pale, but otherwise the same. His green eyes still revealed a tenderhearted nature, his expression warm with delight to see her. She summoned a warm smile for him, too, and returned his brief embrace of greeting.

"Lady Elaine tells me good wishes are in order, Reina. Was this the urgency implied in your letter, a summons to witness your marriage?"

Reina accepted this excuse gladly. "Indeed. I had so wished you could have attended the wedding."

She immediately regretted the choice of those words and their double meaning, which she had *not* intended, but which was apparent when she heard her steward smother a snort. She noticed Theo leaning nonchalantly against the wall and saw him roll his eyes. Simon and Guiot turned quickly away to hide their expressions.

But what else could she have said? John might have been thrilled at the idea of having her to wife, especially since the power behind Clydon could have more easily alleviated his present difficulties. To tell him now that she had wanted him for husband, when it was too late to do aught about it, was apt only to cause unnecessary bitterness on his part.

"Why the secrecy, Reina? Why could you not be more specific in your letters?"

"What? Oh, that. Trouble with one of my neighbors, intercepting my messengers," she said evasively. "He wanted to marry me himself, you see."

"Lord Falkes, I would wager, but we can speak of that later. Do you tell me which of these noble gentlemen is that fortunate lord to win you."

He was looking behind her, at the faces he did not recognize. *Jesú,* how could she have forgotten about Ranulf, even for a moment?

She swung around to find him *right* behind her, so close her nose collided with his hard chest. Curse and rot him, had he heard her, too, and the wistfulness in those words about wishing John could have attended the wedding? But his expression, when she craned her neck to see it, was only curious, and she realized he did not know who John was. Mayhap he would not recognize his name either, having heard it just once.

Reina quickly introduced them, hoping she could as quickly separate them, but that was not to be. She did not know what exactly she had expected from Ranulf, antagonism mayhap, in seeing John as a rival. What she got was a golden brow raised in her direction, and a distinct feeling of amusement just below the surface of his falsely bland expression.

"Now where have I heard that name?" he asked her.

"You would have heard me mention it," she replied tightly, and to John: "Do you come with me and I will see you refreshed before we sit down to table. Sir Henry left this morn, so you can have his chamber."

She deliberately dragged John away before Ranulf

could say any more. He knew, the lout. But what did he find so amusing? So John was closer to her height than his. So he was not as broad of shoulder or thick of arm, was in fact quite thin of frame. At least John was kind and gentle, and *he* would not have tumbled her in the woods.

When she returned to the hall, it was to hear her husband's booming laughter. He stood with his friends, Walter, Searle, and the others, and she flushed with anger, imagining some jest at dear John's expense. She would not have it, and marched directly into their group while her irritation was high.

"I would like a private word, my lord."

"As the little general, or as my wife?"

It could have been said in teasing and likely was, but as he had never teased her ere this, she did not take it as teasing now. And even if he were only teasing, she was in no mood for it.

She glared at him, refusing to repeat her request, but he did not move to come away with her, and appeared unlikely to do so. She stared pointedly at each of his companions until the slow-wits finally took the hint and departed.

"That was unnecessary, my lady," Ranulf said, laughter in his eyes. "I keep no secrets from them."

Why *that* should make her blush, she did not know. He would not tell them of what he did with her— would he? Nay, he would not, for 'twas certainly naught to brag about.

"I am glad you have friends you can share things with. I too have friends, but I do *not* share everything with all of them. Do I make myself clear, my lord?"

"Not precisely."

She gritted her teeth at his deliberate perversity, for

he knew very well what she meant. His grin in reply told her that.

"Then by all means I will spell it out for you. Do not by word or insinuation make Lord John aware of the real reason he was summoned here by me. There is no godly reason he should know now, and every reason he should not. But more importantly, I do not *want* him to know."

"And if I ignore your wishes in this?"

Her eyes narrowed to angry slits. "You want to spite me, do you do so. That is, of course, your prerogative. But like is deserving of like, and I have my own ways of getting even."

She did not care at the moment what reaction he would have to that. But instead of getting angry that she would dare to threaten him, he laughed.

"I have no doubt you could think of something most unpleasant to visit on me, Reina. But you need not worry about your little friend. I will never show you up to be the sweet liar you are as long as your half-truths and deceptions cause no hurt."

She was too shocked at finally hearing her name from his lips to immediately grasp the true meaning of the rest of his words. Then it came to her. He had just offered her husbandly support, not just now, but whenever it was needful. 'Twas something she had not expected from him. Did he really mean it?

Whether he did or not, to have said it, and after what she had just said, made Reina lower her eyes with an uncomfortable feeling of shame. And the feeling increased with her realizing that somehow he had brought her down to his level of churlishness.

'Twas not like her to be so touchy and quick to temper. She knew that incident in the woods was to blame, though she was not sure why. But that was no excuse to deliberately provoke him from his own good mood, especially while they still had guests whom she did *not* want witnessing an argument between them.

Contritely, still with bowed head, she said, "I thank you for that, my lord."

"Nay, I cannot accept thanks for what is your due— any more than I would thank you for what is mine."

Her eyes came back to his with a suspicious glint, and his smile told her she did not mistake his meaning. He was reminding her, without saying it directly, that he had every right to tumble her in the woods or anywhere else if that was his wont. Her contrition dissolved on the spot.

But before she could summon a suitable reply for what she thought of his *rights,* he continued in a new vein. "Now tell me, just out of curiosity, would you *really* have married that little—"

"Do not say it, do not," she gritted out forcefully. "You dare to judge a man by his appearance?"

"His appearance tells me I could blow him over with a deep breath."

She bristled to see the laughter again in his eyes. "You think so?" she challenged. "John may not win many tourneys, but that does not mean he has no skill with a sword, or the speed that bigger brutes lack."

"I am willing to put it to the test."

Her brow rose at a derisive slant. "To pit your breath against his sword?"

"I did not mean that," he snorted.

"Of course you did not. But do you draw your sword at my wedding celebration for aught other than to cut a haunch of meat, and I will box your ears as I would any other fool's.''

''Think you can reach them?''

She could have recalled sooner that he was unchivalrous enough to accept a lady's challenge. ''With a stool if needs be,'' she retorted.

That brought a chuckle. ''You have no need of stools when I am near.''

She jumped back when he moved to prove it, reaching for her waist to lift her up to his level. She put out a hand to ward him off, sparing a glance to see if they were observed in this ridiculousness. That it appeared not did not ease her exasperation.

''*Jesú,* there is just no dealing with you today, and I have better things to do than waste my time trying.''

''Reina?''

She had turned away, but now she swung back, ready to blast him with the full heat of her temper. She did no more than open her mouth before her reflexes had her catching what he tossed at her.

''Yours, I believe?'' he asked, his expression deceptively bland. ''You should not leave them lying about just anywhere, wife. 'Tis likely to give a man ideas.''

She did not understand until she looked down at what she held in her hands, and then she sucked in her breath so sharply she choked on it, adding to the hot color that suffused her face. Horrified, she stuffed her braies up her wide sleeve, gave her husband a fulminating glare worthy of his bizarre humor, and departed ere someone noticed she had shrunk in size, for she felt about two feet tall at the moment.

Chapter Twenty-five

Dusk was a dismal bank of clouds threatening rain, but Reina made it back to the keep ere the first drops fell. She had spent the remainder of the afternoon in the village, tending to the ills and hurts she had neglected this past week. It was her custom to go every few days for an hour or two, unless someone was seriously ill, which fortunately no one was at this time.

Her baker's sister, who had yet to carry a child full term, was pregnant again and needed a new supply of hollyhock. Old Delwyn needed gout weed for his swollen joints. Red Alma, the village light-skirt, had got her foot stepped on by her cow while milking it, and the small cut had become a large sore from infection. Reina left her enough horsetail for several applications, and also the beauty ointments made from cowslip Alma always managed to wheedle out of her, which kept down her freckles. There were the usual colds, sore throats, and fevers to see to, and a dog bite needing madweed, some running cankers and ringworm needing tetter berry. And while she was at it, she made up a mixture of sweet violet for herself, for its calming effect.

She stayed much longer than she was needed. Even after her neglect, she was too efficient for it to take more than two hours to see to everyone. She stayed longer to visit, to answer the many questions about the new lord—and to hide. Without wrapping it up neatly with excuses, she was suffering plain old cowardice, enough to desert her guests for the remainder of the day without the slightest twinge of conscience.

But who could blame her? Dinner had been late because she had been reluctant to come back to the hall earlier. And when she did, she had felt her face coloring every time she sensed Ranulf looking at her, knowing, just *knowing* he was silently laughing at her. She did not think she would ever get over the mortification of not having been aware that a very pertinent article of her clothing had been missing. But he had known, that devil, that miscreant of misplaced humor.

She had escaped as soon as was possible, and was reluctant to return even now. She could only hope that her husband would be gone, that Simon had done as she suggested and convinced Ranulf to leave with him.

She saw Aylmer watching her as she dismounted at the base of the forebuilding stairs and tossed the reins to a waiting groom. That he did not rush forward to greet her as was his custom made her realize she had not seen the boy recently, in fact, goodness, not since the day de Rochefort's men had attacked. True, he did not normally come into the hall, and she had delegated many of her regular duties, in which she was likely to come across him, to other of her ladies to allow her more time with her guests. Even if he had come to the hall to try to gain her notice, 'twas not likely she would have seen him as crowded as it had been.

He was sitting on the side of a storage shed with his back braced against the wall. Once he saw he had

her notice, however, he looked away. She knew then
that something was definitely wrong, and rather than
call him to her, she crossed the ward to him, in no
great hurry to enter the keep even with the first drops
of rain begun. Only when she reached him did she
notice that he had company. Lady Ella was curled up
in his lap.

She did not mention the cat, asking the boy, "Have
you been avoiding me, Aylmer?"

He did not look up at her to reply. "You have been
busy, my lady."

"So I have."

Reina squatted down next to him. The short eaves
of the shed did naught to keep the rain away, and so
she ignored it as the boy was doing, though why the
cat was not running for cover she did not know. The
thing was as stupid as it was ugly.

She said speculatively, "Did you think things would
be different now I have married?"

"Are they not?"

He still would not look at her, and was not much
able to conceal his gloomy expression. She was not
sure what was bothering him, but she had an idea.

"Everything should be back to normal soon now,"
she assured him. "The only difference is that Clydon
has a lord again, and more men to protect us. Do you
not think that is to our benefit?"

"We did well enough—"

"Nay, we did not, Aylmer, and you know it. Now
tell me why you are out here doing naught when you
should be at your job assisting the wafer maker this
time of day."

"He came in the kitchen," Aylmer said in explanation, his voice a mere whisper.

"He? Oh, *him*. So?"

"So I ran off, and now Aldrich will whip me for it, especially since he still has extra wafers to make for those guests remaining."

"Do you let me see to Aldrich," she replied, thinking to herself that if she found out he had been whipping the boy, she would have his ears served up for the morrow's dinner instead of his wafers. "But you knew you were wrong, Aylmer, to run—" She could not finish in that vein, not after she had just done the same thing. "Never mind. Sometimes there is good reason to disappear for a time. Why did you?"

"Why?" He finally looked at her in surprise, as if the answer should be obvious to her. "I—I did not want the lord to notice me. I was afraid did he see my foot, he would send me away from the keep."

Reina groaned inwardly. She wanted to put her arms around the boy and assure him that would never happen, but how could she? He was right. Some men did react despicably toward cripples, as if they saw them as a threat to their own immortality, and she did not know Ranulf well enough to speak for him.

She chose logic, and could only hope it would prove true. "If he sent you away, Aylmer, 'twould mean he feared you. I do not know about you, but I had always heard there was naught that giants feared—except mayhap another giant."

The try for levity was not successful. Instead of giving her a relieved smile, Aylmer was thoughtful for a moment, mulling over what she had said, mayhap even accepting it. But that was not all that was bothering him.

"When he walks, the floors tremble. And you can

hear him inside the keep, even when he is without. Do you not fear him, my lady?''

She supposed a small boy would be frightened of someone with Ranulf's intimidating height. *Jesú*, most men would be.

''We have to take into account that a big man does usually have a big voice, too, and a heavy step. That does not mean he is mean or cruel. Look you at that cat you are holding. Would a mean man keep such a creature for pet?''

Aylmer's eyes rounded. ''You mean it belongs to him?''

''Aye, what did you think?''

''I thought he was a stray in need of care. I found him scrounging around the slop bucket in the kitchen, and thought it best to save him a kick from cook and get him out of there.''

''That was kind of you, Aylmer. But he is a she, and cook would not have kicked this particular cat. He knows who she belongs to.''

''Oh,'' he said, gloomy once again.

Reina smiled at that forlorn expression. '' 'Tis true, however, that she needs looking after. Would you like the job?''

At last he grinned. ''Aye,'' and then the grin failed. ''But will the lord let me?''

Reina could only shrug. ''I will ask him anon. But right now, let us get out of this drizzle ere it starts to rain hard. You can take Lady Ella back to the kitchen for now.''

''Is that her name?''

''Aye, that is her silly name. And, Aylmer, do you tell Master Aldrich that if he lays a hand on you, he must deal with me. But also apologize to the man for leaving him shorthanded.''

''Aye, my lady.''

He limped off ahead of her, Reina following much slower. There was little light left in the sky, but she was still in no hurry to enter the keep. Supper would have started without her, as was customary if she was delayed in the village. She was not hungry herself, too tense in wondering whether her husband would be there or not.

She found out even before she reached the hall, nearly run down by Ranulf as he hurried down the stairs. He was armed and mail-clad, and did not even recognize her, making an annoying rumble that someone should dare get in his way. She was not so nice about being shoved out of the way, laying an expletive on his head. He stopped just below her, recognizing her voice at least.

''So you are still here, my lord.'' It was a statement, not a question, and filled with disgust.

He swung around to glare at her. ''Where else would I be? But more to the point, where have you been?''

''At the village, if you must know. And as for where you should be, Simon mentioned to me that he was going to suggest you ride with him to Forthwick to view those lands.''

''So he did, but I declined. I thought 'twas best I familiarize myself with Clydon ere I go inspecting your other holdings.''

He was absolutely right, though she would not admit it. ''And where do you go now?''

Before he could answer, Walter came rushing down the stairs, with Kenric right behind him. There was nearly another collision, but Walter stopped short in time. Kenric was not so fortunate and plowed into his back.

"So you found her?" Walter said after tossing an annoyed look at the boy. "That was quick work."

Ranulf merely grunted and held out an arm for Reina to precede him up the stairs. She was bemused, realizing what Walter's words meant.

"You were going to search for me?" she asked in a subdued tone.

"You were late, lady," was Ranulf's surly reply. "Henceforth, you will be inside these walls before 'tis dark."

Reina smiled to herself. If her visit to the village had done anything, it had shattered his good humor. Well and good. The grouch was more predictable.

Chapter Twenty-six

"*H*e was only six years and ten when he won his spurs, but 'twas to be expected, the way he wielded a sword even then."

Somehow, Reina was not surprised to hear that. Ranulf's knightly abilities with a sword had never been in doubt. 'Twas his knightly manners, or lack thereof, that she had to wonder about.

As she listened to Walter tell of the battle that had Ranulf knighted at such a young age, she watched her husband across the hall, where he had stopped to have words with his two squires. She was not the only one watching him. It seemed all of her ladies found reason to look that way, too. She sighed inwardly. She could foresee naught but problems in having a husband who was appealing to so many women. Not for herself, of course, but for those poor women.

She had never expected to love her husband. She had hoped to live with him compatibly, to respect him, to be able to depend on him. One out of three was not good.

But she was being unfair and prejudging. She still did not know Ranulf well enough. She hoped there were reasons for why he was the way he was, which was why she had put Walter on the spot to tell her about her husband. And she was right. There were reasons.

She had already learned that his childhood had been

worse than she had thought when Ranulf had mentioned it to her. He had grown up without the care of a woman, subject to a brutish man's temper and heavy fists, shunned by noble and villein alike because of his bastardy. 'Twas not a pretty picture Walter painted for her. And then she learned about Lord Montfort, and that instead of Ranulf's lot improving, he had merely exchanged one churlish master for another.

"You are not listening, my lady."

She pinkened slightly, offering Walter an embarrassed smile. "I am afraid tales of blood and gore have never held much fascination for me. Do you tell me instead why Ranulf has a very real dislike for ladies of rank."

"Why would you think—"

"Do not try to prevaricate with me, sirrah, or has your memory gone to market? You yourself told me of his distrust of all ladies when you convinced me to wed him. I see you now remember. So tell me of the experiences you mentioned then that supposedly soured him against noblewomen."

Walter squirmed uncomfortably. " 'Tis not something he would appreciate your knowing."

"But you will tell me anyway." Her voice was smooth as silk, but her expression was implacable. "Because of your glib tongue, I am wed to a man I am not sure I even like. You owe me, Sir Walter."

To his squirming was added a guilty flush. "He will kill me if he knows I have told you."

"I will remember that."

Her tone was not in the least reassuring, was more like a promise to hold his prediction in reserve should she ever want to be rid of him. But Walter shrugged that aside. The last thing he wanted was for her to hate Ranulf, which might come to pass did she not understand him better. And if telling her of Ranulf's past would touch her woman's heart, then he would not be doing his friend a disservice.

"Very well," Walter said. "But first you should know that Ranulf has always had difficulty with women."

"With that face?" she snorted.

He frowned at her interruption. "Because of that face. Mayhap some men might sell their souls to look as he does, but Ranulf has never been thankful for his handsomeness. Aside from the fact that he is the image of his father, whom you dare not even mention to him, he was teased horribly when he first came to Montfort."

"But that is normal among young boys."

"Aye, and he took it in good grace, thinking he was only getting more than his fair share of ribbing— until the day he first saw his own reflection. There were no mirrors in his village, you see, no clear pools of water to throw back an image. He did not *know* what he looked like until the day one of the older squires at Montfort spitefully shoved a mirror in his face to prove to Ranulf that he was the 'pretty maid' they were fond of calling him."

"And he was horrified," Reina surmised.

"Aye, and soundly trounced the lad for bringing the truth home to him. He was not teased much after that, but he then understood why girls were always following him about, and it disgusted him. He had thought they were interested in him as a friend. He then knew 'twas his looks alone that fascinated the wenches."

"You expect me to believe that did not delight him?"

"Not at that young age, lady. They came in packs—milkmaids, kitchen maids, chambermaids, giggling and disturbing our workouts in the exercise yard. And the knights training us knew who to blame, working Ranulf harder and longer than all the rest of us."

"But when he was older—"

"Oh, he took what the wenches threw at him, never doubt it. But he did not deceive himself that any of the sluts wanted more than a chance to brag to their friends of the conquest—until Lady Anne noticed him. But first there was Lady Montfort."

"His *lord's* wife?"

"Aye, a lady well past her prime, trying to seduce a lad of ten years and five. 'Twas laughable. But the lady did not think so when he refused her bait. She was right furious. And she salved her pride with a little vengeance by informing her husband that Ranulf tried to get into her skirts, earning him a whipping before his peers."

Reina frowned. "Did he not speak up for himself?"

"Oh, no one believed her accusation, not even Montfort. But you do not call the lord's wife a liar, and so Ranulf was whipped, with every noble at Montfort turned out to watch it. And that is what brought him to the attention of Lady Anne, ward to Montfort. She was only a year or so older than Ranulf, and a comely wench, with a smile to light up a room, and eyes like—"

"Do not wax poetic, sirrah," Reina said with mild disgust. "So she was beautiful. Just say it."

Walter smiled sheepishly. "Aye, she was indeed

beautiful, and every page, squire, and knight was a little in love with her.''

''Including yourself?''

He only shrugged in answer. ''But once Lady Anne saw Ranulf, she was blind to all else, or so it seemed. She sneaked down to his quarters to visit him whilst he was bedfast from the whipping, and that is where their affair began. As you might guess, he was thoroughly smitten. The trouble was, he thought she was as well.''

''If you are about to tell me a broken heart caused his mistrust—''

''Would that was all, lady, but if you are not tolerant enough to listen . . .''

Was that how she sounded? What was wrong with her? So she was listening to tales of her husband with other women. She had asked to hear them.

''Do you continue, Sir Walter, and I will endeavor to curb my hasty conclusions.''

As that was as close as she was likely to come to an apology for her interruption, he nodded, his expression now as serious as she had ever seen it. ''Their passion for each other lasted for months, but the day inevitably came when it bore fruit. The Lady Anne confessed to Ranulf she was with child.''

Reina was not particularly surprised. She would have been more surprised to hear that Ranulf had never sired any bastards. That he had one by a lady was not that common, but then again, certainly not unknown to happen. His noble half brother was proof of that.

Without censure, she asked, ''Was it his?''

''Aye; at least he had no doubt.''

''Did they marry?''

"Nay. He was willing, desperately willing, you might say. He wanted her. He wanted his child. But she would not have him. Oh, she played him along for a while more, giving him one excuse after another why they should not tell Lord Montfort they wished to marry. But Ranulf would not let up, and she finally succumbed to the pressure, telling him the truth.

"She would not marry a squire, a landless squire, not for any reason. She had property, you see, just a manor, but Montfort had promised her that because of her beauty, he would find her a rich husband, and that was what she wanted, all she wanted. She laughed when Ranulf mentioned their love for each other, telling him that wealth was the only thing worth loving as far as she was concerned."

"Not very diplomatic of her," Reina said dryly, annoyed with herself for feeling a twinge of sympathy for the young Ranulf. "And the child?"

"Lady Anne returned to her manor to bear it. But when Ranulf got over his reaction to her rejection, he realized he still wanted the child, no matter how difficult it might be for him to raise. Only he could not discover where she had gone, and by the time he did and went there, it was to find the lady had already borne the child, recovered from it, and was living in the north with her new husband."

"She took the child with her?" Reina asked doubtfully.

"Nay, she foisted it on a family in her small village to raise, wanting naught more to do with it."

Reina jumped ahead with her own conclusion again, thinking of Kenric and Lanzo, Ranulf's squires. Kenric was too old to be his bastard, but mayhap Lanzo . . .

Walter was not finished, unfortunately. "I had gone with Ranulf to her manor. He had feared she would keep the child with her, so he was delighted that she had given it away. He had brought a few coins with him and thought it would be easy to buy the child from the villeins. And the family was easy to find. There were no secrets in that place."

"Why do I have the feeling I am not going to like hearing the rest of this?" Reina said uneasily as she watched his expression darken.

"Mayhap I should not go on."

"Nay, you have gone this far. I must hear it all now, good or bad."

"The family the lady brought the child to just a few days after its birthing was poor, verily, the poorest in her village. They were also the largest family there, with seven children already. She knew that. They had protested they did not want the child. She forced them to take it anyway. Within a fortnight it was dead of starvation."

"Oh, God!" Reina moaned.

Walter did not look at her, continuing softly. " 'Twas the only time Ranulf and I ever fought. He wanted to kill the whole family, and burn the village besides. I could not let him. 'Twas not their fault. They were the sorriest lot of villeins we had ever seen, slowly starving themselves. They had too many mouths of their own to feed to spare aught for their lady's cast-off bastard. One of the manor servants later admitted Anne had not wanted the child to be there should she return. She had known what could happen, hoped it would happen. She got what she wanted."

Reina closed her eyes, unable to speak for a moment. She wished she had stopped him. She had not wanted to hear this, not this. *Jesú,* children were the only true innocents. So many died of natural causes, but this was unnatural, deliberate. What kind of woman would do that, when it would have cost her little to find the infant a decent home?

"What—what was it, do you know?"

"A girl child, strong and healthy at birth, which was why it took so long—" .

Reina waved him to silence before she started to cry. She could feel the tears forming and fought them back, pushing the horror from her mind. This had naught to do with her. Whom was she deceiving? It had happened to *her* husband, and he was still suffering from it, which most certainly did affect her. But for him to blame all women for what one heartless bitch had done, that was not fair.

"Let us look at this realistically," she said, managing to sound in control, if slightly pained. "These incidents happened eleven or twelve years ago."

"Eight," he corrected her.

She was startled from her thoughts. "I thought he was older."

"He has always looked older because of his size, but he is only twenty years and three, lady."

"Well, still, eight years is long enough for him to have discovered all women are not the same."

"How would you feel had it happened to you?" Walter countered. "Lady Anne was all that was sweet and gentle. She never raised her voice. She never had a bad word to say of anyone. Her ruthless greed and callousness were concealed from one and all. Think you Ranulf could ever trust another lady's winsome smiles after that?"

"But we are not all like that!"

"I know it, but 'twill take much to convince him of it." And then he groaned. "Smile, he is returning."

"You must be mad. I could not smile now if my life depended on it. And do I do so, he will wonder about it, not the other way around. He has not exactly been in my good graces today, had you not noticed."

"But you will forgive him?"

"What you have told me only explains his distrust of noblewomen," she hissed aside to him. "It does not excuse his deplorably churlish manner."

"*That* is correctable, my lady, do you care to make the effort."

She had no time for another reply, for Ranulf sat down on the bench on her other side just then. Fortunately, Walter gave her time to collect herself by having a brief conversation with Ranulf, but then he made his excuses and departed, leaving them alone by the hearth.

Reina could not look at him just yet. She was confused by what she was feeling now and did not trust herself to speak. Who would have thought such a man could stir her sympathies? He seemed so indestructible, so immune to tender emotions—but had he been that way as a lad? And then she noticed Eadwina across the hall staring at him dreamily and forgot all that.

"Did I hurt you today?"

"What?"

"Today in the woods?" Ranulf clarified. "Did I hurt you?"

It was on the tip of her tongue to tell him aye. But the fact was she had felt anger, disappointment, frustration, but no pain. And lying to him was no way to start out this relationship of theirs.

"Nay, you did not."

"You are certain?"

"Aye."

"You would tell me if I did?"

She looked at him incredulously. What was wrong with him? Or was this more of his bizarre humor? Whatever, she had just passed over the edge to irritation.

"Do you hurt me, you can be sure I would scream loud enough for you and everyone else to know it. Oh, you can be sure of that, my lord."

He frowned at her. Mayhap he should have asked earlier, but she had been in no good mood all day. And now she was turning one thing into another, and coming close to deserving the other.

"Do I turn you over my knee, lady, *you* can be sure I will not care who knows it."

Had she felt sorry for him? She must have been mad.

"Thank you for the warning," she replied tightly, and started to get up.

His hand came swiftly to her arm, detaining her. "I did not mean to—" He stopped, his frown deepening. "Why have you been so wroth today?"

"Do you think about it and the answer will come to you."

"I have done that already, and no answer comes clearly to mind. I would prefer it did you tell me."

"Very well." She glanced around to be sure no one was within hearing before meeting those penetrating violet eyes again. "I did not enjoy it."

"Enjoy what?"

"You *know* what," she hissed.

He started to grin but thought better of it, then made the mistake of saying, "Wives are not supposed to enjoy it."

Reina stared at him, wondering what he would do if she hit him over the head with something. "Who told you that piece of witless nonsense? Nay, let me guess. A priest, and you believe everything priests tell you. Clodpate! A priest is not God. He is a man, subject to the same mistakes as all men. Half of them commit the same sins as we do. Sweet *Jesú*, use your common sense. Nay, better yet, ask any wife here what she thinks of that antiquated drivel. But do not expect me to like being treated less than a whore."

He certainly knew what *his* wife thought of it. He watched her stalk away and had to force back his laughter. Christ's toes, she was feisty, even when she blasphemed. So she wanted to be pleasured? His humor faded. How was he to manage that when he feared touching her with his passion, as tiny and delicate as she was?

Chapter Twenty-seven

Reina crept quietly into the chamber. A night candle had been left burning, giving her enough light to cross the room to the aumbry. She set her basket of medicaments down there and quickly unfastened her mantle.

Ranulf slept on. She did not like it that he had left the bed curtains open. The slightest noise could wake him. But from what she had seen thus far, he was a sound sleeper.

It had been a relief to be called back to the village, though the reason had given her many hours of worry. The baker's sister had taken a fall and had begun to miscarry. But working half the night, and using every remedy she could think of, Reina had gotten the danger down to a mere possibility of losing the baby, which the woman was prone to anyway. If she stayed off her feet for a time, until the baby was well set, she still might carry this one to term.

The relief had come from having an excuse to avoid her marriage bed that night, at least until Ranulf was asleep. She still could not believe she had actually told him what she had in their last conversation. After thinking about it, she had been horrified to realize how it must have sounded to him, and only surprised that he had not laughed in her face. He must now think she lusted after him, or at least that she lusted after the pleasure he could give her, which was even worse. Men never doubted their own prowess, so what else was he to think? Certainly not that she found fault with his jump-on, jump-off technique. Oh, curse and rot her loose mouth.

She yanked open the aumbry, then winced at the creak of the hinge. A stirring of the sheets behind her made her quickly tug off her bliaut without bothering with the laces, carelessly tossing it and her mantle into the wardrobe. She considered making a pallet for the rest of the night. She considered curling up right there on the floor where she was. She did *not* want Ranulf waking, not for any reason, but what excuse could she give come morn if he found her sleeping on the floor?

Her chemise was a tighter fit requiring unlacing. She began to work on the ties in the dim light, but froze after a moment with the sound of Ranulf's voice.

"Come here, Reina."

Her heart where her larynx should be made words terribly difficult. "In—in a moment—"

"Come now."

The order given in that particular tone carried her feet forward. She could only hope he was not completely awake, that he only wanted assurance that she had returned safely, and then he would go back to sleep.

She stopped a few feet from the bed. "Aye?"

She did not even see his hand move. One moment she was being dragged across him, ending up lying flat on her back beside him, and the next, she heard her chemise ripping.

"What—what are you *doing?*" she got out, too late. Her shift tore down the middle, too.

"What you requested," he answered in the most

reasonable tone. "You said we should both be naked. I am already in that state. You were taking too long to get there."

"And that gives you leave to just—"

Her furious question was cut short. She was surprised she had been able to say that much. He had not called her to him for conversation. His mouth moved over hers with a fierce possessiveness, and then so too did his body.

And yet this time *was* different. His thrusts were not so quick and pounding. There was a languor to his movements, a heady undulation that set off a maelstrom of delicious sensations deep inside Reina. And his lips did not concentrate only on hers, but moved over her face, finally to one ear, and *that* intensely pleasant feeling sent such a jolt through her, she bucked under him, driving him deeper into her core—which effectively ended his thrusts.

Her eyes flew open as she heard his roar, and she wanted to scream, *Not yet,* but he was done, and looking down at her now with primal satisfaction in his gaze. That alone gave her the urge to kill him. He had brought her closer than ever this time to what made *him* roar, only to leave her with that aching frustration gnawing at her gut again, her nerve ends raw, her mind sizzling with impotent fury.

He rolled to his side with a sigh. "I did it again, did I not?"

"Aye, you lummox," she bit out between clenched teeth. "That you did."

"I am afraid I was not quite awake. Do you say so, we can try again."

She threw off the hand he moved to her shoulder.

"Do not touch me! I am so furious, all I want to do is hit you!"

"Then hit me."

"Do not tempt me, Ranulf."

"Nay, I mean it. If you will not let me try again, then what better way to ease your anger. Go ahead, little general. You cannot hurt me."

She certainly tried. She pounded on his chest and belly until her fists were sore and there was no strength left in her arms to push him away when he pulled her down to lie close to his body.

"Do you feel better now?"

"Nay," she murmured stubbornly.

He chuckled. "Was it the torn chemise?"

"Ohh!"

He laughed outright. "You are so easy to rile, wife. And now that you have worn yourself out, 'twould also be easy for me to—"

"Do not!"

She could feel his shoulder shrug under her head. "A man is not like to argue when he is already sated, though you cannot expect the same when he is not."

"That is *so* reassuring."

"You dare much with my hand so near your backside, lady." A yawn ruined the effect of that threat.

Reina snorted. "That might be more gratifying than what you—"

"Finish that thought, and you will regret it." This threat was much more effective, particularly accompanied by his hand moving to the curve of her buttocks. "You struck the bargain, and I have upheld my end of it. If you have changed your mind and would prefer that I lust after someone else, do you say so now."

He held his breath, waiting for her answer. He had not meant to give her an out like that, and did not know what he would do if she took it. But she said naught, and he did not press his luck by saying any more.

Reina held her breath, too, and for the same reason, hoping he would not press her for an answer her pride would dictate.

Only after he was asleep did she realize that no answer was all the answer he needed.

Chapter Twenty-eight

*T*he day was humid after the morning rain, but that did not stop children from running through the village in play. Women brought their chores outside of their houses, converging under shaded oaks to gossip as they worked. Few men were about at this time of day when there were fields to tend or ditches to dig, either their own or the lords'. Those present were busy at some labor, repairing plows or other tools, one leading a pair of oxen back to the fields, several men hauling new thatch up to a roof, one gangly fellow chasing a goat through the parish yard. Even the old and lame remained useful, watching the younger children, feeding and collecting eggs from the chickens that scratched in each yard, or working in the small vegetable patches behind each house.

It was the first Ranulf had been there since the wedding, and all labor came to a temporary halt when he was noticed walking down the center street, Lady Ella perched on his shoulder. Only one daring soul called out a greeting. Most were leery of the new lord, wondering what he was doing there when 'twas the bailiff they always dealt with. From longtime experience, it never boded well when a lord showed up. But when he singled no one out for questioning or punishment, they ignored him, or seemed to.

Ranulf was not really sure what he was doing there himself. He had had a vague notion and had acted on it without really thinking it out. One thing he had not considered was the impression it would give when he entered Red Alma's hut.

The place was easy to find from the directions he had from one of his men who had already been there. Two geese were making a honking racket mating in the front yard, ironically appropriate for this residence. The door was open in invitation. A skinny razor-backed hog ran squealing out of it with a wooden bowl sailing after it just before Ranulf ducked down to enter.

"If you come on business, shut the door—if not, we will need the light."

It took him a moment to locate the voice, for the door was the only source of light, and the house was bigger than it looked from outside. Red Alma was changing the linen on a sturdy-looking bed up against the wall on one side of the room. On the other side was tied a cow, placidly chewing on the rushes covering the beaten earth floor. Little luxuries abounded, the fine linen and curtains on the bed, pottery ware hanging on the walls with brass pots, sweet beeswax candles instead of pungent tallow, the aroma of venison stewing in a pot over the open hearth in the middle of the room, venison he recalled being served last eventide in the hall and obviously finding its way here in payment of services rendered.

Ranulf did not shut the door. Red Alma had heard him enter but had not seen who he was yet. It took another moment ere curiosity turned her about to face him. Even then, with the light behind him, she did not recognize him at first. 'Twas his height that did it, making her pale in horror.

"God save me, not you!" she gasped, then paled

even more. "Oh—I mean—please, my lord. The lady has been good to me. She rarely scolds, she brings me special salves, she—"

"Why do you mention her?"

"She—she will hate me does she learn you have come to me."

"Why?" When she just stared at him, Ranulf grunted. "Nay, I did not come for that, and she would have no reason to think it."

This frightened the woman even more. She stumbled to the trestle table and collapsed on the bench there. Her knuckles turned white as she gripped the edge of the table.

"You mean to put me out?"

"What?" He frowned, and then, "Do not be silly, woman. Your services are as useful as any other villein's. 'Tis advice I want from you."

"Advice?" she repeated dumbly.

"Aye." He came forward, removing his gauntlets to tuck into his belt. Lady Ella jumped to the table when he reached it. "More particularly, your knowledge of women."

The smile came slowly, but was brilliant when completed. "Of course! Anything, my lord, anything! Whatever I can tell you, you have only to ask."

"How can I pleasure my wife without hurting her?"

He sat down on the bench next to her. Lady Ella came instantly to be petted. He did not notice Red Alma's eyes round on him in astonishment.

"You hurt her?"

"Not yet—at least I do not think so. But if I touch her as I want, I fear I will. I seem to have lost what control I ever had of my passion since I met her."

"Why do you *think* you would hurt her?"

He held up his hands, frowning at them. "How can I not with these? They are used to large, strapping wenches who do not flinch from a too rough caress. How can they not hurt a woman as tiny and delicate as my lady is?"

Those hands slammed down on the table with that question. The cat was startled, jumping back to his shoulder. He pulled her down to his chest to calm her. Red Alma stared at his hands stroking the cat.

"The cat belongs to you, my lord?" she asked thoughtfully.

"Aye."

"I can see you are fond of it. I had one myself once that I had strong feelings for. I loved that cat so much, sometimes I wanted to just squeeze it, to show it how much I cared for it. Do you sometimes feel that way?"

He smiled, scratching the cat behind its pointy ears. "Aye, often."

"But you do not give in to the urge?"

"Of course not. 'Twould kill it."

"Or badly hurt it."

He frowned again. "What has this to do with what I asked you?"

"If you can be gentle with a cat, because you know that to be otherwise will hurt it, do you not think 'twould be the same with your wife?"

"You compare my wife to a cat?"

"Nay, not at all," she rushed to assure him. "I do merely point out that those hands you fear will hurt the lady do not hurt the cat, a much smaller creature."

"I am not beset with lust for my cat," he grumbled.

She had to bite her lip to keep from smiling. "Of course you are not. What I am trying to suggest is, 'twas not in your mind that you could hurt those other women you are used to, any more than 'twould be in your mind that you could hurt a dog or a horse with a too sharp pat of affection. But you *know* you could hurt your cat. The thought is there, even when you are not thinking about it. 'Tis the same with the lady. You know she is different from those others, that you must be more careful of your strength when you touch her. Even should you lose control in your passion, that thought will be there to temper your strength and protect the lady."

"How can it be? I tell you, I have never known such overwhelming lust as has plagued me since meeting her. It does not even matter where we are. Once it takes me, there is no stopping it, nor holding it back. There are no thoughts of any kind, only this driving need to possess her."

"I see," Red Alma said.

She wondered if he had considered that he might be in love with his wife. She doubted it, and she was not fool enough to suggest it. But if he would not believe 'twas possible to restrain himself in the throes of passion, then how could she help him, or, more to the point, help the lady?

"This puts a different face on the matter," she continued, eyeing his hands again. "The lady might be small and delicate, however, she is still a woman, and we women have more strength and endurance than you men give us credit for. Mayhap your touch would not hurt her at all."

"I do not care to cause her pain to find out."

"Then show me. I think I can fairly judge what a woman can withstand."

At his doubtful look, she smiled to encourage him, though looking at the size of his hands, she wished she had kept her mouth shut. 'Twas a risk, too, that he might not stop once he started. But how else could she ease his concern? That he had this concern was a wonder, and for the lady never to know the pleasure of his caress would be a shame.

"I do not mean to entice you, my lord. Never that. 'Tis no more than a test, and only to determine the strength of your touch—no more than that."

"I understand that," he grunted. "But you are in nowise my lady's small size."

She had to grin. "A breast is a breast. Big or small, it feels the same pain or pleasure. Touch mine as is your custom, and I can—" He did before she finished, and she could not help flinching. "I see what you mean, my lord. You do have a strong grip," she was forced to admit, then dared to add what she had told many a knight. "But a breast is not a sword hilt. It will not fall from your hand do you hold it light . . . oh, God, your lady!"

"What?"

He turned to see his wife framed in the open doorway, her basket of medicinal potions in her hand. But no sooner did he see her than she was gone.

"You must go after her and explain!" Red Alma cried.

"What for? Do I go after her, I am like to tumble her in the woods again, and she does not like that very much."

Red Alma stared at him aghast, distracted for

a moment by that piece of news. "But she will think—"

"Do not be silly, woman," he cut her off. "I told you she would have no reason to think that. She does not deny me even if she does not like it, so what need have I of other women?"

Alma did not tell him that most men would go to another woman for better sport if their wives so disliked coupling with them. But then, too, those particular wives sent their husbands off with their blessings. And his total lack of concern did ease her fears. Mayhap the Lady Reina would be grateful to her. And if she was not, Alma could see to it that she was— indirectly.

"My lord, I fear I have gone about this in the wrong way. You asked how you might pleasure your lady without hurting her, and there is a way, something I have overlooked. Mayhap if you begin slowly. Do not touch her with your hands at first. Use your lips and tongue instead."

" 'Twould not be the same."

"Why not? You can touch her with your mouth anywhere you would touch her with your hands."

"Anywhere?"

"Aye."

"*Anywhere?*"

Red Alma chuckled, gleaning his thoughts. "Aye, there too. I know most men do not think of that, but those few that do find their own pleasure in it. Of course she is like to protest, thinking it strange. But do you insist, she will not only like it, she can be brought to her full pleasure that way."

"How is that possible?"

Red Alma blushed, for the first time in many a long

year. "You will have to trust me, my lord, that it can happen. And in this way, there is no hurry in learning what caresses will please her and how gentle you needs be. There will be time and plenty for that as you come to know her better."

He did not question her further, leaving a silver coin on the table that was more money than she had ever seen, with the promise it would be doubled had she spoken true. Whether she had spoken true depended on the lady. Some women would object violently to what she had suggested, and a man was not likely to insist very long in that case. But the new lord did not seem a man to give up easily. Far from it. He was determined to see his lady pleasured whether she liked it or not. What Alma would not give to be a flea in their bed tonight.

Chapter Twenty-nine

"But why now, my lady?"

"Because now is the perfect time, Aylmer." *While the bastard is steeped in guilt from his infidelity,* Reina added to herself. "He will say aye to anything I ask today."

"I was afraid of that," the boy mumbled.

Reina frowned at him. "I thought you wanted the care of Lady Ella?"

"I do. But I did not think I would have to meet the lord to have it."

"You are not to worry. Wait in the window embrasure until I call you." And then she tousled his hair and gave him a smile to reassure him. "Go on, Aylmer. You will have naught to fear of him."

Her smile crumbled the moment he turned away from her. How her mother had ever managed to do this she did not know. But 'twas one of the things the lady had taught her, that in a world where women had so little governance of their own lives, where they needed a man's yea-say for aught that they did or wanted, they had to take advantage of any occurrence that would help them get that yea-say if they were in doubt of getting it.

Guilt was a prime emotion to play on, her mother had once told her. Not that she had ever suspected her husband of infidelity. She had taken advantage, when alive, of broken promises, neglect, little things like that. She had not had a husband who rutted at the drop of a coin as her daughter now did.

But how *did* she calmly manage to ask for things when she was seething with upset? True, her mother's temper had not been as vitriolic as was hers. She had managed to let her husband know in subtle ways that she was displeased with him, and whether he were guilty or not, he would certainly think he had reason to be and so had leapt at any opportunity to make amends, be it a new gown or a visit to court.

Reina could not picture her giant husband doing anything so normal as trying to assuage a guilty conscience. Neither could she picture herself calmly putting suggestions to him when she would rather break something over his head. But if her mother could do it, she could, too. However, once she had the agreements she wanted, then she would kill him—that swine, that miserable, dog-hearted wretch!

How could he? . . . nay, nay, what was *wrong* with her? She had no business being so furious over something like this. The common belief was that conjugal fidelity was not important. She knew that, had never expected it to be otherwise. What woman did?— except her mother, of course.

The best Reina had hoped for was that her husband would not shame her by bringing his mistresses home, as some men did. And yet was this not as bad? To visit Red Alma in full daylight, in full sight of every gossip in the village, just two days after their wedding. And Red Alma! Reina could understand more readily if she had caught him rutting in a dark corner with Eadwina. Men drooled over Eadwina. Why should her lusty husband be any different?

But Red Alma? True, the woman was not unsightly

with her flaming red hair and come-hither eyes of pansy blue. And she was a curvaceous handful, which Reina knew her husband to be partial to. But he was aware that, unlike most ladies, Reina went among her villeins to tend their ills. He had to know that if he visited the village whore, she would learn of it right quickly, even if he had not imagined she would actually find him with the woman as she had.

So did he want her to know? Was this his way of punishing her for her complaints? And she had been complaining, shrewishly so. Or had he even thought of punishing her? More likely he just wanted a more satisfying ride. Yet she could not forget his question just last night, asking her if she would prefer he lust after someone else. Had he taken her silence for agreement instead of refusal? Could he be that stupid?

"Young Malfed said you wished to speak with me?"

Good. Being forewarned would have him thinking she meant to mention Red Alma. But she had no intention of doing that, which ought to confound him nicely.

Reina composed her features as best she could and turned about to face her errant husband—and was confounded herself. She did not know how she had expected a man to look who was wallowing in guilt, but 'twas not with a mere look of inquiry. Even Lady Ella was purring contentedly in his arms, sensing no agitation in her master.

"Do you sit down, my lord." She indicated the lord's chair, which she had moved in front of the hearth for this discussion. "Wine?"

He nodded, taking the seat. Reina raised her hand and a servant rushed forward with the refreshment.

She had not missed his sigh when he sat down. Was he so tired from his exertions in the village? She had to force herself to hand him the chalice of wine instead of dumping it over his head.

"My bailiff informs me he took you out to view the fields and the mill this morn."

"Aye."

He sipped his wine to keep from meeting her eyes, or so Reina thought. She moved in front of the hearth to look down on him. "I suppose the rest of your day was as productive?"

He choked, spewing wine. The cat hissed, jumping down from his lap. Reina picked her up and smoothed off the wine drops from her fur before setting her down on a nearby bench, where she proceeded to do a better job of cleaning herself. Ranulf was still coughing.

"Mayhap the wine is too strong, my lord?" Reina said in all innocence. "Would you prefer ale?"

With a glower, he rasped, "I would prefer it do you come to the point."

"Point? I have no point to make. There are a few things we needs discuss, but if you are too weary right now from such a *tiring* day, it can wait."

Her emphasis on his exhaustion was not lost on Ranulf. He was tired, but from riding hell-bent through the woods looking for outlaws or any sport that would get his mind off what Red Alma had told him. It was either that or give in to the lust her suggestions had inspired, and he was damned if he was going to let his cursed prick rule him this time.

As long as he kept those thoughts at bay, he was doing just fine, even in the presence of his wife. Her innuendos were proving distracting, however. What

the devil did she *think* had tired him? If she wanted
to know what he had been doing, why did she not
just ask him? 'Twas not like her to dance about a
subject, not this outspoken lady. And he sensed her
upset. She appeared calm and serene on the surface,
too serene, but he could feel the tension of a powerful
emotion radiating from her.

"Has something happened that I should know
about?" he wondered aloud.

The question seemed to baffle her. "That you
should . . . You would know that better than I, my
lord."

Now what did *that* mean? "Never mind." He
sighed. "Just get on with what you wished to tell me
ere I *am* too tired to listen."

Reina clenched her fists behind her skirt. This was
not going as she had expected. Why was he not acting
as he was supposed to? He knew she knew what he
had done. He might have been able to come up with
any number of excuses for being in Red Alma's house
if Reina had not seen him with his hand pressed to
the woman's large breast. *That* signified only one reason for being there.

Did he not care, then, that she knew? Or did he
think she would not dare to upbraid him for what he
had done, was confident she would not even dare to
mention it? Most wives would not dare, too fearful
of a beating should they complain of their husbands'
wrongful behavior. Reina did not have that fear,
thanks to her marriage contract, but even if she did,
'twould not stop her from reviling this man did he
deserve it.

But not yet. She would first see if he was only
pretending to be unconcerned.

"Very well, my lord. This will not take long, just a few decisions I need from you. First, we have had an offer to buy the wardship of the de Burgh heiress. Simon brought me the letter from one of his neighbors, a young lord he vouchsafed is capable of administering to the girl's holdings. I did not wish to mention it until all our guests had departed."

"Then your little lordling has left?"

Her mouth tightened at that derogatory tone. "Aye, Lord John left us this morn."

"I hope you bade him Godspeed for me. I am gracious, after all, to those who lose to me."

"He did not lose to you, he lost by default," she snapped. "And as he does not even know he lost, your being gracious to him on that count is superfluous. Not that he would have noticed graciousness on your part had you been present to offer it. 'Tis rather difficult to discern courtesy when you are being growled at."

"I do not growl, lady."

"If you say so," she replied sweetly, his growl ringing in her ears.

He nearly came out of his chair but caught himself, surprising her by chuckling as he leaned back again. "At least I do not squeak as your little mouse does."

"He is not a—" She clamped her mouth shut, glaring at him. "Very funny, my lord. Now may we get back to the subject at hand? The wardship?"

"How much was offered?"

"Four hundred fifty marks and two palfreys."

"Why so much?"

" 'Tis a small amount actually, when you consider the two manors, each with its own village, owe rents of a hundred and fifty marks annually, making the

income from the farms considerably more than that.
You must also take into account the child's age. She
is not yet two years. Her wardship will continue a
goodly number of years ere she is wed and the holdings given over to her husband's control. That allows
for a tidy profit for whoever administers her fief.''

"Then why sell it?''

"I am not suggesting you sell it. I am not suggesting anything at all. I am merely mentioning an offer
that needs be answered one way or the other. But
something must be done eventually. The widow has
a bailiff and several knights and is managing well
enough on her own, but then she has had no problems
thus far.''

"So you are suggesting I sell the wardship?''

"Nay, I am not,'' she gritted out. "Simon may
know this neighbor of his, but we do not. And there
are other possibilities that would benefit us better.''

"I could appoint my own steward, I suppose,
though stewards not closely watched are like to manipulate profits into their own pockets. Or I could
betroth the child and thereby let the man govern now
what will eventually be his.''

Reina was surprised he did know what options he
had, but he did not mention the one she wanted. "As
you say, a steward cannot always be trusted. But do
you betroth the child now, it must be to a man old
enough to govern, and so you do them both a disservice. He must wait many years yet for his heirs, and
she must eventually marry an old man, which she is
not like to be happy about.''

"Not if I choose Searle or Eric. The lads would be
only twenty and eight ten years from now, no great
tragedy to a marriageable wench.''

That was true, rot him. "But you would gain only one man's service in that way, when you could have two do you arrange a marriage to the widow instead. A stepfather would have the profits of the land now, enough to buy a sizable holding of his own later for his own heirs. I have been considering Sir Arnulph for long now, but I have needed him in Birkenham, so I put the matter off."

"Tell me something, Reina. If that is what you wanted all along, why did you not just say so?"

"Then you agree?"

"I agree the widow should be married. You will allow I should meet this Sir Anulph ere I consider him?"

"Certainly."

"Good." He stood up to tower over her. "But do you get straight to the point next time you want something of me. There is no need to waste time skirting—"

"I am not finished," she cut in, bristling that he should dare to chastise her for anything just now. "There is another matter—about your cat."

"What about her?"

She called the boy forward, feeling her first hesitancy as they waited for his slow gait to reach them. But she had had one success, and so concluded that Ranulf *was* suffering a guilty conscience, even if he did not show it.

She did come right to the point this time. "Aylmer here has taken a liking to your pet. He works in the kitchen, but wants the added chore of caring for Lady Ella, feeding and grooming and suchlike."

"Is this another one like your Theo?" Ranulf asked her.

"I have always looked out for him, if *that* is what you mean. He is orphaned."

He looked down at the boy then, while she stared at him. Her uneasiness grew, even though Ranulf revealed nothing of his thoughts in his expression. She should not have risked this. She should have hidden the boy from him, rather than bring Aylmer to his attention. What if Ranulf did send him away? What could she do?

And poor Aylmer was terrified. He would not look up. She could see his thin limbs trembling. What had been galloping toward panic reared in fury. How did Ranulf dare to put the boy through this with his silence?

Reina drew her foot back with every intention of kicking her husband, when he spoke to Aylmer, and in what was a gentle tone for him. "So you like my cat, do you?"

"Aye, my lord." A mere whisper.

"See that you do not overfeed her."

It took a moment for Aylmer to realize he had the permission he wanted, and he looked up in surprise, which quickly turned to a wide grin. "Aye, my lord!"

It took Reina another moment to put her foot back on the floor. The swine, to keep them in suspense like that. Guilt. He really was wallowing in it. And as long as he was atoning, she might as well go for blood.

"Do you take Lady Ella to the kitchen now, Aylmer. Lord Ranulf has had her out with him all day, so she is like to be quite hungry." She waited until the boy had carefully picked up the cat and limped away before facing her husband again. "As long—"

"You should have warned me ere you brought him forward, lady."

She tensed defensively. "Why? Because you do not want a cripple tending your precious cat?"

"Because 'twas Lanzo's job, and he will not like being usurped by a kitchen lackey."

"Aylmer is no lackey. His parents were freeholders. When they died, no one would take the boy in or even help him. They treated him as if his lameness were a disease they might get from too close association. He was weak and sickly, and twice I nearly lost him to minor illnesses that would barely have affected a stronger child. He is small and defenseless, yet he has his pride. He will not accept charity, but works for his keep. And if he is special to me, 'tis because he has no one else."

"Who else does he need with a general in his corner?"

She ignored that. "While we are still on the subject of your cat—"

"Are we? I thought the subject was the boy."

"The boy is my concern. The cat is yours, particularly where she is to sleep. I do not like waking up with her nose in my face, as I did this morn. She should never have been allowed upstairs."

"She goes where I go, sleeps where I sleep. It has always been so."

"That was well and good when you slept in tents, my lord, but a bedchamber is no place for animals."

"And here I thought you had me in that class. Or do you mean to kick me out of the chamber, too?"

"As if you would go if I did," she snorted.

"Nay, I would not. And neither does Lady Ella go."

"Then we needs discuss it more."

"The subject is closed, Reina," he said, his tone warning that he meant it. "Now do you order me a bath. If you would like to join me, come along. Otherwise, I will see you at the evening meal."

She had to grit her teeth to keep from calling him back as he walked away. She was supposed to have her *every* request agreed to, not the least of them denied. But she had to allow that two out of three was not bad. Only if he thought he had just atoned for his infidelity, he had best think again.

Chapter Thirty

"You will feel better do you talk about it."

Reina did not answer, keeping her eyes closed as Theodric pulled the comb gently through her hair. She wished he were not so perceptive to her moods. She had said naught to him about her husband's visit to Red Alma, nor did she intend to. He would hear about it soon enough once the gossip reached the castlefolk, but hopefully he would not relate that to the upset he sensed in her now. Confession might be good for the soul, but humiliation was not.

She felt like pacing, not sitting calmly on a stool. This nightly ritual was usually so soothing. Theo had the magic touch when it came to easing her tension. But her agitation was mounting, not decreasing, as it grew closer to the time Ranulf might appear.

"Did you get your legs spread again betwixt here and the village?"

"Do not be vulgar, Theo."

"Well, did you?"

"Nay, I did not," she gritted out.

He pulled her hair until her head bent back far enough so she could see him looking down at her. "Who are you wroth with, then, if not the giant?"

"Theo—"

"Tell, or I will go down and whisper in his ear that you are eagerly awaiting him—in bed."

"Do, and you take your life in your hands," she snapped, yanking her head back down.

That hint was sufficient and he said no more. But the ensuing silence only made Reina's nerves more raw. She decided he might as well know half of it.

"You had the right man, Theo, but the wrong reason. I thought I had Ranulf's agreement that he would give Louise de Burgh to Sir Arnulph in marriage. But at supper, he told not only Searle and Eric but Walter, too, to ride over and make the widow's acquaintance."

"So?"

"So I know now he means to give her to one of them, when I as much as had his promise just this afternoon that Arnulph could have her."

"He does not strike me as a man who would break promises lightly, Reina."

"He did not exactly promise," she said grudgingly. "But he knew I wanted the match, and he said he would consider Arnulph."

"Considering is not a firm decision, not by any means. It seems to me he is only preparing ahead does he decide against Sir Arnulph."

"You do not understand, Theo. He owes me his concurrence on this."

"How so?"

"Never mind how so, he just does," Reina said impatiently. "And Arnulph is the best man to place there. He has given us excellent service. He has proved himself most capable of such responsibility. He is deserving of a reward. And besides all that, he knows the lady and likes her, too. They are well suited."

"Ah, but what does she feel about it? Mayhap she

would appreciate having more than one man to choose from."

"Since when is that a matter of importance, especially when the lady is so young?"

"Need I remind you that you were not much older than Lady de Burgh when you very logically and rationally chose John de Lascelles and Richard de Arcourt as the men you would prefer to marry of all those you had to pick from? And not only that, you changed your mind at the last moment."

"Which proves that even at ten years and seven, a woman is an idiot if she thinks she knows what is best for herself," Reina said, her tone disgruntled.

"Now, now, you know the giant is still the best choice, even if you are having your first discord with him. You cannot expect him to agree with you always, Reina, any more than your . . . father . . . would . . ."

Reina glanced up as Theo's words trailed off into silence. Ranulf had entered without a sound and stood staring at them, his expression growing darker by the second. Lanzo stood just behind him, revealing a neck red with embarrassment as he gazed up at the ceiling.

Theo cleared his throat to get Reina's attention, and when that did not work, nudged her shoulder. Only then did she realize what was causing the reaction of the two at the door. Her bedrobe had slid open down her front to expose one breast and a goodly portion of navel.

With a gasp she yanked her robe closed, then glared furiously at her husband. That this should happen once was bad enough. Twice was just too much.

"A little warning ere you enter would not be amiss,

my lord,'' she bit out caustically. `` 'Tis called knocking.''

"At my own door? I think not."

"If you are alone, it makes no difference, but you are not alone."

"Neither are you, lady, and I will know the reason for *that* right quickly."

Too late she saw that he was not just scowling as was his usual wont. He was seething with anger, the cords of his neck taut with it, his violet eyes blazing with it. And those eyes were riveted on Theodric, not on her. But Reina was angry herself, and not just at being embarrassed again.

She came swiftly to her feet to demand, "Just what are you insinuating? You were apprised long ago that Theodric is my personal servant. Why else would he be here except to attend to his duties?"

"And what duties has he that have you sitting before him half naked?"

"Do not be stupid," she snapped. "He looks at me as he looks at you—nay, that is not right. He would rather look at you. Me he does not even notice, any more than Lanzo would notice you when he bathes or dresses you."

"Do you tell me *those* are his duties?"

"Of course."

"Not anymore, by God!" Ranulf snarled, and to Theodric, "Out!"

Reina stiffened and put out an arm to detain the boy. "You do not have to leave, Theo."

"*Jesú,* Reina!" Theo croaked behind her. "Do you *want* me to die?"

"He will not touch you."

"I would not wager on that, wife," Ranulf said,

the softer tone more ominous. "Do you think on it, you will recall that I owe him a thrashing that I will be most happy to administer is he not gone in . . ."

It was unnecessary to continue, Theo already having slipped under Reina's arm to bolt past Ranulf and out the door. Lanzo chuckled at the comical exit. Reina gave him a withering look before turning her back on the pair. She did not trust herself to speak just then. Her temper was that close to making her scream like an idiot.

"You may go, too, Lanzo," Ranulf said in a tone indicating his emotions were back under control. "My lady will help me disrobe."

"And have you accuse me of usurping another of his jobs?" Reina tossed over her shoulder with a baleful look. "Do not count on it, my lord."

"Is it not your duty to assist your husband in whatever manner he bids you?"

"Do not talk to me of duty after that childish display."

"You refuse?"

"*Jesú*, he understands," she said to the ceiling. "Thank you."

" 'Twould seem your Theo is not the only one long overdue a thrashing."

She had not heard him come up behind her, though he was so close his breath stirred her hair. She had not heard the door close either, but they were now alone.

"Mayhap you can frighten Theo half to death with that threat, but I am not so fainthearted."

"What threat? Do I deem it needful, I promise you will find it uncomfortable to sit down for at least a sennight.'' His hand came to the back of her neck to turn her around to face him. "Is it needful, Reina?''

"Are you asking for my permission?''

He grinned. "I would not be so foolish as to leave the matter for you to decide. I asked if 'tis needful. Do you intend more defiance?''

"Nay,'' she whispered resentfully, fainthearted after all.

"Good. 'Twas not in my mind to chastise you when I came in here. I had something altogether different in mind.''

She jerked away from him, her eyes flaring with suspicion. "You cannot mean . . . not after . . . how do you *dare* to think I—''

"So we had a little disagreement,'' he interjected with a shrug. " 'Tis over now.''

"Over? Little?'' she choked. "If that is how you see it, fine. 'Tis no more than I could expect from a barbarous lout. But you will not have your 'something altogether different' from me, not in the same day you had it from Red Alma!''

"Red . . You had best explain yourself right quickly, lady.''

"*Me?*'' she gasped. "You visit a whore, and I am to explain *myself?*''

"So that is the tick got under your skirt today.'' He grinned suddenly, then furthered her outrage by laughing. "And I told her you would not be that silly.''

"You told . . . silly?'' she sputtered. "Aye, then I must be, to think my husband would not shame me so openly.''

He shook his head at her, still grinning. "My lady, you were in nowise shamed—''

"And the pigs will fly on the morrow,'' she

snorted. "Best you inform the falconer to prepare for this wonder."

"—nor have you reason to be wroth."

"So I am to wonder daily whose bed I will find you in next, but never to say aught about it? Is that what you are telling me?"

"Did you find me in bed with the wench?"

"I found you with your hand stuck to her breast. Discussing the rent, my lord?"

Her sarcasm was getting more deadly. He had forgotten that she had appeared at Red Alma's door at just that moment.

"Actually, we were discussing you."

"Certainly." Her tone turned dry.

"The door was open, if you will recall."

"Which only proves what you told me was true. You do not care whether you have privacy or not. In the woods, in a whore's hut with the door wide open, what difference?"

She *would* have to remember that just now. "You know, little general, you could have saved yourself this jealous grief had you just answered my question yestereve. If you do not want me to lust after anyone but yourself, you should have said so."

"So you admit it?" she asked with little triumph.

"Do you?" he countered.

"Since you cannot be discreet, I suppose I must, though 'tis pointless after the fact," she replied bitterly. "And I was *not* jealous. I was appalled and humiliated, but not jealous."

"Very well, you were not jealous," he allowed, though his smile said he did not believe it. "You still could have avoided any upset at all by simply asking me what I was doing there."

"There is only one reason a man visits a whore."

"Then why did I only talk to her?"

"Talk?" she snorted. "As in putting your hands on her breasts?"

Instead of squirming in abashment, he chuckled. "How else was she to determine whether or not my touch would bruise you?"

"Me? You expect me to believe you caressed her for my sake?" she sneered. "Do you try again."

At last he frowned. "Was I in need of a woman, I would not have had to go to the village to find one. There are plenty here who would not tell me nay, including yourself. What I was in need of was an answer that only a woman of vast and varied experience might know. That is the only reason I sought out Red Alma, and that is all I got from her. Even when her answer aroused me, I did not stay to take advantage of her profession. But had I found you waiting outside, lady, you can be sure you would have had proof that you assumed wrongly."

She did not mistake his meaning, which brought color to her cheeks. And she believed him, unwisely or not, because she wanted to. Only that meant she had made an utter fool of herself with her accusation. She should be grateful he had not lost patience with her completely. But he was still frowning, which added to her present discomfit.

"Will you—" She had to clear her throat, nor could she meet his gaze just now. "Will you tell me what answer you sought?"

He took a step closer, and his voice was a low, husky rumble. "How I might pleasure you without hurting you."

Reina's head snapped up, hot indignation rushing back to the fore. "You asked her *that?*"

"Aye."

"But you have never hurt me."

"I have never touched you as I would like, either, too afeard that these hands would cause you pain when I lose control, as I have repeatedly done with you." He became exasperated at her doubtful expression. "Look at you! Do you know how breakable you seem to me? You are the tiniest, most delicate woman I have ever taken to my bed. Lifting you puts no more strain on me than lifting Lady Ella."

That was an exaggeration, but neither of them noticed as he grasped her beneath the arms and lifted her high to prove his point. She was looking down on him now, but he looked no farther than her chest, mesmerized by the parting of her robe. Both breasts were revealed, the large, dusky rose areolas in sharp contrast with the creamy white skin, the nipples puckering even as he watched, as if reaching for his lips. He obliged, bending his head just enough to taste one, and then sucking it deeply into his mouth.

Reina saw it coming when his eyes darkened to indigo, held her breath waiting, and now let it out in a soft moan. Her head rolled back as heat swirled in her belly. Her hands, lightly resting on his shoulders, reached up, fingers digging into his golden mane. That her body was not braced against his, was just dangling from his hands, was of no moment. Her limbs had turned to mush anyway. His remained rock-steady; even his arms still holding her aloft did not tremble.

He finally let go of her breast, only to lick his way to the other, drawing a deeper moan from her as he flayed this virgin nipple. The feeling became nearly unbearable it was so intense, but Reina would not have cried mercy even did she think to.

Then suddenly she was being lifted even higher. His lips did not leave her skin, pressing hot kisses across her belly, stopping briefly at her navel for his tongue to delve inside. She barely caught her breath from this onslaught when she was lowered again, slowly, with his tongue now licking a path from belly to neck, to cheek, finally into her mouth for a scorching kiss that curled her fingers and toes.

When he at last set her back on the floor, she would have crumbled at his feet were she not still gripping fistfuls of his hair. As it was, she collapsed against his body and hardly noticed when he untangled her fingers and lowered her arms to her sides, pushing her robe off her shoulders until it slithered to the floor. She did notice being lifted again, this time cradled in his arms, and vaguely knew where he was carrying her. But no other thoughts intruded through the misty haze of pleasure she was still feeling.

Nor did the pleasure abate. Even when he placed her on the bed and stepped back to strip off his clothes, the tingling continued as she watched him, his golden flesh revealed, the strength that had held her aloft for so long magnified in each ripple of muscle. She wanted to touch his skin, to taste him as he had her. She had never known such trembling anticipation. And when she met his eyes, still another thrill of sensation shot through her, for his eyes smoldered with passion, telling her, as she had already suspected, that this time would be different. But she could not have imagined how different.

When he joined her on the bed, his lips came to her again, tantalizing her with soft kisses, alarming her with rougher nips, inflaming her wherever they touched, until she was in a welter of heat and wanting. She was also thoroughly frustrated that he would not let her touch him as well, but held her hands firmly in his and would not release them.

At last he prepared to fulfill her need to have him inside her. He knelt between her legs, bestowed one more kiss on her quivering belly, and then . . .

"Ranulf, what . . . nay, do not . . . *nay!*"

He did, and it felt as if she shot right through the ceiling. Half her body did come off the bed, her back arching of its own accord, trying to escape the fire of his tongue where it had gone. But she could not, nor could she twist her hands free. She tried sitting up, only to have one of his arms press her back down and stay there, resting across her belly to keep her down and at his mercy.

He had none. He continued to taste the essence of her, burning away the shock and fear, to let a wild, primal satisfaction burst forth that was shocking in itself. This response seemed not her own, and yet she felt it, exulted in it, and, with helpless abandon, let it take her where it would, which it did right quickly. A new, glorious heartbeat exploded between her legs, wringing from her a cry to rival Ranulf's customary roar.

And while she floated on the breathless aftermath, he entered her, keeping her crested on a wave of pure sweetness as he surged to his own release. Only the wave unexpectedly built to tidal proportions, and at the last moment, her cry joined his in another burst of throbbing ecstasy.

Chapter Thirty-one

*I*t was rather a shock to wake up from a most pleasant sleep with a cat's rear end staring her in the face. Reina could not immediately comprehend what she was looking at, but the ghastly smell that assaulted her nostrils a moment later she had no difficulty identifying. She shrieked, leaping out of bed. But when she swung about to glare at the offensive creature reposing on her pillow, she was arrested by the sight of her husband.

Her outraged scream had awakened Ranulf, and with a warrior's reflexes, he was already standing on the opposite side of the bed with his sword in hand. That he was unable to figure out what had alarmed her was obvious by the questioning look he gave her, one golden brow crooked just so.

Reina's chagrin did not abate, was considerably added to instead by the fact that they were both standing there naked. Memories of yestereve also crowded into her mind to further vex her. So when he finally asked what had disturbed her, she did not care how foolish her answer might sound. The cat was to blame for this new embarrassment, and the cat would get the blame.

"That feline rodent farted in my face."

He did not laugh. She almost wished he had, for it might have relieved the tension the absurd situation was building. Instead, he very calmly returned his

sword to its scabbard and got back into bed. His lack
of any comment at all was enough irritant to prod her
temper. That he picked up Lady Ella and began to
pet her was the push over the edge.

"Well?" she demanded.

"Well, what? 'Tis a normal occurrence. Animals
fart just as we do."

"*She*"—Reina stabbed a finger at the culprit—"did
it apurpose!"

"Ridiculous. Why do you hate cats?"

"I do not hate cats. I love cats. I hate *that* cat, and
I refuse to sleep in the same chamber with her any
longer. Either she goes, or I do."

When he said naught, but simply stared at her as
if she had gone mad, Reina stormed out of the room,
pausing only long enough to swipe up her bedrobe
from where it had been left on the floor. Not until
she was out in the passageway did it occur to her that
she had nowhere to go. She had already given her old
chamber over to Elaine and Alicia to share, and did
not care to disturb the other women in their quarters
at this early hour either. Nor could she go below
dressed as she was. 'Twas only just dawn, but some
of the servants would have risen by now.

The torches in the passageway had burned out, and
the light coming through the deep window embrasures in the wall was barely discernible. 'Twas even
darker in the stairwell, but Reina moved in that direction anyway. The floor was cold, and at least sitting on the stairs she could wrap her feet in her
bedrobe. Hopefully no one would be coming up just
yet to find her there, nor going down, for she could
not think of a single excuse to explain a desire to sit

in the dark on cold steps wearing naught but a bed-robe.

After a moment her breathing calmed. It took a bit longer for the turmoil of her thoughts to quiet down, but when they did, she dropped her head to her knees with a groan.

I did not do that. Jesú, tell me I did not say or do any of that.

No divine voice answered, and Reina groaned again. Ranulf would think he had married a crazy woman, and not be far wrong. She had to be crazy to let her temper run amok like that, and for no good reason. Yesterday she had reason, or thought she did. This piece of idiocy had no excuse. So a cat was smart enough to wage a subtle war. No one would believe it. She would doubt it herself had she not seen Lady Ella's particular style of maneuvering ere this. And . . . *Jesú,* she was doing it again, making crazy excuses. No one in his right mind would attribute human motives to a cat.

Reina had to face it. She was jealous of Lady Ella—but with reason. That absurd ultimatum she had given Ranulf proved he cared more for his precious cat than he did for her, for she was the one sitting here on cold steps, while that feline was being cosseted in a warm bed—her bed.

Suddenly Reina started as something brushed against her thigh. Just barely, she saw a small dark shadow move on down the stairs. Lady Ella? But she had closed the door to the antechamber. How, then . . . ?

Reina tensed, her senses finally aware that her husband stood on the step just behind her. Now was the time to apologize, to beg him to forget this morn's

silliness, but no words could get past her mortification. It seemed to be becoming a habit, humiliating
herself in his presence, though she could not reason
why. But this time was the worst, and she was loath
to imagine what he must be thinking right now.

"Do you come back willingly, or do I carry you?"

She stood up and turned to face him. All she saw
was his silhouette, no expression to discern his
thoughts by. His low-pitched voice gave no clue either.

"What does that mean?" she asked hesitantly.

"It means I concede, little general. I would prefer
it did you try and tolerate Lady Ella, but if you cannot, you cannot. Henceforth she can sleep with
Lanzo."

Reina should have been magnanimous and said she
had not been serious, that he could keep his cat wherever he liked. But she had won, and without guilt to
aid her. The feeling was worth savoring without con-
cessions.

"Thank you."

"For what? You left me no choice."

She smiled to herself, for that was not exactly true.
He could just as easily have dragged her back and
forced her to accept his will regardless of her feelings
on the matter.

"You are not angry?"

He did not answer that, but stepped aside for her
to pass. Better she count her blessings and leave the
subject be. He had not sounded angry, though by
rights he ought to be. Men did not usually like ulti-
matums of any kind.

She tightened her robe against the chill of the stair-

well and moved up to his level—and found herself
scooped up into his arms. "I thought—"

"Be quiet," he interrupted. "I had not realized
you were barefoot."

What could she say to that? Her feet *were* terribly
cold. He had had sense enough to put shoes and
chausses on to come after her. She had just barely
thought to grab her bedrobe. This chivalry on his part
was unexpected, but nice. She would savor it, too,
while it lasted. Besides, she rather liked being held
in his arms.

Lanzo slept on, undisturbed by their comings and
goings through the antechamber where he nightly
spread his pallet. He was attuned to Ranulf's voice
raised in summons, but Ranulf had not once raised
his voice this morn.

The bedchamber had lightened up considerably
since Reina had left it, dawn giving way to sunrise.
Ranulf did not put her down until he reached the bed,
where he could set her. Only then did she glance at
his face to determine his mood. His grin was self-
explanatory.

"So that is why you are not angry. You found my
behavior amusing?"

He sat down next to her but avoided looking at her,
staring instead at his feet stretched out before him.
"I have had women fight over me before and throw
jealous tantrums, but never over my cat."

"Is that so?" she replied indignantly.

The laughter he had been holding in burst forth.
He fell back on the bed with it. He rolled from side
to side with it. He roared with it. Reina glanced
about for something to hit him with.

"I swear," he gasped out, clutching his stomach

now, but still laughing, "I have never seen . . . or heard anything so funny . . . as you accusing a cat . . . of farting just for your benefit!"

Had she really done that? 'Twas not even logical. Animals could not control such things any more than people could.

"I will allow I may have been hasty in that accusation. I should have said she would have done it apurpose if she could have."

That brought on another paroxysm of laughter. Tears were now streaming from his eyes. Reina had to bite her lip to keep it from curling. His humor had become infectious.

"Enough, Ranulf," she said in exasperation. "So I behaved like an idiot. You do not have to rub it in."

"Nay, not an idiot." He pulled her down next to him and leaned over her, smiling. "You were utterly delightful."

"And silly," she said, feeling warmed by the way he was now looking at her.

"Silly, aye. Know you that I have never before laughed like that? I am glad you are so silly, little general."

Her hand came up to wipe the moisture from his cheeks. "I am sorry."

"Why?"

"That you have had so little to laugh about in your life."

He caught her fingers and brought them to his lips. "Careful, lady, or you will find out firsthand what I do to women who wish to cosset me with sympathy."

"I know exactly what you do," she snorted. "You take complete advantage of their sympathy to lure them to your bed. A shameful male tactic."

"No more shameful than those female tactics you worked on me yesternoon, when you assumed I was suffering a guilty conscience."

"Never did I—" she started to deny, but his knowing grin brought an answering one to her lips. "It always worked on my father."

"I am not your father."

Her brow arched. "You do not care whether you have peace in your household or not?"

Reina tensed as he bent his head to grasp the edge of her bedrobe with his teeth and pull it open, then melted when his tongue slid out to swirl about the exposed nipple. When he glanced back at her, his eyes gleamed with male satisfaction.

"I believe," he said in answer to her question, "I have discovered a more delightful way to make peace."

"Mayhap you have," she agreed in a husky whisper, but then sat up and was able to add matter-of-factly, "But as we are already at peace . . ."

"Not so fast," he chuckled.

A finger in the neck of her bedrobe brought her back down. It also brought the opened robe off her shoulders. Both breasts were now visible, and the look on his face as he gazed at them told Reina this conversation would not continue much longer.

"Are you still angry that I sought out Red Alma?"

Reina squirmed uncomfortably. "You could have brought your question to me."

"Would you have told me how to pleasure you as I did?"

"How could I when I did not know such was even possible?"

"Neither did I."

His lips grazed her cheek on a path toward her mouth, but he did not kiss her. He ran his tongue tantalizingly over her lower lip until she was teased enough to press her lips to his. Then he leaned back, grinning.

"Now tell me you enjoyed it."

"You have doubt?" she asked incredulously.

"Nay, but I want to hear you say it. Say it, Reina." He punctuated the demand with another kiss, leaving his lips hovering just over hers. "Say it."

"I did—enjoy it."

"Do I do it again, you will not protest?"

"I did not say *that*. Ranulf, wait! 'Tis morn . . . daylight . . . sweet *Jesú,*" she ended with a blissful sigh.

Chapter Thirty-two

Reina snipped off the last thread and stood up, shaking out the finished garment for inspection. She had to smile. Trimming the blue velvet with strips of brocaded ivory silk had produced a bedrobe worthy of a king. Whether her husband would consent to wear it was the question, however, and not just because he was not used to wearing a bedrobe. All of his clothing was nondescript, plain woolens and linens without embellishments, most in need of repair. You could not accuse the man of being showy or ostentatious, even though he had long been able to afford grander clothing. That he preferred simple attire said a lot for his character.

She had indulged her own fancy with the bedrobe, since only she and the few servants allowed in the bedchamber would see him wearing it. The rest of the new wardrobe she intended making for him would be of fine quality, but much more modest—at least until she could accustom him to the idea that wealthy lords of the realm were expected to be grandiose, at least more splendidly arrayed than their own vassals.

The comments she had gotten from her older ladies as she was working on the bedrobe were typical ribbing for a new bride, and she had taken them in that vein.

"Are you sure you want to cover those magnificent shoulders in that?"

"I would be taking it off him, not putting it on."

"You will be sorry if he takes after my William and decides to sleep in his." That from Lady Margaret.

"If he is not used to wearing one, why tamper with a good thing?"

What they did not seem to realize, and Reina was not about to tell, was that having a man with a body like Ranulf's parading around the bedchamber in the altogether played hell on a woman's equilibrium, at least on hers. She did silly things when he was naked, like stare with brazen discourtesy, or accuse a poor cat of being spiteful. Before long she would succumb to the sensual urges all that golden skin manifested in her, to touch him, caress him, taste him, whether he bade her to or not. What would he think of her then? After all, his frequent bedding of her now was no more than a fulfillment of their bargain. Once she was with child, it would end.

Putting him into a bedrobe now was a safeguard to temptation. It assured that he would not think her pining away for loss of his body later on. If he had gone on as he had to begin with, there would have been no doubt of that. But his new techniques had gotten to her. *Jesú,* how they had gotten to her. And he knew it. He was also sweetly endearing in his delight over this great feat, a typical male reaction, she supposed, like a little boy winning his first victory against insurmountable odds. So it was up to her to make him believe she was still basically indifferent. She was going to come out of this with her pride, if naught else.

Reina draped the finished garment over her arm to take to her chamber. She would leave it on the bed for Ranulf to find. Hopefully he would feel obliged to wear it simply because 'twas made for him. If not, she would have to see about making the chamber drafty by removing some of the wall coverings. A little cold would curb his lack of modesty if naught else would.

"I would reconsider were I you," Dame Hilary called out in a singsong voice, setting the younger ladies to giggling.

Reina smiled despite herself. Were the circumstances of her marriage different, she would indeed reconsider. But she was not likely to forget that Ranulf had practically had to have his arm twisted ere he would agree to wed her. He might have new loverlike skills that he was inordinately proud of, but he would no doubt prefer to practice them on someone else.

"If you must give it him, lose your own," Florette suggested, straight-faced. "That will assure he will not wear his too often."

They finally managed to get the blush they were after. But before Reina could give a suitable reply, Wenda appeared in the doorway to interrupt the merry laughter. She was out of breath, with a hand to her chest indicating she had come at a run. Nor did she mince words once she had caught her breath.

"My lady, best you come quickly. Lord Ranulf's knights have returned, and two are grievously wounded."

There was not a single sound heard in the sewing room after that. Reina's heart had dropped with those first words, thinking something had happened to Ranulf. Why she should react like that she was not sure, but as her color returned, her mind turned efficient.

"Hilary, Florette, do you both come with me."

She tossed the bedrobe to Wenda. "Put that in my chamber when you fetch my medicaments. Margaret, do you gather what is needful and meet me below. Elaine, send someone after my lord. This will not await his return."

"Where is he?"

"In the village, I believe." *Making Red Alma rich,* she added to herself, for she was not sure Ranulf had been teasing when he had said the woman's advice was worth her weight in gold. "Florette?"

The young widow had not moved to join her, was in fact still staring ashen-faced at Wenda. "Was—was Sir Walter one of the wounded?"

"I know not, madam," Wenda replied. "They were still being carried into the keep when Master Gilbert sent me to fetch Lady Reina."

Florette's color did not improve with that answer, and Reina had to wonder if the lovely brunette had developed a tender for Walter de Breaute. Obviously, her own problems had made her lose touch with what was going on around her in her own home. She had not even been aware that Ranulf's men had left Clydon today.

"Florette, mayhap you had best remain here," Reina suggested, deciding the woman would be more hindrance than help if she did indeed hold Sir Walter in her affections and he was one of the two wounded. "Margaret can—"

"Nay, I need to know."

"Certainly, but—"

"Please, my lady, I was only surprised," Florette insisted. "I am fine now."

Reina hesitated, but finally nodded and left the sewing room.

Even before she reached the hall she could hear
Searle of Totnes blasting the men carrying him with
invectives. He had taken a pike in his thigh, and although the metal spearhead had been removed, he
had links from his mail chausses embedded in the
wound that were agitating it with each movement.
From the volume of his voice, however, she determined his condition was not as grievous as Wenda had
implied. Walter, on the other hand, and he was the
other man hurt, was unconscious. His color was not
good, and he was bleeding from more than one
wound.

Eric Fitzstephen followed behind them, and it was
to him Reina directed the questions she needed answering, while the bearers deposited the knights in
their separate chambers off the hall. "How long has
Sir Walter been bleeding?"

"Too long," Eric replied, his voice raspy with
worry. "He took that gash on his side early in the
fray, yet continued to fight. And we were a goodly
distance from Clydon when we were set upon."

"Did he fall from his horse when he received that
head wound?" she asked with concern. "I must know
if he has aught to tend from within."

"Nay, no cracked ribs or the like. That wound did
not fell him, nor the other. 'Twas the sight of his own
blood when 'twas over that—ah—"

"I understand," Reina cut in, realizing how difficult it was for one knight to claim another had fainted.
"Know you who did this?"

"We were on the woods road, my lady."

Explanation in itself, she supposed. "Very well. I
have sent for Ranulf. Best you have one of my ladies

attend your scratches ere he gets here, for he will want a full accounting of what happened.''

She found Florette already bent over Walter in his chamber. Her face was colorless again, but she was not rendered useless. Carefully, she was removing the makeshift bandage that had been wrapped about his head.

"Leave that," Reina said briskly. "The bleeding has stopped there, but his side still seeps."

"Will he—die, my lady?"

"Why should he do a fool thing like that?" Reina said, though until she saw the wounds, she could not really say for sure.

The most difficult task was removing Walter's heavy hauberk so they could get to the wound. It took two men to manage this with the least amount of movement. The rest of his clothes were quickly cut away, to reveal more clearly the extent of his blood loss.

Too long, Eric had said, and had not exaggerated. Walter's whole left side was soaked red clear down to his boots, the wound ragged and still dripping. The weapon, whatever it was, had pierced the hauberk just above the lowest rib. But instead of entering the body for a death wound, it had been deflected off the rib to slice a long tear straight across beneath his hauberk. 'Twas deep, but did not seem dangerously so; at least it would not be had it been closed up sooner. The danger now was in whether he had lost too much blood, and so would be too weak to fight off infection.

Reina worked swiftly, cleaning the wound and then applying a salve to immediately stop the blood flow. She let Florette do the stitching while she then saw to the head wound. This was just a small break in the skin, though there was a thick lump under it. A helmet could have prevented it, had he been wearing one at the time. As he was certain to have a splitting headache for a goodly number of days, he was not about to leave Clydon without a helmet again.

Walter did not awaken once, which was fortunate as there were so many stitches to apply, but 'twas not so easy getting the tonic she had prepared into him. She left Florette to see to that while she checked on the younger knight.

Searle's loud complaints, grown louder still while Hilary worked on him, were heard clearly in the next chamber. He had only quieted down now that she was almost done with him.

When he saw Reina, however, his voice rose again. "You are cruel, lady, to set this witch on me."

"That witch has gentler hands than I, sirrah, so be grateful I was too busy with Sir Walter to attend you myself."

That shut him up nicely and brought a chuckle from the stout dame. "Did you ever hear a boy make so much fuss over a little prick?"

"Little?" Searle choked.

"Only three stitches, my lady," Hilary informed her.

"So few? Sir Walter had nigh a full score. Did you hear him screaming for mercy?" Reina grinned then, taking pity on the young man now blushing. "Nay, Searle, we only tease you. Yelling ofttimes eases the pain. You should have heard my father when he would get a mere splinter from the exercise yard. We had to stuff our ears with cloth ere we could remove it."

"Is Walter—will he—"

"You have no need to worry over him. He is still

unconscious, but that is a good thing just now. His wounds were not as bad as they seemed, but they will be very painful once he rouses. Now drink this.'' She handed him a decoction of white poppy mixed in warm wine. '' 'Twill ease your own pain and put you to sleep, which is what you also need just now.''

''But Ranulf—''

''Eric can answer all his questions.''

At that moment, the door in the next chamber crashed open and Searle swiftly gulped down his tonic. ''How quickly will this work?''

Reina frowned at him. ''What is wrong with you?''

''He is going to be furious. I would just as soon sleep through it.''

''But why should he be angry, unless you three did wrong? Did you?''

''We have one dead and two wounded. There were only fifteen of them. We should have given a better accounting of ourselves, lady.''

''How many rode with you?''

''Six.''

Reina gave him a look of disgust. ''Go to sleep, lackwit. Hilary, see to it my lord husband does not come crashing in here to disturb him.''

''You do not ask for much, my lady.''

Hilary got a disgusted look, too, for her unneeded sarcasm. ''Very well, I will see to it myself,'' and Reina left, mumbling, ''*Jesú*, three to one is even odds? Does he think his men are all giants like himself?''

Eric slumped weakly against the wall outside Walter's chamber, apparently already having told Ranulf what had happened. The door was still open, and Reina became hesitant now on seeing Ranulf within.

He stood next to Walter's narrow bed looking down at him, his body so still it could have been made of stone, muscles bunched, fists clenched at his sides. She could not see his expression yet, but he must indeed be angry to have frightened Florette into leaving her patient, for she, too, was waiting without the chamber.

He still did not move or glance her way when she reached his side. "You cannot truly be angry with him for getting wounded, Ranulf. Think you he did it apurpose?"

"The fool knew he would be traveling through the woods, lady. He knew the place swarmed with brigands, and yet he only took three men-at-arms with him."

"But they were besides three knights fully armed. The outlaws rarely set upon travelers with any strength in their group."

"They did this time."

What could she say to that? So he did have reason to be angry. But when he finally looked at her, 'twas not anger she saw in his eyes, but a deep, terrible dread.

"My lady, please, do not let him die," he said with heartfelt gruffness. "Do you aid him to recovery, you will have my deepest gratitude."

Reina felt her throat tighten. She had the overwhelming urge to put her arms about him and assure him he had naught to fear. But sympathy and trite assurances were not the way to deal with this man.

"Whatever can you be thinking, my lord?" She made her voice deliberately stern. "Much as I would like to have you beholden to me for a time when I might find it useful to have you so, I must tell you

de Breaute is not dying. His wounds are trifling compared to some I have seen.''

"Then why does he not awaken?''

"Because I gave him something to make him sleep,
as I gave to Sir Searle. 'Tis the best way for a man
to get his strength back after losing a little blood. But
neither of them is so sorely wounded that he will not
be full of complaints at the long bed rest I will insist
on.''

She was not sure her husband would swallow that,
but after a moment he nodded curtly and left the
chamber. Reina sighed in relief that was short-lived
as she glanced down at Walter. He was still terribly
pale. No wonder Ranulf had thought him dying.

"Best you hear me, de Breaute.'' She bent over
him to whisper sharply by his ear. "You make me a
liar by dying now, and I will spend the rest of my life
praying you spend the rest of *your* life rotting in pur-
gatory. For whatever misbegotten reason you are dear
to him, for his sake you will recover right quickly.''

Whether he somehow heard her or not, she felt
better for having said it.

Florette was still hovering anxiously outside the
chamber, so Reina sent her back in, instructing her
to watch for fever and send for her at the first sign.
A glance about the hall found Ranulf in conversation
with Eric again, but Reina only heard the last of it as
she approached them.

"Send a messenger you can trust to the castellan
at Warhurst. Tell him does he send a large force after
the outlaws on the morrow at first light, he will at
last have them.''

"Will he?''

"Aye. After he chases them into our hands, he can

have whatever is left of them to do with as he pleases.''

Reina turned away ere Ranulf noticed her, not that he would call her to him if he did, when he had only bloodshedding on his mind. She had never heard him speak in quite that tone before, but knew that whatever it was he planned for the morrow, 'twas not something she wanted to know about. She could almost pity the outlaws, if they had not long needed getting rid of.

Chapter Thirty-three

*T*he overcast sky kept the heat at bay, but did naught to alleviate Ranulf's impatience as the morning progressed. They had left Clydon under cover of darkness in the middle of the night, and at intervals in small groups. Riding south first before turning back to circle the woods had been another caution, enough to satisfy him the trap would not be suspected.

There had been a total of sixty-eight horses at Clydon, and Ranulf took every one, including his wife's dainty palfrey. Still, the smaller men had had to ride two to a horse to accommodate the full hundred men he was utilizing and get them where he wanted before first light.

Eric and Sir Meyer had taken half the men east, Ranulf riding along the western edge of the woods. Being unfamiliar with the terrain had not been a detriment to the plan, at least on the western boundary. The stream that paralleled the woods here for about a league had a low enough bank to conceal the horses, even spread out as they were to allow for whichever point the outlaws chose to exit the woods. They needed that concealment for surprise, and he could only hope Eric had found a like concealment.

The wide field of oats running between the woods and the stream was newly planted, low enough not to give the outlaws any cover once they were caught in the middle of it. According to one of the Clydon men,

285

the field belonged to the widow de Burgh, so Ranulf did not feel the least hesitant in littering it with dead bodies and trampling the crop to do so. He had even considered sending a man to her manor to enlist what men she could spare, but decided against it for such easy sport. If and when Lord Rothwell came to see what had happened to his bride, or if there was any more trouble from Falkes de Rochefort, would be soon enough to call on his vassals for aid.

"Think you something has gone awry, Ranulf?" Kenric asked beside him. "Mayhap the men from Warhurst got lucky this time and caught them for us."

Ranulf did no more than grunt, for the thought had crossed his mind, too. The woods were only several leagues wide, so how long could it take a man running for his life to exit them? True, these outlaws were wily. They might be even now on the edge of the woods, cautiously watching for a trap ere they decided to make a run for the next stand of trees farther west.

And then he saw movement, though it took a moment for him to be certain. No wonder these men had eluded capture for so many years. Without horses, and dressed in the same colors of the woods, they could easily blend into the foliage around them, even get up a tree to become almost invisible. If their pursuers were not many, they really had no reason to leave the woods entirely. So Warhurst must have sent forth a large enough patrol to make them nervous enough to risk it.

There were now two men, now three. They were in no hurry. The first man turned about to say something to the others, while still more emerged from the woods. If they had scattered to run from the Warhurst soldiers, then they obviously had met up again before risking the open field, which was more than Ranulf could have hoped for. He had been half afraid they would come out singly and he would get only a handful or so, for stragglers would either see his men or hear something, and blend back into the woods.

Ranulf passed the word down the line to make ready, though the band of outlaws crossing the field was hard to miss now. Their numbers had increased until they were nearly fifty, odds more to Ranulf's liking. Thirty-four of his men would ride out to meet them. The rest were positioned with crossbows to take down any within range. He did not intend to lose a single one, and so being, he had to first cut them off from escaping back into the woods.

What ensued was a farce like to sicken a seasoned warrior. The element of surprise worked. To see a line of horsemen charging over an embankment right in front of them had the outlaws gaping for long, suspended moments ere they spurred their feet to turn about and run. They were reached just past the middle of the field, which undoubtedly made them lose heart, seeing the woods and escape such a long distance away. A goodly number were struck down in the pass to cut them off, but when Ranulf turned about, it was to find the entire band prostrated on the ground, what weapons they carried thrown away, and the whole lot of them screaming for mercy, as if they had long practiced this ploy.

Ranulf was disgusted, but short of outright slaughter, there was naught to do but accept their surrender. Yet he was not to be denied the retribution he was here for. Eric had said five of the group that had attacked them on the road had given up and run back into the woods when they saw they were losing the fight. He would have those five for hanging, as well as the leader of this bunch. The rest could be sent to Warhurst.

Ranulf dismounted and signaled Master Scot to tell him what he wanted. He did not have long to wait, but the brawny master-at-arms returned with only one man. Square jaw smooth, mustache neatly trimmed, brown hair even shorter than Ranulf's, he was not what one might imagine an outlaw to look like. There was nothing even to indicate he lived out-of-doors. He was not filthy. His clothes were in decent repair. And if he had moments before been crying for mercy with the rest of them, there was no fear in his gaze now, which was entirely too direct.

"Claims to be their leader," Master Scot said, though Ranulf had already come to that conclusion.

"Know you who I am?" he asked the outlaw.

"I make it my business to know all my neighbors and what they are about, Lord Fitz Hugh, new and old."

"That would indicate you have some intelligence, yet if that were so, you would have watched and waited until you learned my mettle ere you attacked me or mine," Ranulf replied harshly.

"So I did. I had men watching Clydon and both roads to its gates. The men who attacked those wearing your colors were not mine. They had followed your men whence they came and waited until they were well inside the wood to set upon them."

"Followed with horses, but attacked without?" Ranulf scoffed, then added in a lower, more menacing tone: "Do not think you can weave fanciful tales to color yourself guiltless. You know not where my men come from or you would not try to place the blame there.''

''They came from the narrow track that allows anyone from Keigh Manor to reach either Warhurst or Clydon without going leagues out of the way taking the western road, both your men and those who followed them. I know that much, for one of my men was hunting in that area and saw them coming out of the track. Whether your men had been to Keigh Manor or beyond that, as you say, I do not know. But the woods road does not travel a straight line, Lord Fitz Hugh. It turns this way and that to avoid the older trees in its path. According to my man, those who followed kept well inside the tree line, and when the sharpest curve in the road was reached, they cut a straight path through it to come out ahead of your men, left their horses concealed in the bush, and ran to intercept them. 'Tis unreasonable, as you bethought, to attack without horses, especially against mounted riders, unless you want someone else blamed for the deed, someone known not to possess horses.''

''Yourselves?''

''I see you are still doubtful, but common sense would have arranged a better ambush. There are several points along the road where trees overhang and the foliage is thick. I would have placed my men there, on both sides of the road, even along the tree limbs above, to come at my target from all sides for a quick end to it, and assured success. But ask your men and they will tell you it happened much differently. They could have easily turned about and ridden away instead of fighting.''

''John!'' Ranulf bellowed.

The man-at-arms who had ridden with Walter yes-

terday was near enough that Ranulf did not have to
ask the question. " 'Tis true, my lord. They came all
at once at a run and from only one side of the road,
giving enough warning that we could indeed have ridden on in either direction to avoid them. Now that I
think on it, 'twas not well done for men supposedly
adept at robbery.''

"Where is the Clydon man?'' Ranulf called out.

"Here, my lord.''

"Algar, is it not?'' At a nod, Ranulf asked, "What
think you of this brigand's story?''

" 'Tis true enough, what he says of his methods.
All the robberies we have heard tell of, the victims
claim the outlaws surrounded them in moments, even
falling from the sky. They rarely have time to draw a
weapon, yet we had time and plenty to do so.''

"Could you have been followed from Keigh Manor
and not know it?''

"Aye,'' Algar admitted, if a bit reluctantly. "Truth
is, we were none of us paying overmuch attention to
the road. We were laughing so much we were not like
to have heard anyone following behind either.''

"Explain yourself.''

"Sir Searle had seemed well and truly taken by the
widow, and your other two knights were wont to rib
him about it, especially since she did not return his
interest.''

Ranulf had not thought to ask ere this how they
had been received at Keigh Manor. Their reason for
going there had been forgotten in light of the outlaws'
attack—if it had been the outlaws who had attacked.

"How was Lady de Burgh otherwise?''

"Now you mention it, my lord, I remarked to Wat,

God assoil him, that the lady seemed different from when last we saw her at Clydon.''

"How so?"

"She was courteous enough, but her manner was right chilly. Her being a woman in need of a husband, you would think she would welcome three handsome knights with gladness, but she was more glad to see them depart."

"Was she told why you were there?"

"Sir Searle might have told her. As I said, he was fast smitten."

"Did he insult the lady?"

"With declarations of undying love?"

"So he was a bit tactless," Ranulf snorted. "What had the lady against Eric and Walter, or were they likewise offensive?"

"Not at all, which is why her manner was so strange."

"Can you think of a reason why she might behave so?"

"I might." This from the outlaw, not the least hesitant in gaining Ranulf's attention again. "Rumor has it Louise de Burgh has set her affections on William Lionel, one of her household knights. With a husband firmly in mind, would she welcome other prospects?"

"How would you know this?" Ranulf demanded.

The man shrugged. "We have our ways of learning things, just as we knew of your first coming, just as we knew who it was you sent fleeing from Clydon that morn."

"We already know who attacked Clydon."

"Do you, my lord?"

It was said in such a way as to leave no doubt that

the outlaw knew something that Ranulf did not, and Ranulf had never been one to enjoy being toyed with. In a trice, he had the man lifted by the front of his leather jerkin to bring them eye to eye.

"Best you spit it out right quickly, ere I recall why I had you summoned to me."

"They fled to Warhurst!"

"You lie," Ranulf hissed. "I have it on good authority the castellan there is an imbecile. Did he not prove it by accepting a message last eventide and acting on it without knowing from whom it came? The proof is that you are here."

"He is as you say, but his lord is not, and Lord Richard was in Warhurst all that week, as well as on the road that morn with a large troop of men, none of whom wore his colors, nor did he. I saw him myself returning to Warhurst with a wound on his right shoulder. I am not like to mistake the man who had me outlawed for the simple reason that he coveted my wife."

Ranulf slowly set the man down. Then to the bafflement of his men and their prisoners, he burst into laughter. Could his little general have erred that badly about the man she had hoped to wed? Could the lordling have erred that badly, wanting her, unaware that she wanted him, too, deciding to take her by force? Christ's toes, that was rich!—if it was true. He sobered, eyes narrowing on the outlaw.

"You are a veritable font of information, Master Brigand."

The man drew himself up stiffly now that color was returning to his cheeks. "What I know of the de Burgh widow is merely rumor and speculation. She is young and still a child in many ways. I would be the first to doubt she sent her men after yours. Yet I do know my men were not involved, and those who were came from the direction of Keigh Manor. The answer is no doubt simple—I just do not myself see it, or pretend to know it. What I know of Richard of Warhurst, however, is truth.''

"So you say, but you have yourself admitted to having good reason for blackening his name," Ranulf pointed out.

"So I have—so does every man with me. He is a man with a powerful father, and so he thinks he is above the law. In Warhurst he is, for there are none to gainsay him. If anyone tries, they quickly find themselves joining our band."

"You are saying you are all of Warhurst?"

"Aye, banished without fair hearing and denied our families. If not by Lord Richard, then by his castellan or those fat merchants in his favor, who all liken their ways to his, charging a man falsely because they want something of his or simply do not like him. And all that I have said can be proved by questioning anyone at Warhurst."

"If that is so, then why did you never seek redress in the shire court?"

"Against a lord, and one who still holds our families within the walls of his town, subject to his whims?"

Ranulf grunted. He knew the power of petty tyrants firsthand. Montfort was one.

"You are no villein. What were you in Warhurst?"

"Lord Richard's clerk," he replied in disgust. "Not even my knowledge of his ill-gotten gains prevented him from getting rid of me."

Ranulf's brow rose. "Ill-gotten gains, as in stolen cattle and sheep?"

"Aye, that, too, among other things."

"As in *Clydon's* stolen cattle and sheep?" Ranulf clarified.

"I know not where the stock came from, only that 'twas taken north for sale."

"Tell me one thing more," Ranulf demanded. "Why has no one in Clydon suspected this lordling's tyranny, when they are such close neighbors?"

"Why should they? The lady herself has no need to frequent the Warhurst markets; her own merchants at Birkenham supply all her needs, so she would not hear any complaints. But Lord Richard would ofttimes visit Clydon, and he is a different man when he leaves his little kingdom, a man adept at fooling anyone who does not truly know him into believing there could not be a nefarious bone in his body. He is young, clever, and has been Lord of Warhurst only these four years past. If the lady or her father had ever heard rumors about him, they would be quick to defend him, not believe them. You will yourself doubt all I have said do you meet him, for he has that effect on people, appearing trustworthy and virtuous when he is anything but."

"I do not have to meet him to doubt you, sirrah. All you have said is in doubt, or did you assume I would blindly accept the word of an outlaw as truth? But your tale has put off your hanging for the while, at least until I hear what Lady de Burgh has to say of this. Do I find you have done me no harm, I will then look to the rest of your tale."

Chapter Thirty-four

Louise de Burgh stood in the open doorway of her hall, staring in horror as man after man rode through her gate to crowd into the bailey. She had been told Lord Fitz Hugh had come, but told too late to close the gate against him. Not that that would have kept him out, she realized now as his men continued coming, fifty, sixty, still more, and she saw the giant among them, sitting his huge destrier that refused to stand still, staring directly at her.

She saw one man she recognized, Sir Eric Fitzstephen. At least he was not dead. But what of the other two who had come with him yesterday? Did their absence mean they had not survived the ambush?

God help her, she must have been mad. She had known it not long after she had sent her men to attack those knights. She had sent another to call them back, but it had been too late. And now her overlord had come for retribution, and 'twas all Searle of Totnes' fault, that wretched cur. If he had not told her Lord Ranulf would give her to him did he but ask, and that he would ask, she would not have been driven by anger to do something so stupid.

Of course, she could blame William, too, for proving so difficult and refusing to marry her. Had she been wed already, Searle of Totnes could not have upset her. But she could not blame William. She loved him. In time she could have convinced him that they were right for each other. Now it was too late.

Or was it? Lord Fitz Hugh might have come with a small army, but could he know for certain what she had done? How could he know if she did not confess? The men who returned yesterday, few in number, would never admit their guilt either. And William, who might be guided by his cursed honor to tell all, did not know. She need only . . .

"Louise de Burgh?"

She nearly jumped out of her skin. He had not dismounted, had not even drawn near. His voice carried across the yard like a trumpet.

She would have to shout or approach him to answer. She preferred to do neither, and for now simply nodded.

"Is this all the men you have, lady?"

Louise glanced about to see that everyone had come out to get a look at the new Lord of Clydon, even the servants. But of course they had naught to fear of him; at least they did not think they did. William was there, too, standing with the men-at-arms, and frowning at Lord Fitz Hugh's manner. These were the men Fitz Hugh referred to. She had only twelve here at Keigh Manor after losing ten yesterday.

Before she could nod again to answer his question, Lord Ranulf demanded, "Which of you is William Lionel?"

Louise came down the steps then, at a run. "What do you want with Sir William?" she cried. "He was not even here yester . . . day . . . ."

'Twas too late to take back the words that as much as condemned her, if the look Lord Ranulf gave her now was any indication. He dismounted at last, and

Louise paled to see that he really was a giant, and coming straight toward her. She would have run were she not paralyzed with terror that he meant to kill her right then.

"I would have sworn 'twas not you, lady. When Eric suggested 'twas more like to be your man Lionel acting on his own to eliminate any competition, I was inclined to agree, even though he did not recall meeting the man."

Ranulf had not expected Eric to show up just as he had dispatched half his men to escort the prisoners to Clydon and was about to ride for Keigh Manor with the rest. But as Eric had told him, there was no point in his waiting any longer for the outlaws to emerge from the woods on the east side, when the patrol from Warhurst had done so. So he had ridden straightaway to join Ranulf with the rest of their men, and after hearing the outlaw's story, was quick to defend the widow.

"She is beautiful," Eric had told him. "Did Searle not fall to Cupid's bow so quickly, I might have asked for her myself. A man could easily be driven to murder for want of her, and this knight of hers no doubt saw his chances threatened when he learned why we were there."

So Ranulf had been tempted to believe, but it just was not so. He should have stayed with his instincts that would doubt any lady first and foremost, simply because they were all deceitful and capable of treachery. And she was lovely, this one, with her corn-silk hair and eyes like sapphire, young, and afraid—with good reason. He ought to hang her, but he supposed his little general would object to that.

"What is this about, Lord Fitz Hugh?"

Ranulf turned to face the knight he had noticed earlier, and assumed rightly that this was Sir William Lionel. Tall and handsome, with sooty black hair and keen gray eyes, he supposed the man could easily inspire passion in a lonely young woman. The question was, who wanted whom?

"Your lady decided she had too many suitors and ought to kill off a few," Ranulf replied in disgust.

"That is a serious charge, my lord."

"She is guilty all the same."

"Not until proven, and I will stand her champion to decide the matter."

Ranulf's interest perked immediately. He looked the man over more carefully. He was big enough, near six feet, brawny enough, and willing. Ranulf had been denied the fight he had waited half the night and all morning for. Would he have it now?

"Against me?"

There was a start of surprise, but Sir William quickly recovered and tendered a curt nod. Ranulf's smile came slow and was chilling in its implication. Lady Louise promptly burst into tears and threw her arms around William's neck.

"You cannot fight him, not him! Please, William, I did naught—at least he cannot prove it. And Lady Reina will protect me."

"Stop it," William said harshly and set her aside.

"But he will kill you!"

"You should have thought of that ere you acted with your usual childish impetuosity."

He turned away from her then and walked to the center of the court. Ranulf nodded to Eric to restrain the lady should it be necessary and went to join him. There was a short wait while Sir William's squire went to fetch his helmet so he would be as fully armored as Ranulf, but once it was donned, Ranulf drew his sword and attacked.

The hope was strong that for once he had a worthy opponent, and William Lionel did acquit himself well at first. His movements were swift, his instincts good, his blade or shield blocking every swing. But that was all he was able to do. As usual, Ranulf's offensive gave no opportunity for counterattack. His powerful blows continued nonstop until Lionel was brought to his knees by sheer exhaustion, unable to raise his shield even once more.

He bowed his head, awaiting the death blow, too done in to overmuch care. He heard Ranulf sheathe his sword instead and looked up with surprise. The giant was grinning, his breathing labored only the slightest degree. William shook his head in bemusement and chagrin.

"It does you no merit to enjoy this win, when the lady's fate hung in the balance."

Ranulf laughed at the man's misconception. "I have done naught to turn your belly, sirrah. The lady's fate was set whether you fought for her or not."

"Then why did you accept my challenge?"

"I needed the exercise. With my usual partner bedfast thanks to the lady's treachery, 'twill be long ere I have someone capable of standing against me. But you do not ask after her fate. Did you love her so little?"

"I love her not at all. She might be comely, but she is a spoiled, vain child and much too willful for my liking."

"Did you know she wanted you?"

"Aye, but I never encouraged her. Far from it. I

did all I could to show her I was not interested, including begging leave to depart her service. She would not believe me.''

"Then why stand her champion?"

"She might be a spoiled little bitch and foolish in the extreme, but I am still her man until she releases me."

Ranulf bit back another chuckle at the rancor in those words. "Very commendable. I can use a man of such convictions in my own service, are you willing. But as for the lady's fate, Sir William, you need have no further concern. She will be wed to my own man who will assure she makes no more mischief. She may not like it, but she will learn loyalty to her overlord even if her bottom must suffer in the teaching."

"A lesson she should have had long ago," William snorted in full agreement.

Ranulf turned away then, tossing his helmet to Kenric. His eyes happened to light on the widow, who was too far away to have heard what was said of her. She was pale, anxious, and fair trembling with fear now that her champion had failed to acquit her through combat. But as he approached to tell her of his decision, he watched her change with her first clear sight of his face. Her expression softened, her body relaxed, her eyes turned sensual in appraisal, and he could almost hear the wheels turning in her mind. He had seen that look too often to mistake it, the look of a woman about to seduce a man to get what she wanted.

"Do not even think it, lady," he growled at her and turned about again.

She could wait until Searle was recovered enough

to come here and tell her her fate. She could stew with worry in confinement until then, which was far less than she deserved for the lives she had cost. Had her mischief not led to other discoveries, he would not be even that lenient.

Chapter Thirty-five

"*He* comes, my lady."

Reina did not need to hear more. She ran from her chamber and down the stairs, across the hall, down more stairs and still more, reaching the bailey just as Ranulf dismounted. With no thought to the war-horse whose reins he still held, she charged forward and threw her arms about Ranulf's neck.

Hearing him swear most foully was the first indication she should not have been so impulsive. Feeling his whole body jerked by the reins was the second. And then she heard the horse as it geared up to do what it did best, stomp anyone foolish enough to run toward it, including its master. Reina gave a small gasp and let go to scurry out of the way.

Ranulf was furious by the time he finally got the animal under control. But one look at Reina's ashen face, reminding him of Louise de Burgh's fear of him, and he tucked his anger away to draw from at another time. He walked to his wife and picked her up.

"That was a fool thing to do, lady," he said simply.

"I know. Stupid and thoughtless and it will not happen again."

"Good," he replied, still quietly. "Now do you tell me why you did such a stupid, thoughtless thing."

Her eyes lowered shyly, while her hands hesitantly touched his shoulders, slowly slipped around them, until she was again clinging tightly to his neck. "I was worried," she whispered by his ear. "When the men returned with prisoners and said where you had gone and why, I became afraid. I remembered William Lionel, and he is no small man. I was afeard you would fight him and might be hurt."

The shaking, she discovered after a moment, was laughter. It very effectively dashed her concern and replaced it with chagrin. So, too, did the tight squeeze she got before she was set back on her feet.

"Do not be silly, woman."

The grin he gave her was all the prod her temper needed. "Aye, I must be to worry over a lackwitted lout with no more sense than to ride into a place suspected of treachery with so few men at his back!"

"Eric's men had joined up with me ere we got there." He was still grinning.

"Oh," Reina said, but was not completely satisfied. "Still, you should have waited."

"For what purpose? I was there and had ample men to go up against a mere handful. And as for Lionel, he might be a man of considerable size, but look at me, Reina, and tell me which of us you would place your wager on."

She gave him a sour look for that piece of conceited logic. "It takes only one man with one arrow to fell a giant, Ranulf. You are not invincible."

"Mayhap not," he agreed. "But I am not an idiot either. I have been taking keeps and defeating armies for other men these past seven years. Think you I will be careless now that I fight for myself?"

"I suppose not," she grudgingly conceded.

"Then what were you worried about?"

"A woman does not need a reason to worry," she retorted irritably. "I felt like worrying, so I did."

"Lady, before you go much further and make even less sense to me, I have to tell you I am not much longer on my feet. You should be offering me a bath, a meal, and a bed, instead of railing at me for a good day's work. Do you know how long it has been since I last slept?"

Hot color flooded her cheeks. "Sweet *Jesú*, why did you let me go on like that? Come inside, my lord, and you will have what you desire."

He stared at her hips swaying as she preceded him up the stairs and shook his head. He wished she had not used those particular words. For once he was too tired to take advantage of them.

Reina was not sure what had awakened her, but she was immediately aware that the bed was empty beside her, even before she turned to see that it actually was. She felt a moment's qualm, followed by a start when she saw that Ranulf was still there in the room. But where he was, leaning against the post at the foot of the bed, the bed curtains pushed out of his way for an unobstructed view of her, brought back her disquiet. So, too, did his nakedness, bathed bronze in the light of the night candle. If he had noticed his new bedrobe draped over his clothes chest, he had ignored it.

"Is something wrong, my lord?"

"Nay."

"Then what are you doing just standing there?"

"Watching you sleep," he said simply, adding just as simply, "You snore, you know."

Her mouth dropped open, but she was quick to snap it shut. "I do not!"

"Aye, you do. Not loudly, but 'twas snoring just the same."

What a terrible thing to tell a woman, and rot him, she could not even say the same about him. "Thank you. I would have been aggrieved had I gone on much longer without learning that."

He chuckled. "Do not be wroth with me, little general. I am still wallowing in the glow of your earlier concern. No one has ever taken such tender care of me as you did."

How could she be wroth with him after hearing that? "I did no more than bathe and feed you."

"And warmed my wine and my sheets, and covered the windows to darken the room, and chased all your ladies below so no noise would disturb me at that early hour. Lady, you even tucked me in ere you tiptoed from the room."

Was he teasing her or thanking her? Reina blushed all the same. She thought he had been asleep by then, he had been so tired. And she was so relieved that he had come home without even a scratch that it had been a pleasure to make him comfortable. But had he really never been tucked into bed before? That urge to put her arms around him and just hold him was back again, but he was no child to comfort, and she was being silly even wanting to.

"I thought surely you would sleep through to the morn, my lord. Did something disturb you?"

Aye, you did, he thought to himself, *snuggling up close to my body.* But he had already made her blush once, so he would not say so.

"Nay, a few hours was enough to restore me. I am

not yet adjusted to the luxury of having a normal night's sleep. Yet I was so tired, I did not ask of Walter. How does he fare?''

"He awoke and started complaining, as I predicted he would." At least this time she spoke true. "Will you tell me now what happened at Keigh Manor?''

"You mean you did not pester my men for that information once I was abed?''

His knowing grin was annoying, but after a moment she returned it, conceding, "So Eric told me, also that you did fight Lionel.''

"And?'' he prompted.

"Very well, so there was no contest and I had no reason to worry,'' she said grudgingly. "But I told you a woman does not need good reason.''

"That you worried at all, lady, is what intrigues me.''

"Think you I want to go through the trouble of choosing another husband?'' she retorted.

"Then you are pleased with your present husband?''

"Satisfied.''

He gave a rumble of laughter. "A word of many meanings, that.''

Reina gritted her teeth. "You have strayed from the subject, my lord. Eric did not say what you intend doing with Lady Louise.''

He came forward to sit on his side of the bed. For a moment she stared at his broad back, and the strength indicated there gave her a pleasurable shiver that sent her thoughts straying from the subject as well. Then he leaned back on one elbow placed next to her hip, and she was surprised by how serious his expression had become.

"The widow will remain confined in her chamber until Searle is well enough to wed her—that is, if he still wants her after learning of her perfidy."

Reina stiffened. "Then you did not even consider Sir Arnulph as I asked?"

"Nay, I did not. I have Birkenham in mind for him."

"But that is too much!" she gasped in amazement.

"Why, if he is as loyal as you say and acceptable to me once I meet him?"

"But—but I thought you would give it to Walter."

"He does not want it."

"I know he said that, but surely he was jesting."

Ranulf smiled. "He was most serious. He knows that I will always have a place for him without weighing his shoulders down with responsibilities, which he does not want. Did I try to do so, he would just as soon go home, where he is welcome and would not be asked to do aught more than fight when he is needed."

"Then why did you send him to Keigh Manor?"

He shrugged. "To keep the younger two lads from coming to blows over the lady if they both decided they wanted her."

"And what if he had taken a fancy to Louise?"

"That would have been unlikely, as Walter has already shown a keen interest in one of your ladies here, or had you not noticed?"

"Eadwina is not a lady."

He chuckled at her indignant snort. "Not her. His interest in her is no more than a necessity. A man must still see to his needs while he is contemplating marriage. Or would you countenance his sneaking into Dame Florette's bed?"

"I countenance neither action, if you must know. I do not see why a man cannot control his lustiness for a short time. If Walter wants Florette, and I can assure you she would be delighted to have him, why can he not wait until they are wed? You did." For the second time, she saw her husband's face flush with color, and concluded, feeling unreasonably hurt, "You did not?"

He heard the catch in her voice and put his hand to her cheek. "Lady, would I have been so impatient to have you after that second wedding ceremony if I was bedding one of your wenches? But I was annoyed enough with you for closing your door to me that I will not deny I thought about it. And if you say thinking about it is just as bad, I will beat you."

She grinned helplessly, knowing full well he did not mean it, and too relieved to care if he did. "Nay, I would not say that, or else every man alive must be condemned."

" 'Tis good you can be reasonable," he grunted and sat up again.

He also knew she trusted him not to beat her, but he was not sure if that was good or not. How did you control a wife who did not fear reprisals? If he ever did see the need to punish her, she was like to feel betrayed and never forgive him, and that was not worth any lesson she needed learning. But why he should feel that was so was the question.

"Is something wrong, Ranulf?"

"I have just recalled the prisoners," he said gruffly, disturbed by the direction in which his thoughts had gone and needing a distraction. "Where were they put?"

"In one of the wall towers. I must say I was surprised to see them brought in."

"Why?"

"I did not think your plan would work after you changed your mind about sending a messenger to Warhurst, to send a letter instead, and that unsigned. Only a complete fool would act on such unreliable information."

"I counted on the castellan being the imbecile you claimed him to be, and so he was."

"But why take that chance?"

"I did not care to be cast as the fool if the plan went awry."

She had to force back a smile at that bit of vanity. "Oh, very wise, my lord."

He frowned, sensing her humor anyway. "Wise or not, lady, it still worked. And because I did send only a message, Warhurst is unaware that I was even involved, or that I now have the outlaws."

"Yet I heard you say you meant to turn them over to Warhurst. You have changed your mind about that, too?"

"For the while."

"Do you tell me you mean to hang them yourself?"

"You need not sound so appalled, lady. Do they deserve to hang, they will hang. But I am inclined to believe a lesser punishment is called for, or even none at all, if what they said about Warhurst is true. 'Tis that truth I mean to get at on the morrow."

"But you cannot believe aught from an outlaw," she protested.

"So I thought, yet what their leader had to say about Keigh Manor proved true enough."

"And what have they said about Warhurst?"

"Only that your esteemed Lord Richard has been there these past weeks, that he left Warhurst with a large force the same morn I found a large force attacking Clydon, and that he returned to his town that same morn, wounded. The man had a lot more to say, but . . . You laugh? I fail to see aught humorous in what I said."

She tried to control it, but another peal of laughter rang out. It was his steadily increasing glower that finally sobered her, though not completely.

"Tell me you did not give credit to that ridiculous tale."

"And why is it ridiculous?"

"For what possible reason would Richard attack me?"

"For the same reason you thought Falkes de Rochefort attacked you."

"To marry me?" She grinned. "You forget I was willing to marry Richard."

"Nay, I do not forget. But tell me, Reina, did he know it?"

That sobered her completely, and that he was obviously pleased to have made that point annoyed her as well. "Whether he did or not, you will never convince me that Richard would do me harm. You do not know him, Ranulf. He is the most affable, sweet-natured—"

"Is he?" He cut her off with a sneer. "You are so certain of that? What if he is a completely different man inside the walls of his little kingdom? Have you ever seen him inside Warhurst, to know how he behaves there, or how his people behave toward him?"

He went on to tell her the rest of what the outlaw had

to say of her Lord Richard, ending, "What if even a
little of that is true?"

"Because an outlaw says so?" she scoffed. "Of
course he would tell you true about Keigh Manor
when you were after his neck and he knew it. And
since that worked out so well for him, he spun another tale of injustice done him to work on his next
hope, full freedom, which you have already admitted
you are considering. Oh, he is a clever one. But you
will not convince me that Richard is aught but good.
And I know why you want to believe this nonsense."
She did not even give him a chance to challenge that
statement, but went on heatedly. "For the same reason you delighted in belittling Lord John. You want
me to be ever grateful that I got you instead of one
of them. But I am grateful for that, so you do not
need—"

He put a sudden stop to this tirade by rolling over
and landing half on top of her. A finger across her
lips kept her from even gasping, while he grinned
unabashedly.

"You have worked yourself into a huff for naught,
lady. I did not say I believed any of that, only that I
meant to get at the truth. Do you say your Richard is
a saint, I will consider it so until I see proof to the
contrary. But let us now examine this gratitude you
have just confessed to having. Does it carry with it
certain benefits?"

When Reina saw the direction his thoughts had
taken, as well as his eyes, she could not get any words
past her throat. Her breasts tightened under his gaze,
and she flushed hot. When his eyes came back to
hers, she could only stare, drowning in the look she
now recognized.

She waited breathlessly for his mouth to begin its magic, and so was surprised when his hand covered her breast instead, his eyes still locked to hers. His fingers were warm, and gentle, and infinitely exciting, teasing her nipples to hardness, giving her the tiniest alarm when his grip began to strengthen, intensifying the thrill when it relaxed.

Still he watched her, and listened to her gasping breaths, and finally whispered, "Am I hurting you?"

"Nay."

"You would tell me?"

"*Jesú,* are you going to start that again?"

She heard his laugh just before his tongue came to lick at her lips, and during the course of the next hour, Reina managed to demonstrate those benefits he had asked about with a good deal of mutual pleasure.

Chapter Thirty-six

Reina saw the giant crossing the hall toward her with her steward, but she doubted her eyes, knowing very well that Ranulf was still abed, his few hours' restorative sleep having turned into the rest of the night and the entire morning besides. She had just come from the kitchen to delay the midday meal because of that, and Theo, who had not left the hall until her return, had shaken his head when asked if she had missed Ranulf.

So if not her husband striding toward her, then there were two as huge, when she would have sworn there could not possibly be another as tall and broad and fearsome. And as happened when she first met her husband, she saw only this man's size. She did not notice his face until he had almost reached her, and then that golden mane of hair when he shoved back his coif. Gilbert must have introduced them ere he slipped away, but Reina was too bemused to hear a word of it.

Golden hair and skin, deep violet eyes, a face the same—Ranulf's, but not Ranulf. 'Twas too incredible by half. Was this his brother, then? Nay, he had said the brother was younger. This man was older, though not by much. Surely he could not be old enough to be the father, and yet he must be. But no loving father this, and recalling that, she also recalled her outraged reaction when Ranulf had told her about this man.

" 'Tis all right, Lady Reina. I ofttimes have this affect on women."

A line he must say by rote, meant to ease a lady's embarrassment for being rendered deaf, blind, and dumb by his extraordinary looks. But he had the wrong reason this time, and Reina could be excused for her shock. 'Twas not every day you met an older, identical version of the man you had wed.

"Are you here to see Ranulf?"

"Ranulf?" 'Twas his turn to appear bemused, but then he smiled, understanding. "So that is why you stared. The resemblance. 'Tis uncanny, is it not?"

"Very," she replied, still not quite believing two men of different years could look so much alike.

"But I was unaware Ranulf was even in this area. Last I heard, he was fighting for one of the marcher lords. Of course, that was last year, and he does not like to stay in one place very long."

How would he know that? According to Ranulf, he had spoken with this man only twice in his entire life. Did the man like to pretend a familiarity and fatherly concern just because anyone who saw him and knew Ranulf could not mistake they were father and son?

"That may have been his habit, but he is not like to leave Clydon anytime soon," Reina said stiffly.

The man seemed confused by her manner, yet more curious about her words. "Clydon and its many holdings are well known to me, Lady Reina, yet I had not heard you were having the sort of trouble that would require my son's particular skills. However, I can assure you that you have hired the best."

Was that true pride she detected in his voice? By what right did he take pride in a son he had all but forsaken?

"We are naturally grateful for Ranulf's exceptional abilities, my lord, but I fear you are under a misconception. I did not hire Ranulf, I married him. He is the new Lord of Clydon."

Reina did not feel quite so foolish for her own earlier shock, now that she witnessed his. He stared at her incredulously for long moments, but then he threw back his head and laughed.

"You doubt me?" she bristled.

'Twas another moment ere he found breath to answer. "Nay, I do not doubt you at all, my lady. I always knew Ranulf would do well for himself, but I never suspected he would surpass even myself. If he is here, I would indeed like to see him."

"But that is not why you came. Why are you here, my lord?" ·

"My baggage wain dropped a wheel just down the road. I thought to borrow your smith to expedite the repair, and to pay my respects to you while 'twas being worked on. Now mayhap you will tell me why you are being so defensive."

"Defensive? I thought I was being quite rude, but if you wish to call it by another name . . ."

She got another burst of laughter instead of the expected rancor such discourtesy would ordinarily cause. Verily, 'twas not easy to insult father or son. Now she felt embarrassed for having tried. The man was a guest under her roof after all, albeit uninvited. He did not deserve her antagonism for past deeds that had naught to do with her. And what if Ranulf would be glad to see him? There would be hell to pay did she chase him away ere Ranulf had the opportunity to decide one way or the other. All in all, she had behaved abominably toward a man she did not even know. What was his name? *Jesú,* to ask now would be akin to another insult.

"I must beg your pardon—"

"Nay, do not," he interrupted, still smiling. "I like your spirit, lady. 'Tis a trait needful in dealing with my son, as disagreeable and intimidating as he can be. A woman with less mettle would likely be overwhelmed by him."

Again Reina wondered how he could know that when he had himself had so few dealings with Ranulf. But she would not ask. Nay, just now the best thing she could do would be to exit right quickly, ere she proved more ungracious than she had thus far. But the man's remark deserved a comment first.

"Ranulf is not as fearsome as he appears, once you become accustomed to his roar. But you must know that for yourself—" She stopped, appalled that she was doing it again, but hopefully he had not detected that last bit of sarcasm. "Do you make yourself comfortable, my lord." She indicated a bench by the hearth, away from the bustle of servants still setting up the tables. "We will have dinner soon, as you can see, and you are welcome to join." She hoped that was the truth, but could not really predict how Ranulf would receive him. "Do you excuse me now while I locate my husband for you."

She gave him no chance to reply one way or the other but hurried off, stopping only long enough to send a servant to fetch wine for him. She felt flustered, and anxious, and contrarily, still annoyed by the man's behavior. The way he acted, you would think Ranulf a beloved son, when the truth was he was a son barely acknowledged. Or did the man think to share in and make use of Ranulf's good fortune?

Aye, that would explain his delight that Ranulf was Lord of Clydon—but not the pride in Ranulf as a man that she had detected ere he learned he was not merely a mercenary she had hired.

In truth, she knew not what to think. She had to acknowledge that Ranulf might not have told her all the facts. Yet she had not mistaken his bitterness when he told her what he did. That was real and what had stirred her own dislike of this uncaring father. If Ranulf bore no love for the man, there had to be good reason, whether she knew all the facts or not.

Recalling that bitterness, Reina became even more anxious. In her shame over her own behavior, she had made the man welcome. She should not have done that. If Ranulf refused to receive him, worse, demanded he leave, she would be even more shamed, regardless that she had herself tried to insult him into leaving. Once hospitality was extended, it was tantamount to an offering of peace. 'Twas not rescinded except by deeds done after the fact which might destroy that peace.

But all of these thoughts went right out of Reina's mind when she found Ranulf still abed, though quite awake and watching her rush toward him. She immediately checked for pallor or brightness in his complexion, indications of sickness. There were none, yet he had to be ill and seriously so, to keep him abed this long when he was not sleeping as she had assumed, especially since he had spoken of sending one of his men to Warhurst to question the townspeople, also of further interrogating the prisoners. She berated herself now for not checking on him sooner.

"You should have sent for me." The terseness of her tone was at odds with the gentle touch of her hand on his brow, then his neck. "You are not hot," she added with a worried frown. "What ailment do you feel?"

Ranulf stared at her blankly for a moment, then replied, " 'Tis lower."

Her eyes moved down him, settling on his stomach, bare above the bed sheet gathered loosely around his hips. Her hand followed, but only to hover over the area. She saw his muscles tighten in anticipation of her touch, a sure indication he was in pain. Dread washed over her, for this was more serious than she thought.

Her throat was suddenly dry with fear for him, making her squeak, "Here?"

His own voice was not steady when he rasped, "Lower."

Her eyes shot lower, then as quickly filled with suspicion and came slowly back to meet his. "There, eh? And what could possibly ail you there?"

"A most painful swelling—"

"Ohh!"

"What?" He grinned at her outrage.

"Curse and rot you, Ranulf, I thought you were grievously ill! Do you ever scare me like that again—" The urge to hit him was too strong, and as he continued to grin at her, she gave into it.

"Ow!"

"Serves you right," she grouched. "Now I have something to treat."

He rubbed his shoulder as if she had actually hurt him, complaining, "You had something to treat, lady."

"Aye, your sense of humor could use a good purge.

Now do you tell me the real reason you are still abed. Did you only just wake?''

He shook his head at her. ''I have been practicing patience, little general. I have been lying here waiting for you to come and chastise me for laziness.''

''Will you be serious!''

''But I am. Would you rather I came below, just to drag you back up here? Think you your ladies would not have raised a collective brow at that?''

Her own sable brows came together. ''You would not be so—so—'' He would, and his arch look was proof of that if past experience was not. And 'twas too late to pretend she did not know what that collective brow raising would have been about.

''Should I thank you?''

''It never fails.'' He chuckled. ''If you are not snapping my head off, you resort to sarcasm. But in this case mayhap you should thank me, little general. I will not always be so considerate. There will be times I am rushed and—''

''And any dark corner will do?''

That sneer got her pulled down onto the bed. ''Aye, anywhere, though I do prefer this soft bed.''

''Better than the woods?''

''Much.''

She refrained from grinning, but she could not stay angry with him when he was like this. She would never have imagined there was a playful man inside the churlish giant, but she was coming to appreciate that there was. She was also like to become addicted to the amorous side of him, but that was her problem. While it lasted, she meant to take advantage of it— but not just now.

Before the nibbling he was doing at her neck made

her forget again, she blurted out, "Ranulf, this must wait."

"Not unless the keep is burning down, lady."

He did not stop nuzzling her, and now that he was no longer afeard to caress her, his hands were quite busy, too. "Ranulf, I came to tell you . . . there is someone below you should . . . ought to . . . Ranulf!" She gasped as he latched onto her earlobe. "It can wait," she decided, then in the next breath, with a sigh, "Nay, it cannot. Ranulf, 'tis your father."

He became very still, but after a moment, slowly leaned back to look down at her. "My what?"

"Your father is below and has asked to see you."

Surprise was there, and for a fleeting second something akin to gladness, though Reina could not be certain. But whatever these first reactions were, they were quickly masked by a much darker emotion, one she had seen that day he told her about his father.

He got up from the bed, she thought to dress. Not so. He began to pace, or more like prowl as a restless animal would. The bedrobe she had made for such times lay ignored atop his coffer. She did not care much at the moment. So he was a man of little modesty, and the robe was apt to never get any use. He was magnificent to watch. Such raw masculinity brought a response to her body that was wholly primitive, making her wish she had kept her mouth shut.

But 'twas too late for that, and although she hated to interrupt his prowling, she still had to ask, "Will you see him?"

"How the devil did he find out so soon?"

Reina had the feeling he was not speaking to her at all, that he had not heard her question. Still, she answered, "If you mean about our wedding, he did not know, leastwise not until I made mention of it."

That got his attention right quickly. "You told—then why is he here?"

" 'Tis no great mystery, Ranulf. His baggage wain broke down in passing. Otherwise, he would not even have stopped at Clydon. Gilbert brought him to me and—"

"And you guessed who he was," he finished in disgust.

"Guessed? *Jesú*, there was no guessing to it. You did not tell me he was so young, or that you are a near exact copy of him."

"Think you I am pleased by such close resemblance? You cannot imagine how many times I have been mistaken for him by acquaintances who have not seen him for long. There were even a few who refused to believe I was not him. Know you what it is like to be taken for a man you . . ."

He would not complete the thought, so she did it for him. "Despise? Do you really?"

That got her a scowl instead of an answer. "What does he want, lady?"

"To congratulate you, mayhap?" The scowl darkened. "Well, how should I know?" she added testily. "Why not go down and ask him?"

"Bite your tongue, woman!"

She blinked; then her lips curled the tiniest bit. She had heard him speak just so to Walter, and knew it to be more an endearment than an expression of anger. She might be the recipient of his roars, but not of his temper, leastwise not yet.

"Then you will not see him?"

"Nay, I will not," he growled.

"That is too bad," she replied lightly, as if the matter were settled. "I was hoping to learn how he could know so much about you."

"What do you mean?"

"Somewhere along the way you must have given him reason to be proud to call you son. I cannot imagine how . . ."

"Reina—"

"I was only jesting!" she cried when he started toward her. She scrambled off the bed and moved toward the door before adding, "But you should have heard him singing your praises when he thought I had bought your services. I suppose he wanted to assure me that I would be getting my money's worth. 'Twas a pleasure to correct his mistake. I must confess, however, that I was terribly ungracious at first. I know not what came over me. But you will be glad to know he is as thick-skinned as you are when it comes to insults. He simply would not take offense."

"Through no fault of your own, I am sure, since you are so good at going for the jugular."

She smiled inwardly, aware that he had himself just taken exception to her remark. Still, she stepped closer to the door ere she made her final confession.

"He was still a stranger to me, and I had no excuse for being so inhospitable—which is why I thought to make amends by inviting him to join us at table."

"You did what?" he exploded.

That was her cue to exit right quickly.

Chapter Thirty-seven

*R*eina had to clamp her hand over her mouth to hold in the giggles as she rushed toward the stairs. Ranulf's expression had been so comical, half surprise, half fury. But she really should not have done that to him. He was certain to get even in kind for her putting him on the spot like that, and it might not even have worked. Just because she had him thinking she meant to make his father welcome did not mean he would put in an appearance to do otherwise. What had she hoped for, anyway? That they would see each other and all would be well? That was not likely to happen, and in truth, she simply did not want to be the one to ask his father to leave. She had been rude enough for one day. Did Ranulf want him gone, he should be the one to tell him.

Reina stopped at the top of the stairwell, for *she* still had to tell the man something when she returned to the hall without Ranulf. An excuse, a lie, the truth? Which would he believe? If he knew Ranulf as well as he implied, then would he not half expect the re-action she had gotten from him?

She was still frowning over this new problem when a hand clamped down on her shoulder and she nearly jumped out of her skin, not having heard anyone approaching from behind. She saw why she had heard nothing when she swung about. Ranulf stood there barefoot, and bare everywhere else as well. Reina's mouth dropped open. She would never have dared to goad him as she had if she had not been certain she could escape his wrath by simply slipping out the door; he would not *dare* to follow her, at least not directly.

"Are you mad?" she demanded, feeling her cheeks heating with the embarrassment that *he* should be feeling. She imagined ten servants appearing out of nowhere to witness her husband's total lack of modesty. "Sweet *Jesú,* you are naked!"

"What I am is far beyond my quota of patience, lady," he growled in reply. "You have just earned yourself a chastisement long overdue."

"Will you at least clothe yourself first?"

She regretted that flippancy immediately. If anyone was mad, she was, to tempt his temper further. She expected to be dragged back to their chamber for her "punishment" this instant, or to be pulled across his lap right there on the stairs. She certainly could not blame him after that unwise remark.

But he did neither, fortunately, for he had not forgotten the main reason for his anger. "Just now you will return to the hall, lady, and withdraw your invitation."

Reina sighed inwardly. Why did he have to be so—so unyielding? Her answer, the only one she could give, was going to make him even more furious, but this time just with her.

"I cannot do that, my lord."

"Cannot? I did not ask you, woman. That was an order."

"I know." She cringed. "And I would like to comply, but how can I? This is no longer just a matter of what is between you and your father. I was wrong to make him welcome without first learning your wishes, but I did it, and as your wife, I speak not only for myself but, in your absence, for you as well. Do you ask me to take back an offer of hospitality, you shame me as well as Clydon. Is that what you are demanding I do?''

He glared at her for a long moment, but finally said, "Feed him, but then I want him gone."

Bless him, he was not so unyielding after all. "Aye, my lord. And may I tell him—"

"Lady Reina?" Florette's voice drifted up to them.

Reina gasped, looked down at her husband, and flushed crimson. "Go!" she hissed at him.

"We are not finished," he replied stubbornly.

"Ranulf, you . . . are . . . *naked!*"

"So?"

"Lady Reina?" Florette appeared around the bend of the stairs. "Dame Hilary wants to know—"

"Not now," Reina snapped at the lady as she swung about to spread her skirt wide in front of Ranulf, knowing even as she did it that that was not sufficient to hide his towering frame.

"But—"

"Not *now*, Florette!"

The woman retreated right quickly then, but whether she had first gotten a good look at them or, more to the point, at Ranulf, Reina could not say. The situation was still exasperating enough to ignite her own temper.

She swung around again to glare up at her husband. "That was the most lackwitted piece of stubbornness I have ever witnessed. Do you want to parade yourself before my ladies, you might as well come below now.

Why treat only one? I am certain they would all be thrilled to see you bare-assed naked.''

"Do not change the subject, Reina."

It infuriated her more to see that for some reason he was now amused. Though he did not go so far as to actually grin, she saw it was an effort not to.

"Very well, my lord," she gritted out. "The subject was your father, I believe? May I tell him you will join us presently?''

That got his frown back, she was glad to see. "That would be a lie, lady. You invited him. You eat with him."

"As you wish." She descended several steps ere she tossed back at him, "Your presence is not needful for me to appease my curiosity.''

"Reina, come back here!"

She continued down the stairs. "I will have food sent up to you, my lord."

"Reina!"

She did not answer again, hurrying now, only half certain this time that he would not follow. She had no urge to giggle, but could not deny a good deal of satisfaction in thwarting him a second time. She would pay for it later, she knew, for he was not likely to forget his promised chastisement now, but she would worry about that later.

Chapter Thirty-eight

*B*etween directing the servants to begin the meal and attending Dame Hilary's minor crisis caused by Sir Searle's insistence that he was well enough to leave his chamber, Reina had not yet returned to Ranulf's father ere Ranulf came charging down the stairs, still in the process of fastening his belt. She had not expected this in response to her last defiance, and for a moment had the urge to run, thinking his rage was so great he had come to punish her now. But he came to nearly a skidding halt when he saw her by Searle's chamber, alone, and must have realized she had not yet spoken again to his father. His gaze then searched for the man and found him by the hearth in conversation with several of Reina's ladies.

Reina bit her lip, watching him grapple with indecision and other painful emotions she could not even guess at. He did not move, just stood there staring at his sire, making her realize how insensitive she had been to taunt him on this of all subjects. Verily, she deserved a thrashing. She did not know what it was like to hate one's own father, but it could not be an easy feeling, going against the grain.

And then she saw Ranulf stiffen, and knew that his father must have finally noticed him. Sure enough, she looked and saw the older man stand up and start toward Ranulf. His expression was one of pleasure, immense pleasure. Ranulf's was suddenly inscrutable. Yet his body was still stiff. Not a single muscle moved.

Reina held her breath even as she moved toward them to intercede. She could only hope her presence would prevent an angry confrontation, but she could not be sure. The two men seemed unaware of anyone else in the room, both for different reasons. But every eye in the room was on them, watching in fascination two men of such extraordinary size, and so identical. Mayhap this was why Ranulf did not say what he would have said were they alone.

Ranulf suffered a hearty embrace but did not return it. His father did not notice, or if he did, it did not dampen his mood.

"By the rood, I am glad to see you settled, Ranulf, and settled so well."

"Indeed? Did you think I would remain a mercenary all my life?"

"Not at all. I knew you had more ambition than that. How could you not have when you are so like me? What delights me is that you have surpassed even my expectations for you, and much sooner than I could have hoped. How did you manage such a feat?"

"The lady was smitten by me and would have no one else." Reina's gasp clarified that piece of sarcasm for what it was. Ranulf smiled at her mockingly. "Do you have a problem with that summation, lady?"

"It matters not how it came to pass that you are now Lord of Clydon," the father quickly amended. "You still have my congratulations."

"So you are happy for me?" Ranulf replied coldly. "Is that what you want me to believe?"

The older man hesitated, unable to ignore Ranulf's hostile reception any longer. "You doubt me?"

"Give me one reason why I should not."

"I can do that," Reina interjected, annoyed that he was being so churlish. "Because he is your father. 'Tis reason enough for him to want only your good."

"Lady, you got me down here with your sly machinations, and that is mischief enough from you. Get you gone now. This does not concern you."

"Whatever concerns you concerns me," she retorted. "And I will not be ordered from my own hall, Ranulf. You want me gone, you will have to drag me out of here. But I warn you, do you make a scene like that before my people, you will regret it much longer than I regret taunting you."

An apology and a threat all in one? Ranulf's scowl darkened for a moment, then smoothed out. After another moment he was chuckling, and there was nothing of derision in it.

"You congratulate me, Lord Hugh? Mayhap you should offer sympathy instead."

That he was teasing was not in doubt, so Reina did not feel *too* chagrined by that remark. And his father was amused, too, which was a good sign considering Ranulf's attitude thus far. Lord Hugh? She should have realized, being married to a Fitz Hugh, that this would be his name.

"My lords, might I suggest you continue this reunion at table? Dinner has been delayed long enough due to some people's laziness."

Ranulf did not mistake that dig, and replied in kind. "Is that what you call lust these days, lady?"

Reina had turned away, but now whipped about with a gasp, two spots of color staining her cheeks. She started to say something, made a squeak of noise instead, and clamped her mouth shut. But her icy blue eyes spoke volumes, and Ranulf knew better than to think he had gotten the last word in. When his guts spilled out on the floor later, he would know she had retaliated in kind.

For now, he at least had rendered her speechless, which was no small feat. With a fulminating glare, she huffed off, leaving him standing alone with his father, who seemed actually embarrassed by that last exchange.

"That was . . ." he began carefully, then changed his mind. "Never mind."

"You might as well speak your mind here," Ranulf replied in a neutral tone. "I intend to."

Hugh winced at the implication, even given unemotionally as it was. "Very well. That was rather unchivalrous of you. She is your wife, after all."

"Exactly. *My* wife. And you are not qualified to judge what passes between her and me when you know not what has gone on before. Suffice it to say the lady was deserving of much worse than that, and well she knows it, or she would have cut into me then and there with that sharp tongue of hers. I understand you have already had a taste of it yourself, to know of what I speak."

"Actually, I had forgotten about that," Hugh admitted. "She does indeed have a way with words."

"She said you were too thick-skinned to notice."

"Did she?" Hugh chuckled now. "Not at all. Enchanted is more like it. 'Twas refreshing to meet a woman who was not either impressed by my rank, intimidated by my size, or charmed by a simple smile. That has never happened to me ere now."

"You are not losing your touch, old man, if that is

what you think. She was not very impressed with me either when we first met.''

''Still, Ranulf, you have missed my point. A lady can be a veritable shrew, but a knight must still refrain from chastising her or insulting her, at least in company.''

''Chivalry again?'' Ranulf snorted. ''And where do you get the idea that I learned such things at Montfort? I assure you no such niceties were taught there.''

Hugh had the grace to flush. ''I told you I knew not the kind of man Montfort was, Ranulf, leastwise not until I met him at your knighting. My father arranged your fostering. Lord Montfort was a friend of his from old. I was assured you would be well received and taught by the best. And I was kept apprised of your progress, which was nothing short of remarkable. It came as little surprise that you earned your spurs at such a young age. I was nine years and ten ere I was myself knighted. Even my father was impressed by your abilities.''

''Think you I care what that old man thought?'' Ranulf could no longer keep the bitterness from his tone. ''In all the years he came to the village to check on my development, I had not a single kindness from him, not even—''

''What did you say?'' Hugh cut in sharply.

''Was that too much for a boy to hope for, one kind word or look from his grandfather?'' Ranulf snarled.

''Dear God, what are you saying, Ranulf? He did not know of your existence. *I* did not know of your existence. You were nine years old when he told me, and he swore he had only just learned about you himself.''

Ranulf could do no more than stare at him, feeling as if his guts were being twisted apart. To have the crux of his true bitterness ripped asunder, that his father had so despised him that he would not even acknowledge his existence those first years of his life. He had never once thought he might not know of him. How could he not? His grandfather had known. But he was forgetting the rest of his life, and other bitter disappointments. Nay, not forgetting. The rest was simply not as important.

In a voice devoid of inflection, he said, "He lied."

"He would not!" Hugh insisted.

"Very well." Ranulf sighed, too torn apart to care just now. "I lied."

A brief look of raw anguish crossed Hugh's face and shook Ranulf to his core. "Nay, I know you do not. Sweet Christ, no wonder you were so distant and unresponsive to me that day we first met. My father told me that was natural, that you had not known of me either. He said to give you time to get used to the idea."

"Aye, seven more years is time aplenty, especially when I needed no getting used to the idea. I knew who my father was from the day I knew what a father was and that mine was unwilling to acknowledge me."

Hugh paled at the accusation in those words. "Is that what you thought?"

"What else was I to think? I lived on your land, in your village. Everyone on the demesne knew I was your bastard even before my face and body fleshed out to prove it."

Reina had heard enough, too much. She had returned to prod them into eating ere the food grew cold, but had stood there and listened instead, aware that they were both too engrossed in this painful dredging of the past to notice her or anyone else. But she could not bear to hear any more, and she did not think Ranulf could either. His face was ravaged, the misery of a wretched and lonely childhood evident in his voice, his eyes, his every word. He was hurting inside and she felt it, hated it, and hated his father for causing it, much more than he did, if he did, for he would not be in such pain if it was only hate he felt for this man.

She could not take the pain away from him, but she could prevent more. "If you have not noticed, Ranulf, we have a hall full of people like to starve, waiting for you to take your seat at table."

She got a potent glare for the interruption, but also the desired result. He nodded curtly and strode off toward the dais. When Hugh started to follow, she detained him with a hand to his arm. That the violet eyes he turned to her were nearly as tormented as Ranulf's had been did not sway her.

"I swore I would make amends for my earlier rudeness to you," she said in a low, though no less fierce tone. "I find I cannot, not after what I just heard. I want you to leave Clydon now, this minute."

He did not seem surprised by this demand, but he did not comply with it either. "I cannot leave this thing unsettled, lady."

"You refuse to go?"

He gave her a weak smile for the incredulity that erased her frown. "I believe your words were, 'Do you want me gone, you will have to drag me out of here.' I seriously doubt you can manage that yourself, my dear."

"Plague take you, then," she seethed, knowing full well she could not have him thrown out, at least not without Ranulf's permission, which she was not likely to get now, or he would have done it himself. "But I warn you, Lord Hugh. Do you hurt my husband anymore by word, deed, or otherwise, I swear I will destroy you and your house and all you hold dear."

"And if what I hold most dear is your husband?"

"You have been unable to convince him of that. What makes you think I would believe it?"

"Because 'tis true. I love him. I have from the day I first saw him looking at me with my own eyes, my own image. Before I leave here he will know it, if I have to beat the truth into him."

So saying, he left her standing there in a quandary of doubt and confusion. She did not know now whether to interfere or let him try to convince Ranulf of his sincerity—if he really was sincere. But even were he not, should Ranulf believe him, would that not ease some of this bitterness he had carried inside him for so long? But beat the truth into him? She had to smile at that choice of words, for Lord Hugh was perhaps the only man alive who possibly could.

Chapter Thirty-nine

*T*he eel in a savory herb sauce was still warm, as were the chicken with pine nuts and the spicy creamed rabbit. Ranulf did not touch the fare before him. Hugh did not touch it. Reina was not one to let any emotion affect her hearty appetite, but in deference to the two men on either side of her, she merely sipped her wine.

It was a silent table in comparison to the norm. Walter's merry wit was sorely missed today. Though Reina's ladies spoke quietly among themselves, they were subdued by the brooding atmosphere at the center of the table. Even the servants were on their best behavior, sensing the tension in the air.

But it did not continue for the duration of the meal, much to Reina's misfortune. She had assumed Ranulf's thoughts were solely on his father, but some small portion must have been spared for her. He rose and with a hand under her elbow, brought Reina to her feet as well. And then without a word of explanation to his father, or to her for that matter, he escorted her from the table. She would not have questioned him if their direction were not the stairwell leading up to their chamber.

"What are you doing?" Reina demanded in an anxious whisper when she could not manage to break his hold on her arm.

"I need a distraction, lady, ere I explode."

She immediately thought of his lusty nature and cried, "Not *now!*"

"Aye, 'tis no better time, for I would not have you dreading the night. Or did you think I would forget what I promised you earlier?"

Promised? Dreading? Sweet *Jesú,* he spoke of the chastisement he felt she had earned this morn, not lovemaking. Her color receded, only to flood back with visions of what he intended to do. The way she saw it, did he punish her now, 'twas likely to be quite painful, *very* painful in fact, for he needed an outlet for the turmoil raging inside him that his father's visit had thus far caused. But if she helped toward a reconciliation first, his emotions were like to be less turbulent, so would he not go easier on her, mayhap even just give her a severe scolding instead?

She did not try to stop him, but she did glance back at the table and silently beckoned Lord Hugh to follow. Fortunately, he was watching their departure. And just before they reached the stairwell, she saw that he had stood up. But his expression seemed uncertain. Curse and rot him, was he remembering what she had last said to him? *He* was the one who had said he would not leave here until he had settled things with Ranulf. Did he expect to find a better opportunity to get his son alone?

Reina was dragged up the stairs, not at all certain now that she would have a reprieve. A tight knot formed in her belly, the dread Ranulf had mentioned. She did not want to become acquainted with the palm of his hand, as he had once promised would happen did she provoke him, especially when that hand had been naught but gentle to her since she received that warning. Yet she did deserve some form of punishment. She had deliberately provoked him, as well as forced him to confront his father against his will. But, *Jesú*, she had never believed he would actually do *this* to her. Too often he had threatened her with this same consequence, but naught had ever come of it.

He did not let go of her until they were inside the bedchamber, and then only to close the door and bolt it. Reina's trepidation increased tenfold. Common sense said it would be over with quickly, that if children could suffer this, so could she. Common sense be damned.

"Ranulf, can we not talk about this?"

"Nay," he said flatly and crossed to the bed. He sat down on the edge of it, sideways, and patted the spot next to him. "Place yourself here, lady, and raise your skirts."

Reina blanched. "You mean to humiliate me as well?"

"Humiliation is the foundation of this lesson. You will forget the discomfort right quickly, but the humiliation you will long remember."

"I will also remember that you took pleasure in this!" she snapped.

"Not even a little, lady. I like this no better than you, but you have defied me one time too many. Now come here." She remained rooted to the spot. "Do not make me come after you . . ."

Or it will go worse for you, he could have finished, but did not. The warning was clear enough and she heeded it. But it had never taken so long for her to walk a few spaces. Her hands had already begun to sweat. 'Twas not so much the stinging bottom she feared, but the telling blow to her pride, and she could not think of any way to . . . unless . . .

She had reached him, and in a desperate move, slipped her arms around his neck. "Ranulf, you wanted a distraction. Make love to me instead."

Fire leapt into his eyes, but only for a moment. His lips were a hard, straight line, unyielding. Slowly, he unwound her arms and placed them at her sides.

"I will—afterward."

Fire leaped into her own eyes then, but of a different kind. "Curse and rot you! If you touch me afterward, I will never forgive you!"

"Meaning you will forgive me for this lesson you have earned?"

He was right and she was wrong in this instance. Of course she would forgive him. But she would not assure him of that.

"You do not have to do this now!" she cried. "At least wait until you are not so angry."

"I am not angry with you any longer," he replied patiently. "I even understand what you tried to do." But then his voice hardened and she knew she was lost. "But I will not be manipulated like that, lady, and best you learn it now."

She wondered if tears would help at this point. Likely not. He was too barbarous a lout to appreciate them.

"What if I promised to be the boring, silent, cowering wife you apparently want? I will give you no more reason to call me little general. Will that satisfy you?"

Obviously not, if his frown was any indication. *Jesú,* what had she said to bring back his anger? But she had no chance to find out. The reprieve she had hoped for came at last in the sound of a knock at the door.

With a relieved sigh, she told Ranulf, "That will be your father, and none too soon."

His frown darkened considerably. "He would not dare."

Reina cringed inwardly, afraid her next words were going to make her situation even worse. "I—ah—I believe I invited him."

Ranulf came to his feet with a growl, making Reina jump back with a gasp. But he did not say anything. The look he gave her said it all, giving her no doubt that he felt she had again contrived to manipulate him.

"I—I will send him away," she offered in a small voice.

"Nay, you will let him in," he replied, his own tone rough but controlled. "And you will stay also. I do not intend to hunt you down when this is finished."

She winced but complied, opening the door. For the briefest moment she thought of defying him again and fleeing. Her own curiosity put the thought aside. And she still had one hope, that Ranulf would reconcile with his father and thereby forgive her for her part in bringing it about. A small hope, but one that put her on Lord Hugh's side again.

"Do you come in, my lord," she said, closing the door when he did. "You can speak privately here, do you deign not to notice me. Unfortunately, I cannot leave. I am to be punished as soon as you are finished, you see."

"Reina . . ." Ranulf said warningly.

"What difference if I tell him?" she retorted with a baleful glare. "I am going to scream loud enough when it happens that the whole of Clydon will know anyway."

"Thank you for the warning," Ranulf said low, with distinct menace. "I will be sure to gag you first."

Hugh cleared his throat at this point, looking decidedly uncomfortable. "If this is not a good time—"

"There *is* no good time for the opening of old wounds," Ranulf snarled. "But you are determined to see mine bleed, so have your say and be done with it."

"Think you I like this any better than you, to learn after all these years that my father lied to me? I even realize now that he deliberately kept us apart, before I knew of you and afterward. He was still an active man when you were sent to Montfort, yet he turned over the management of all his holdings to me at that time. I was barely older then than you are now, Ranulf, nor did I know the first thing about stewardship, for I had practically lived at court with my wife up until then, thinking I had many years yet ere such responsibilities would be mine."

Ranulf said nothing to that, and the look on his face was no indication whether it made any difference as to how he felt. Reina felt like kicking him for his silence. If he had no questions, she certainly did.

"Why would your father do what he did?"

"I cannot say, lady, and his reasons died with him several years past. Mayhap he did not know of Ranulf's birth until much later, and then—"

"He knew," Ranulf cut in. "My mother told him, which was why he wed her to the village smith."

"And near half of all village babies die in the first or second year," Reina pointed out. "Could he have kept the knowledge from you to spare you the loss if Ranulf had not survived?"

"Lady, had I known of Ranulf from his birth, he would have been brought into the keep to raise, given every care. I simply do not know why my father would leave him to the care of villeins."

"*Jesú*," Reina whispered, recalling another who had given her baby to villeins with the hope it would *not* survive. She glanced at Ranulf and wondered if he was recalling the same thing, or if he had already surmised that possibility but thought it was his father who had hoped he would die. 'Twas better not to mention that, but Hugh had not finished anyway.

"And I can think of only one reason why he still kept the knowledge from me. I had another natural son, whose mother's family was very powerful. They would not let me marry the lady. She was already betrothed. But I was forced to make her son my heir."

"Forced?"

"The concession was wrung from me at the boy's birth. My father was in concurrence, for 'twas either that or they would make war on us, which he could ill afford at the time."

"But you were so young," Reina said. "Surely they expected you to marry and have legitimate children."

"Aye, but in either case, I was still to provide for the lady's son. That kept them from having to do so, and unofficially allied our families, which in fact delighted my father. For that reason he may have wanted Ranulf's existence kept from me, and from Lady Ella's family."

"Ella?" Reina looked sharply at Ranulf. *"Ella?"* His scowl made her burst into laughter.

Hugh did not see the jest. "Do you know the lady?" he asked Reina.

"Nay, my lord, though I am well acquainted with her namesake." A low rumble from her husband wiped the grin from her lips. "But that has naught to do with this. Why would your father finally tell you about Ranulf?"

"I was home that summer after several years' absence. The court was traveling, and my wife thought she was with child, so I was in no hurry to leave. Ranulf had reached an age where I would only have to see him to know he was mine."

"So your father feared you were like to discover him for yourself, and possibly suspect that he had already known and deliberately kept it from you? Telling you and swearing he was as surprised as you would effectively put your suspicions to rest ere they even formed."

"So I must assume."

"But why keep you apart after you knew of him?"

"Again I can only guess, lady, that he wanted no bond to form."

"Did you form a bond with your other son?"

"Nay." Hugh sighed. "Ella's family raised him and he is nothing like me. Sometimes I even wonder if he is truly mine. And yet he is closer to me than Ranulf, for Ranulf has never let me get close to him."

"Can you blame him? As I understand it, my lord, this is only the third time in his life he has ever spoken with you. For the first nine years of his life, he thinks you do not want him. For all the years of his fostering, you never sent for him or visited. Considering that, I can see why he doubts your sincerity. I doubt it myself."

She got a frown from both of them this time. Well, that was just too bad. She did not hear Ranulf asking his own questions. And she had yet to hear anything to truly support what Hugh had told her earlier. If he really cared about this son of his, he would have ended their estrangement years ago.

"I happen to know, lady, that Clydon has been under your control these past several years," Hugh said defensively. "Tell me how often you found the time to travel for your own pleasure."

She had the grace to blush. "In truth, not once."

"Neither did I. My father had never been one to delegate his power to others, and in those first years that I took over his duties, I had not yet found men I trusted enough to share the burden with. I think now that he had a lot to do with that, but I have no proof. But I do know that he discouraged me from interfering with Ranulf's training. And since I was being given regular reports on his progress, and was kept so busy anyway . . . but that is no excuse. I was wrong, and readily admit it. I should never have let so much time pass before seeing him again, nor left communication to letters."

"What letters?" Ranulf finally broke his silence to demand. "I received but two from you, and those after I had left Montfort."

"Nay, you must have had others. I wrote to you at least a half-dozen times each year the entire time you were at Montfort. I did not expect replies. I knew how grueling a squire's training could be from my own experience. I simply wanted you to know you were not forgotten."

Reina nearly cried out at the look of anguish on her

husband's face as he shouted, "I tell you I had no letters from you there!"

Hugh was also shaken by Ranulf's obvious pain. "Then my father must have intercepted them."

"Or Lord Montfort," Reina said quietly. "Did you not say he was a friend of your father's?"

Hugh did not answer or look at her. He stepped closer to Ranulf. Reina had the feeling he desperately wanted to embrace him. She wanted to herself. But Ranulf had his emotions under control again, and his expression did not invite any overtures of that sort just then.

"I did write you, Ranulf," Hugh insisted. "I swear to you I did. I also sent for you four times, but each time I had back from Montfort excuses why it was not a good time to release you. I suppose you were never told that either?"

For answer, Ranulf merely scowled. Reina hesitated to interfere again. Ranulf obviously did not believe everything he was hearing. But then why should he? He had only his father's word, and that word could be false. Still, they were not getting close to a reconciliation, and if that was to come about, there had to be something to support Hugh's word.

"You claim to have had reports on Ranulf while he was at Montfort, Lord Hugh, even if he did not write to you himself. What I do not understand is how you could know so much about his doings after he left Montfort."

For a moment she thought he would not reply. He seemed more than just hesitant to do so, more embarrassed.

"One of Ranulf's men is actually my man."

"A common man-at-arms who can write?" Reina scoffed.

"He was my clerk. He did not like the duty I assigned him, but he has been well paid for the risks of soldiering. He has even come to finally enjoy it."

"So you spied on me?" This from Ranulf, and without much surprise.

"How else was I to know what became of you? I wrote to you after you left Montfort, if you will recall. You admit you at least received *those* letters. But still I had no answer from you, and, coupled with your coldness the second time we met, I was finally forced to accept that I was not like to ever hear from you."

"I was your sin, grown to your image." The bitterness was back in Ranulf's tone. "You were naught but ashamed of me."

"Never that," Hugh swore. "How could I be ashamed of a son so like myself?" And then in a burst of exasperation, "Sweet Christ, Ranulf, what must I do to convince you that you are dear to me?"

Again Ranulf did not answer. Reina had an answer, but she was likely to be throttled by one or the other of them did she give it. When had that ever stopped her?

" 'Twould seem you must beat it into him, my Lord Hugh."

"Lady," Hugh growled, "you are being no help to me."

"Did I say I would help you?" she asked with arched brow. "As I recall, I asked you to leave Clydon ere you caused him any more pain. You were the one who said you could not go with this unsettled. You said you love him, that you have from the day you first saw him and knew him to be yours. Well, you also said that before you leave here he would know it, if you have to beat the truth into him. Your words, my lord, not mine. And 'twould seem that is the only recourse you have left—unless, of course, Ranulf finally has some doubts that what he has believed to be true all these years might not be true. What say you, Ranulf?'' She changed the direction of her attack. "Can you believe him? His father is dead and cannot verify what he says, but is Montfort? Or will you question this clerk of his turned soldier? Or will you simply accept his word and the love he seems determined to give you? It might behoove you to try, for he appears to be the one man you cannot be completely assured of besting. 'Twould be a shame were you in no condition to deliver my promised chastisement.''

"A shame, indeed, so do not count on it," Ranulf said darkly.

Reina shrugged. She had gone this far. She might as well do her worst.

"You have not answered my question, Ranulf, but before you do, you should be aware of something I have noticed that mayhap you have not. This man is very similar to you, and I do not speak now of resemblance. His temperament is the same as yours. He is as stubborn. *Jesú,* you both even scowl at the same things. Could not your sense of honor also be the same? I also wish to point out that had I not believed you when you told me about Rothwell, we would not now be wed.''

"Christ's toes!" Ranulf exclaimed. "What has that to do with this?"

"It has to do with trust. I had never heard of Rothwell, nor has he come here to verify what you claimed. I took you at your word without proof that you spoke true. You owe the same trust to your father, especially since most of what he claims can be verified and he knows it, so he would have no reason to lie. And did you not say yourself that your grandfather had never shown you a kindness? It does not take much sense to see that you have unknowingly blamed the wrong man, Ranulf, and this is no time to remain stubborn about it. Do you ask me—''

"No one has asked you!" both men said at once, and with a good deal of exasperation.

Reina grinned, satisfied she had made her point. "True, but you see," she told both men, "I would not be here to give my opinion were I not awaiting punishment. And I would not be awaiting punishment if I had not forced my husband to see his father. If I am to suffer for arranging this meeting, you can both suffer my opinion."

"Which we have done, but no longer," Ranulf rumbled. "Get you gone, lady, now."

"You have decided to forgive me, then?"

"What I have decided is to let you dread the coming night after all. Go about your duties, Reina. I will attend you later."

She gave him a sour look ere she stalked to the door. "I always knew you were a dog-hearted clodpate. See if I ever do you another favor!"

There was silence after the door slammed shut. Hugh deliberately avoided Ranulf's eyes, fearing he would laugh did he witness his son's chagrin after that set-down. Did he have a sense of humor, it would not matter. But that was one of many things he did not know about his son, he realized. And if the lady had done anyone a favor, 'twas him. He would not like to see her hurt for it.

"Do you intend to beat her?"

"With these hands?" Ranulf snorted. "I mean to lesson her, not kill her. Besides, she has it in her marriage contract that I cannot take my fists to her."

"The terms of a marriage contract bear little weight in the heat of the moment."

"I have lived with this strength all my life, my lord. I was afeard to even touch the lady, she is so tiny. There is naught that she could ever say or do to make me forget that, so you need not be concerned for her. She will have no more than the flat of my hand on her backside."

Hugh chuckled. "A method I have found the need to use on occasion myself."

"Does it work?"

"Aye, though the result is not always worth the months of regret a woman can make you feel afterward—that is, if you bear feeling for her."

Ranulf grinned. "Then you might find interesting a suggestion I had from a whore . . ."

Reina had gone no farther than the antechamber, where she paced in an effort to work off her temper. When she heard the deep laughter, she stopped and relaxed. So her gamble had paid off. She went below smiling, certain she no longer had to worry about any punishments.

Chapter Forty

Reina went about her duties that afternoon feeling a good deal of smugness. Learning that Ranulf had taken his father out for a tour of Clydon only increased that feeling. He might not like her methods, but at least they bore results. He was reconciled with his father. The bitterness that had long festered inside him would be gone, leaving him a happier man, and thereby one easier to deal with. Could she pat herself on the back, she would have done so.

She spent some time with Walter and apprised him of what had happened, both yesterday and today. She no longer worried about his wounds. He had developed no fever, and Florette was keeping close attendance on him, which had much to do with why he was not complaining about the needed bed rest. In a week he should be up and about, though he would still have to go easy for a while.

It had been a surprise, however, to recall the prisoners, Warhurst, and Lord Richard in the telling. She could not even answer Walter's questions, for she did not know whether Ranulf had sent a man to Warhurst as he had intended. He had as like forgotten, too, considering all that had happened this morn.

She still could not believe Lord Richard was capable of such despicable tyranny. She decided to speak with the outlaw leader herself, and did, but came away unconvinced. Yet the man was so very

sincere, he did manage to plant a few doubts and
"what ifs," but not enough to matter. It came down
to her own instincts, which rarely failed her, as well
as her father's keen judgment of character, which was
even less fallible. He had liked Richard, had approved
of him as a husband for her. They could not both be
so wrong about a man.

Reina did not brood on it for long. That smugness
was still there to make her think of other things, her
husband in particular. She was not going to let Ranulf
forget that he owed her his gratitude, especially since
he had come so close to punishing her instead. He
would not have admitted it, but she had known he
carried deep feelings for his father despite the resentment that was on the surface. The man would never
have been able to hurt him otherwise.

Reina was back in the hall when they returned and
had an opportunity to watch them cross the long room
unawares. The difference in manner was remarkable.
They laughed, they touched, they were as two never
separated, and in looks, they were more like brothers
than father and son. Verily, Hugh was not even two
score in years yet. He was a man any maiden Reina's
age or even younger would look on with favor—just
as her husband was. And as usual, every woman in
her hall was doing just that. 'Twas something she
would simply have to get used to, she supposed.

A nod to a servant brought forward a platter of
sweetmeats and cheese. She had not forgotten that
neither man had touched his dinner earlier, and supper would not be ready for a while yet. She had satisfied her own hunger with a simple trip to the
kitchens, where she had also collected Lady Ella. It
was a veritable devil inside her that made her toy with

the idea of introducing the cat to Ranulf's father. The
only thing that decided her against it was the risk that
Hugh might not see the humor in the name Ranulf
had chosen for his scrawny cat. She did not want to
upset this boat she had set on such a steady course.

Lady Ella was now curled at her feet by the hearth,
having held no grudge over losing her sleeping quarters. At least she was still as friendly as ever whenever Ranulf was not around. But his voice woke her
ere he was even half across the room, and she went
bounding toward him to leap into his arms. Typical.
Heaven forbid he should happen to see her resting
companionably at someone else's feet.

Reina wondered if Ranulf felt at ease enough with
his father to introduce the cat. Whether he did or not,
she did not think the matter of a name had come up,
though they were talking cats as they drew nearer.

"Nay," Hugh was saying. "I have become accustomed to them over the years. My wife has three that
she even allows in our chamber. I have tried numerous times to get them ousted, but with no luck."

"My lady could tell you just how to get rid of them,
for she managed to oust mine right quickly."

"Ah, but what works for her would not work for
me, or have you not realized yet that though we men
have the final say, our ladies will win most every argument in the end to get what they want."

"Bite your tongue," Ranulf retorted, though there
was laughter in his violet eyes. "I expect to win at
least half the arguments in this household—one way
or another."

Reina was blushing by the time they reached her.
That was not a discussion she cared to hear or get
involved in.

"Did you have a pleasant ride, my lords?"

"Indeed," Hugh replied. "Though I must confess I was hoping to find a few areas where my advice might be needful for improvements. Instead I learned a thing or two I intend to implement on my own lands. You have my compliments, lady. Clydon is as prosperous as I had heard."

"That is to my father's credit, not mine," Reina replied. "He was at heart a farmer, and loved the land."

"And his daughter is too modest," Ranulf added. "She has kept the entire estate running so well there is little for me to do other than see to its defenses."

"Do not belittle the importance of that, my lord. It takes only a single act of aggression to lay waste to years of hard work."

Hugh grinned. "She has you there, Ranulf. No demesne can prosper long without a lord capable of protecting it. I am sure the lady took that into consideration ere she allowed herself to be 'smitten' by your charms."

Ranulf guffawed with laughter. Reina smiled herself. "So you told him of our unusual courtship, did you?"

"He managed to wrest a few details from me," Ranulf admitted as he dropped Ella on the bench beside her.

"I can well imagine which ones," Reina snorted, though she was in fact amused. "But come, rest yourselves." She stood up to pour them each a goblet of wine. Handing one to Hugh, she said, "I do not intend to be remiss in my duties again, my lord. I have a chamber readied for you do you care to refresh yourself before the evening meal. Theodric will show you the way when you are—"

"Theodric will not," Ranulf interrupted sharply. "Lady, you would not dare."

"Would not dare what?" Reina asked sweetly. "Eadwina awaits to assist your father. Theo will only show him the way to the east tower when he is ready."

"Oh," was all Ranulf said to that.

"Is something amiss?" Hugh asked.

"Not at all, my lord," Reina assured him, picking up her own goblet, but sparing a wry smile for her husband. "And now I would like to propose a toast. To new beginnings—" She paused, and her smile turned to a satisfied smirk. She really could not help it. "—that need only a tiny nudge to get started."

Hugh chuckled. Ranulf did not. And then a new voice was heard from that gave Reina a start, as well as her father-by-marriage.

"I hope I am not interrupting."

"This is a surprise, Richard," Hugh said, and he was indeed surprised, uncomfortably so under the circumstances. "I believe you are well acquainted with my son, Lady Reina?"

Reina did not answer. She had spewed her wine as she made the connection and was now busy choking. She sat down heavily but was quick to wave away Ranulf's assistance. She did not care to be pounded on the back by him and end up sprawled on the floor just now. He, fortunately, did not yet realize who Richard was—other than he was his brother.

"Are you all right, lady?" both Hugh and Richard asked.

"Indeed," Reina rasped and set her goblet down. "A bad brew," she added by way of explanation.

Hugh nodded and glanced at Ranulf, but as he looked only mildly curious over this turn of events, Hugh gave his attention back to Richard. "How is it you discovered I was traveling to Warhurst?"

"I did not," Richard replied. "Actually, I was on my way to Lyonsford, but wanted to pay my respects to Lady Reina, as I have not visited Clydon for sometime. I was not aware you were acquainted with the lady, father."

"I was not, until this morn. My baggage wain broke down, or I would not have stopped here, with Warhurst so close."

Reina was not paying attention to this conversation. She was watching her husband and knew the moment his ignorance ended. He was sitting next to her on the bench, so that she heard his sharp intake of breath and the even louder expulsion. Then his eyes came to her, glowing with furious accusation, and she could do no more than flinch.

Well, 'twas her own fault. Had she been paying attention when Gilbert introduced Hugh to her, she would have known he was not only Ranulf's father but Richard's, too, and she could have given Ranulf warning. Lyonsford, the very family her own father had approved an alliance with, and she had made that alliance unawares.

This was too funny, though she did not dare laugh just now. She had wanted to marry one brother, had ended up marrying the other, and did not even know it—and neither did they. And now her husband thought she had deliberately tried to keep the truth from him and would continue to think so until they were alone and she could explain. Nay, why should she wait? They were all family, after all.

" 'Tis not what you think, Ranulf, so you can stop scowling at me like that. I was so surprised when your father walked in here this morn that I did not hear him introduced to me. 'Tis as simple as that.''

"Is it?" he growled.

"Very well, give me one reason why I would not tell you your brother is now your neighbor if I knew it. You were like to find out soon enough, if your father did not tell you first, so why should I keep it from you?"

"For spite."

"I am not Lady—" *Jesú,* she almost said "Anne," but she was not supposed to know of her, and she could not betray Walter's confidence. "Never mind," she finished stiffly, annoyed that she could offer no better defense, further annoyed that she should need one. "If you think that, then you do not know me at all."

There must have been enough disappointment in her voice to make an impression, for the moment she turned away, Ranulf's hand drew her back. "I am sorry," he said gruffly, and she knew it was not just words, that he actually was. He looked too embarrassed not to be. "There is just too much converging on me at once here."

She knew exactly how he felt, and so smiled encouragingly. "Naught that cannot be dealt with, my lord." And then she leaned closer to whisper, "The key is to take the situation in hand and assume control of it—like this." His alarmed look made her add, "Relax. *You* will not be on the receiving end this time."

Reina turned to the two men still standing. They had ceased their own conversation, though how much they had heard of hers she could not guess. But Richard did not look at ease, not in the least.

He was a half foot shorter than his father, with curly brown hair and gray eyes usually as merry as Searle's, but there was no humor in them now. Hugh was right: this son of his bore absolutely no resemblance to him. That was not unusual. What was unusual was the striking resemblance Ranulf bore to Hugh, which Richard could not mistake. He had once told her that he had cousins and uncles on his father's side whom he had never met. Had he assumed Ranulf to be one of these when he first saw him, she could understand his disconcertion now if he had heard her say they were brothers. Even if he had not heard that, suspicions would not be long in coming.

''Well, Lord Hugh, as well as your father managed to keep Ranulf a secret from Richard's relatives, you must allow the secret is now ended. Do you intend to introduce your sons to each other, or should I?''

Suspicions might have been forming, but confirmation sent Richard stumbling toward a seat. Hugh frowned at Reina, but she ignored him, ignored Ranulf, too, who was also frowning at the abruptness of her disclosure. She was more interested in Richard's reaction, which was not just surprise, but alarm. Now why should that be? He was his father's heir, so named in his will. Did he think that would change now? He might, if he thought his father also had only just discovered Ranulf's existence.

''You really did not know, did you, Richard?'' she asked more gently, remembering belatedly that this man had always been a friend to her.

''Nay,'' he replied, and looked to his father. ''Did you?''

"For many years now," Hugh admitted.

"And you never thought to tell me? You did not think I would find it of interest to know you have another bastard, one older than I?"

He made this heated accusation in a tone and expression so unlike himself that Reina was startled. Ranulf was not, she saw, but of course Ranulf did not know Richard's usual easygoing manner. Hugh was not surprised either, however, so mayhap he had been witness to such an outburst before. But Reina had not been, and this Richard was so different from the one she knew that she was forced to recall all the outlaw had told her in a new light. She had thought it impossible that Richard could be of two such different characters, but in fact it was not.

"I never found a reason to tell you," Hugh was saying. "Due to unfortunate misunderstandings, I have been estranged from Ranulf all these years."

"And now you are not?" Richard demanded.

"I am pleased to say that is so," Hugh replied, and then more sharply, "Your upset is understandable but uncalled-for, Richard. This does not change your own circumstance. What I was coming to Warhurst to tell you does, however. You learn today that you have not only a half brother but also a half sister, Elisabeth, born to my lady wife last month."

Richard paled at this news. Reina glanced quickly at Ranulf to see he was not surprised. Hugh had obviously already told him he had a sister, and he was not in the least displeased. Well, it did not matter to him one way or the other, did it? But to Richard it did, and where an estate the size of Lyonsford was concerned, it no doubt mattered a great deal.

But Hugh was not finished. "The terms wrested

from me at your birth, Richard, were unreasonable and never meant to fully apply. That my wife remained barren for so long mayhap has led you to anticipate more from me, but that is not to be. I gave you Warhurst. You needs be satisfied with that.''

"Why? Because 'tis more than a bastard should expect? You forget who my grandfather was!''

"Nay, I do not forget,'' Hugh said coldly, finally giving reign to his displeasure with this son. '' 'Twas my father who gave a damn, not I.''

Richard could not deal with all of this at once. A sister was not real to him. A baby, and babies died. Ranulf was real, however; there, watching him make a fool of himself, which he could not seem to help.

"And what do you give to *him*, father?'' Richard sneered, glaring furiously at Ranulf.

He paled again, however, when Ranulf stood up to accept the unspoken challenge. Reina stood up, too, to step between them. There would be no fighting in her hall if she could help it. But 'twas Hugh who defused the sudden tension.

"Not that it is any of your concern, Richard, but what I give to him was given long ago, when he reached his tenth year, so 'tis no longer a part of Lyonsford. The transaction was approved by the king, the property to be turned over to Ranulf when he reached twenty years and five. 'Tis no town like Warhurst, merely a small keep, but I know for a certainty he will be well satisfied.''

"Will be?'' Richard laughed derisively, obviously seeing some humor in this. "You waited this long to even tell him?''

Reina could have kicked the young lord. Sweet *Jesú*, had she really thought to marry him, this greedy, vindictive, whining boy-man? More and more she was beginning to give credence to the prisoner's tale.

She said in a whispered aside to Ranulf, who stood behind her, "He told you of Elisabeth. Did he give you warning of this, too?" He did not answer, forcing her to turn enough to see him. His expression was answer enough. "So he did not," she hissed.

Once more Reina could not help feeling an unreasonable anger toward his father. Richard had been gifted with Warhurst when he was only eighteen, to do with as he would, but Ranulf had been given an even smaller property, and not told of it at all. And he still could not have it, not until he was twenty years and five. Not that he needed it now, but what kind of reasoning was that, to make him wait? He could have made use of it before, could have won a wife with it, started a family . . . and she would not have met him. *Jesú,* what was she getting angry about? Hugh's reasoning, whatever it was, had worked to *her* benefit, if not to Ranulf's.

Still, Ranulf was to have had no more surprises here. She had been lax in letting the talk get away from her control. Hugh too noticed Ranulf's adverse reaction and came closer, so close that Reina was near pressed between them. Not that they should notice her way down there. Sometimes a lack of height was a very real disadvantage, which she had never felt so keenly as just then.

"You hold it against me?" Hugh asked Ranulf carefully. "I was told that you might when I made the decision, but I had my reasons. I did not want you to be satisfied with your lot and strive no further to improve it. You were so like me, Ranulf. I wanted to see how you would fare on your own first." And then he grinned, that pride Reina had earlier detected in him there for Ranulf to see now. "I would say you have done right nicely. Farring Cross has become insignificant."

"Farring Cross!" Ranulf began with a gasp, but ended in a burst of laughter.

Hugh also laughed, and Reina could not for the life of her figure why until he added, "De Millers had the devil's own time trying to keep you from learning he was only the steward there. 'Twas rather disconcerting for him that you were trying to purchase your own property. He thought surely you would kill him when he was forced to again raise his price to keep you from buying it, but I would not let him tell you the truth."

Reina squeezed out from between them to shake her head at the irony. Richard did not understand what they found so funny, however.

"You tried to purchase this Farring Cross?" he asked his brother.

"Aye."

"It must be richer than our father implied, then."

"Not richer, just in excellent condition and suitable to my needs at the time," Ranulf said placidly, but suddenly his demeanor changed, as did his voice, which turned mocking. "Unlike you, I did not desire an estate of the extent and magnitude of, let us say— Clydon?"

Reina noted Richard's distinct unease at this insinuation. She wanted to applaud her husband, but first she would see what further reaction could be wrested from Richard.

"Oh, you poor man," Reina said to Ranulf. "How

unfortunate you should be encumbered with such an estate after all.''

"What estate?'' Richard was quick to demand.

"You see, Lord Hugh,'' Reina chided gently, "you should have introduced them as I suggested; then Richard would already know that his brother is Lord of Clydon.'' And to Richard, whose face was swiftly crimsoning with fury: "We were wed less than a sennight ago.'

"But he is a bastard!'' Richard exploded. "How could you marry a bastard?''

There it was, more clear than if he had come right out and admitted the truth. He had assumed she would not have him because *he* was a bastard, and so had decided to take her by force. But Ranulf's fortunate arrival had ruined his plans. She wondered if Richard had thought to try again, mayhap today even, and that was really why he was here. Some pretext to get her to leave Clydon with him, and he would have had her. Too bad he had not thought of that first. Nay, not too bad—thank God.

"I do not see what the circumstances of Ranulf's birth have to do with it,'' Reina said calmly enough, though her eyes had become frigid. "Verily, did that matter, I would not have considered you for my husband first.''

"What?'' he fairly shrieked.

" 'Tis true, Richard. I sent you numerous letters, both to Warhurst and to Lyonsford. Had you come to Clydon as I requested, you might have agreed to my proposal, and I would be wed to you now instead of your brother. But I was pressed for time, you see, and needed a husband right quickly. I knew not where you were and could not wait indefinitely to hear from you. So when I met Ranulf last week and found that he would suit me as well, I put my proposal to him."

She had rendered Richard speechless for the moment. Not so Hugh. "You actually wanted Richard?"

"Why does that surprise you, my lord? He has been a good neighbor to us, my father approved of him, and I thought we would deal well together."

"Then why could you not wait?" Richard burst out. "Or give me an indication of why you were trying to reach me?"

One sable brow rose inquiringly. "I assumed my letters never reached you, Richard. Do you tell me now they did, but you simply ignored them?"

"Nay, nay, I did not mean to imply—I have been traveling a great deal—"

"Well, it does not matter now, does it?" she cut in silkily. "I am well satisfied with the husband I have. And he has already proved how capable he is at defending Clydon. 'Tis how we met, you know? He arrived here in time to rout a despicable band of miscreants who dared attack us. He has also sworn to run the villeins to ground as a warning to others who still might think Clydon without a new lord. I told him 'twas unnecessary, but he was a mercenary for many years, and you know how they love fighting and killing, and generally making war."

"I am not so bloodthirsty as all that, lady," Ranulf protested gruffly, though his eyes were laughing at her.

"Well, of course you are not," Reina agreed, and then saw her chance for the crowning touch in the bit of fluff twining about his feet. She stooped down to pick up her nemesis. "No man can be all bad who would keep a scrawny, ugly thing like this for pet, and even give it the esteemed name of—''

"Reina!''

His warning came too late, though she would not have heeded it anyway. "—Lady Ella,'' she finished with a sweetly innocent expression that earned her a fierce glower from her husband.

It was all Hugh could do to keep from laughing, but once again furious color rushed to Richard's face. "Lady Ella? You named your cat after my mother?'' he asked in disbelief, and then in outrage, *"You named your cat after my—"*

"Whatever are you shouting about, Richard?'' Reina cut in sternly. "You cannot think your brother would be so currish as that.''

He did not answer her, but turned his fury on his father. "Will you let him insult her like that? She was your . . .''

"My what?'' Hugh prompted when he did not finish, and then he shook his head in disgust. "Nay, we both know what she was, and she has not exactly endeared herself to me over the years, Richard, and well you know it. As it happens, I have several bitches in my kennel by the same name, so do not expect me to upbraid a man whose humor is so like my own.''

"My uncle will hear of this!'' was all Richard could think to say after that.

"Oh, for Christ's sake, Richard—'' Hugh began in exasperation but ended with a sigh as the boy stalked off. He looked apologetically at Ranulf. "I had best go after him to calm him down. He always was a hothead, but what can you expect after he has been raised by those infuriating relatives of his?''

"Much more—" Reina started, then gasped as her bottom was pinched.

"Go ahead, my lord," Ranulf said, even as Reina turned around to glare at him. The byplay was not lost on Hugh, so Ranulf added, "My lady does not know when to quit while she is ahead."

Hugh nodded with a grin. Reina barely waited until he was out of hearing ere she hissed, "Why did you stop me, Ranulf?"

"What you would have said cannot be supported."

"Then you have not sent a man to Warhurst yet?"

"Nay, and I will not."

"Will—but why?" she cried. "Did you not see the look on Richard's face when I mentioned you would hunt down the villeins who attacked Clydon? He is guilty!"

"So he is.";

"And your father must be told."

"Not by me, lady."

She stared at him incredulously. "Why? Because he is your brother?"

"Exactly. A brother I have resented most of my life, and now—now I do not know what I feel other than contempt, but I will not be the one to carry tales to my father of him."

"Of all the lackwitted . . . Very well, I will send a man to Warhurst. *I* at least will not be accused of spite, though you do your father a disservice to assume he would think that of you."

"You will stay out of it, Reina, and I mean that," Ranulf said coldly. "I will attend to the matter in my own way once my father is gone."

"But he needs be told!"

"Not by us!"

Chapter Forty-one

*R*eina thought about it. She really did. And she came that close to defying Ranulf and doing as she thought best. But then she remembered how deadly serious had been his order not to interfere, and she decided it would behoove her to obey her husband in this instance. She had to begin trusting in his judgment at some time anyway, and now seemed a likely time to start. As it happened, she had reason to be thankful for that decision, for the matter resolved itself, and right quickly.

When Hugh could not catch up with Richard in time to speak with him, he determined to follow him to Warhurst, sending a message up to Ranulf that he would return later. 'Twas much later when he did. The hall was quiet, so he was taken straight up to the chamber prepared for him. Reina had food warming at the hearth, where a small fire had been laid to also heat water for a bath. The man was tired, but not only from fatigue. One look at him was enough for her to realize he had learned the truth about Richard for himself. The townspeople had, in fact, converged on him with their complaints, laments, and charges of tyranny as soon as he passed through the gates.

"This is Ella's doing," Hugh said after he had repeated some of the outlandish things he had been told. "She would not wed me, thank God, but she would not let me have the boy either. She wanted him raised at court, as she had been.''

Reina had intended to just sit by and listen, to let Ranulf and his father work this out between themselves, but when Ranulf made no comment to this, her curiosity could not stand it. ''I thought you said Richard was raised by his mother's family, my lord.''

''He was. Ah, I see your confusion. Did I neglect to mention Ella is a Plantagenet? From the wrong side of the blanket, of course.''

Reina's mouth dropped open. Ranulf did not even blink. He obviously had known this from the time he first learned of his half brother.

''One of Henry's?'' she asked when she found her voice.

''Just so. And now you know why my father was so pleased by the association. But the uncle Richard mentioned is not his namesake. King Richard barely knows him. 'Twas Prince John who took an interest in the boy, more's the pity. And you can see where *that* influence has led him.''

''But what if he speaks to John as he said?''

Hugh gave a derisive snort. ''John is too busy with his machinations to wrest the crown from Richard. It has been his obsession since their father died. Think you he would really care about some harmless insult to a bastard sister? Nay, lady, my younger son likes to think he has influence at court, but in truth, he does not, nor does his mother any longer. The man she wed might once have held power, but he lost it when Richard Lion-Heart became king. What my son has, he has from me.''

''What will you—what *can* you do, then? Warhurst is his by your own generosity.''

"Nay, not quite. Unlike Farring Cross, which was given outright, Warhurst still belongs to Lyonsford, and will until my death. My mistake was in allocating control of it to Richard, with the hope that the responsibility would help develop a more honorable character, or at least some integrity. Instead he corrupts the steward I sent to guide him, and emulates his all-powerful relations to the worst extent."

"But what of the castellan, Chaucer? We have dealt with him."

Hugh shook his head. "Chaucer was my steward, Lady Reina. *Richard* was castellan."

"Why, that liar!" Reina said indignantly. "He had everyone in the area believing him Lord of Warhurst."

Ranulf chuckled at her rancor. "Come now, lady, you were befooled by an expert who learned from the best deceivers in the land. 'Tis no fault of your own that you could not see through his duplicity."

"That is easy for you to say," she retorted. *"You* did not almost marry him!"

Ranulf grinned. "I should hope not."

"At any rate," Hugh was quick to intervene, "you will have no more trouble from my younger son, lady." And then he could not help a grin of his own. "I cannot guarantee the same of this one, however. Richard is even now being escorted to a cousin of mine in Ireland who has no tolerance for dishonesty. A few years there should turn him about, or so I can only hope."

"He actually agreed to go?"

"I did not ask," Hugh replied baldly.

"Oh—well, that settles that, except for—"

"That settles everything, Reina," Ranulf cut in sharply. "Get you to bed now. I will join you anon."

Her lips tightened. She was ready for battle at being summarily dismissed. The man really must learn some manners. But suddenly she remembered what she had just barely escaped that morning and thought better of provoking him anymore today.

Still, she had had a tiny devil inside her the entire day, and 'twas that wicked creature that prompted her to retort as she crossed to the door: "You need not hurry on my account, my lord. I am like to be fast asleep."

"Nay, you will not be, for we still have unfinished business, if you will recall."

Her mouth opened, then abruptly shut. Nay, he could not mean that. Not *that*.

He did mean it. No sooner did he enter their bedchamber than Ranulf asked, "Have you dreaded this moment, lady? Nay, there is no need to answer. Your behavior this day speaks for itself. But you have concluded wrongly, for whatever reason."

Reina sat on a stool by the hearth, where she had been combing her hair. Ranulf crossed to the bed and took up the exact same position on it he had assumed that morn. She could do no more than stare at him in total dismay.

"Come, Reina," he said in the most casual tone. "This will not take long."

Oh, just like that? The lout, the brute! How dared he be so calm about it?

"And if I refuse?"

"Then 'twill just take longer—much longer."

He was not counting the time he would have to

chase her about the room, she was sure. "If I had let you have your way this morn, you would not now be reconciled with your father," she said bitterly. "Does that count for naught?"

"The means do not justify the end, Reina. You totally ignored my wishes and forced me to accept yours. What we do here is assure that never happens again."

"What you do here is barbaric!"

"Did I fetch a whip, lady, *that* would be barbaric."

He came to his feet as he said it, and Reina jumped to hers also. When he did not come after her, however, she realized he was still giving her a chance to make this easier on herself. Did she want a worse punishment just for the sake of a little, useless resistance?

Reina forced herself to close the distance, stopping before him with bowed head. Her stomach was queasy with dread, her heart pounding. It did not feel right, this weak submission, but what else could she do? A wife simply did not go against her husband, taunting him and provoking him until she had her way. And this husband was going to make sure she remembered that, rot his inflexible stubbornness.

"A wise decision," he said as he sat down again and drew her onto his lap. "You may retain the robe you are wearing. 'Twill be a simple matter to lift it out of the way."

She had the feeling he said that only to increase her distress and humiliation, and it worked. That he was not being rough with her, or sharp in his tone, only seemed to make it worse. His voice was husky, his hands gentle as he turned her over so that she rested across his thighs. Reina dropped her head down to hide her face, and placed one hand against the bed, the other on his left knee. Did she feel the need to push herself out of this horrible position, she would have the leverage. Or so she thought. His left hand, coming to rest in the center of her back with a subtle pressure, seemed to say otherwise.

Alarm bells of a different sort went off in her head when he began to raise her robe. He did it by setting his hand on the back of her calf and slowly gliding that hand up her leg, the robe perforce coming with it. 'Twas a caress, plain and simple, and it gave her the strangest sensations. Her body no longer knew what to anticipate, pain or pleasure. Her mind was reeling with the same confusion. Was this a punishment?

Soon the robe was gathered at her waist, his hand removed, and Reina braced herself, her eyes squeezed shut. Her face burned to have her bottom bared to him. Her heart was now racing. Only he did nothing immediately, and the suspense was terrible, the wait worse than aught that he could do by way of punishment.

When the smack finally came, 'twas almost anti-climactic. Almost, but not entirely. Hot and stinging, it brought a gasp from her that was only half surprise, and a tensing of her muscles to receive another. But there was no other, only his voice coming to her softly.

"In case you wondered, little Reina, that was the extent of the punishment I intended to give you when I brought you up here this morn." Her reaction was immediate, every muscle relaxing in relief. "But while I had you in this convenient position, I meant to do this." Her eyes flew open when she felt a kiss on the reddened imprint left by his hand. "And this." Reina sucked in her breath as his fingers slid inside her body with no difficulty at all. This was what that other caress had prepared her for, and she had no resistance against the heat that flooded her. "Of course, I am forgetting that you warned me not to touch you afterward, something about not forgiving me." He paused, his fingers tormenting her. "Is that right?"

Reina was throbbing, on fire, could barely speak. "Mayhap . . . I was a bit . . . hasty."

"Or mayhap it no longer matters?" His fingers brought forth another gasp. "Does it?"

"Nay."

"Red Alma was right again, it seems," he said with a note of satisfaction. "Fear combined with the correct stimulation can increase a woman's pleasure to the point that she will overlook whatever small punishment she receives."

Reina tensed, but not enough to combat the haze of pleasure he had created with such unbelievable swiftness. "You went to her again?"

"Nay, 'twas a bit of information she volunteered in her gratitude for the large sum I gifted her with for her help. And she has been most helpful, has she not?" His fingers withdrew, thrust back, withdrew, bringing Reina to the very edge of ecstasy. "Shall we put it to the test?"

She thought he already had, but then she was not thinking clearly at the moment. "How?"

"What I mentioned was what I originally meant to do." His change of tone gave her warning. "But since then you have earned at least another . . ."

"Ran—nulf!" Her voice rose before she got his

name out, for she heard the crack of his hand ere she felt it, and the stinging pain was much worse than before. "What did I do?" she shrieked.

"You had at me again in this very chamber, lady. Rail at me in front of my father, will you?" Again his hand descended.

"Ranulf!"

"Call me a dog-hearted clodpate, will you?" Another wallop.

"Stop!" Her cry rose in volume. "Sweet *Jesú,* gag me. You said you would gag me!"

"There is no need," he said brusquely. "I am finished."

Reina was set on her feet, which were not at all steady. A glance at her husband showed how furious he had become, to which her bottom could well attest. His next words only confirmed it.

"Do not ever make me do that again, lady," he growled low.

She shook her head, but she was not sure whether she was saying she would or would not. Not that it mattered just then. Her backside was on fire, but it blazed not half as much as that other fire he had created. Without another thought, Reina crawled back onto his lap.

"I am duly chastised, my lord. Now finish what else you started."

He did not have to be asked twice.

Chapter Forty-two

*L*ess than a sennight later, Reina slammed into her bedchamber in a fine temper. Theodric, who was there giving the room a good cleaning, glanced up with a start, fearing 'twas Ranulf. He stayed out of that one's way, and no longer attended Reina at her bath. But he refused to allow anyone else to usurp the rest of his duties. However, he saw to them only when the lord was not likely to be around, as now in early afternoon.

Seeing Reina, he relaxed. In another moment he noted the torn sleeve of her bliaut, the mussed hair minus the silk caul she had been wearing earlier, the bloom to her cheeks that was not entirely temper.

"Another tumble in the bushes, eh?" he inquired with a wicked grin.

Reina swung about to glare at him. "He's a brute! An animal!"

"The best ones usually are." Theo sighed.

She ignored that. "He rode out to fight Rothwell." But not before he had pulled her into an empty stall in the stable and made swift, passionate love to her— for luck, he had said. With a whole troop awaiting him? The grooms sent running with a single growled order? Everyone undoubtedly aware of what had delayed her? But 'twas his lack of sense that truly infuriated her. "He would not listen to a word I said."

"What did you say?"

"That he should not go, of course."

She told the mighty warrior not to go out and fight? Theo nearly laughed, but did not think his lady would appreciate it at the moment.

"Rothwell? Is that not—"

"Aye, *him!* Ranulf said he might come, and now he has."

"Where is he?"

"Reported about an hour's ride north, and with an army three hundred strong. Ranulf took only fifty men with him!" she cried. "He is mad! What was wrong with letting Rothwell come here? Clydon is well manned now. We can withstand thousands! But nay, he said does Rothwell get a good look at Clydon, he will never give up. He means to stop him ere he gets any closer and turn him back with words! Mere words, Theo! When have you ever known a man set on war to listen to, much less heed, mere words?"

"When they come from a giant set to stop him."

Reina glared another moment, then frowned thoughtfully. "I suppose that has some merit," she allowed. "Rothwell knows Ranulf, knows what he is capable of. 'Twas why he was willing to pay so much to hire him. But, *Jesú,* the old man is going to be furious does Ranulf tell him that *he* wed me. What if he then thinks to make me a widow?"

Theo chuckled that she had now found something else to worry about. "Reina, think you Ranulf has not considered all this? He is a man of strategy. Fighting is what he does best. 'Tis why you wed him, is it not?"

"I know, I know, but I hate the odds, Theo. He is only one man, regardless does he think he is more.

Why can he not be reasonable and close the gates when he is so outnumbered?''

If Reina had known that Ranulf rode forth to meet Rothwell with only Eric and Searle at his side, she would never have forgiven him for the fright that would have caused her. This was not one of Ranulf's concerns, however. He took note of the dozen men who separated from the ranks to intercept him with Rothwell. Three he recognized from his first meeting with the old lord. The others were likely vassals he had coerced into joining him. They did not appear too pleased to be on this campaign, but that was what Ranulf had counted on from what he knew of Rothwell.

As he had also figured, the ranks were filled mainly with mercenaries; several of their captains Ranulf recognized from past association. They stirred uneasily at the sight of him. He had to wonder if they even knew what they came here for. To steal a bride was not something one would want bruited about.

Ranulf had left his own men concealed in the wood behind him, some visible, some not, so their numbers were in doubt. He had waited here for Rothwell in order to gain that advantage, but he did not really think he would need it.

"I did not expect to find you still in the area, Fitz Hugh," Lord Rothwell said as they drew abreast. "When you did not return, I assumed you had decided not to accept my offer. Or will you tell me you never even gained access to Clydon and are still trying?"

This last was said with a sneer that rubbed Ranulf

on the raw, but his tone was level when he replied, "Your first assumption was the correct one."

"Then what are you still doing here?" the old man blustered.

"Seeing that you do not make a serious mistake. The lady you wished to avail yourself of is no longer available. She has already wed."

"So *that* is why you did naught," Rothwell chortled, then drew closer to add, "You should have come back and said so, but never mind. She can as like be made a widow. My offer still stands are you interested."

A golden brow rose questioningly. "Five hundred marks to kill the husband?"

"Aye."

"That would be a bit difficult, my lord, as I am that husband."

Rothwell's eyes bulged. For a moment, he choked on his own spittle. When he did find his voice, it came out in a roar.

"Devil's spawn! You stole my bride! Kill him!" he shouted at those men closest to him.

Eric and Searle put their hands to their sword hilts, but Ranulf did not move. Neither did Rothwell's men, other than to control their mounts that were spooked by the noise the old man was making. And he got louder, his face blotched with color, enraged that his orders were ignored.

"What are you waiting for? Are you all cowards? He is only a man!"

"He is also Lord of Clydon," one of his men hissed at him. "Think what you are saying."

"He stole—"

"Enough, Rothwell," Ranulf growled menacingly.

"Naught was stolen from you, and well you know it. The lady was never betrothed to you. She had never even heard of you. But she is now wed to me, and I will keep what I have made mine. Do you wish to dispute that, challenge me now and name your champion."

Rothwell was delighted with the offer, until he looked toward his men to see who would fight for him, and not one would meet his eyes. Again his face suffused with color.

"Cowards all, that is what I have!"

"Nay," Ranulf said. "What you have is honest men whose misfortune is to have you for an overlord."

"You have not heard the end of this, Fitz Hugh."

"Then you court your own death," Ranulf said in a tone as ominous as the words. "For I will give you only this one warning. Go home and forget Clydon, or I will ignore how old you are and kill you myself."

He did not await a reply, yanking his horse about and riding off. But he had seen the fear in those old eyes. Rothwell would find himself another bride.

Chapter Forty-three

Reina was nearly four months pregnant. For long and long she tried to deny it, finding one excuse after another to convince herself it could not be so. She had to stop trying when her waist increased, but her appetite did not. That day she was impossible to deal with, a veritable shrew to one and all. Her temperament had not improved much since. Fortunately, Ranulf had been gone a good deal of this time and missed her truly bad days, when she would be so beset by conflicting emotions that she would either rage at the least little provocation or burst into tears.

She had been told again and again that this would pass, that 'twas the changes in her body making her so emotional. Each of her older ladies had assured her of this. They all knew about the child. Everyone knew about the child—everyone except the child's father. But no one was aware of what was really bothering her. 'Twas not something she cared to discuss, even with Theo.

That lackwit was as excited about the baby as 'twas possible to be. You would think he were to bear it. Not that Reina was not excited herself. She wanted this child, more than anything. Already she loved it, imagining it not half formed as it was, but as it would be, a life to cherish, to protect—to spoil. Her little giant, exactly like Ranulf, but unlike Ranulf, needing her.

Oh, sweet *Jesú*, there were those cursed tears again. Reina angrily swiped them away and left the brewhouse, the unlikely place where Lady Ella had decided to deliver her litter of five. She had been missing for a week, causing a castle-wide search and panic, at least on Reina's part, to find her ere Ranulf returned. He had been so silly over the cat's pregnancy, so delighted yet anxious, she had almost told him about her own, but could not do it. Now, she had waited so long, she would not have to tell him. Her body had done its changing during this three-week absence of his. He would know as soon as he saw her, or at least as soon as he took her to bed. God, how she was dreading that.

The past few months had been so idyllic and uneventful. She had had no trouble with Ranulf since his father's visit. Hugh had sent a new steward to Warhurst, whose duty it was to wade through the mess Richard had left behind, and recompense all those who had suffered unjustly. The prisoners Ranulf had held had been turned over to the new man to be retried, this time fairly, and nearly all had been cleared of any wrongdoing. And Ranulf had kept busy, which was why he had not been witness to any of Reina's recent uncharacteristic swings in mood.

He had made a tour of all the Clydon fiefs. He would be gone a few days or a week, return for a short time, then leave again. Reina had gone along the first few times, until the riding began to cause her a queasy upset, and she made excuses to remain at Clydon after that.

This last and longest absence of Ranulf's was a trip to London at his father's invitation. All was going well with them, or so the letter she had indicated.

This was her first correspondence from Ranulf, but in no way personal. 'Twas in fact written by Walter, who had gone with him. But Reina had learned from Ranulf himself that he could neither read nor write. Thus her reply lacked intimacy as well, since it would have to be read to him. She had already determined something should be done about that, though Ranulf was likely to balk at learning what there were clerks aplenty to do for him.

None of that mattered, naught did, in light of what would happen once Ranulf learned he had done his duty and given her the child she had demanded of him. The only reason she had been the recipient of his lust thus far was because he took seriously the duty fulfilling the terms of the marriage contract. That lust would be gone now, and with it the closeness she had come to feel toward him. She had never guessed, when she had decided to enjoy it while it lasted, that she would in fact be devastated when Ranulf no longer had a need to bed her.

She wondered if he would ask her to move back to her old chamber. She wondered how long it would take him to find a mistress. She wondered if she would be able to forgive him and accept him back when it was time to produce the next child, for she had asked for children, not just one child. She was driving herself mad with the wondering. Sweet *Jesú,* she was not supposed to have cared about any of this. 'Twas not the way she had ever imagined her married life to be. But then she had never imagined she would come to feel lust herself, intense, insatiable lust, and for a husband no less.

She had been selfish to put off the telling. It could not have been easy for Ranulf to remain faithful to her all this time, and she believed he had been, even when he was gone from Clydon. A man who returned and immediately took his wife straight to bed, no matter the time of day, and did not leave it for hours on end, was not a man who had been getting his pleasure elsewhere. How she was going to miss that, and so much more.

Reina was so weighed down with these dismal thoughts, she almost did not notice the visitors who crossed her path, making their way toward the keep. They in turn paid no attention to her. Why should they? She had put on her oldest bliaut when the ale-wife came to tell her she had heard the mewling of kittens coming from behind the ale barrels. And without her calling out a dozen servants to move the huge barrels, and possibly get a few squashed kittens in the process, the only way to see if 'twas Lady Ella back there was to climb atop the stacked barrels and crawl around until she found in which narrow crevice the mother cat was holed up. Subsequently, she was covered with dust and grime, but at least she was assured that Ranulf's cat was alive and well. A moment of humor broke through as she imagined him crawling across those barrels to see for himself, and he would, too.

So who were her unexpected guests? There was a lady and a lord, but they had already passed her; thus she had missed seeing their faces to identify them. Their ten-man escort was smartly dressed and equipped, but that gave her no clue. Well, she was in no hurry to find out, for even if she ran now, she was not likely to get into the keep before them. Once again she was caught ill-prepared to receive company. The last time she had met her husband. This time would be no less embarrassing, looking as she did, no matter who the visitors were.

Their arrival had caught the interest of several of the knights in the exercise yard. Practice had stopped for a moment, but resumed when the visitors passed through the inner gate. The quintain was getting good use, and the clanging of swords echoed across the full width of the outer bailey. Since Ranulf's coming, 'twas a familiar sound this time of day.

Clydon now had seven new knights in service, with as many new squires. She noticed Sir William instructing one. He had not enjoyed himself so since her father had left for the Holy Land. Searle was there, pitting his skill against one of the new knights. She had watched Ranulf and Walter challenge each other just so, and Searle, who had been taught by them, used the same technique. There was no contest. The new knight was disarmed in moments.

Eric and Aubert were there, too, watching two squires in similar mock combat. One she recognized as Lanzo, with his bright red hair. He should have been helmeted, for he was using a true sword instead of the wooden ones the newer squires used. His smaller opponent was not fully armed either, and was taking a beating, barely able to keep his sword up, much less his shield, and even as she watched he went down. That Lanzo kept after him even though he had fallen annoyed her, however. She knew a knight had to learn to defend himself even from the ground, for many died in just that position were they not so trained, but Lanzo seemed particularly brutal about the lesson.

Her heart then seemed to stop as she thought she recognized the boy on the ground. Aylmer? Nay,

Lanzo could not be that cruel. True, Aylmer loved to watch the knights in practice. But Lanzo would not dare entice him onto the field, to actually give him a sword and then attack him. Would he?

She started forward, calling out the squire's name. He could not hear her, still pounding his sword against the downed boy's shield. She was soon close enough to see that it really was Aylmer taking this beating, and a blind, red fury consumed her. She was upon them in moments, with no thought for the danger of that swinging sword, just the need to stop it—which she did with a mighty shove that sent Lanzo sprawling.

She immediately helped Aylmer to his feet, pushing back the sweaty brown curls from his eyes, quickly examining him for any hurts. She felt some relief that he was not bleeding anywhere, but she was still furious, and that he looked at her as if she were crazy did not help.

"Lady, why did you do that?"

"Why?" she fairly shrieked. "You are being pummeled nigh to death and you ask why?"

Those knights who noticed her there and started to come forward to see what had happened quickly resumed their practice at the sound of her fury. Eric, who had tried to intercept her when he saw her charging toward danger, backed away, unwilling to draw her attention to him. One look at Aubert said they were all in trouble, though they could not fathom why.

Aylmer was the only one there who realized that Reina was merely concerned for his welfare. 'Twas embarrassing in this instance, but it never failed to fill him with warmth that such as she could care for him.

Quietly, hoping she would be glad for him, he said, "I am to be a squire, lady."

Reina's heart constricted at the pride in those words. Oh, God, this jest was crueler than she had thought.

"Who told you that? Did Lanzo?"

"Nay, he was teaching me by Lord Ranulf's order. But Lanzo was going too easy on me. I told him I would never learn that way."

"So he pounds you to the ground?" she said, but the words were automatic, for her mind was actually reeling.

Aylmer had the nerve to grin, not noticing Reina's loss of color. "In another month I will do better."

"You want this?" A stupid question. A boy with no hope of aspiring to aught, offered a chance at knighthood? Of course he would want it. "Never mind. I see you do. How did this come about, Aylmer?"

"I thought you knew, lady. Lord Ranulf simply asked me. He said some knights carried so many wounds they might as well be cripples, but they could still wield a sword and fight. He said my foot should not stop me, and he is having a special boot made for me in London that might give me more balance." And then Aylmer added with the most pride yet, "Do I do well, he has promised to train me himself."

Tears came to Reina's eyes. What other knight would think to take on such a task, much less do it? She knew Ranulf was not the insensitive brute she was fond of calling him, but this? For her? She did not think so. He was just that way. No wonder she loved him. . . .

Aye, 'twas true, she realized with a start. Sweet

Jesú, when had that happened? When she had discovered his sense of humor? When she had realized his gruffness was all bluster? When he had gone to a whore to find out how to please her? That long ago? Or when he could not punish her without making immediate amends for it by turning it into an incredibly erotic experience she was not likely to ever forget? What a lackwit she was, to have fooled herself into thinking 'twas only lust all this time. And what difference did it make, when he did not feel the same?

"Lady?"

She swung about to find Lanzo still on the ground where he had fallen, watching her warily. She was then hit with the horrible realization of what she had just done. She had interfered in knightly business and attacked a squire. *Ranulf's* squire. He was not hurt, just leery of getting up with her still there and like to attack him again. But he really became afraid when she dropped to her knees beside him.

"Lanzo, I am so sorry."

His eyes flared with shock that she would demean herself to apologize to him. "Lady, please get up."

"Nay, you must tell me you can forgive me."

"Lady, just get up," he beseeched her. "Does Ranulf hear of this, he will kill me!"

She made a face at that. "I am at fault here, so does he kill anyone, 'twill be me." Then, with concern: "You are all right?"

"Of course," he replied with a snort of indignity.

She smiled, relieved, and offered him her hand so they could both rise. "You will forgive me, then?"

"There is naught to forgive, lady," he assured her, uncomfortable that she would not give up. "You misunderstood, is all."

"So I did. But for my peace of mind, could you go a bit easier on Aylmer—until you feel he can take it, that is."

Lanzo grinned and nodded, and Reina left them. But she knew Aylmer had been told her wishes when she heard him call out, "Lady," in the most complaining tone. She did not stop. The boy was only seven, after all. He had many years ahead of him to get battered and bruised.

Chapter Forty-four

Reina had forgotten about her guests until Gilbert, looking for her, met her in the forebuilding. Lord Roghton and his lady wife were requesting lodging for the night, on their way to London. It was a common enough occurrence. When the court was in London, they would get parties of travelers as often as two or three times a week.

"I have not heard the name before. From where do they come?"

"Northumbria."

"*Jesú*, as far away as that? Well, make them welcome, Gilbert, and find a chamber for them. And if I can manage to get through the hall without their notice," she added with a grin, looking down at her filthy clothes, "tell them I will join them at the evening meal."

"Aye, my lady, but the lord has stopped here before, many years ago, I believe it was," Gilbert felt it necessary to warn her. "He asked for a night's lodging then, too, but ended up staying nigh a sennight."

Another common occurrence, a practice of those with large retinues or only one estate who frequently exhausted their own stores, and so would travel about for months at a time, stopping at one keep or another until they had worn out their stay, all at little or no cost to themselves.

"One of those, eh?" She chuckled, not minding for the simple fact that Clydon could afford such extras at table.

She still could not place the name, but she did remember when she came down to supper later that day and saw the man. She had been five or six at the time of Lord Roghton's last visit and she had thought him the ugliest creature alive. He was still hard on the eye, though she was no longer a child to be frightened by it. A man nearing two score years, he had been overweight before and was even more so now, but that had naught to do with it. He had cruel eyes, there was no other word for it; a large, bulbous nose that distracted from them if you let it; and two hideous scars, one that twisted his mouth into a permanent sneer, and one that puckered his cheek and pulled down the skin near his left eye.

His wife was not yet present. Reina could only pity the woman such a husband. 'Twould be different were there any kindness in him, but she was remembering more and more of his first visit, and that was not the case at all. In fact, she believed Roghton had made himself so obnoxious with his subtle insults and little cruelties that her father had finally asked him to leave. Well, she would see if he had changed any, but she wished mightily that Ranulf were here to deal with him instead of her.

He stood with Sir William and Lady Margaret. Reina's younger ladies were all mysteriously absent from the hall. She could not blame them. Roghton really was the stuff of nightmares.

Searle and Eric both appeared simultaneously at her side ere she reached the group by the hearth. They were ridiculously protective of her whenever Ranulf was away and they were left behind, and had been the recipients of her sharp tongue more than once since she had become so testy. But for once she was grateful for their presence.

Searle had married Louise de Burgh as Ranulf had intended, so Reina did not see much of him anymore, except when Ranulf was gone. That match had worked out rather well, considering the lady had had to be dragged screaming and kicking to her wedding bed. The last Reina had seen of her, she had been blissfully contented. Whatever Searle had done or said to her, it had had a magical effect. Would that she could do the same with Ranulf.

"Ah, Lady Rhian, is it not? The child with the witch's black hair. Do you remember me, lady?"

Reina stiffened. Two insults in as many sentences? Did the man think she was a complete idiot, that she would assume his words an innocent mistake? Gilbert would have told him her name. *He* had to be an idiot could he not remember a simple first name given him mere hours ago.

"Actually, Lord Ralston," she replied, paying him in kind, "my name is Reina—Reina Fitz Hugh. Do you care to forget it again, you may simply call me lady, as is my due. And were I a witch, you would not feel safe to sleep under my roof, so 'tis fortunate I am not."

She was not her mother, to ignore innuendos and sly taunts, and pass them off as unimportant in deference to keeping the peace in her hall. If Roghton thought he could get away with that nonsense here, now, he had better think again.

She had managed to surprise him. He had not expected to have his disrespect tossed back at him, not by a woman at any rate.

Disconcerted as he was, his reply was civil. "I understand you are newly wed, Lady Reina."

"Aye, if you can call four months newly wed. My husband is away to London, however, with his father, Hugh de Arcourt."

"Lyonsford?"

"The same."

She did not hear another offensive word after that, which was amusing did she care to think of it, since Clydon was more powerful than Lyonsford. This just went to prove that a lady in charge of a small kingdom was not as impressive as a warlord owning much less—unless she cared to mention the names of those warlords as being relations.

His wife arrived, and Reina, like everyone else who had not seen her yet, went into mild shock. In complete contrast to her husband, she was a woman of stunning, incomparable beauty. Blond, fair-skinned, with the face of an angel. Even Eadwina had cause to be teeth-gnashingly jealous.

'Twas inconceivable that this vision of loveliness could be wed to a man like Roghton. Who could be so cruel as to have arranged a match between such opposites?

Searle and Eric were both awe-struck. Actually, every man in the room had gone silent and still, in some way affected by the lady. Reina was mayhap the only one to notice the delight of the husband in the reaction to his wife. He enjoyed the sensation she caused, and then the horror that such a desirable, exquisite thing could be his. Despite that, he took the lady to task for being late, embarrassing her and anyone near enough to hear his deliberately harsh scolding. And Reina was sure it was deliberate. 'Twas more a demonstration to dispel the disbelief and clarify for anyone still in doubt that she really did belong to him.

Reina had little opportunity to talk to Lady Roghton, at least not until supper was nearly finished. Roghton had dominated the conversation, and his lady had sat meekly to his left, uttering not a word and looking as miserable as she must feel. Reina tried to imagine herself in the lady's position. Had she not had a loving father, such could have indeed happened to her. It made her sick to think about it.

When Roghton, who had stuffed himself with everything near to hand, was finally replete, his interest was snared by the more uninhibited talk among the men at the lower tables. Reina was left alone with Lady Roghton, who moved closer on the bench as soon as her husband left. But she was now faced with the dilemma of what to say that would not smack of sympathy. She need not have worried. The blond beauty was not at all hesitant, now that she was no longer cowed by Lord Roghton's presence.

"I was told your husband is Ranulf Fitz Hugh?"

"Do you know him?"

"I am not sure," Lady Roghton demurred. "Is he tall, very tall, and all golden?"

Reina was amused. "Aye, that could well describe him."

"Then he *is* my Ranulf," the woman said excitedly. "This is incredible! Ranulf? Lord of Clydon? 'Tis a shame I missed him, but I heard someone say he is in London, so I will be sure to find him there."

Reina could do no more than stare. Had the woman forgotten whom she was speaking to? Was she even aware of that possessive "my" she had let slip? 'Twas difficult to tell. Her manner had completely changed. She was fairly bubbling with excitement.

"When—when did you know Ranulf?" Reina asked.

"Oh, 'twas long ago, but he will not have forgotten me." She laughed, a sweet, musical sound. "Of course you can guess our relationship. Every woman at Montfort wanted him, he was so beautiful to look at. How could I resist him? I even bore him a child."

Anne? Sweet *Jesú*, this was Lady Anne!

The shock must have been apparent in Reina's face, for the woman added mistakenly, "You did not know? But 'tis naught to concern yourself with. Men are never faithful, you know. They spread their bastards all over the countryside. Why, Ranulf is one himself." And then she smiled. " 'Tis why I am so amazed he has come to be Lord of Clydon."

Reina took a sip of wine, hoping it would defuse the fury she suddenly felt. What kind of woman would say such things to a man's wife—unless she hoped to make trouble between them? Walter was right about the lady. She was naught but a calculating bitch beneath the sweet smiles and angelic looks. And *she* had pitied her?

"You did not say what happened to this child you bore," Reina said tightly, realizing Anne wanted her to think she had this link to Ranulf.

The lady was disconcerted by the question. "Did I not? He died, poor thing. I was so devastated."

"He?"

"I believe—" she started doubtfully, but was quick to correct the impression. "Well, of course 'twas a boy. I would know what I gave birth to."

Sweet *Jesú*, she actually did not know, had not cared. To Reina, as an expectant mother, that fact was nearly as inconceivable as what the lady had done with the child, her daughter, her flesh and blood—oh, God!

Reina stood up, unable to bear another moment of Lady Anne's presence. " 'Tis fortunate Ranulf is not here," she said and walked away.

Anne smiled, misunderstanding what had been a warning were she smart enough to realize it.

Chapter Forty-five

Ranulf bounded up the stairs to the Great Hall, uncaring of the noise he made or of the hour, which was late. He had missed Clydon. Three weeks was too long a time to be away from—well, he might as well admit it. 'Twas his wife he had missed, not Clydon. She might be willful, temperamental, at times extremely aggravating, but when he was with her, he felt more special than he ever had in his life—cared for, important, needed. She saw to his every comfort, nursed him when he was ill, scolded him when he pushed himself too far, worried over him. He did not have to be on his guard with her, or suspect her every word and motive, for she had proved herself to be different from what he had come to expect in women. Even his new relationship with his father did not come close to the way Reina made him feel.

He ought to tell her, but he knew not the courtly words a lady would expect to hear. Did he try to wax lyrical, she was more like to laugh at him than take him seriously. Besides, she must know how he felt. Women were supposed to be intuitive about such things. And he knew how she felt, had known since she first called him lackwit, a name she reserved only for those she cared about.

Aye, he knew her well. The only thing he did not know was why she was taking so long to tell him of the child she carried. But as his father had warned him, and Walter, too, who had been at home for the birthing of two younger sisters, 'twas not unusual for a woman to behave strangely in that condition.

Considering his thoughts and where he was rushing to, Ranulf was ill prepared for the woman who stepped into his path as he crossed the darkened hall. She appeared so suddenly he nearly knocked her over. He started to apologize, then saw who she was. The words died in his throat.

Anne had seen him coming. She had been trying to wake her drunken husband, who had fallen asleep by the hearth. Now she was glad he had drunk himself into a stupor. The opportunity was heaven-sent. She would not waste it.

"So you do remember me, Ranulf," she said with satisfaction, and added for good measure, knowing no man liked to be taken for granted: "Your wife would have had me believing you had forgotten all your previous lovers when you wed her. She claimed to have your affections firmly in hand."

All of Ranulf's old wariness came rushing to the fore. He knew his wife would intimate no such thing, leastwise not to a stranger, but that only proved that once a liar, always a liar. This woman had not changed at all. She was as beautiful as ever, nay, more so with the added fullness of maturity. Her soul was still black as sin, however, and if she had been in Reina's company for any time at all, there was no telling what mischief she had caused.

He decided to play along with her for the moment, though his hands itched to close around her throat. She was a woman who picked her words carefully. Everything she said was for effect, good or bad. She had to have a reason for wanting him to feel resentment for his wife's loose tongue.

" 'Tis a surprise, lady, to find you here."

"Did you think we would never meet again? I always knew we would." She stepped closer to whisper, "You cannot imagine how often I have thought of you, Ranulf, remembering the passion we shared." Her hand came to rest on his chest. "Is there not somewhere we can . . . speak alone?"

It was a seductive offer. At one time it would have had the power to inflame his senses and make him mad with lust for her. All it did now was make his skin crawl with revulsion.

He looked about him at the servants in the shadows, fast asleep. "For all intents and purposes, we are alone."

"I meant—never mind." She pouted. "You must have forgotten how often we sought dark corners."

He was growing tired of waiting for her to get to the point of what she wanted. He knew 'twas not him, so it had to be something he could do for her.

"I am a man now, Anne. I prefer a warm bed."

"I have one in my chamber."

"Which brings to mind the question of what you are doing here."

For a moment her carefully controlled expression wavered to show her irritation with him. "Is that all you can think of? We were in love, Ranulf."

"I was, or thought I was. You chose a different path, however."

"For which I have been punished ever since!" She then stated her plea with appropriate feeling. "Oh, God, Ranulf, you cannot know the monster Montfort gave me to." She stabbed a finger toward the hearth, where a candle was lit and Roghton could be seen sprawled on a bench. "There, that is my husband, and his soul is as grotesque as his body."

"The man did not matter, as I recall," he replied coldly. "Only his wealth."

"Can you not see I am trying to tell you I was wrong?" she cried. "He is wealthy enough, but all the wealth in the kingdom cannot make up for the hell he has made of my life all these years. Do you know he trains falcons to attack people, then sets them loose on his poor villeins for sport? That is the kind of man he is, and I cannot bear it anymore."

Whether that was true or not, Ranulf was unmoved. "Then leave him."

"Do you think I have not tried? I am kept as a prisoner—watched, followed, locked in my chamber whenever he is not about."

Ranulf looked again at the sleeping man. "Go now. I see no one to stop you."

"He would only find me and drag me back as he has done before."

As Ranulf had thought, this was not what she was after. "Why do you tell me all this?"

"You could help me, if you would."

"How?"

She moved closer again, this time to brush her breasts against his forearm. "Kill him for me," she pleaded huskily. "He has told his men that does he die by suspicious means, I am to be tortured to death. And they will do it. They are as mean and vicious as he. He could choke to death on his food and they would kill me. He must be challenged fairly, die by the sword. Please, Ranulf, free me from him."

So there was justice after all. He almost laughed

aloud. She wanted him to free her from a hell she well deserved? Not likely, but he did not tell her so just yet.

"For what reason would I challenge him? I see no marks on you to show you are mistreated. In fact, Anne, I find it hard to believe the man does not cherish you."

"He did, at first, but I could not stomach his touch and he knew it, and came to hate me because of it. Then he found me with a—with a lover, and he killed him with his bare hands."

"But he did naught to you?"

"He—he waited until my grief had lessened. He wanted me to grieve. He was glad of that. He did naught as long as he thought I was suffering, but as soon as I began to heal, he beat me. He wanted me to remember, you see. He thought my grief was so strong at first that a beating would not have mattered in comparison, so he waited. That is the kind of diabolical man he is. And now he beats me if I even look at another man. Oh, please, Ranulf," she begged, throwing her arms around his neck. "I cannot live like this any longer. Can I not be free of him soon, I am like to kill myself."

"You think I would care?"

She leaned back slowly, frowning, but disbelieving his meaning. "You loved me once," she pointed out.

"Now I love another."

"Who?" When he did not answer, her eyes widened incredulously. "Certainly not that little mouse you married!"

"Mouse? She is more beautiful to me than any woman I know—or have ever known."

"You do not mean that," Anne scoffed, and became bolder in her desperation, pressing her hips to his. "You must remember all we—"

Ranulf reacted with violent disgust, shoving her away from him. Then he closed the distance again and caught her hair at the nape of her neck, yanking her head back. At last she saw what he had kept under tight control. Hatred blazed from his eyes and sent a cold shiver down her spine.

"Lady, you killed my daughter," Ranulf said in a deadly snarl. "You did not even kill her with mercy, but let her starve to death. *That* is all I remember about you. Now get out of my home ere I take the retribution you truly deserve."

"I cannot leave without my husband!"

"Then best you wake him right quickly—or I will."

"And what am I to tell him? 'Tis the middle of the night!"

"You will think of something, lady. Lies are your specialty." With that he walked away and did not look back.

"That miserable whoreson," Anne hissed, but only after he was gone. "How can he care about a bastard that was not even his own? I should have told him. That would have put the stupid wretch in his place."

"Aye, you should have," Walter said quietly behind her. "But I will be sure to correct the matter. 'Twill not take away the pain he has carried all these years, but it might lessen the memory of it some small bit."

Anne had swung around at his first word and now smiled at him. "Sir Walter, is it not? Were you standing there long?"

"Long enough, lady," and he too walked away, not hiding his contempt.

She glared after him until she heard the cruel laughter by the hearth and turned around with a gasp to see her husband sitting up and watching her. "Not having much luck tonight, are you, my dear? I see I should have come to bed sooner, for now I have no bed to go to at all. How do you think I should thank you for that?"

Anne paled and fled the hall to the chamber they had been given, to cower there in a corner. Her husband's laughter could still be heard, which meant that he had been titillated by what he had heard and seen, which meant that he would want to bed her ere they departed. And that was far worse than any beating that might come later.

Chapter Forty-six

Reina woke to the gentle caress of a hand as it slid the sheet off her body. She sighed dreamily, but then her eyes opened and she gasped until she realized it was her husband and not some other slipped into her bed.

"*Jesú*, you gave me a start, Ranulf."

"That is not what I intend to give you, lady," he said in reply, grinning.

Her cheeks pinkened just the slightest bit. She was still not quite accustomed to his lusty talk, though she surely did not object to it.

"Did you only just return?" 'Twas morn, if the light beyond the bed-curtains was any indication.

"Nay, Walter and I rode in late yestereve. You slept so peacefully, I decided not to wake you."

As he said this, his hand moved across her navel, reminding her of what rested beneath.

"Do you—notice aught different about me, Ranulf?"

"Not a thing." His fingers tweaked a breast to watch the nipple come to life.

"Nothing?"

"Nay, why?"

"Never mind," she said, disgruntled.

"Do you notice aught different about me?" he teased.

"Only that you are missing a few more wits," she snorted.

Ranulf laughed heartily and pulled her close to hug her. "Why do you not just say it, lady?"

"What?"

His hand covered her belly again, and then he leaned down to kiss it. "What Walter told me about nigh two months ago."

"You know?" she gasped. "And you did not mention it?"

" 'Tis a wife's privilege to tell her husband. I waited for you to do so."

"I am sorry. I know I should have, but . . ."

"But?"

"The reason is silly," she hedged. "I would rather not repeat it."

He accepted that. "Never argue with a pregnant woman," his father had warned him, "for you will not believe some of the nonsensical things they will say at such a time." And besides, he had other things on his mind just now, like thoroughly acquainting himself with the new fullness of his lady's luscious body.

He did just that, amazing Reina that he would still want to make love to her even knowing of the child. She was not fool enough to question him about it, but the confusion, which went away for the next bliss-filled hour, returned when Ranulf finally lifted his head from her breast to get up for the day. Did this mean he had gotten used to her during these months of marriage, and whether she was pregnant or not, had decided to still avail himself of her? If that were so . . .

Reina's smile was brilliant, full of joy and contentment, until: "Oh! I almost forgot. We have guests, Ranulf, that you should know—"

"We *had* guests, lady," he said as he crossed to the door and banged on it to rouse Lanzo. "They left last eventide."

"They did?" she said in surprise. "Why would they do that?"

"I believe the lady realized 'twas not safe for her to stay here," was all he said.

Reina stayed silent. As long as that pair was gone and not likely to return, she was satisfied.

'Twas two months later that the messenger arrived with a call to arms from Shefford, and Reina's bubble of contentment burst. She was in the hall playing a game of chess with Walter when Ranulf came in to tell them. It appeared that Lord Rothwell had found himself another heiress, Lord Guy's niece, no less, who was also his ward. Her keep in Yorkshire had been under siege for several weeks now, but Sir Henry had only just learned of it and had decided that Ranulf was needed.

Reina objected immediately, and quite strenuously. " 'Tis no more than a test, and I do not like it. Sir Henry could have summoned half a dozen men closer to York to see to this, and I will tell him so. You do not have to go, Ranulf."

"Bite your tongue, lady," he replied incredulously. "My arm will grow rusty for all the use I get of it here."

"You would fight for the wrong reason?" she shouted at him.

"I will fight because I like to fight!" he shouted

back. " 'Tis what I am trained for, and what I enjoy best—aside from taking you to bed!"

Brilliant color shot into her cheeks, and her temper exploded even more. "You do not care how I feel, do you? Who am I but your wife!"

"You are being unreasonable, lady," Ranulf rumbled. "Rothwell is an utter ass. He will turn tail and run as soon as he sees reinforcements arrive."

"And if he does not?" she stormed. "I love you, you lackwitted clod! Think you I want to see you bloodied in some meaningless battle?"

"I love you, too, lady, but I will not give up my pleasure in a good fight to appease you!"

"Then go! See if I care!"

She stalked off, but no more than a few steps ere she turned back to run into his arms. "You love me?"

"Aye."

"Really?"

"Aye." He grinned.

"I love you, too."

"I know."

She hauled off and hit him. "Well, I did not know you did! You could have told me!"

"Now who is the lackwit, lady? I tell you every night I take you in my arms. I tell you the only way I know how."

"Nay, my lord, you just said it more plainly," she said with tears of happiness in her eyes. "Even if you did shout it at me, 'tis still what I longed to hear."

"Those words?"

"Aye."

"But that says so little," he complained.

"My lord, do I want to hear what a troubadour has

to say, I will hire him. From you I only need 'I love you,' every so often.''

Ranulf chuckled. ''As you wish, little general.''

She drew his head down for a lingering kiss. He had stopped lifting her up to his level when he had nearly dropped her earlier this month in surprise at being nudged by one of his son's more exuberant kicks.

''Now,'' she said with a purr of contentment. ''Will you forget about this silly war?''

''Nay.''

''Ranulf!''

''But I still love you,'' he offered.

She glared at him furiously ere she stalked off again, this time without coming back.

''She will not stay angry,'' Walter said, unable to hide the amusement in his voice. ''She never does.''

''But I will be gone ere she decides to calm down.'' And then Ranulf grinned. ''I hate to miss that. She is always so—expressive in her forgiveness.''

Walter hooted. ''Someone ought to tell her you said that.''

''Bite your tongue. Do you have her guessing why I so often tease her temper, and I will take my loss out of your hide.''

Chapter Forty-seven

*W*inter closed in around Clydon with a white blanket of snow that was not likely to melt completely until spring. Reina secretly liked this time of year, even though viands grew stale and moldy, and men's tempers snapped from inactivity. 'Twas a time when women could do things there was never enough time for otherwise. Tapestries were started and completed ere the season ended, clothes made for the next year's special occasions, new talents discovered, recipes discussed and experimented with. 'Twas a warm, cozy part of the year with all hearths blazing, a time when relationships developed more strongly. Did a woman want to take the supreme luxury and just lie abed for a day and do naught, she could do that, too.

Reina did that often, simply because her small frame had difficulty carrying so much added weight. Ranulf teased her unmercifully about her new size, insisting he liked it so much he would see to it she was often kept overweight. Surprisingly, he came home more often than she would have expected, considering Sir Henry was still in the field. He showed up for every feast day, and was home for the Twelfth Day celebration to pass out the perquisites, or bonuses, to the manorial servants; the food, clothing, drink, and firewood that were their traditional Christmas due. He stayed that time until Plow Monday, the first Monday after Epiphany, when the villeins raced their plows across the common pasture to determine how many furrows each man could sow that year.

But Ranulf did not arrive for the one holiday she was sure he would not miss, Candlemas, at the start of the second month of the new year. 'Twas now a week after, and Reina was due to have her baby any day, but he had still not shown up. After he had promised he would be there for the birthing, what was she to think except that something dire had happened?

Walter was quick to tell her she was being silly to worry. He had not gone on this campaign with Ranulf, nor did he mind staying behind, being newly wed to Florette. But what did he know of a woman's fear? And yet, realistically, Reina knew he was right.

Rothwell had scurried home as Ranulf had predicted he would, but that had not been the end of it. Sir Henry had decided he needed lessoning for his audacity and had taken the Shefford army west to besiege Rothwell's keep, and so it had been under siege these past two months, with very little actual fighting.

Ranulf's forty days' service had expired, but what did that matter when a man was enjoying himself? That he had stayed on to fill the ranks had caused another fight between them, which he, of course, won, and she, of course, forgave him for. The lout simply loved a challenge, any challenge, and she would perforce have to get used to that aspect of her life with him. It would become easier as the years passed. There would be times when he would be home so much she was like to wish him gone. And there would be times when he was late again in returning and she would worry herself sick. There would also be the times of loving to make up for it all.

Verily, what did she have to complain about? That

Ranulf was not there for the birthing of his first son, who arrived on time and without undue complication? Aye, she would not let him hear the end of that. And yet 'twas forgotten when he entered their chamber a mere hour after the ordeal was over, and came directly to the bed to take her in his arms.

He was contrite and elated all at once, and how could she scold him when he showered her with love? His excuse for being late was a good one. Lord Guy had finally returned to England and had summoned Ranulf to Shefford for their first meeting, which had gone very well. He had even insinuated that he would not take it amiss were he asked to be godfather to this first child of theirs. Reina could only laugh. 'Twas not like her overlord to be subtle about his wishes. Ranulf must have duly impressed him, which meant she had naught else to worry about on that score. Her father's little deception for her sake would never come to light, and his last wish was fulfilled. She had married the man of her choice, as he had wanted.

Theodric hummed softly as he rocked Guy in his arms. The three-month-old infant was fast asleep, but he was in no hurry to put him down in his bed. Wenda was combing Reina's hair, still slightly damp from her bath. Theo no longer complained that the girl had usurped his duties, not since he had taken over the care of Guy, whom he adored. He was worse than any mother when it came to fretting over the baby. Reina sometimes thought that he envied her the nursing of him, and would do that, too, if he could.

Lady Ella preened herself in the center of Reina's bed. Her most recent batch of kittens cavorted on the floor, making Wenda giggle every so often. Reina was amused by them, too. She had not liked it when her nemesis had decided to have this litter under her bed, sneaking into the room to do so. Reina had tried moving them at least into the antechamber, but Lady Ella would cry and scratch at the door until it was opened, then pick up the kitten she had carried there and rush into the room with it. Ranulf had said not a word, leaving the decision to Reina. What decision? The cat had made up its mind and there was naught anyone could do about it.

When the door opened and Ranulf walked in, Reina was delighted. She had thought with Lord Hugh's arrival this afternoon that Ranulf would not retire until much later. But one look at him staring aghast at Theo holding Guy and she groaned inwardly. That he had not discovered ere now that Theo had taken charge of Guy was due only to Theo's clever timing.

Ranulf did not mince words; he simply bellowed, "Out!"

Theo was no longer frightened to death by Ranulf's roars. He gently laid Guy down in his basket and walked stiffly from the room. Reina gave a nod to Wenda to fetch the basket and leave them. The argument she was about to commence would probably get loud enough to disturb Guy's sleep.

"You have offended Theo," she began quietly enough.

"I will do more than that do I find that catamite near my son again, lady. I will not have Guy influenced—"

"Do not use *that* excuse, Ranulf," she interrupted sharply. "The only one like to influence your son is you, and well you know it. You would have it no other way, and that we *both* know. As for Theo, he has lived here his whole life. In that time he has had the care of two babies and three children, myself included, and I might add that I was the only female he has attended. He has not influenced any of us adversely, nor is he ever like to.'' Then, on a softer note when she saw he was actually listening to her and no longer frowning quite so sternly: ''He loves Guy as if he were his own. He would never do aught to hurt him. Now which is more important? That your son receives the best care? Or that you continue to hold a grudge because Theo admires your magnificent body?''

That caught him off guard. ''Magnificent?''

''Aye.'' Her smile broke through.

''I did not know you thought so.''

Was he embarrassed? Sweet *Jesú,* how she loved this man, with all his quirks and faults and endearing qualities.

''Have I not told you, my lord?''

''Nay.''

''I must have shown you.''

He really was embarrassed. Reina grinned and slowly crossed the room to him. Deliberately, she let her bedrobe slip down one shoulder, and saw his eyes ignite. He might have been disconcerted for the moment, but 'twould not last long, and in fact, lasted no longer than it took her to reach him. She was lifted off her feet to dangle in the air. This was how they had met, the only difference being the passion that smoldered in his eyes now was not anger.

''Christ's toes, woman, when you look at me like that . . .''

''What are you waiting for?'' she asked thickly,

and wrapped her arms around him until there was not a breath of space between them. "Want me to drag you to bed for a change?"

She did not have to ask twice.